COSMIC
LOVE
at the
MULTIVERSE
HAIR SALON

COSMIC
LOVE
at the
MULTIVERSE
HAIR SALON

ANNIE MARE

ACE
NEW YORK

ACE
Published by Berkley
An imprint of Penguin Random House LLC
1745 Broadway, New York, NY 10019
penguinrandomhouse.com

Book design by Daniel Brount

Library of Congress Cataloging-in-Publication Data

Names: Mare, Annie, author.
Title: Cosmic love at the multiverse hair salon / Annie Mare.
Description: First edition. | New York: Ace, 2025.
Identifiers: LCCN 2024040611 (print) | LCCN 2024040612 (ebook) |
ISBN 9780593817483 (trade paperback) | ISBN 9780593817490 (ebook)
Subjects: LCGFT: Romance fiction. | Lesbian fiction. | Science fiction. | Novels.
Classification: LCC PS3613.A7388 C67 2025 (print) |
LCC PS3613.A7388 (ebook) | DDC 813/.6—dc23/eng/20240930
LC record available at https://lccn.loc.gov/2024040611
LC ebook record available at https://lccn.loc.gov/2024040612

First Edition: June 2025

Printed in the United States of America
1st Printing

The authorized representative in the EU for product safety and compliance is
Penguin Random House Ireland, Morrison Chambers, 32 Nassau Street,
Dublin D02 YH68, Ireland, https://eu-contact.penguin.ie.

For Ruth, time after time after time after time

COSMIC LOVE
at the
MULTIVERSE
HAIR SALON

OCTOBER 1

. . . .

T RESSA FAY ROBESON FLUFFED HER DARK FRENCH BOB AND slapped two Post-its over her nipples, then bent one arm over her head and grasped her wrist with the opposite hand. She widened her stance and lifted her chin at her phone on the stand, popping off a series of pictures with her remote.

Right now, everything was perfect.

There was butternut-squash-and-cheese-tortellini soup on the stove. All her plants—and she had dozens—were perky and vibing cheerfulness. Epinephrine, her best boy orange tabby, had obliged her photo sesh by hanging on the back of the sofa, just in view of the camera.

Her pictures would have looked even hotter if she hadn't had to use the Post-its to escape Instagram's censors, but they were still definitely solid.

Someone knocked on her apartment door.

Damn.

"Tressa Fay!" Mary shouted through the door. "We know you're hygge-bating in there, but we're your best friends, so you have to let us in."

"I'm naked!" Tressa Fay called out.

"So? You cut hair at the salon today with visible underboob."

That was unfair. Tressa Fay had worn a full-coverage bra under her tiny crop top. Her eponymous salon was always a little warm.

Also, her clients took a lot of pictures. Many of them waited for months for their booking with her, and some drove long distances or even flew into Green Bay to have their hair cut because they followed her platforms or had read about her in a magazine. To reward their efforts, she liked to put on a little bit of a show.

She opened the door.

"Good *night*." Guy put their hands over their eyes. "Some advance warning would be appreciated."

Mary, Guy, and Linds came in, Guy keeping their eyes resolutely on the floor. Linds trailed a finger over Tressa Fay's shoulder blades as she walked past. Linds was like a crab—she explored her environment by feel and liked to sun in a pile of other bodies.

Tressa Fay grabbed a cardigan off a chair and put it on. "I told you I was naked."

"Naked, I could handle." Guy sat in Tressa Fay's rocking chair, their hair out of its characteristic bun and tumbling in pale waves to their waist. "Naked is natural. Whatever it is that you have on suggests something outside of nature."

Guy liked to play the part of the prim miss. Tressa Fay shrugged, reached into the cardigan, and plucked the Post-it pasties off the black mesh bra top of her brown velvet bodysuit. She'd received it gratis, along with the matching thigh harnesses, from an indie lingerie designer who wanted to be on her feed.

"Being outside of nature is what makes it so good." Linds collapsed her long legs and spread out along the floor, smiling at Tressa Fay.

"It's a bodysuit," Tressa Fay told Guy. "Which is perfectly regular."

Linds wrinkled her nose. "*Bodysuit* is the worst word ever. Like, you're getting out of bed, and you're a skeleton, and then you tug your legs into a *bodysuit*."

"That's how I felt before I got top surgery," Guy said. "But now I just feel myself." Linds laughed, and they leaned over and high-fived her.

"I have an agenda." Mary directed this stern remark to Tressa Fay. "Which is you, out with us at the taproom." Guy and Linds and Tressa Fay went all the way back to elementary school, but Mary had only joined their group four years ago, after Tressa Fay hired her to work in the salon. Mary's agendas kept the rest of them from snuggling into a rut.

"No." Tressa Fay lay down on the rug next to Linds, who reached out to hold her hand. "Your agenda will mess up my plan."

"This is your plan?" Mary circled her finger around the apartment, which Tressa Fay had mood-lit with a million candles as soon as she got home before putting on her mom's old Bikini Kill record, misting the plants, and making the soup.

All of which was better by an enormous factor than numbing herself with her phone or streaming shows while wondering why she couldn't find a girl to make soup and listen to records from the nineties with. Tressa Fay loved this cozy world she'd made for herself. She also loved how the mythical girl in her imagination wasn't cheating on her, complaining about cat hair, or wishing Tressa Fay were something she wasn't.

"It's hopeless, Mary." Linds put her head on Tressa Fay's shoulder. "Once our girl here starts taking sexy pictures with soup on the stove, she's only getting freaky with herself."

"True," Tressa Fay said. "True, true." She deliberately did *not* look at Mary. Despite how emotionally close Tressa Fay was to

Linds and Guy, they didn't know every part of the sad story of her last relationship, whereas Mary had greater knowledge and also had caught Tressa Fay opening dating apps a couple of times. Mary knew Tressa Fay's wound was now a healed-over scar and that she was a romantic, couldn't help it.

Also, Mary had brokered more love matches for her friends and family than it was safe to ignore. She had powers.

"I told this extremely fine girl about you last night, and she said she'd probably be at the taproom around nine," Mary complained.

There it was. "I don't do bars. As you know." Tressa Fay ignored the small flare of interest, low in her belly, that had fired in response to the words *extremely fine girl*. It had been a long time since she looked at an attractive person across a table and tried to figure out if they liked what they saw while her nerves fluttered. A long time since she held someone, their body fitted against hers. She did, in fact, need that. But she did not want anything to do with the usual ways to get there. Bars. Apps. Loud restaurants with heavy menus.

"But it's not a bar. It's the taproom!" Mary said. "Very low-key. Like, the key of low. Only dogs and very chill, hot people can hear in this key. And you haven't been out in forever, so it would be good for you even if you're not interested in this painfully gorgeous person I found for you and didn't even keep for myself."

Mary fluffed the dark honey-blond shag Tressa Fay had touched up before they closed the salon today. She should have known that if Mary was begging for a cut at the tail end of the day, she was dreaming up one of her agendas.

"She's not going," Linds said, fixing her false eyelashes in her selfie camera.

"I'm not going." Tressa Fay smiled. "But I love you very much."

"What am I supposed to do about this dishy woman who was going to meet us there?"

Tressa Fay narrowed her eyes. "You said she was probably going to be there. As in, incidentally."

"Same thing."

"You can give her my number."

Mary sighed, then stood up. "I love you, so I will try to understand."

"I could loan you some books about introversion." Guy stretched their arms over their head. "There are different types."

Tressa Fay had a dusty stack of books Guy had given her when they were worried about her after her breakup. Guy was a lawyer. They genuinely believed any problem could be studied its way out of.

After a quick round of hugs, Tressa Fay briefly finger-styled Mary's new cut and kissed Linds's glossy brown pixie, and her friends left.

She put her back to the door, smiling to herself. The evening was hers.

She strode across her tiny living room, dropping her cardigan, then ladled herself an enormous bowl of soup with lots of parmesan, flipped over the album on her turntable, and curled up on the sofa, nearly purring over each tortellini.

It had taken her such a long time to figure out that the best way to give other people what they wanted was to make sure she had everything she needed.

When she started working toward her cosmetology license her senior year, it was mostly because she'd taken every art class that her Green Bay, Wisconsin, high school had to offer, and she knew she wanted to keep doing something creative, but she didn't want to go to college. Plus, she had to earn money, because her dad had made it clear she'd be on her own once she walked across the school's stage with a diploma in her hand.

To her great luck, she was a natural, at least at cutting hair. Maybe it was because of her name, which her mother had given her to honor a particularly transcendent house party frontwoman's band named Tressa and the Over It Alreadies, with the addition of Fay to appease her dad, whose mother's name was Fay and who also, as an observant Catholic, fervently believed in the power of two-name names.

Tressa Fay didn't *love* talking to people, at least beyond the first conversation when they told her about their hair, and she especially didn't love anyone telling her what to do. None of that was a deterrent, though. Lots of people preferred a stylist who wasn't chatty. What almost ruined her career before it even started was that it turned out almost everything in the salon that she touched, smelled, rubbed, brushed, sprayed, or scrunched into someone's hair made her sick.

So while it wasn't long before she surpassed her classmates with a pair of scissors, a clipper, or a blade, she did the bare minimum she needed to do when it came to everything else, wearing gloves to protect her peeling hands and a mask against the onslaught of airborne chemicals. Her teachers acted like she was exaggerating. Most of her classmates simply didn't get it. After four years working at three different salons—each one promising a "natural" and "organic" environment—two different allergy specialists she couldn't afford, and prescriptions for steroids, inhalers, and immunomodulating topical creams, she ended up in the emergency room hooked up to a nebulizer after a coworker tripped and dumped a texturizing solution on the floor.

Tressa Fay was fired via text while she was talking to the hospital's billing department. She then failed to make rent, and her next bed was her dad's sofa, with a very firm thirty-day deadline.

She did the only thing she could do. She cut hair. Illicitly.

From her dad's kitchen and deck while he was at work, she cut and barbered for cash. Ten bucks for short, twenty for long, no other services. Just her, her client, blades, and the birds that fluttered onto the deck, stealing bits of hair for their nests.

Tressa Fay loved it.

She loved figuring out what the natural texture of a person's hair could do, sometimes showing the client the possibilities for the first time in their lives. She loved the different colors hair came in and the color clients had done somewhere else, or at home themselves. She loved making shapes, making statements, figuring out what was sharp, what was throwback, what was French, what was rock, what was queer.

She made enough money to nab a sketchy one-bedroom on the west side of Green Bay's downtown, and she kept cutting. Other than the moment she had to convince her landlord that the steady stream of foot traffic to her place didn't mean she was selling drugs, she was happy. Even better, she was healthy. Her skin cleared and stopped hurting. She could breathe. She didn't wake up worried she was coming down with the flu because she was congested, fatigued, and foggy.

When a commercial space across the street from her apartment became available, she had a stack of cash, but she was twenty-six years old with no credit, no references, and very creative tax returns. She met with the real estate agent anyway, and while they were in no way willing to give her the space, they did connect her to a business incubator that changed her life.

Now she owned her own salon.

All it had was white walls, plants, a shampoo station with the blandest hypoallergenic product ever made, her chair, and her blades. Mary washed hair, booked appointments, and worked viral marketing. Tressa Fay made shapes and helped people feel how they wanted to feel.

It was everything she needed, and she had to believe that giving herself what she needed in her private life—quality time with her cat, good food, an occasional gloriously dirty bit of lingerie to remind her sex existed—would lead to her someday getting what she wanted. Someone who loved her for exactly who she was. Someone who chose to stick by her through good times and bad. Someone she picked for herself and who picked her back, over and over again, forever.

Just that.

She'd finished her dishes and was considering making a half batch of cookies when her phone buzzed with an incoming text.

> Hey! So I'm the worst, but I don't see you, and I have done a complete turn upstairs and down. Help!

Tressa Fay didn't recognize the number. **sorry!** she replied. I don't think I can. wrong number?

Three dots floated up, then slammed back down.

> Look, it's okay if you changed your mind, it's even okay if you ghost, but the wrong number bit is just, no.

Uh-oh. Tressa Fay smiled sympathetically. Dating was extremely and very awful.

> hey, so . . . this is the wrong number, for sure. my name's Tressa Fay, and I'm at home communing with my cat and soup, and I didn't have a date tonight or anytime in the foreseeable future, actually, but good luck out there, it's the level worst

> !!! I have the wrong number.

> yes

> I just realized. I used the wrong first three digits.

> oh, no. numbers are so tricky

> I'm an ENGINEER.

Tressa Fay laughed out loud. remind me not to drive over any of your bridges.

> One collapsed bridge and a girl's got a reputation.

She laughed again. This stranger was funny. did you find your date?

> Yes. Well, no. She just texted. She "remembered she was supposed to do something for her sister" and she, in fact, has a lot of family stuff going on right now so . . . maybe she can circle back some other time?

oof, sorry. like I said, rough out there

at least I think it is?

> Cat. Soup.

yep

> You have the right idea. Sucks, too, because it's such a gorgeous evening. I was looking forward to the Canyon Tacos patio to enjoy the last bit of light.

This engineer was very optimistic about her night, because it was cold and dark outside. Or she was being sarcastic.

Also.

Tressa Fay tapped her lip. Funny. Into girls. Hmm.

Hmm.

get a taco, and I'll be your phone date

> I just walked out!

don't stand me up, get back in there and let's do this thing

Pretty good game from the couch, there.

I do my best work from the couch

what are we having?

Got a seat at the bar. The special is their black bean and avocado tacos. I'm ordering three. And churros with the chocolate dipping stuff. And a Jarritos.

what flavor?

Watermelon.

thatta girl. come here often?

Yes. It's why I picked the place. So I would feel comfortable. She . . . was really hot and, um. Came on strong? Not in a bad way? I needed the courage that only comes from someone hot having to eat a messy taco in front of you.

I thought that's what happened after a date went really, really well

Three dots came up and went back down multiple times while Tressa Fay wondered if she had gone too far.

> Everyone is looking at me like I've lost my mind because I'm laughing so hard all by myself.

Tressa Fay grinned. **What's your name, hot stuff?**

> Meryl. And you're Tressa Fay. Wait.

what

> You have that ultra-cool tiny salon on the west side.

I do

> Wait.

what

> Um. I am looking at your Insta. Oh no.

Tressa Fay glanced down at herself, still clad in just the body-suit with the black mesh top. And only straps in the back. She had not put Post-its on her butt for the pictures.

Well.

oh no, what?

You are very much so very hot. This picture of you in the roller skates should win a Nobel Peace Prize.

Well, well, *well*. Tressa Fay grinned and let out a tiny squeal. If you built the cozy, the babes, they would come. However, it was interesting that Meryl had gone months back into her feed. Mary had taken that picture of Tressa Fay in short shorts and roller skates way back in April, during a freak warm-almost-hot day.

Tressa Fay was not complaining. She posted thirst traps for a reason. This, right here, was the reason. Trapping.

thank you. engineering and a sense of humor are too much hotness for me already, she typed. but if I were to openly spy? is there a handle?

@ItWasMyGrandmasName

Tressa Fay opened Insta, wiggling.

Oof.

Meryl hadn't posted since a hashtag-tax-day-so-sad post forever ago, but hello, big-brown-eyed, curvelicious, freckly-nosed *nerd* trap. Tressa Fay scrolled through, sighing contentedly at her luck.

Meryl probably hadn't thought about a haircut for her wavy, frizzy, elbow-length pale auburn mane in years. It was messy. Everywhere. It matched her amazing eyebrows over those Bambi eyes. She made math jokes. There was more than one fandom T-shirt barely containing her juicy. Sometimes she wore glasses, murdering Tressa Fay where she sat. Meryl had one of those mouths with a slightly bigger top lip than bottom, which fired Tressa Fay's kissing imagination into a frenzy.

Yes, please. All of this.

She'd eaten a lot of soup, but maybe she could go for a churro?

Meryl

Yes.

I think we should take this somewhere IRL. what do you think?

I think I'm going to get this man next to me to give up his stool come hell or high water. Which I can do. I'm a stormwater engineer. High water is a real motivator.

Tressa Fay bit her lip and typed, don't move. stay exactly, exactly, right there.

I'm a statue. A citizen protesting eminent domain. A stumped chess player.

Tressa Fay laughed out loud again. just be for real, and I will be there so fast, Meryl.

She jumped up from the sofa with enough urgent intention that Epinephrine complained at her.

"I know, baby boy, but this is an emergency. I have a funny engineer on the line, and you know how I feel about redheads.

You, for example." She scritched between his ears and then dashed into her bedroom, digging through her closet until she found her lucky jeans and a clean button-down. She put both over the bodysuit, pulled on her boots, and was on her way to Canyon in less than ten minutes.

Tressa Fay cursed downtown parking but eventually found a spot for her tiny green Fiat. Even with the cold, damp weather, people were spilling out of the restaurant. She jogged to the narrow two-story building, which sat in the same row as the old theater. On warm days, Canyon would open its entire front wall of windows to let people sit at an open-air bar looking out at the street, but right now it was closed and fogged from the people and food inside, the light casting a square on the dark sidewalk and the smokers huddled there.

It was packed. She looked over the bar and didn't see Meryl at first glance.

"Can I help you?" The hostess widened her eyes. "Oh! Hi. Um, Tressa Fay? You cut my hair and changed my entire life." She grinned.

"Katie?" Tressa Fay had to shove her hands into her own pockets to keep from fixing one of Katie's curls near her face.

"Yes! You remember. I love this haircut so much. I have never loved my . . ." She gestured around her face. Tressa Fay remembered her self-consciousness over her acne scars. "Not ever. But I've felt completely different about that since I left your chair."

"Can I?" Tressa Fay reached out.

"Yes!" Katie leaned forward, and Tressa Fay played with the hair near Katie's face, changing her part, then stepping back. "You're amazing. What can I help you with?"

"I'm meeting someone. She said she would be at the bar. Meryl. She ordered the black bean tacos, a Jarritos, and churros."

"Be right back." Katie winked and wove her way into the crowd.

Tressa stood on her tiptoes to look over all the people. She pulled out her phone when she felt it buzz in her pocket.

> I just bought a mini pitcher of their limeades. So when you get here, I'm the girl in the red mathlete T-shirt with a pitcher of limeades at the downstairs bar.

Mathlete, God. Tressa Fay wasn't going to survive this. She saw Katie weave back out of the crowd toward her. "I didn't find any Meryls or see anything like that order in the system. Are you sure you have the right place?"

"Huh? Yes. I'm sure. Look." Tressa Fay held up her phone. "She said she just got a mini pitcher of limeades, and only you guys do those. She's wearing a red shirt and . . . hold on." Tressa Fay pulled up Meryl's Insta again. "This is her."

Katie looked at the picture, her brow furrowed. "Okay. Yeah. Hold up. I'll look again, and just in case, I'll check the bar upstairs."

> it's so busy. can't find you

> I'm by the door, and the hostess is helping me

> raise your hand or come get me?

> I'll come get you!

Tressa Fay grinned and rose to her tiptoes again, waiting for her first glimpse of Meryl coming through the crowd. She hadn't felt this ignited for a date in a long, long time, and they'd only flirted over text. Butterflies were racing so fast from her belly to her sternum that she had goose bumps.

Katie came back shaking her head. "I didn't see her anywhere, and we haven't had a limeade pitcher go out for an hour." Her expression was apologetic.

No, not apologetic. Sad. For Tressa Fay. Because Katie believed that she had been stood up.

Tressa Fay's phone buzzed in her hand.

> I'm right here by the door! Where are you? Did you go someplace else? Or outside? It's hot in here, even with the front windows wide open.

Tressa Fay shook her head slowly back and forth. Everyone talking was too loud. Suddenly, the hits of cold air from the door behind her as even more people piled into Canyon weren't exciting but annoying. She wished she'd brought a coat. She looked at the tables by the front—tables that had been placed there once the restaurant moved the bar out of the front windows for the season. The big front windows that were completely closed.

I'm right by the door, Tressa Fay typed. my hand is on the red coat rack.

She was fairly tall. Five seven. Her dark, exaggerated French bob wasn't a subtle look. It was her signature, in fact. And she had a port-wine stain birthmark that spilled from her left temple to the place where her ear and jaw met and over her neck, collarbones, and arm. It was in every picture of her. She never covered it up.

> Hey. I am standing right by that coat rack? Did you move?

Three dots.

> Or change your mind?

She shook her head again. She hadn't changed her mind! She was right where Meryl said *she* was! Tressa Fay looked at Katie in desperation. "Is there another Canyon Tacos? Like maybe in Appleton or something?"

"Oh! No. There isn't. This is it." Katie tipped her head sympathetically. "Look, I'll take one more tour around." She reached out and squeezed Tressa Fay's arm before she melted into the crowd.

> I swear I'm right here. and there isn't another Canyon Tacos

> on washington street next to the theater

> with a red coat rack and big windows that open, and you said they were open, but I'm looking at them right now, and they're closed. it's cold and windy and miserable out

> Call me.

Tressa Fay waited a few moments to catch Katie coming back from her round and thanked her. She stepped outside and tapped the call button. It seemed like forever before the phone started to ring, and then it was a jerky, broken ringtone before someone picked up.

"Hey! Hello? Meryl?"

"Tress . . . so it . . ." Her voice was cloaked in static.

"I think we have a bad connection. Can you hear me?"

". . . connec . . . do you . . ."

Tressa let out a short, frustrated growl and disconnected the call. Tried again. Same jerky ringtone. "Meryl? Is this better?"

"Hi!" Meryl's voice came through clearly, but then the call dropped with another rush of static.

Tressa Fay pulled her phone away to look at their text messages. The bubbles were the color that indicated she and Meryl had the same kind of phone, and in Green Bay, they were likely to have the same carrier. Tressa Fay had a strong signal. Meryl's number was local.

Her phone buzzed with another call. Unknown. Tressa Fay picked it up.

"Hello . . . Tre . . ." The call dropped.

Tressa Fay opened up the chat again.

we are not connecting

This is so ridiculous. Why this night?
It's so pretty out.

Tressa Fay looked around at the dark street that was acting like a shaft to direct freezing-cold air from the nearby Fox River right through her shirt. The navy-blue sky was covered in black clouds, and the air was so damp, it made the wind colder when it hit her in cruel bursts.

She felt sick.

It had been a long time since she'd been catfished like this, if ever. She was thirty-one. She hadn't used apps to date for several years now. When she had, that was the last time she'd run across people who were so hurt, they would use another real human being to entertain themselves.

She toggled back to Meryl's Instagram, wondering if this person on the other end of the phone was even Meryl. It was possible Meryl herself didn't know that someone was using her name and profile to catfish strangers.

This was why Tressa Fay didn't go out.

She swiped back to the chat, furiously blinking tears out of her eyes, freezing in the dark, cold wind. **never contact me again**, she typed.

She sent the message and stared at the screen. No response.

She scrolled back to the beginning of their chat, touching Meryl's first funny message. **One collapsed bridge and a girl's got a reputation.** She was about to block the number when she stopped.

Touching the message, she'd seen something strange. She slid it over.

7:25 p.m. May 1

Weird.

She slid each of the messages over, and the times got later, but the date stayed the same. She shook her phone, closed all the apps, and double-checked her time/date settings. They were correct. Then she opened the chat again. Still the first of May.

Today was October 1.

Tressa Fay felt as if she were floating just enough to not fit in reality. It had to be some kind of random misfire. Or, if it wasn't that, then it was something more ominous related to the upsetting and bizarre game this stranger had played with her. It was so dark, and she was so cold. She needed to rest. She'd gotten badly keyed up. Hopeful.

In the event this Meryl was a victim, too, she DMed her on Instagram with the bare details and the phone number she'd been messaging with. Then Tressa Fay blocked the number.

The drive back to her apartment barely made an impression on her.

Nothing bad ever came of staying the fuck home.

OCTOBER 3
. . . .

TRESSA FAY HELD HER BONE-HANDLED STRAIGHT RAZOR AGAINST the taut, pale ribbon of hair between the fingers of her opposite hand and carved. The curls she released sprang away from her blade like something alive, rousted from the underbrush.

She stepped back and narrowed her eyes.

"When you do that," Guy said, "I want to stick my tongue out at you."

"I wouldn't notice if you did." Tressa Fay stepped forward to sift the precise layers and pieces she'd made in Guy's elven hair, checking if her cut was perfect.

It was.

"You're finished." Guy smiled at her in the mirror. "I can tell because your imperious aura has mellowed. It's back to its ordinary level of bossiness."

"Yeah, yeah." Tressa Fay focused on disinfecting, then polishing her blade on the leather strop that hung from her bench. When she was satisfied, she folded it into its handle and snugged it into the holster she wore on her thigh. "Let me take pictures. People are always interested in how a cut can make waves like yours curly."

Guy was already standing in front of the mirror, running their fingers through their hair and posing, then rubbing their hands over their tight gray Henley shirt. "I look like a sexy snow fairy who left the fae to front a band called Slink and the Bloods."

"Is that good?" Tressa Fay set up her ring light.

"Very. What do you call this cut?"

"'Guy.'"

Guy rolled their eyes at Tressa Fay in the mirror.

"It has some shag," she said. "Some mullet. Depending on how you style it, some faux-hawk vibes."

"I love it. I don't know why I waited so long for you to do this." Guy stepped into the light, pursing their lips, letting Tressa Fay snap pictures.

"I like it when people don't get in my chair until they're ready. That's when the magic happens."

Guy pointed their chin down and looked up, trying a sexy, menacing glare that was actually pretty affecting. "I think I needed to get into my feels after starting testosterone before I was ready for something like this. Honestly, it does feel a bit magical."

Tressa Fay's eyes started to water, and she stopped taking pictures. "*Guy.*"

"Don't start crying, because then I will. Do you want one where I'm pulling my shirt up a bit? I hit core hard this morning."

"Absolutely I do."

Tressa Fay finished taking pictures, admiring how her cut made Guy's cheekbones sharp, their silvery blue eyes impossible to ignore. "I'm AirDropping this set to you. You'll want these."

Guy opened them up on their phone and looked at them, smiling. "Yes, I will. Thanks, Tiff."

She smiled at the old nickname, a pronunciation of her first name's initials. "Where are you headed after this?" Tressa Fay had already mostly closed down the salon for the day, leaving only Guy's hair to sweep and her chair and station to clean.

"Michael and I are going to see that classical guitarist at the university theater. You?"

Michael was a man who Guy had gone to law school with in Michigan. Back then, Guy hadn't transitioned and was presenting as female, and Michael identified as gay—but there had always been chemistry, close friendship, and deep feelings Guy hadn't known how to express. They'd reconnected six months ago when Michael moved to Green Bay to accept a partner track at a law firm. It was a love story about timing, and probably about being who you were supposed to be, because when they'd started hanging out this time around, it wasn't long before they were both head over heels.

"I've got a date with Netflix tonight. Still a little wobbly." Tressa Fay started spraying down her chair and station.

Guy sat on the live-edge bench along the wall, crossed their legs at the knee, and leaned back. "I'm sure. But what about it hurts the most? Because when you talked to me about it, I felt like it wasn't the catfishing, at least not entirely." They patted the bench next to them.

Tressa Fay sat down next to Guy and started idly playing with the wavy curls she'd just cut. "You caught that, huh?"

"I've known you for more of my life than I can remember."

She leaned her head against the wall. "I liked her."

"The fake engineer."

"She felt real to me. Obviously, she wasn't. It was just some text messages and pictures. To be honest, I'm not sure why I ran to Canyon like that without checking myself even once." Tressa Fay fiddled with a fingernail, sending a deep breath past her racing heart to soothe it. Guy had been honest with her. She wanted to be honest with them.

For so long, the time since Amy had felt like no time at all. Six months ago, Tressa Fay still slept differently. Sometimes when she needed to settle back to sleep, her leg reached for Amy's in the night to hook itself around. Except she didn't find Amy. So she didn't go back to sleep.

But lately, she'd been sleeping through the night. She'd felt *better*, all the way better in a way that was tough to pin down but easy to appreciate. And she *had* rushed out of her apartment to meet Meryl.

"Actually, that's not true. I am sure," she said. "You know how they say 'it just takes time'? I needed the time after Amy. It's like time is the *only* thing that could've given me the space to get to know myself."

"And the Tiff you know now didn't hesitate to haul ass downtown to meet up with this woman."

"No! She didn't. When Meryl wrong-number texted me, there wasn't any coyness, no nerves or game. No dancing. I felt like I knew her, or recognized her. Of course not actually, but also, *actually*. So I didn't hesitate. I had to get to her."

"And then when she wasn't there . . ."

"I left my apartment feeling *yes* like a gong through my whole body. I had no doubt she was something for me. So when she wasn't there, wasn't *real*, can you understand how I would doubt that I've really gotten to know myself better at all?"

"Have you considered that maybe the reason she had this effect on you is not so much this Meryl, but more that you *are* so ready to get out there, to meet people and be vulnerable and let yourself get introduced to hot women, that any connection feels like *the* connection?"

Tressa Fay let her hand drop into her lap.

Guy sighed with understanding. "I know how hard it's been, and I'm the very last person to suggest getting back on the apps or heading to the bar. But going out with your friends, getting introduced to someone? Maybe that's the everything you're feeling ready for."

"There's something else." Tressa Fay reached around and slid her phone out of her back pocket, almost expecting it to feel hot or electrified, or to release tiny knives.

"You showed me the date discrepancy," Guy said. "More than once. You told me the tech person at the phone place said it could be a lot of things."

Shaking her head, Tressa Fay reminded herself to feel her feet against the floor—something a therapist had told her to do when she was anxious or overwhelmed. She swiped open a paused video. "It's this. Watch this."

Guy took the phone from Tressa Fay. It was a local news segment from a couple of years ago. The reporter and the woman she was interviewing were both holding umbrellas and standing in the middle of Main Street on the east side, which had experienced terrible flooding through the night. There was a stranded car behind them, water up around its wheels.

Guy pointed a finger at Tressa Fay. "You cyberstalked her! Or at least you cyberstalked the person whose identity was stolen by a catfisher. So this is a catfisher, or the victim of one, who you found an old video of."

Tressa Fay heard Guy, but mostly she heard the soft audio from the clip, which she'd watched enough times to almost have it memorized. Meryl Whit's husky voice carefully explained storm drains to Audrey Hatsinger of WBAY News. "She posted this on her Insta. I didn't stalk. I don't do that. But that's not why

I'm showing you. Keep watching, but look there, at the top of the street, where there isn't flooding. By the green awning."

Guy raised their eyebrows but watched the video. Then their hand covered their mouth. "That's—"

"That's me." Tressa Fay reached over and tapped pause. "I remember this day. I had been booked by the salon with the green awning to teach a class on curly cuts, and I thought they'd cancel because of the flooding, but they called me and told me I could still come because they were dry. I remember seeing the news crew. I remember noticing her hair."

Tressa Fay had noticed more than Meryl's hair that afternoon. She'd looked down the street, clocking the news crew, and seen her immediately. Peach and gold hair in two fat Dutch braids, tall green rubber boots. An *interesting* person.

She'd opened the salon door with a smile on her face.

Guy restarted the video, watching Tressa Fay get out of her Fiat and open her blue umbrella with black cats on it. You could see her red jeans, a flash of her dark bob. Her face, looking down the street, was shadowed under the umbrella, but it was definitely her, in the same place as Meryl, at the same time.

"I think the person who texted me *was* Meryl Whit." Tressa Fay took her phone from Guy. "I think if it hadn't been raining and I didn't have somewhere to be, or if the news crew had already finished up, I probably would have found an excuse to talk to her *then*."

They let that sit between them in the quiet salon, Tressa Fay's fingers wrapped around the solid shape of her phone. She didn't say anything more. She didn't know what the video meant.

She only knew how it felt.

"I want to tell you," Guy said slowly, "that it's not a great idea to look for signs and wonders. Especially when something like this happens, like what happened to you the other night. Or to search for reasons, to try to solve some mystery or assign something you found on the internet to fate." Guy ran their hand through the new, tumbling curls at their brow. "I *want* to tell you that, except I can't. You were there with me that night I realized I wanted Michael. You heard me, so you know what I really believe behind all my professions of logic and reason and my love for research." They smiled.

Tressa Fay grinned back at them, glad to be understood. Guy had practically made one of those maps with red string laced all over it with thumbtacks, connecting dozens of points along the course of their whole friendship with Michael as inevitably leading to their moment of understanding.

The bell on the front door jingled. Tressa Fay had thought she'd locked it. She stood up, Guy right behind her, then in front of her, protectively leading the way toward the door. Two people came into the dim salon, looking around. One was a Black masc-presenting person with beautiful throwback Jheri curls that made Tressa Fay wonder what genius was cutting their hair, and the other was a short, gorgeous redhead wearing what looked like a vintage square-dancing dress that showed off how delicious their cleavage and round belly were. Neither one of them looked threatening. In fact, they looked very much like Tressa Fay–type clients.

"Hey, sorry," she said. "I'm closed. I could help you real quick to grab my next available booking, though." She started toward the reception desk.

"Are you Tressa Fay?" Jheri Curls asked.

"I am." She smiled and walked to the books. "Let me get your name."

They shook their head. "I'm James. This is Gayle. We're here about Meryl."

The smile froze on her face. She tried to find the sensation of the soles of her shoes against the floor, but she couldn't. The hair on the back of her neck was actually standing up. "Sorry?"

"Why are you fucking with her family like this?" Gayle asked this in a soft voice, but her face had gone pink. "What could you possibly be getting from it?"

Guy had moved to Tressa Fay's side. She was still rigid, her thoughts spinning. If she hadn't felt Guy's hand on her elbow, warm and sure, she might have fainted, and she hadn't done that since she'd ended up in the hospital after her allergic reaction to the spilled perm solution.

"Could you help us out and explain what's happened?" Guy was using their easy, calm lawyer voice, and Tressa Fay made herself take a breath. She wished she could turn on more lights, make this feel more real.

She watched as James made eye contact with Guy, clearly trying to assess them. "Gayle is Meryl's sister. I'm Meryl's closest friend. Ex-boyfriend." He looked at Tressa Fay as if that previous status should add some kind of meaning to his explanation. "All we have left to do at this point is monitor her social media. Her email. And it's basically hopeless, obviously. Then you left that DM, and we couldn't figure it out. We knew about when you stood her up last spring, but to DM her about it with everything that's going on now? It was so cruel. We talked about taking it to the police. We still might."

James's jaw was tight. He was angry. Gayle was angry. Tressa Fay had two angry people in front of her, angry at her for a reason she couldn't understand, but it had something to do with Meryl and the other night, except they were talking about "last spring."

May.

Tressa Fay gripped the edge of the desk where the booking

calendar was. She was glad Guy was here, but she wished Mary were, too. Mary didn't use a computer. She used this calendar. She didn't like that computers made mistakes in a way that meant no one could tell if it was the computer or the person who made the mistake. Mary wanted any mistake with a booking to be *hers*. Tressa Fay didn't even have a website. She had Instagram, but if people messaged her there, she just gave them the salon's phone number. When Mary made an appointment, she put it in the booking calendar, then copied it into a day planner for Tressa Fay.

That was what Tressa Fay was thinking about, wildly. Mary. Her ways. If she were here, she would be able to figure this out, because difficult people, angry people, didn't ruffle Mary. She was good at them. Tressa Fay looked at James and Gayle, these two people who she'd thought were *her* people, her kind of people.

"I don't think we understand," Guy said. "This sounds very serious, and I promise, we want to help."

"I thought I was catfished two nights ago," Tressa Fay heard herself saying. "I got a text, but me and the person who texted me figured out she had the wrong number. We started chatting. The person I was texting with directed me to Meryl's Insta to show me what they looked like."

"We read your message." Gayle bit the words out. "We know what you said." She didn't sound as though she believed that what Tressa Fay had said was true. Or reliable.

"Meryl has been missing for a *month*," James said, his voice breaking. "Don't you read the paper? Meryl Whit."

Tressa Fay did not read the paper. Her dad did, and at their weekly diner meals he sometimes told her about the latest Green Bay crime news, but she didn't remember anything about a missing woman, and she was sure she hadn't heard of Meryl Whit—or any Meryl—until the other night. She had seen her and her braids and her boots in the rain a couple of years ago, but she hadn't known it was Meryl then. She hadn't lied to Guy about not stalking Meryl other than looking at her Instagram, feeling sad and at sea.

"She was out with us downtown last month," James said. "We were at Speakeasy. She went to use the restroom and never came back. We've been searching for her ever since. There's a police investigation."

Tressa Fay put her hand to her throat. "I'm sorry. I'm so sorry. I'm sorry someone used her pictures like that. I blocked the number. You can—" Tressa Fay pulled her phone out of her pocket, and this time her phone felt heavy and cold and useless, and her hands were shaking. She fumbled the phone, nearly dropped it. "I'll unblock the number so you can see everything." She set the phone on the reception desk as if it were an animal that might bite her, went back to her blocked numbers, unblocked the number that had texted her, and opened the chat.

Gayle slid the phone toward herself and briefly scrolled the chat. She shook her head. "No. Stop it. I know what this says. She already showed it to me. We talked about it."

Guy stepped forward. "I'm sorry, but you just told us she's been missing for a month."

"That's right," Gayle said. Tressa Fay could see the strong resemblance between Gayle and the Meryl on Instagram. The red hair, although Gayle's was a few shades darker. The same full upper lip. It made her chest tight.

"Then I don't understand. This conversation"—Guy put their fingertips on Tressa Fay's phone—"happened two nights ago."

"No," James said, insistent. "Meryl had a date back in May. It was May Day. I remember because she had given me a bouquet of flowers, left it on my doorstep. She likes traditions like that. She had a date with a woman she'd been talking to on one of the apps. She talked to me while she was getting ready. We dated a long time ago, but we've been friends since. She got stood up, texted her date, but instead she got you." James looked at Tressa Fay.

It wasn't May now. It was October. October 3. It was cold. It was dark. Tressa Fay wanted to *shout* this.

But also, also, she couldn't help remembering what Meryl had said. *It's hot in here, even with the front windows wide open.*

"Just really look at it." Tressa Fay moved Guy's hand out of the way and woke up the chat. She pushed her phone even closer to Gayle. "Please."

Tressa Fay wasn't sure what she thought Gayle could see. The text dates were wrong, just as they had been before. May 1, May Day. She sat down on the chair. Was this some kind of elaborate, multistep scam? A terrible prank? Her face felt hot, but everywhere else, she was cold. She couldn't stop thinking about the braids under the umbrella. The green boots. Just a few minutes ago, she'd been talking to Guy about fate, or serendipity, feeling like she already knew Meryl.

Gayle gingerly picked up Tressa Fay's phone, tapping and swiping. A tear rolled down her face, but she didn't brush it away. As though she were used to tears.

Of course she would be.

"This doesn't make any sense." Gayle looked at Tressa Fay. "What are you playing at?"

"Please tell me what you see," Guy said.

Their calm lawyer persona must have been working, because Gayle nodded. "This is everything Meryl showed me. Back in

May. Including the last message, where Tressa Fay told her not to call her again. This is Meryl's number. *Her* messages are from May. But"—Gayle looked at Tressa Fay—"*hers* aren't. They're from October first. Like the DM."

"Tressa Fay's timing is consistent between the chat and Instagram," Guy said, sounding less than easy for the first time. "May I see the Instagram message that you saw?" they asked Gayle.

She pulled out her phone, tapped and swiped it, and handed it to Guy, who studied the screen. "Had Meryl seen this message before you did?" they asked. "I mean, was it marked 'seen,' or—"

"No. It was new. Boldface. Meryl didn't read it. How could she? She left her phone on our table when she went to the bathroom. Last month. Don't you read the paper? Watch the news? Have the internet?" Gayle rubbed the tear away now, her sadness and anger trading places so fast, it made Tressa Fay feel uneasy and helpless.

"I'm sorry. I don't know anything about it." Tressa Fay closed her eyes. She'd thought the mismatched dates in the chat were messed up from a problem with the messaging app. "Is it my phone?" she asked. "Can it do that? Can it mess up date stamps? I called the tech people. They told me it wasn't a big deal. Lots of things could cause it." Tressa Fay could barely hear the words coming out of her mouth. She couldn't tell if it was that she was speaking softly or her ears were closing up.

"What I'm telling you is that I talked to Meryl about this back in May. When it happened." Gayle reached into her bag and pulled out a manila envelope, then slid out a cutout from a newspaper and put it on the reception desk. "Look."

It was a *Gazette* article about Meryl. The picture in the article was a professional portrait, probably from Meryl's workplace.

Her pale red hair was smooth. She wore a pretty blouse with a tie, and her freckles were so numerous, some of them grouped together like watercolors. Her glasses had big frames, pink-to-orange glitter ombre. She was beautiful. She had gone missing.

SEARCH CONTINUES FOR CITY ENGINEER MISSING FROM DOWNTOWN BAR SINCE SEPTEMBER 4

Tressa Fay looked away from the newspaper clipping. Gayle picked it up and carefully slid it back into the envelope, stowing it in her purse. "Does it sound like her?" Tressa Fay asked. "The chat, I mean."

"Yes. She has a red mathlete T-shirt. She showed me this chat on her own phone, trying to figure out what went wrong."

Tressa Fay looked at Guy. *Do you think these people are trying to hurt me?* That's what she wanted to ask. But she didn't feel it. She couldn't actually imagine anyone, in real life, staging such an elaborate prank. Such a devastatingly cruel one. She thought, really, they were right to suspect *her*.

Everyone around the reception desk seemed to figure out they'd reached the end of this conversation. Either James and Gayle would tell the police about Tressa Fay or they wouldn't. What else was there to do?

The screen on Tressa Fay's phone lit up. It was still on the text exchange she'd had with Meryl that Gayle had just looked at. Three dots popped up.

Cold prickles washed through her body.

Her phone buzzed, and everyone in the room jumped.

"There's a text," she said. "Where's Meryl's phone?" Her voice sounded loud now.

Gayle clearly wanted to snatch up Tressa Fay's phone, but she reached into her purse. "Here." She pulled out a phone with a blue plastic case that had a picture of a glass half full of water on it beneath the legend NEITHER, THE GLASS IS TWICE AS BIG AS IT NEEDS TO BE.

Tressa Fay couldn't help it. She choked on a laugh. "I'm sorry." She pointed at the phone case. "The engineering joke. It's . . . funny."

She felt terrible. But James smiled at her for the first time.

Meryl's phone was dark.

"It's charged. I keep it that way." Gayle woke it up and put in a passcode.

Tressa Fay picked up her own phone.

Hey. I'm really sorry, the first new text said.

Then more.

> Oh! You unblocked me.

> I was just here with my sister, trying to figure this out. I told her I didn't think Tressa Fay would do a prank? And I couldn't help apologizing to you. Even though I knew you wouldn't get my texts anymore.

Tressa Fay shook her head. *No*, she thought. "No."

Gayle was white. She looked at James, who had stepped back and crossed his arms, obviously upset.

"What?" Guy asked.

"I remember," Gayle said. "But I don't understand, because I remember this *not* happening, too." She said this to James, and he nodded.

"Please say what this is." Tressa Fay held up her phone.

"I remember sitting with her. Talking about the date. I remember her realizing she was unblocked and typing something to you."

"Two days ago," Guy confirmed.

"No. In May."

What Gayle was saying was impossible. She was saying the text Tressa Fay had just gotten was a text Gayle had watched her sister send five months ago—but until it showed up, Gayle hadn't remembered that happening.

Because it hadn't happened.

Tressa Fay growled in frustration. **what's today's date?** she texted.

> **Um. Okay. May 3?**

"I remember her laughing because she told me you asked her what the day was, and if I thought this was going to turn out to be some kind of queer *While You Were Sleeping*. Like maybe you were waking up from a coma." Gayle was almost whispering.

"What *is* this?" Guy stepped forward. Their voice was angry. Tressa Fay never heard Guy angry. "Both of you are seconds from being asked to leave."

> **you're not playing a joke?**

When Tressa Fay sent this text through, Meryl's phone didn't buzz or light up like it was receiving texts. But a response came up on Tressa Fay's phone.

No. No. No. I swear. God. I don't know what happened! My sister's convinced you're pranking, but I feel like that would be so bad for you. Because you're kind of famous. And . . . I don't know. I don't get that vibe.

"Did she write back to you? What did she say?" Gayle couldn't see Tressa Fay's phone now.

Tressa Fay held out her hand for Meryl's phone, and Gayle slid it into her palm. When Tressa Fay woke it up, the chat was still there. Meryl's last text was on the thread, dated May 3.

I'm not pranking you, Tressa Fay wrote, watching Meryl's phone. There weren't three dots. When she sent it, her message simply appeared on Meryl's screen. Sent October 3.

She looked up. Everyone had seen it. Guy's breathing was ragged.

James made a horrible noise in his throat. "Tell her not to come to Speakeasy with us on September fourth. Tell her to stay home. *Please.*" His jaw was tight. Gayle leaned against the desk as though she couldn't trust her legs to hold her up.

Tressa Fay put Meryl's phone down on the desk next to Gayle.

can I ask you to do something? she typed with clumsy, icy-numb fingertips on her own screen. don't go to Speakeasy with your sister and James on September 4.

Then Tressa Fay set down her own phone on the reception desk as if it were radioactive and she couldn't hold it for too long. Her message appeared on Meryl's chat screen. No buzz. No dots.

"God." Gayle took the manila envelope out of her purse again, looking at James, who appeared genuinely horrified. She shook out the newspaper article. Then she dropped it on the floor.

Guy picked it up and looked at what Gayle had seen.

Tressa Fay watched them as her phone buzzed again.

> Don't block me, and I won't, but that is the absolute weirdest. Clue me in, please. And how you know I have a sister and a friend named James. Gayle's calling James, certain he's in on something.

"I remember that call," James said. "Right now. But I also know that I definitely didn't remember it a minute ago."

Guy showed Tressa Fay the newspaper.

SEARCH CONTINUES FOR CITY ENGINEER MISSING FROM HER HOME SINCE SEPTEMBER 4

Missing from her home. Not from Speakeasy. The story had changed.

Tressa Fay pulled up the *Gazette* on her phone. Guy was already pulling it up on theirs. She tapped in Meryl's name in the search box.

The online article was the same. The same new headline.

"Her phone's gone. Oh my God. It disappeared." Gayle was looking at the spot where Meryl's phone had been sitting on top of the desk. Where Tressa Fay had put it.

Where she remembered putting it.

But now she *also* remembered that Gayle had told them she didn't have Meryl's phone. She'd said the police had it. They had taken it from Meryl's house as evidence. Gayle had only seen the Instagram message because she logged into Meryl's accounts on her own computer once a day.

Tressa Fay knew that wasn't what had happened. It wasn't what Gayle had said at any point since she walked into the salon. But now, suddenly, she remembered it happening, exactly as though it had. Just like the headline seemed to have changed, her own memories had, too.

Both things had happened. Both memories felt real. And that had to be because there had been one reality, and then, just by asking Meryl not to go to Speakeasy, they'd made another one.

But the experiment hadn't worked. Meryl was still gone.

"Shit," Guy said.

"I don't understand." James was shaking his head.

"Oh my God." Gayle put her hand over her mouth.

Tressa Fay didn't know where the sudden calm in her body came from, the calm that put her phone in her back pocket and pulled her keys out of the other one. "Let's go to my apartment and figure this out," she said. "Call whoever you think should be there."

Her phone was buzzing in her pocket as she locked the door.

OCTOBER 3, LATE

. . . .

TRESSA FAY'S APARTMENT HADN'T SEEN THIS MUCH ACTION IN A long time.

Gayle and James had come on their own. They'd told Tressa Fay there was no one else they would want to invite. He was Meryl's closest friend, and she was Meryl's only family in town. Gayle was curled up on Tressa Fay's sofa with Epinephrine on her lap, while James occupied one side of a big beanbag chair that Tressa Fay had pulled out from under her bed.

Mary was on the other side of the beanbag, and Guy sat in Tressa Fay's rocking chair with Michael between their legs on the floor. Michael's sharply barbered dark hair was messed up from running his hands through it so much.

It had taken a while to bring Michael and Mary and Linds up to speed. Tressa Fay wasn't completely sure it was fair of her to have called so many people here—to have *all* her people here to support and help her—but she didn't know how she could possibly handle the utter mindfuck of this situation without them.

She sat on the other end of the sofa from Gayle, her phone on her knee.

Linds, of all people, was holding court in the middle of the rug. In addition to teaching creative writing, Linds was the author of numerous self-published eight-hundred-page queer fantasy and sci-fi books, which was turning out to make her uniquely qualified to clarify what the hell was going on.

"Multiverse theory." She made an expansive gesture, the sleeves of her loose sweater sliding down and revealing her brightly tattooed arms. "Obviously not a theory. Einstein has been right about everything so far, plus we've successfully sent subatomic particles into a parallel universe. Parallel worlds are for real."

"But you have to explain it like we're five," Guy reminded her.

"And without any examples from books we haven't read, movies we haven't seen, or from what people talk about on your D&D Discord," Mary chimed in.

Linds smiled at Guy. "I will if you tell me I'm pretty."

"You're gorgeous. But also." Guy made a *get on with it* motion with their hand.

Tressa Fay's phone buzzed on her knee. She didn't let herself pick it up to look, hating how it made Gayle stiffen. Once they'd all gotten to her apartment, more than an hour ago now, James had firmly requested, for the time being, that they not do anything else in the category of what he called "creating additional reality." Everyone had agreed Tressa Fay could continue texting with Meryl, but she needed to keep it light, not say anything else about where Meryl should go or not go on September 4, and definitely say nothing about Gayle or James.

Tressa Fay adjusted her body, sliding her phone into her hand, hidden by her thigh, and glanced at the screen.

> I know you said you were with your friends and probably couldn't text, but I worked out nothing was stopping me from texting you.

So far, the keep-it-light strategy was working. Everything was holding at Gayle and James remembering two versions of the night Meryl disappeared. Two different sets of memories—the version where Meryl went missing from Speakeasy, and a new version where she went missing from home. Tressa Fay and Guy also had doubled memories of the consequences of that experiment, including Meryl's phone disappearing from the reception desk and the newspaper headline changing.

What was weird to Tressa Fay was that having two different memories about the same event didn't feel *unfamiliar*. It felt like wondering if she'd left her bag in the break room or in her car, because she remembered leaving it both places. The only difference now was that she had proof that both things had happened. The bag was in the break room, and the bag was in the car. Experimenting with the fabric of reality, it turned out, felt disconcertingly *normal*.

But if she were Gayle, it still wouldn't be long before she decided she didn't give a fig about reality and would rather talk to her sister again. So Tressa Fay jumped when her phone buzzed, even as she glanced down and couldn't help her smile.

> Because I can't stop now that I know we obviously had some kind of epic missed connection the other night and you don't think I'm a troll.

She had managed to successfully hold off Meryl from asking too many questions by telling her that the night they were supposed to meet at Canyon had been a "very weird evening" and that she was "with friends right now" but would give her a real explanation later. Meryl was clearly happy to pick up their flirting where they had left off and get her questions answered later.

It was a testament to the power of Tressa Fay's weakness for Meryl's freckles and game that she was more preoccupied with getting back to Meryl than she was with hearing about evidence of alternate realities. It was *tough* out there. Surely space-time was a smaller hurdle to dating than, well, *dating*.

> Unless you like that kind of thing. I could roleplay a troll or an orc or a mage so hard. Fur corsets, leather panniers, fairy wings, whatever you want.

Tressa Fay bit her lip to keep in the giggle, looking around to see if anyone noticed. Mary had her eyes narrowed right at her. *Oops.*

She let the phone drop to the sofa cushion. Screen side up, though.

"Quantum physics," Linds said. "But before you look at me like that, please let me say that quantum phenomena aren't rare. It's not science fiction. It explains so much of what we are otherwise unable to explain." She put her hand on her chest. "Right now, this second, we are living in one of many extremely similar universes happening alongside this one."

Michael leaned forward. "All right, but there's esoteric scientific theories on the one hand, and then there's a phone disappearing right before our friends' eyes on the other."

"I hear that, but I'm trying to tell you there's nothing esoteric about these theories. Take the quantum theory of superposition.

That's when an object isn't *just* an object that you can see and hold. It is that object, the object you expect it to be, but it's *also* a combination of multiple possible objects at the same time."

"Ugh," Mary said.

Linds gave her a wide-eyed-professor look that meant *Stay with me.* "The reality of the theory of superposition was demonstrated in the nineteenth century. A guy made two cuts parallel to each other in a piece of paper. He covered one cut and shined a beam of light through the paper to hit a photographic plate. Then he did the same thing again, but he covered the second cut, and he used a second plate. He developed the two pictures. One had a white bar of light on one side. The other had a white bar of light on the other side. Exactly what we'd expect. This is the reality we think we live in, where what we feel and what we see is how it looks. A bar of light on the left, a bar of light on the right. So what happened when he didn't cover either cut? When he shined the light through both cuts at the same time to expose the plate?"

"There were two white bars in the picture," James said. "Do I get an A, Professor?"

Lindsey smiled. "Not this time. It seems like there *should* be light coming out of each cut the way it did the first time, streaming to the plate, making two straight lines. But remember, light's both a particle and a wave. It's *moving* in a wave. So when you have two streams of light next to each other, the projected light beams *interfere* with each other. And in the time it takes this light to travel to the plate and expose it, the particle waves of light interfere in uncountable different ways. The light takes *every possible trajectory* on its way to the plate and is in multiple states at once."

"We can't see that," Michael said. "But if the beams of light coming through the paper are close together, we can see that they're merging. They'd look more like one beam of light than two."

"Exactly correct," Linds said. "We can't see it. The photographic plate can. The picture this photographer developed looks like a wide area of many gradations of white and gray. It shows all the possible solutions, like a math problem where x equals ten *and* x equals forty-two. We can't see it, but the photograph records it. The photograph is what's real. The photograph is a picture of what the universe really, actually looks like, which is something we can't see. We don't even recognize that what's in the picture *is* the universe we're living in."

"So the phone is like the photograph?" James asked. "It's showing us two universes we expect to be separate, but they aren't. Because we're here. Meryl's there"—James pointed at the phone—"and not here. *And* we're here, talking about Meryl while Meryl blows up Tressa Fay's phone, so it's like Meryl is here. The phone is showing us reality. And the reality is that Meryl is alive and well. That's a solution." James crossed his arms and dared Linds to say different.

Michael took Guy's hand when Guy reached it down to him. "But we need a *solution* solution. Happily ever after or nothing."

Linds nodded. "My limitation here is that the language of physics is math. The math is way *more* right than the phone, because humans are so unreliable. However, none of us know how to do math like that, so offering up a solution is beyond me." Linds winced at Michael's exasperated expression. "But also, there are ideas like entanglement. It's such a beautiful idea. The theory is there are objects that can't be described on their own. They can only be described, observed, exist, by describing the other, observing the other, and vice versa. If two things are entangled, they are linked together forever, no matter how far apart they move from each other in space."

Tressa Fay felt something inside her go still and quiet, listening.

"Think about your first love," Linds said. "No matter how long you live, how far away you are from that first love, you're linked to them. Your story can't be completely told without them. You're entangled." She shifted her position, looking up at the ceiling, and blew out a breath. "That doesn't seem hopeless to me."

"No," Mary said solemnly. "I like the way that sounds."

"Like, even Schrödinger's box was asking us to think about quantum reality," Linds said. "It's probably the most famous example. Schrödinger was the scientist who explained all of this by asking us to imagine a cat closed in a box with poison. Until we open the box, we don't know if the cat is alive or dead. Until we see the cat, the cat is both. There is no alive cat without also dead cat, and I don't mean in our imaginations. I mean if you see a dead cat in the box when it's opened, there is a you in another universe who finds a living cat. There is a you who never opens the box. All of those are real. They're entangled. Nothing in the universe is truly lost."

Tressa Fay shook her head. "But." She fished around for the question she wanted to ask. "*But* is all I got. Consider it a question that breaks this whole thing open."

"Maybe your question is why?" Linds tipped her head to the side. "As in, why us? Why now? Why Meryl?"

"That's *my* question," Gayle interjected. "I've been struggling to come to terms with what the police have told me is Meryl's likely death while I'm still desperately trying to find her. Forgive me if observing my sister text in actual, real time with an actual, real person right in front of me brings up more buts and whys than a desire to get out a calculator." Gayle glanced at Tressa Fay's phone. "She's there, so my heart tells me she's *here*. Or at least she can be."

James pointed at Gayle. "That's where I'm at."

Linds's eyebrows arched with fascinated interest. Tressa Fay was glad that at least one of them was in their element. "The why question is actually a how question. How have we come to experience two universes at the same time? Or managed to travel from one to the other? Because that's what we're talking about."

Mary groaned. "*How*, then? I'm starting to feel the way I felt in Mr. Arts's science class in high school. Which is angry."

Now James pointed at Mary. "What she said, also."

"I'm afraid the only answers I have to offer aren't going to help anyone's feelings." Linds wrapped her arms around her knees. "Most people don't seem to find the multiverse exactly comforting. Many-worlds theory is very hotly debated. So, okay, hang in with me. Say we're observing an electron."

"I would never do that," Mary said. "Ever."

"I know, but pretend. Pretend the electron is a little star. And when you're looking at it, it's waving up and down. A bright star moving up and down and making a wave across the night sky."

"Okay."

"But as soon as you look away, the wave collapses, and it goes back to being a star. A single point of light. *You* determine what something actually is. The phenomenon we're observing is changed by us. It's changed by everything we can imagine it could be. It depends on us. *Because* we know a cat can be alive and it can be dead, our knowing that matters and affects the cat. Us. Everything. Absolutely everything."

Tressa Fay reached over to put her hand protectively on Epinephrine, who had left Gayle's lap and found a good spot on the back of the sofa to watch the proceedings. "No cats may be harmed."

"Agree," Linds said. "Schrödinger went about explaining many-worlds theory in the most gruesome way possible, and we do not approve."

"No," Gayle said. Her tone made it clear that she wasn't talking about cats. "*No.*"

"No," Linds said softly. "We don't need an experiment that hurts a cat, or a person, to give us permission to simply wave a hand over what is happening and make a good guess that something *like* this theory, at least, is what's happening. There's a world where a series of events unfolded that led to Meryl's disappearance. Our world, we can call it. And there's probably worlds where she didn't disappear. And there's hers"—she pointed in the direction of Tressa Fay's phone, which vibrated softly as though in response—"where she hasn't *yet*, because time unfolded a different way. And maybe in that world, Meryl won't ever disappear. We can't know."

> Was that too much? Not enough?

> I was teasing, but now I'm interested in the answer because my bedroom's just dim enough I can't be embarrassed.

> Instead of the golden hour, it's the mood lighting hour.

A picture popped up in the chat. A *good* picture—twilight making all those coppery waves fade to a pale fawn, glasses, oversized T-shirt draping in a way that suggested little other clothing.

Tressa Fay let her hair fall forward to conceal what was probably her flirt face, the one Guy teased her about because she went literally heart-eyed when pretty girls paid attention to her.

"But Tressa Fay talked to her," Guy said. "She's *still* talking to her." Guy cleared their throat as Tressa Fay looked up guiltily. "And Gayle and James remember two versions of what happened. That makes it seem like we're in the same world as Meryl. Let's call it the world where Meryl talks to Tressa Fay."

Linds smiled. "Yes. Schrödinger thought that once you opened the box and the cat was alive, then the world where the cat was dead collapsed. But other folks have decided that those other worlds don't collapse. They carry on. So far, people haven't traveled to another world, experienced it, and then returned to the world they started from. Some think we could. Wormholes. Dimensions between worlds. String theory has some ideas. Books and movies use magic or machines."

Gayle stopped scratching Epinephrine, who had moved back into her lap. "Isn't a phone a machine?"

"Yes. And there's evidence that simple circuits, like the kind you make with potatoes and copper wire, can learn, entirely on their own. They have sentience. Maybe."

"A smartphone is way more complicated than a potato clock," James said. "And I know what I know, and I saw what I saw. I don't like it, but that's happening." He jabbed the air in the direction of Tressa Fay's phone, which buzzed again, though Tressa Fay didn't dare look. "Events were set in motion, and my guess is they'll stay in motion, so someone tell me how to get them moving in the direction of Meryl being right here." James pointed to a spot on the floor in the center of their group. "ASAP."

Mary had her honey-dark head bent. She looked up. "Okay. Here's something." She patted her palms against her knees a few times. "When I was a teenager, my mom and I were fighting constantly. Like, bad. The kind where I would take off to a friend's house, and she would put up 'my daughter is missing' posts on Facebook. Lots of drama."

"But you guys are close now," Michael said.

"Yeah. Super close. The reason why we're close now is actually something like this stuff we're talking about."

"Wait, really?" Tressa Fay had not heard this story, and Mary told a lot of stories.

"Yes. Kind of. So, one of the things that set us off were those kinds of arguments where one person is super fucking positive one thing happened, and the other person is sure that something else happened. You know what I'm talking about?"

Michael and Guy, both lawyers, looked at each other ruefully. Everyone else nodded.

"Yeah. So that kind of argument is treachery. There is no way to resolve it without one person just, like, either agreeing to put their own version of reality away or gaslighting themselves. I don't know what it was, but it felt like this was always happening to me and my mom, and we couldn't even work it out with this counselor who my grandma made us get, who I think was always trying to figure out which one of us *was* gaslighting the other one." Mary took a deep breath. "Then everything changed."

"Magic phone?" James asked.

Mary laughed. "No. My mom told me a story."

"Give it," Gayle said.

"Yeah. We were both crying at the kitchen table over one of these fights. Usually once we got to that point, I'd lock myself in my room, and my mom would take a water glass of box rosé to the sofa and turn on the TV. But this time, she told me about a time *she* had snuck out of the house. She'd had a big fight with her mom about this pool party she wanted to go to and a bikini she wanted to wear. My grandparents are kind of religious, so it was a no-go. The day of the party, she was grounded, but her parents were in Appleton at a church thing. She got herself downtown on her bike. This was back when the mall was where the riverfront stuff is now. Her plan was to buy the bikini at the mall, and then a friend would pick her up for the party."

"We have all had this plan," Guy said. "You'd think it would be more foolproof."

"No lie. So she gets to the mall, and she's on the sidewalk near one of the entrances, and then it happens."

Tressa Fay held her breath.

"The entrance she was getting ready to use was in the wrong place. She thought she got turned around, but then she figured out the entrance wasn't the entrance to the mall, but a glass door on a small shop next to other shops. The mall wasn't there."

"Oh, I think I know where this is going," Linds said.

"She's looking up and down the street, freaked, but also thinking she had been *so* nervous about sneaking out and going to the party and not being home if her parents called that she must have taken a turn down the wrong street, even though she's never lived anywhere but Green Bay. Except the street name was right. The street *sign* was wrong."

"How?" Gayle's voice was hoarse.

"It was the wrong color. Not a green street sign. Black with white letters. Then she noticed the cars. They were old fashioned. Some of them had the big fins on them. One of them was teal. That was the car a woman got out of, and she was wearing a hat. Not a ballcap or a sun hat, but a little white straw hat that was pinned into her hairstyle. It was an older lady, so my mom's like, okay. It's just a grandma who still wears her old clothes. Except there was also a girl walking down the sidewalk, about her age, wearing a dress, but not any kind of dress my mom had seen at the mall in, like, 1990. My mom was wearing a Bon Jovi T-shirt that she'd cut into a crop top and jean shorts, and she had one side of her hair shaved, and this girl looked at my mom and actually laughed out loud and crossed the street, yelling something at her about what she was wearing."

"Rude," James said.

"My mom got scared and panicked, didn't know what to do, so she opened the door into the shop and walked in. She told me she didn't know if she was going to ask for help or what. There were two ladies looking at a top that another lady was holding up for them. More old-fashioned clothes. Everywhere, this time, because it was some kind of clothing store. She told me the store smelled like perfume, and it was really quiet. The lady holding up the top gasped and dropped it, then started walking over to her, asking her who she was and what was wrong. If she was hurt, something like that."

"Jesus," Michael said.

"So then she started talking to the lady—she didn't even know what she was saying—and the lady asked her, 'Do you want the bikini or not?'"

"What?" Gayle said. "What, what."

"The lady isn't a lady. It's a college-aged girl in a Roxy T-shirt, with the bikini my mom wanted on the counter. My mom had her wallet open."

"Was she—" Guy started.

"She swears she wasn't daydreaming. And she's never had

some kind of medical problem, and nothing like that had ever happened to her before. The store in the mall she was in was pretty far from the entrance, and she went from talking to the lady in the clothes store to standing at the checkout with her wallet out."

"Was there a . . . technology?" James asked. "A phone? Or, like, a watch? Magic boom box?"

Mary laughed. "No. She didn't even buy the suit. She walked out of the mall, and her friend was there in the car to pick her up for the party. She threw her bike in the trunk and told her to take her home. Maybe none of it had happened—that's what she was thinking. Except then her friend complained that she reeked of perfume, which my mom wasn't even allowed to wear. When my mom smelled her own arm, it smelled like the clothing store in bizarro old-fashioned world."

"That is weird," Gayle said. "But." She put her hand on Epinephrine's back, resting it there. "I have a pop-up vintage goods business. I'm part of this women-in-business group in Green Bay, and we have presentations all the time, and there *were* little shops down by where the mall entrance used to be." Gayle sighed. "Her mom, your grandma, would have known that. She probably told her."

Mary shrugged. "I can't make it any more believable than what my mom told me. When she told me, in the middle of a fight we were having, she said she'd never wavered about going to the party. She didn't think anything could stop her, but this did. And what happened was as real as any of her other memories. Her friend still remembered the perfume smell years later. My mom never had anything like that happen again, except fighting with me and feeling certain about one version of how something happened, and my being certain about another. But it made her think that maybe everyone was living different versions of life all the time. It was a story that turned things around for us, because we could accept that there was more to living than what we think, and there are things that happen that no one can believe, or they think what *they* believe is true. Or more real."

"And that was what fixed things with your mom?" James asked.

Mary smiled at him. "It's more what made us realize that nothing was busted. I liked believing in her story. I liked her story. I felt like she trusted me with knowing something about her, especially something about her that wasn't cut and dry."

"Everything has gotten so messy since Meryl disappeared, it's as if I've never thought in a straight line, ever," Gayle said. "I don't even know if I give the same answers to the cops when they ask me the same questions over and over." She looked down at Epinephrine, who was purring so loud, he sounded like a mechanical cat. "I'm already not sure what answers I gave when Meryl was gone after that night at Speakeasy, versus what I said when we figured out she was gone from home. They're both true. True here." Gayle put her fist over her heart. "It's awful."

James leaned back, his hands over his eyes. "I could talk to Meryl *right now* with that phone. And I could make a plan with her to save her. It feels like I could. She's smart. The smartest of anyone I've ever known. She'd get this stuff. We do what she says—that's what my heart is thinking. We'll build a fucking lightning tower, or we'll break into a lab, or we'll set off a nuclear weapon. Whatever it is that will let Meryl walk through the door."

Tressa Fay looked at her phone, lit up with another text.

> I should say that I'm not shy, but I'm usually a little more circumspect.

Circumspect. God. And all of this excellent grammar. Periods at the ends of her texts. If Meryl hit her with a literary allusion, Tressa Fay could not be held responsible for what happened between her legs.

"Dude!" James leaned forward in Tressa Fay's direction. "Stay with us. I'm perfectly aware of the power of Meryl's game, but we're trying to science."

Tressa Fay turned the phone over. "Sorry," she whispered. Her phone buzzed again. She lifted the edge, just a tiny bit, so she could read as soon as James looked away.

> But it felt good when I wrong-numbered you the other night. Better than good. Like it was supposed to happen. I've hated being blocked and knowing you must be hurt.

Tressa Fay put the phone back down, swallowing. This was so terrible in the best way possible.

"What about what Mary said?" Guy asked.

James raised his eyebrows. "What about it?"

"About there being more than one version, or more than one reality. If there isn't a single truth, and also, we're living, because we can't *not* do that, then we're going to make choices, and so is Meryl. And that's going to start fucking with everything even more. What can our brains even deal with? How many versions of reality can we hold on to?" When Michael winced, Guy squeezed his shoulders in response. "Look, I'm a lawyer, so I have to consider a different version of the same reality every time I go to work. I can hold multiple things in my head at the same time. But each of us experiencing different realities as they happen because there's a wormhole or a portal or a magic phone is different."

"Maybe not, though," Linds said. "It's actually mathematically impossible that the first time we recognized the existence of another world, or even interacted with it or experienced it, is right now. More than one reality is always possible."

"More than one reality is making me angry in exactly the way Mary said. It makes me *angry* to get into that argument with my husband about something we have different memories of how it happened," Gayle said. "I want a grown-up to walk into this room and tell one of the realities it has no choice but to agree to disagree."

"Yes." Linds nodded. "But what I'm trying to say is that if science is right, and there's communication with other worlds, other universes, that we commonly experience in many different ways, then our brains and our hearts *already know* how to experience it without letting it break us."

"To be perfectly honest," James broke in, "I'm having a hard time hanging on to what happened at the salon already. As if I'm having to repeat it inside my head like a number I need to memorize."

"I don't feel that way," Gayle said. "Every time I think about it, I'm horrified all over again."

Linds tapped her mouth with her fingertips. "Maybe because what happened is always true in your worlds. She's your sister. In every one of your worlds, she has you and you have her in some way. Everything that happens at any time with Meryl is always connected to you, more connected than it is to James."

Tressa Fay swallowed. She could remember *exactly* what happened in the salon. In high definition. She felt it all through her body.

What did that mean?

"We forget," Michael said. "We know how to forget because this happens all the time. We possibly *evolved* to forget. We can only perceive everything happening at once until it gets to be too much, and something in there"—he tapped his head—"hits the kill switch and replaces it with an acceptable narrative."

"Because we're *storytellers*," Linds said. "We'll make a *story*. We're making one now. We have no choice but to live this, because these are the scientific laws that rule us, so we have to do what Mary and her mom decided to do. Put down arguing about reality and simply live whatever this is."

"This is not special. This is something that happens all the time. We know how to do this." Michael said it like he was repeating a new mantra.

"We're just human," Linds said. "It might be impossible to get Meryl in this room with us. It might be possible, but not yet. Or it might have already happened."

Tressa Fay looked at her croton plant, the spotted leaves spreading out for light, its life as unmistakable as her own. Just like Gayle and James, she couldn't make it feel real that Meryl was gone while her phone gently buzzed with texts from Meryl that she desperately wanted to read. What felt real was that Meryl *was* here. That she wasn't gone.

She didn't want to be reckless with herself or anyone else. Tressa Fay was a cautious person. She wasn't one to leap into the unknown, but she also trusted herself. Opening her salon had been a gut decision she knew was real and right and would be amazing. Recognizing her queerness had felt the same way. And something about the way Meryl had talked to her that night—how it was easy and electric at the same time, even over text—felt like it was worth trusting. Something about the video clip from the news that Tressa Fay had shown Guy, and Gayle and James walking into her salon, and texts from Meryl popping back up on her phone as though she hadn't stopped talking to Tressa Fay for even one minute, told her that *this* woman, *this* time, was different.

If that was simply Tressa Fay's alive, human, animal self making a story, she found it hard to care.

"Okay. Okay. Okay." Tressa Fay needed to make something happen. "I'm with Gayle. And James. And Mary's mom. It isn't acceptable that Meryl disappearing is a part of our story, so we have to prevent that. Also, James said Meryl is smart, and, as some of you know, I wouldn't have left my place on a cold night with soup on the stove if I didn't think that was true."

Mary snorted. Tressa Fay's sapiophilia was legend.

"There are ethics to think about," Michael interjected. "If what is being suggested here is that we try to take actions that will, let's say, *reunite* us with Meryl, then we also have to consider who could be harmed by those actions. It's obviously a terrible harm that Meryl disappeared, and if we can repair it, we should. But not without thinking about what other harm we might do."

"Extremely, very lawyer-y," Mary said.

Michael sighed.

"That's if we're assuming that *this* Meryl"—Guy pointed at Tressa Fay's phone—"is on one timeline with us. That she's five months back from us, as opposed to the idea that we're creating multiple Meryls every time we interact with this Meryl."

"Oh my God." Gayle covered her mouth with her hand.

"You know what?" Mary asked. "The only thing to do, for the sake of ethics *and* preventing harm *and* preserving our mental health, is to believe Meryl's timeline is ours, five months back, and we're five months ahead. There is a Meryl who is there, in May"—she nodded toward the phone—"who can talk to Tressa Fay here, in October. And in September, Meryl disappears. The end. The *end*." Mary glared a warning at Michael and Linds, who both looked like they were about to say something. "Old school," she said firmly. "That's the only way we can do this. We have to believe that what we've seen, heard, and experienced is true. We have to believe in each other's experiences. And we figure out how to make the most of what we know without causing more harm."

That helped.

Gayle lifted her hand. "If I know my sister, she's going to do all kinds of experiments, I bet." She paused, then looked at Tressa Fay, her eyes a little narrowed. "How much did you guys get into over text, anyway?"

"I mean, more than I have in some time." Tressa Fay looked at her phone, smiling. It gave her an idea. "My phone." She held it up. "The phone can be a thing to *do*. I almost talked to her, remember? The bad connection? And she could only see my Instagram as far as she had got on her timeline, and hers stopped in April, but I think she just doesn't post much, so I should be able to see them. Observe! Right? And act on that. I bet there are other things to try. Because my phone is more than a potato clock."

As if to confirm that it was magic, her phone buzzed again. She absolutely had a hot engineer on the line. Facts.

Gayle pressed her lips together. "Until we all decide together, though, don't let Meryl tell *us*—the us back then. We keep talking, and we watch out every minute, and we hope that one of us figures out what will keep Meryl out of danger and keep her here. Maybe it's not going to be about making decisions so she stays safe. Maybe we're going to actually have to rescue her. I want to be ready for anything."

"Yeah. Also, I'm going to church on Sunday." James stood up, then held his hand out to help Mary up from the beanbag. "I need something omnipresent to help me sort this out."

"No one keeps anything to themselves." Gayle looked at Tressa Fay. "Please tell her, too, that if there is any way she can try to talk to me?"

The grief in this request was palpable. "I could," Tressa Fay said. "But I wonder if, while you're here, shouldn't it be you who tells her about . . . this reality?"

The color in Gayle's face drained, leaving behind two hot spots burning on her cheekbones. "Now?"

Tressa Fay held out her phone. "You're her sister."

Gayle took the phone with trembling fingers. She looked at James.

"It's okay," he said. "Don't worry about all the other stuff. Just talk to her how you really want to talk to her."

Gayle sat down and started typing, tears on her face. Tressa Fay gathered up everyone's coats and bags, packed up some cookies for Mary, and fussed with Guy's hair.

Finally, Gayle stood up and cleared her throat. "Okay. She's got it." She looked like she would say more, but Tressa Fay was pretty sure she was trying not to cry.

James shoved his hands in his coat pockets. "What did she say, though?"

She laughed, a short, barky laugh that sent a few more tears down her face. She read from the screen of Tressa Fay's phone. "'Tell me that you haven't gone through anything at my house.'" Gayle rolled her eyes. "Then she said, 'It will be okay. Nothing can be as bad as the wind effect on the lake that flooded the entirety of the east side, with a giant rotting-fish clog in the Main Street storm drain to boot. If I can get through that, I can get through anything.'"

"Mercy." James looked at the ceiling. "Meryl."

"Does she really understand?" Michael sounded worried. "Should Linds or somebody try to explain it again? Because it sounds like she's maybe not worried enough."

"Explaining problems to Meryl is easy," James said. "Making her worry about them is hard."

"Linds maybe can explain it better, but I explained worse," Gayle said. "By which I mean, I explained it in the most catastrophic language possible and tried to make her feel guilty for how much she's made me sick with fear. I told her to fix it, and I told her not to let some girl with long legs distract her from getting her ass up here. Alive."

Michael rubbed his hand over his mouth. "So you've got it handled, then."

Gayle held out Tressa Fay's phone to her. "You were the first person she's talked to me about in years, maybe." When Tressa Fay reached for the phone, Gayle moved it away. "Don't fuck it up."

Tressa Fay couldn't be sure if she meant the multiverse or Tressa Fay and Meryl's infatuationship, but she could tell Gayle was serious. She gingerly took back her phone.

Linds shrugged into her coat. "I just have to say one more thing." She pushed her hands through her pixie cut. "If you can, try to think about this extraordinary glimpse into how time operates as proof that you never really lose anyone. You don't. All your love exists everywhere, all the time."

"Okay," Gayle said. She picked up her bag and went to the door. She didn't say anything more, just shoved her way out as if she couldn't get away fast enough.

Tressa Fay understood. It was hard to accept what Linds said. Tressa Fay's mom had died before she'd even had a chance to remember her, and "lost" was the right word for how her absence felt. What they'd glimpsed tonight didn't change that.

It was a while before everyone left. When Tressa Fay was alone again, her apartment felt chilly without all the people, even quieter than usual.

She swiped open her phone. She didn't let herself read Gayle and Meryl's conversation with each other. That wasn't right. Instead, she swiped up to reveal the long string of messages from Meryl that she hadn't been able to look at.

> I just learned about your environmental allergies from your IG. You'll have to tell me if I should change anything I use.

> I don't wear perfume or dye my hair, and I already use unscented deodorant and laundry detergent because I think it's weird when those things have a smell, but but but I have such a weakness for lotion that smells like dessert. Right now, I smell like salted caramel, for example. It makes me happy, but not happy enough that I'd want you to have to stab an EpiPen in your thigh if we . . .

Those ellipses were fill-in-the-blank sexting. Choose your own adventure. Did you like those books? The ones where you could turn to a page for one thing to happen, or turn to another for something else to happen? I loved them more than any other kind of book.

Tressa Fay smiled.

hey there, caramelicious. everyone just left

Right here, right now, in the glow of these texts, it felt exactly like it should. Like passing notes with a pretty girl who you knew might like you, and you might like back. It was completely the same feeling as always.

Every single universe there was in the infinite infinite had *this*.

okay, I got the same thing I always get when I try. *Number is no longer in service.* but it's kind of crackly

All right, but back up a second. When I called you before you tried to call me, you didn't get anything? Not even a small blip? Did you stare at your phone like I said?

lol. I stared at my phone and got no indication you were calling me

It rang and rang on my end. You didn't answer. I guess I really can't call you.

You can't, and I can't call you, but I can send you texts and pictures, and you can send them back. no videos, no real-time DMs, only five months apart ones. the universe only wants us to see one part of the picture the cut paper and the light makes. but here I am

Not for me, I guess?

except if there was anything like the universe telling you that you ARE for me, I feel like it would be finding me via text outside of time in a world where you're not here

Oh! There's a video you posted this morning, my morning, but your five-months-ago morning? Hair washing?

gah

It just arrived! Brand-new for me. Obviously, for you it's way back in your IG timeline. You really posted a video of yourself in the shower.

to show people proper hair washing technique

Shhh. I'm very busy learning how to massage my scalp.

I'm excited you get to see something that got me temporarily banned and was taken down

save it while you can, the only evidence left of it here is in my notification history from the IG hall monitors

there's not even that much nipple, just the top half, if that, for maaaybe two secs

though maybe it was because of my butt, there is all of that

in my defense, I thought butts were perfectly fine, just no nips

what is even nudity?

Philosophically? A lot of things. But I don't have a lot of philosophical thoughts after watching that video. I'm not even sure I remember it was about hair washing.

OCTOBER 4, 12:11 P.M.

I'm eating at that tiny place on the east side of downtown with the sign that just says HAMBURGERS, but I'm having grilled cheese.

that place is closed

What? I love HAMBURGERS!

not forever, probably. it caught on fire so

What?!? Was it the fryer? Because I'm looking at it right now, and it can't be right to have all those postcards hanging up right over it, soaking up grease and transforming into Girl Scout fire starters.

hm. I think it was a mouse or a rat chewing something electric

Oh, well that's fine, then. Obviously it wasn't a rodent that lives here, right now, with access to the cheese in my sandwich. Probably a mouse that lost its way gathering acorns outside for its den where it has a sofa made from a matchbox.

I just sent you the Gazette story about it since I feel like my casual recollections won't satisfy you

Nope.

nope, a news account won't satisfy you? how high are your standards?

No, I mean I didn't get it. Try again.

now?

Still no.

can you see this screenshot of the burned building from the article?

Yes! Oh. Hm.

oh, hm?

It seems a direct link from the future is not for me, but YOU are for me.

that makes perfect sense to ME, is the thing

OCTOBER 4, 3:35 P.M.

I only have a minute because Mary is starting to leave marks with the looks she's giving me when I text you from work

she knows what I'm doing, Meryl

Good. Because do WE know what we're doing?

I'm talking to this girl

That you met?

at the past. ever heard of it? we've all been there

I've been doing some research.

I thought you were at work

I am. But I have an office, and the only people here who understand what I do are the other two stormwater management people, but they're out looking at damage to a jetty in the bay.

you can go harder

With what??

the sexting. I can take it

...

you'll figure me out. go on

Um. Okay. So I was thinking about how I couldn't see the link to an article that doesn't exist in my time, or your IG except the ones you posted when you were in my time, but how you could send me a screenshot. And how I can send you anything through text, but I can't call you, but I'm not sure if that's because I'm not there or because I don't know you here?

Like, maybe your phone rings in my time but you don't answer because the you here doesn't know me. Although it doesn't go to voicemail, and it should if my call was going to your actual phone here.

But it makes sense that you get the *no longer in service* message, because where you are, I'M no longer in service, because Gayle and James's experiment to keep me away from Speakeasy zwooped my phone into another universe.

And I can't stop thinking about how there was a moment we were in the same timeline. The interview about the flooding. I want that to mean that we're possible. That I'M possible, beyond September.

Texting is a loophole. Or a wormhole. But how much of a hole is this?

That sounds bad. What I mean is, is this more than just one string between two tin cans stretched across time and space?

you're really pretty

Sorry. It's just that the internet and the library are RIGHT THERE.

Gayle said you would do this

Oh, what did Gayle say, now?

that you would experiment

Look, I didn't cry in AP Calculus to not use it. And maybe if I'm just talking to this girl, I shouldn't admit the other thing.

what other thing?

The thing where every time I pick up my phone, I'm afraid you won't be there. That the universe will block me. And here, I have no one to talk to about this, so if that happened I would be sad and scared and alone with it, unable to reach you in any way, and I haven't even got stock numbers from you yet so that I can splash out on our first date.

Meryl . . .

If we experiment, I want to experiment to make us as real as possible to each other. I want it to be the kind of real I could show someone else, and they'd have to believe me.

you're at work downtown?

Yes.

you know the elementary school that has part of its playground under the mason street bridge?

Yeah. Hamilton Elementary.

take a walk

there's a sidewalk that runs against the outside of the fence where the big play structure is

six of the sidewalk squares on this sidewalk look a little lighter and newer than the other ones, look at the one right in the middle

when I was in fourth grade, I was walking to school and realized they had poured that new section and the concrete was still wet. there's a handprint inside a heart and it's labeled with my initials TFR

Tressa Fay . . .

I have to go. but I'm not going anywhere, and if I'm coming on too strong, just know that it's not because I don't know we have miles to go, it's not because I don't know all the things we'd really have to experience together to KNOW, but because I can't see any reason not to make everything of THIS right now. if it's all we ever have, I'm going to have all of it

but I promise I'll stay right here for you

OCTOBER 4, 9:27 P.M.

this is my favorite part. where this nerdy forensics detective lady realizes the seeds in the tire tread casting are the same as the seeds recovered in the trunk carpet and that the seeds are the seeds of a grass native to Ohio that has only recently been reintroduced at the safari nature preserve

When you said that you wanted to simulwatch something, Forensic Files was not on my bingo card.

shh, she's about to explain how this seed is definitely the special grass seed because of the color of its husk when she drops the science liquid from the beaker on it. gives me tingles

Obviously we don't have detectives this smart in Green Bay.

alright, you gorgeous nymph, that's enough. we're turning off the show. talk to me

I don't mean to kill the vibe of watching a woman's murder get solved with botany, but it does bring up some . . . feelings? right now.

I can see that. I'm sorry

Oh! Don't apologize.

okay, I won't. but I know your brain has been working just as hard as this hot grass detective. what experiments have you thought of?

The grass detective who's at least sixty and favors turtlenecks printed with a pattern of fir trees and bears?

imagine my horniness when I ran across a stormwater engineer who favors math tshirts that are holding on to her smoking body for dear life

it's occurred to me more than once that I could walk to your apartment right now, wearing one of these T-shirts, wait until you come out, and drop my handkerchief in your path.

oh

Tressa Fay?

no, it's okay, it's only that I had to calm down my instant spike of green-hot jealousy

Of yourself?

no, of the other woman you want to flirt with when they come out of my apartment

Who is you.

not anymore. I'M me, now, and it's ME-ME that thought about your upper lip in great detail coming home from work today

So . . . back to the subject at hand. Which is not your jealousy, but the idea I was having about doing another time experiment.

with ME

With YOU. I want YOU to have evidence of me. I want evidence to exist in my world and yours of the versions of us who know each other.

i don't understand, but you're so pretty. braiding your hair would be like holding a big bouquet of those fire-colored dahlias they sell in the farmer's market in september

That's a lot more poetic than my thoughts about licking you behind your ear and biting my way down to your shoulder.

!!!

So, my IG. Which is ordinarily pretty . . . staid.

disagree. the one of you in a navy suit talking to the city council is now my phone's wallpaper to give me a sensual lift when I'm flagging

You are a notable exception. My point is that I think we can use IG to make an artifact that doesn't *just* live on our two phones, that proves my knowing you and you knowing me has changed reality for everybody, including the fifteen other people who look at my IG expecting another post of my Keens-clad feet on the riverbank.

those are absolutely precious. like little snacks. give me a minute to pull up your insta. okay

Jesus Pete

.... Tressa Fay?

okie doke, the fire department came and hosed me off

my entire body is evidence of your existence right now

that's one way to do it, detective

MICHAEL

HE WATCHED GUY WALK ACROSS THE STAGE AND TIP THEIR head to receive their juris doctor hood. The light caught the part in their freshly barbered hair. The crusty dean of the law school unwittingly smiled—*unwittingly*, because he never smiled— at Guy's blinding, infectious grin.

Guy was Michael's best friend. Michael had tied their tie be- fore the ceremony, wondering if best friends noticed their best friend's abs when their shirt pulled up from their trousers. He had, in fact, taken his best friend to shop for their first suit, nav- igating Brooks Brothers with Guy, shooting daggers at the tailor whose mouth made a disapproving frown when he saw Guy's binder. He'd found a fresh spot that Guy couldn't reach under their shoulder blade to apply a T patch, realizing he was lingering too long over it, letting his fingers rest against Guy's skin.

He had taken Guy to a gay bar for the first time and nearly ground down his back teeth in jealousy, watching them put their hand around the nape of some shirtless nobody, someone who wasn't Michael, who was supposed to be their friend. Michael had been Guy's friend since the first day here, when Michael helped them carry boxes to their apartment in the same building Michael had just moved into, Guy's hair long then, clipped up, their blue eyes uncertain. It would be months before Guy told Michael where that uncertainty came from. Why they weren't as happy as they made everyone else.

After the ceremony, Guy found Michael in the crowd, waving madly, so completely *Guy* that it made Michael's stomach tighten and goose bumps wash down his spine, and before they knew it, he was taking Guy's hand and pulling them down a cool marble hallway away from all the people until Michael stopped in a dark corner and faced Guy, putting his hand on their chest, curling his fingers into the cords of their graduation hood.

"I don't want to be friends anymore." That was what Michael said, and it broke his heart and made his heart at the same time to say it, right against Guy's mouth.

"Oh, thank God," Guy said, kissing Michael and finally, finally, completing the world that they'd made together.

OCTOBER 5
....

HOLD STILL." TRESSA FAY PUT HER HAND ON THE TOP OF HER dad's head and directed her clippers at his neck, careful to keep the line sharp.

"You about done, then?"

She pulled her fan brush out of her denim apron, swept it over the back of his neck, and removed the strip of cotton she'd tucked into the collar of the drape. "Done."

"And you didn't do anything weird." He touched the sides of his head.

"I've been giving you this same haircut every four weeks for almost fifteen years. I could do this haircut if someone propped up my corpse." She pulled the drape off her dad, and he stood and headed immediately to the coffeepot in his kitchen.

As he poured his coffee, he watched her fold up the drape and move his step stool chair back into the corner. She grabbed his kitchen broom to clean up. "Business good?" he asked.

"It is." It was better than good, but her dad would never be able to believe that a hair salon owned by a woman could generate the kind of income Tressa Fay's did. She'd tried to tell him, but it just wasn't possible in his worldview, which had been handed to him, she assumed, on a stone tablet as soon as he was born and as-signed male at the Catholic hospital in Green Bay, Wisconsin, fifty-six years ago.

Her dad got down a second mug, breaking with his routine. "You have time for a cup of coffee?"

Tressa Fay stopped sweeping.

Her dad never invited her to have a cup of coffee with him af-ter she cut his hair. She cleaned up, they made an agreement to meet at the diner downtown for their Wednesday lunch as though they might choose some other place to eat—though they never had before, not once—and then she went on her way. "Sure. Let me finish up here."

She tipped out her dad's hair into the bin and put everything away. He handed her the Snoopy mug that had been in his kitchen cabinet as long as Tressa Fay had been alive. "I don't have any-thing fancy to put in it, so you'll have to drink it the way God intended."

She took her coffee black, as he well knew. She wondered if he would ever concede that despite her sexual identity, her choice of profession, and her politics, she was a lot more like him than he obviously found comfortable. "Thanks."

"So." He put his hand in the pocket of his canvas pants. He worked as a foreman at Green Bay Box and Corrugation, which manufactured packaging, and he had for the last thirty-odd years. Since she was five years old, she had known about his plan to retire at sixty-five, fully vested, and buy a boat and an ice fish-ing shack. She couldn't imagine what he had to talk to her about that might affect these plans in any way. The man's wife had died when he was twenty-eight, and Tressa Fay assumed he'd decided this would be the last unexpected thing to ever happen to him.

"What's on your mind, Dad?"

"I'm getting married."

Tressa Fay's very hot, very black coffee came shooting out of her nose. It took a full minute for her to stop coughing and for her eyes to stop watering from the searing shock of coffee in her sinuses and her dad's news. "Warn a girl, huh?"

"I'm sure you're surprised." Her dad had only sipped at his coffee while she fought for her life after inhaling Folgers. "But I thought you might want to know."

"I didn't even know you were *dating*. You didn't think I might want to know something about this before you're sending out save-the-dates?"

"Why do you need to know about it? A man's social life is his own business. No reason to talk about it until it's settled. No need for people to get riled up and stick their noses in where they don't belong."

Tressa Fay widened her eyes. "What people? Your daughter?"

He didn't respond.

She let out a slow exhale. "What do you want from me here?"

"Jen wants to meet you."

"Jen."

"That's her name. Jen Sluslarski. She's coming with me to the diner on Wednesday, if you still want to meet at the diner."

There were so many things Tressa Fay could say or ask, but none of them would get her any further than simply agreeing to meet her dad *and Jen* at the diner on Wednesday. "If she hadn't wanted to meet me, would I have just showed up someday to cut your hair and found Jen here making the coffee?"

He rolled his eyes but didn't respond. This meant he thought she was being *contrary*, which was her dad's priest's term, as far as Tressa Fay could tell, for women generally.

"All right, then." She picked up her bag. "I'm gonna bolt."

"See you Wednesday. Watch the mailbox on your way out."

One time. When she was sixteen years old, *one time*, she'd grazed the mailbox pulling out of the driveway, and this meant she had to hear this reminder every single time she left her dad's house forever.

"Yep."

She got in her car, and because she knew that her dad had moved to the living room to watch her out the front window and make sure she didn't hit the mailbox, she left, drove around the corner, and parked.

She pulled her phone out.

Ordinarily, this situation would land itself immediately in her group chat with Guy, Linds, and Mary, who would be truly prepared, after years of dealing with Phillip Robeson, for how extraordinarily *landmark* the news was.

But she didn't put the news on her group chat with Guy and Linds and Mary like she normally would have. She also didn't put it on the new group chat that included Gayle and James and Michael, which she had been dutifully keeping up to date.

It hadn't even been two days since everyone left her apartment, but there was only one person Tressa Fay really wanted to talk to, to text, to think about, and to imagine in a dozen different scenarios that involved sustained eye contact and burning-hot incidental touching followed by extremely not-incidental touching.

That night, the night they'd found out, after she'd spent several minutes responding to Meryl's long string of texts with flirting and jokes that didn't entirely, authentically, express how freaked she was, Tressa Fay had realized she was avoiding talking about all the universe stuff, the time stuff, the impossible stuff—

and maybe Meryl was, too. Maybe she was flattened by what Gayle had told her, but it sounded to Tressa Fay like Meryl had focused on making *Gayle* feel better. Meryl's response hadn't been about *herself*.

It seemed to Tressa Fay that Meryl deserved to be asked how she felt, considering she was the one who had disappeared. Would disappear.

And so Tressa Fay had opened her Notes app, just like she used to when she was young and fighting with a girl over text, so she could make everything perfect before dropping a hard message like a fat folded letter through the slits of someone's locker.

Give me a sec, Meryl had written back almost immediately.

Tressa Fay had fretted until she saw Meryl's three little dots, and then she held her breath.

> **Sorry!**

> My neighbor has this thing about where the trash and recycling bins are placed by the curb, and when your message came and I was halfway through reading, he knocked on my back door. No matter how many times I tell that man that I work for the city and it is FINE if I put the bins on the apron of my driveway, he moves them onto the easement and then has to tell me about it like he donated a kidney to my mother.

Tressa Fay had laughed then, relieved. but are you okay, for real? you can tell me because I'm new.

> Yes. The thing is, I wasn't entirely surprised. I noticed the date stamps on your texts the night at Canyon when you said it was cold and windy, and I had already been idly thinking that this was either a very elaborate invitation to a LARP or a parallel universe problem.

oh my god

A little bit, Meryl had been joking. But also, it was true. She did believe Tressa Fay, at least as much as Tressa Fay believed what she had seen and felt, which was completely, but also not at all.

Then she and Meryl had texted until they were falling asleep, waking up to the other's texts until they finally said good night. And that was all they'd been doing since. So far—gloriously—it didn't seem to *matter* about the particulars of this long-distance relationship.

my dad's getting married, she typed, turning up the heat in her car. She'd bought an external charger for her phone just in case her phone's being charged, ready, on, *always*, was what kept Meryl with her.

Tell me everything, Meryl wrote back. So Tressa Fay did.

She told Meryl about her dad.

She told her about how she'd known Linds even longer than

she'd known Guy, because their mothers met each other while pregnant, at the doctor's office for prenatal appointments. When Tressa Fay's mom, Shelly, died when Tressa Fay was three, it had taken her dad several years to really get it together. Linds's mom, Carla, had stepped in to help. What Tressa Fay mostly remembered from that time was giggling in the back seat with Linds on the way to school, her dad lifting her sleeping body from Carla's sofa when he finished second shift and arrived to take her home, and how her dad would let Linds and Tressa Fay play video games for hours and hours on a Saturday and put candy in microwave popcorn for lunch.

Good things. But also things that gave Tressa Fay the ability to gauge, now, the depth of her father's grief.

She told Meryl so much, in several blurting texts, trying to synthesize what it was like to be that man's daughter, always, forever, and still be herself.

And still try to feel like *herself* could ever possibly be good enough.

As Tressa Fay talked about her dad with Meryl, she was glad that she and Meryl weren't avoiding anything anymore. They had been experimenting instead. First, they'd done a series of experiments so that Meryl could observe the situation for herself. Meryl was an engineer. That meant she didn't rule anything out, but she certainly didn't rule anything *in* until she was certain it was correct.

Tressa Fay found this behavior extremely attractive.

The Instagram Experiment, as Tressa Fay called it in her head, consisted of Meryl with her long pinky-red strawflower-colored hair in braids, wearing turquoise cat-eye glasses and a pale blue tank, striking a pose that suggested Meryl was *only* wearing the tank, due to the glowing curve of thigh uninterrupted by even a single bow on a pair of panties.

Meryl's hypothesis was she never, ever would have posted it if she didn't know Tressa Fay, which meant that her posting it and having it appear in her feed in May was a way of confirming the reality of her connection to Tressa Fay. And Meryl's hypothesis *was* confirmed when Meryl's followers started populating the comments with a lot of big eyes and exploding-brain emojis.

But that experiment got less fun when Tressa Fay noticed, beneath Meryl's friends' comments, the notation in small gray text. 21w.

Twenty-one weeks ago. That was when the comments had appeared. The comments that Tressa Fay could see rolling in, in real time.

You're remarkable, Meryl wrote back to her blurt about her dad. Look at you.

> but you can't. not actually,
> actually

Hmm.

> hmm?

I have an idea for an experiment.

> you know what? I've said this already,
> but I feel like you're taking all of this
> super well

I like to feel powerful. And look! I have all the power. I'm the only one, in all of this, who can know everything. I know myself, I know my sister and James, and I know what they did and what they're doing now. I know what's coming for me, or at least that it's tenacious and not moved by a simple change of venue, which gives me a lot of information. I'm starting to know you. Where I am, and where you are.

Tressa Fay shivered. There was something big and centering about Meryl claiming so much power.

what's your idea? for the experiment?

Book me.

what do you mean?

I mean, look back in May, preferably soon because I'm impatient, and book me into your salon.

Tressa Fay took a moment to breathe, her mind and heart racing. I couldn't, really, you'd have to be a walk-in

Pick a day that you'd take me as a walk-in.

She put her hand over her chest. I wouldn't know you!

> No. But I would know you. And then we could see each other, and then October Tressa Fay would remember me. Maybe.

Oh. *Oh.* Tressa Fay took a deep breath, her stomach flipping over, flipping over again. *Now* she was warm.

> if I cut your hair the way I cut hair, then we might mess with Gayle and James's past. maybe more people's. my cuts have a signature, are usually dramatic. I don't know

> Then give me a trim. I'll ask for a trim.

> is this an experiment, or is this... something else?

> It's something else. And an experiment.

Tressa Fay touched that text. She took a deep breath. you'll know me then and now, she wrote.

> I won't know anything, while I'm cutting your hair, but the present moment. if it works like it did before, you'll walk out of my salon and I'll only have memories of trimming your hair. I won't know who you are to me

She remembered Michael in her apartment asking questions about how much their minds could handle, talking about how they had to try to avoid doing harm. But she wanted to have the memory of meeting Meryl. To know how she looked in person. How her voice sounded.

We're both here, Meryl wrote. **My guess is we've already done this, and it turned out okay.**

god. you . . .

I know. But I want to see you. Already, it's been almost impossible not to go and see you. I nearly left work to drive to your salon.

I don't know how to say no to this idea, anyway. I don't. I can't

maybe that's weird, that it's barely been a week and it's just texting, but the idea of not giving you something you want if I *can* feels more impossible than doing THIS

It's a bad idea for us to do this, but now that I've thought of it, there's no way I won't unless you don't want us to. Because it's the only way we can meet in person—and because, what if it means we can keep talking to each other and figure out how to really be together . . . even if?

> I hate hate that "even if"

> I hate it too, but it's hard to resist this now that I've thought of it. BECAUSE it will change everything, and that's what we want. Because we can know each other.

They could know each other.

They could have this.

In the hush of her car on this overcast street, knowing Meryl felt like the only thing Tressa Fay wanted. But she had to consider, minimally, what Michael or Guy or Gayle or Mary would say to this plan if she told them about it.

> you would think that we would use these experiments to figure out how to keep you safe in September

> I don't feel like I'm in danger. I don't feel anything like that. How could I? Right this minute, all this time so far, I want to use these experiments so that I never stand you up again.

She wanted to argue with Meryl, who *was* in danger. Her future was uncertain. What was Tressa Fay going to do, come February, if Meryl disappeared in her own September . . . *really* disappeared? Off her phone? Out of her own life?

I think your sister is going to want to know that you're applying the full nancy drew treatment to your life right now

Yes. But the number I misdialed was yours. So I'm taking you with me.

Tressa Fay squeezed the phone. Then she reached into her bag and pulled out her day planner and flipped back to May. She tried to fill herself with Meryl's confidence. She studied the calendar, because it wasn't enough to simply find a cancellation or the rare unbooked appointment. She wanted to know how she *was* that day. She pulled up her Instagram, too.

But it turned out to be simple. May 6. That afternoon, she had been alone, because Mary had gone to an appointment to get a tattoo. She confirmed this on Mary's Insta. Yes. May 6, in the evening, Mary posted her raw tattoo, covered in film, on her hip. The salon had been quiet from three o'clock on, and Tressa Fay had a lot of no-shows.

Why? She didn't have a May 6 post on her Instagram, so she looked at her camera roll.

Oh, right. It had been a beautiful day. She sometimes had no-shows on beautiful days. Wisconsinites so rarely got beautiful days that they never failed to take full advantage. Her photos were of the street outside her salon, a group of people walking in tiny summer clothes, a panting dog tied up outside the deli next door.

come at three. Tressa Fay was shaking. **tomorrow. your to-morrow.**

Yes! Yes. Yes.

go easy on me, I'm incredibly nervous. I feel a little sorry for my may self, taking pictures outside on a warm day and polishing my tools and listening to music. she doesn't know what's coming

More than that, it was hard not to wonder if she had the right to consent to this experiment on behalf of May 6 Tressa Fay. But that wasn't the kind of question she could get an answer to.

Still. Maybe they should let that Tressa Fay be. She'd already navigated that day, and she remembered it, even now, as a bit of a golden day.

Of course, that Tressa Fay would always exist, wouldn't she? She had already folded into the whole big mess that was time. What Meryl was proposing was something that hadn't, exactly, happened to Tressa Fay yet. It would happen to a different Tressa Fay. When she knew about it, it would make *her* a different Tressa Fay, now. *God.*

Meryl was proving to be a force of nature, even through this strange chain of notes they passed back and forth. Tressa Fay was inclined to believe that Meryl was right, that she did have a lot of power, and she could use it to experiment, and she could deploy it to stop what was coming for her in September and also find her way to Tressa Fay.

I will be kind in every way. And I'll do my best to protect you and the people I love without setting off red flags for you. I think the only risk is that . . . well. No matter what, I think we'll be friends.

Also! This is an adventure, right? I'm working on an idea. On another kind of experiment. When I have thought about it more, we should talk.

Tressa Fay turned the dial up on the heat.

She *was* Phillip Robeson's daughter, truly. She loved her apartment. She loved her routines in it, making it just so. She loved her job, making it what she needed. She'd known the two most important people in her life since before she could remember.

But obviously there were things about her dad she didn't know and hadn't guessed. She should probably give herself the same scope of imagination. She had never wanted nights out or a bar or a dating app or anything like that to get her out of . . . she didn't want to say her *rut*, because that was unkind, but her habits. Her comforts.

Right now, she had a perspective on her life that she'd never had before, the kind of perspective that poets thought about. Untraveled roads. What ifs. She was a very unlikely hero in this kind of an adventure, that was for sure. But she *was* the person Meryl's misdirected text had gone to, and Tressa Fay couldn't pretend it meant nothing that she was more interested in talking to a woman—more willing to shake off her habits, her routines, and her comforts for this particular woman—than she'd been in forever.

this is an adventure, Tressa Fay wrote. I will repeat that to myself until it feels like one.

Three dots came up and disappeared more than once. It made her nerves feel drawn out, fragile, and like too many signals were running up and down them.

What she held in her hand right now was the only thing she and her people had of Meryl, and it couldn't be more tenuous. She'd had dreams of the chat going silent, going gray, being scrambled, of hearing staticky snippets of Meryl's voice.

But the next message arrived, just like the other ones had.

> I'm scared, too. I wanted to say that. And I don't want to push you, and I'm taking seriously what my sister and friends and family are dealing with up ahead. I don't want anything to happen to me, of course. I like my life. I love my life. I'm happy. The idea of anything bad happening to me seems so remote, but I'm taking it seriously. I'm thinking so much about how to use everyone we can to help without hurting anyone in the process. It's all the thinking that's keeping me steady. Also, you. You. Your humor and how easy you are to talk to and how beautiful. How much I *like* you. It's making this situation way, way more easy, if not to accept, then to live in.

Tressa Fay looked up from Meryl's long text, out the windshield at the gray October day. Somewhere out there, in the time she was experiencing and moving forward in right now, was Meryl. But this Meryl wasn't using her bank accounts. She wasn't reaching out to anyone.

Tressa Fay hadn't let herself really think about it, because how could she? How could she take in the reality that Meryl Whit wasn't here anymore in a way that was utter and final and meant her loved ones were already grieving?

And how could she pass up a chance to meet Meryl, however she could, whenever it was possible?

I'm all in, Tressa Fay typed. maybe you SHOULDN'T make it so easy on me tomorrow.

> To be honest, I might be all talk. Who knows what will happen when you're *right there.* You don't happen to remember what you were wearing that day, do you? For example, there's a picture of you from a couple of years ago cutting hair in a leotard. I might not be able to speak if that's what I run into.

They flirted for long enough that Mary had to call her and tell her to get her ass back to the salon.

For long enough that Tressa Fay forgot to be worried, and she was just a girl teasing her girl about their first date.

MAY 6

. . . .

TRESSA FAY HUMMED ALONG WITH THE CRANBERRIES, TAKING A moment to circle her ass and close her eyes, to put her hands over her head when the beat hit against the rising layers of sound in the chorus.

Unlike the yearning lyrics, she was happy to let herself linger in this moment.

Mary had left early for a tattoo appointment, having finally saved enough money for a piece on her hip inspired by nudes in art deco posters, and due to the gloriously warm, sunny, dry afternoon, with a blue sky that was literally glowing, Tressa Fay's appointments had been dropping off the book in favor of a boat ride on Lake Michigan or a beer in a lawn chair with friends.

As it should be, she thought, opening the door to the salon and propping it with a rock. She snapped a few pictures of laughing groups of people in small clothes that were really a bit too small for May in Wisconsin—it would probably be in the high forties tomorrow—and of a dog, panting, leashed outside the deli next door, which was doing a brisk business in brightly colored granitas.

She had also worn too-small clothes today, cutoffs that were largely cut off from being proper pants *or* shorts and a crochet halter top that had been her mother's, had in fact been made by her mother, which she'd recently found in a box of things her dad wanted to get rid of. The transfer of this box, and then of other boxes that her dad also gave her, was shocking. Tressa Fay hadn't thought her dad would *ever* get rid of her mother's things. She wasn't sure why now as opposed to any other time in the last almost three decades.

She loved this top. The boxes and what they contained had sent her on a journey of thinking about her mom, her life, her dad, and what she wanted from him, which was making Tressa Fay feel hopeful and . . . better.

Actually very good. For the first time since Amy.

She finished taking pictures, turned up the music, and started to mist the plants in the salon as the warm breeze through the open door ruffled their leaves and her hair.

So the door didn't jingle, because it was propped open, and Tressa Fay didn't hear the greeting, because of the music, and her professionalism could not be located, because she had arched her back, wiggled her hips, closed her eyes, and started spraying her face and chest with the plant mister in time to the beat.

She did, however, feel the tap on her shoulder.

"Eye-yikes!" she yelped, turning around.

"Sorry!" A long-haired, freckled, curvy bit of *business* stepped back and held their hands up, grinning. "Um, you couldn't hear me."

Oh. This person was extremely *yes*.

Tressa Fay shunned her libidinous warm-day brain and turned on her fancy-salon-owner brain. She didn't ordinarily hit the *a-woo-gah* horn so hard for a stranger. "Oh, God. No worries. Let me turn down this music." She used her phone to slide the volume down to the background, where it belonged. "I'm so sorry I

didn't notice your coming in! I'm Tressa Fay. Here, follow me."
She walked over to Mary's reception desk, where she kept her
book.

This person, who had waves of peachy auburn hair that Tressa
Fay couldn't wait to get her hands on, wore a tight red shirt
that . . . yes. It was an East High mathlete shirt. She wondered if
it was a thrift store find or if this person was mathy and adorable.
If so, that would be bad, because Tressa Fay generally did not ask
clients on dates. It wasn't a rule, and she had done it a lot more
when she was starting out, but as her platform grew, she couldn't
be sure it would be a fair start even to something casual.

If Tressa Fay were someone who did casual. Which she
was not.

"Okay. Let me find you here." Tressa Fay slid the book toward
her client. "What's your name?" She smiled and hoped her question didn't sound like a come-on. "Once I find it, you can write
down in the entry any or none of the info we request. You know,
email. Pronouns." *General status of the romance-y type.* Tressa Fay
sternly slapped that thought away.

"Um. Meryl Whit, she and her, and, well, that's the thing. I
was walking by and saw the salon, and the open door, and okay,
so, I've been meaning to get a trim forever, but work has been a
lot lately. I was kind of hoping for a walk-in appointment?" The
question was accompanied by a hopeful smile that wrinkled the
bridge of this confection's nose, making the glittery glasses
perched there slide down. Then *Meryl*'s pretty eyes swept over
Tressa Fay in a manner that belied sweet politeness.

Well.

"I don't usually take walk-ins, but . . ." Tressa Fay motioned to
the empty salon. "And you only want a trim?" She had to assume
that her walk-in didn't know about the salon and its reputation

for haircuts that sometimes took Tressa Fay a couple hours to get right. Aside from her dad's monthly clipper cut, the only trims she ever did were to freshen a repeat client's look, and even then, Tressa Fay didn't strictly believe they were *trims*.

Every cut changed things, at least a little.

"For the moment." Another nose wrinkle and smile combo from Meryl. "An inch or two, and I'll be out of your . . . well."

Tressa Fay laughed, and so did Meryl while she looked around the salon like people did when they *did* follow Tressa Fay's socials and needed a moment to make everything they saw line up with the way they'd expected it to be. When she turned back to Tressa Fay, she still had that expression, excited and expectant, as though she knew something amazing was about to happen.

It was a direct hit to Tressa Fay's professional intentions. "Okay, but you'll have to promise to look at my Insta and maybe book something in the future. I'd love to work with your hair." She turned the calendar around and held out a pen. "If you'd just fill in those three lines for me." Tressa Fay tried not to openly stare as all of that hair fell from shoulders over arms, breasts pushed against the nerdy T-shirt, but it was difficult. Meryl adjusted her glasses for the second time, and Tressa Fay got a sprinkling of hot prickles across her nape.

Did she have a bit of a thing for smarty-pants types? Yes. Yes, she did. And redheads. And women who looked at her like she glowed, like they had already spent hours with her. Probably, in truth, Tressa Fay had never been looked at by a woman like that until now, but she liked it. So much.

Normally, for a trim, the service wouldn't include a shampoo unless the client requested it and was paying for it. However, there wasn't anyone scheduled for the rest of the afternoon, Tressa Fay could trim a single inch in her sleep, and also, Meryl's arms must get so, so tired washing all of that hair. A shampoo would be the real service of this appointment.

A service to *Meryl*, she reminded herself.

"Lemme just shut the door while you hop up in the shampoo chair." Tressa Fay shut it and flipped the sign over to CLOSED, trying not to overthink that move, then grabbed one of the organic cotton drapes Mary organized on hooks and a waffle towel from the stack on the live-edge shelves. "Here." Tressa Fay put the drape around Meryl, lifting the hair at her nape away from the closure with practiced fingers.

Meryl's goose bumps met Tressa Fay's fingertips. So that was fun. Tressa Fay took a deep, slow breath as a way to bank excitement and feelings and anticipation that were doubtless mostly the result of how long it had been, which was a *while*. And the sun was out. The music was good.

Meryl looked up at her and smiled.

It was not just the music and sun and deprivation.

"And then you can lie back. I've got the towel right here." Tressa Fay guided Meryl's neck over the lip of the shampoo bowl. "If you'll let me." Tressa Fay slid Meryl's glasses off gently. "I'll put them at my station."

Was taking off a woman's glasses undressing her? She thought about this, and about the gentle clench between her legs, as she set Meryl's glasses on the shelf of her station. Probably not. But also, it would be what happened before other things could happen with a woman who wore glasses. So.

"I really appreciate your fitting me in." Meryl had a pretty, husky voice. "I was afraid it wouldn't work."

Tressa Fay stopped in the middle of setting the temp for the water on the faucet's digital display. *I was afraid it wouldn't work.*

It made her feel like she'd missed a step going down a flight of stairs.

But Meryl just meant that she hadn't been sure Tressa Fay would agree to trim her hair, didn't she? "It's no problem. I wasn't busy."

"But you were getting down." Meryl smiled as the little light on the faucet told Tressa Fay it was ready.

She laughed. "I was."

"Bit of a smoke show, actually." Meryl's grin was not shy or polite.

She's flirting, Tressa Fay thought with delight. She turned on the water and smiled. "I will absolutely take that. Is this temperature okay?"

Meryl closed her eyes as the water sluiced over her hairline and seeped into her waves, darkening them to deep auburn. "Yes. This is perfect."

"Are you allergic to anything? We use a very ultra-hypoallergenic co-wash here, which is a great shampoo alternative for curls like yours, but it's okay if only water will work for you."

"I'm not allergic."

Tressa Fay lifted up Meryl's hair, heavy with water, directing the spray over it in slow sweeps. Meryl's eyes were closed, so Tressa Fay gazed at her freckles, noticing how there were so many in so many different colors, and the way her eyebrows and eyelashes matched her wet hair.

Oof.

Tressa Fay hadn't washed a client's hair in some time. Mary typically did it. But she had no complaints about washing Meryl's hair. She poured out a handful of the creamy co-wash from the aluminum bottle and dunked her other palm into it. The steam from the water meant that she could smell Meryl—sunscreen and windy sun and something sweet that reminded her of vanilla. When her hands were full of product, she picked up the dripping rope of Meryl's hair and slid her hands down it, making it as slick and soft as the weeds growing up through the fine sand at the lake in Algoma. Then Tressa Fay slowly moved her fingertips into the hair over Meryl's scalp, rubbing the rest of the clinging product through but mostly, mostly, massaging her warm scalp.

This is perfect. The satisfied echo of Meryl's words kept her company as she worked her hands through Meryl's hair, watching her throat hollow when she moved her thumbs in twin circles at her temples. Clients were typically very quiet and still when their hair was washed, taking it in with a tender mix of relaxed pleasure and social anxiety, but Meryl felt completely present and alive, pushing back against Tressa Fay's hands like a happy cat.

Meryl sighed, her face soft. Her upper lip was a little bigger than her lower, and her lip line had been invaded by freckles. That was what Tressa Fay stared at while slowly moving her strong fingers over Meryl's head in wide rakes, sometimes pressing her thumbs and holding them against Meryl's soft temples and those lower edges of the skull that get sore at the end of a long day, always brushing her fingertips lightly against her nape when she moved to the back before returning to stronger strokes.

"God," Meryl said, keeping her eyes closed. "This feels so good, I might fall asleep or float away or kiss you."

Tressa Fay swallowed, then scratched her nails over Meryl's scalp. Meryl made a noise in her throat. "Too much?" Tressa Fay asked.

When Meryl opened her eyes, they looked a little drugged. She shook her head, and Tressa Fay made her close her eyes again by running her nails over her scalp another time.

Meryl wore shorts. Ordinary black chino shorts with a little cuff and a button and fly. But there was a hot pink flush over her legs from her knees right up to the cuffs. And under the cuffs.

Tressa Fay had to take a moment. She'd turned herself on washing Meryl's hair, bending over her in the steam, touching her, breathing her in. Not professional behavior, obviously, but the rough, shocky tingles over her skin and between her legs did not care even the tiniest bit.

"I'm going to rinse now." Tressa Fay pulled her hands from Meryl's hair slowly, then tapped the water back on with her elbow. She pointed the water with one hand and picked up, tugged, and slid Meryl's hair through her fist with the other, over and over again. Meryl had one of her arms draped across her middle, the other at her side. She'd bent a leg up. She was wiggling around with her eyes closed. Tressa Fay lifted, pulled, and stroked while watching Meryl, knowing she should be stern with herself but unable to muster the effort.

Meryl opened her eyes. "I'll pay you a thousand dollars to wash my hair again."

Tressa Fay went still, then laughed, but she could tell she was blushing as she finished rinsing Meryl's hair. She carefully put her hand at her warm nape and got the towel up and over it, squeezing it damp. "I'm a cheaper date than that." She quickly looked away, her embarrassed gaze landing on her barrel cactus, solemn as a soldier in the front window, her hand still on the back of Meryl's neck—but Meryl was laughing again.

"I'll keep that in mind." She raised her eyebrows.

Tressa Fay choked only a little. She guided Meryl out of the shampoo chair and to her station, where she readjusted the drape and touched the button on the floor to raise the chair up. She picked out a big wide-toothed comb and started detangling, comforted that her brain had kicked back on and determined where the hair was trained to part, where the ends were uneven, what condition it was in. Tressa Fay didn't talk, and Meryl didn't, either, but that was nice. The music had moved on to Tracy Chapman, and the quiet hush of the empty salon felt comfortable.

Cozy. Like a bowl of her favorite tortellini soup and a record playing on a blustery fall day while she snuggled on her sofa with Epinephrine and a redheaded woman.

Tressa Fay came back to herself enough to give herself a lecture. *This is a client. She came in here for a trim. Yes, she is fire. She flirted, possibly first. She smells like eating ice-cream cones at the swimming pool. No one would argue that her T-shirt isn't a felony. However, Tressa Fay Catherine Louise Robeson, you are a licensed stylist with the State of Wisconsin and have built a spotless reputation. This is not the moment to get goatish.*

She leaned over where she kept her tool holsters and grabbed the one for her shears, buckling it on.

"Wait," Meryl said.

Tressa Fay met her eyes in the mirror. "Yeah?"

"You put your scissors in a holster?"

"And my comb."

"You, right now, are strapping a leather holster to your hip."

"This one. The one for my razor goes on my thigh." Tressa Fay pulled a comb and her shears from the drawer where they had been placed after disinfecting and put them in her holster, then fastened several clips to her waistband to be ready to section Meryl's hair.

"But that's unfair." Meryl's dark eyes were so pretty, looking into hers from the mirror, like she knew how Tressa Fay was fighting for her life here.

"Why?" Tressa Fay parted and flicked out and sectioned the smooth, damp locks.

"Because you took away my glasses, and now I can't watch you *holster* about with all the detail that I need to really take it in."

Tressa Fay's belly was damp with water from the shampoo bowl, and her self-mastery had been cut from her like the dusty piles of hair they swept from the floor all day. Something was *happening* with this woman. It felt like the time Linds had talked her into skydiving—how Tressa Fay's heart had hammered in her chest as she looked out the open door of the plane at the patchwork of Wisconsin farmland below. "I'm sorry. I have to ask, are you flirting with your stylist?"

God, she'd loved that jump, though.

"Absolutely I am." Meryl smiled. "Is that okay? I could retire to my thoughts."

Tressa Fay dusted Meryl's ends with her shears, glad she hadn't given Meryl's glasses back, so Meryl couldn't look in the mirror and see Tressa Fay grin and bite her lip and privately rejoice. "It's okay."

They both went quiet again while Tressa Fay trimmed Meryl's hair. Changing her, one *snick* of the scissors at a time, and who could say what those changes would bring about in Meryl's life?

"What do you do?" Tressa Fay asked after a while. "I see that you're a mathlete, but I wasn't sure if maybe you were just at the amateur level."

Meryl laughed. "I'm a stormwater engineer for the city."

Oh. Well. "Sure. Just hit me with your game without warning."

"You're teasing me."

"I'm not, actually." She checked her line, then tipped her shears into the disinfectant, grabbed an airbrush, and plugged it in. "I might have a bit of a thing about, you know. The smart girls." She pulled a section of Meryl's hair around the airbrush, going slow.

"You're really not kidding about that." The way Meryl said it, she sounded almost fond, as though Tressa Fay had proven . . . she didn't know what. Something *between* them.

"Mm-mm. I don't joke about girls with brains." Tressa Fay brushed out another section, the warm air of the brush against her palm as she slowly smoothed Meryl's hair dry. "Tell me everything about what a stormwater engineer does."

Meryl smiled. "It's a type of civil engineering. I'm responsible for quality control of stormwater projects, like city storm sewer upgrades and studies on where stormwater goes, where it floods, where it gets hung up. We try to responsibly plan our natural watershed and wetlands areas. And I plan the maintenance for the stormwater facility." Meryl said all of this with her eyes closed as Tressa Fay slipped sheets of glossy hair through her fingers and over the humming airbrush.

"I didn't even know that was a thing. But of course it is. Wow. Look at you. That's amazing."

Tressa Fay thought about those girls in high school with their organized folders and binders and long hair in low ponytails, rushing to classes with "AP" and "Honors" in the name, their heavy backpacks almost tipping them over. Those girls had always been her favorite. She'd loved their serious faces as they walked down the halls. They seemed so precise, even how they unzipped their backpacks, pulling out pencil cases and bags with skinny mechanical pencils and writing in their notebooks, bent over them with complete concentration. They carried cello cases to school. Put little red-and-yellow tubes of Carmex in their pockets and slid it over their lips in class on an unpredictable schedule.

Tressa Fay had *yearned* for those girls, and when they grew up, they were even better. They had serious jobs and serious senses of humor and were seriously, secretly wicked and delicious, and Tressa Fay could bask in them forever.

Meryl was watching her, something careful in her expression. "I have a confession."

"Tell me everything." Tressa Fay put down the airbrush and dipped her ring finger into the little metal tin of hair wax she kept in her holster, rubbing it into her palms to finish styling Meryl's hair.

"I knew about you."

Tressa Fay pulled her hands away from where she had been piecing the waves. "Me?"

She nodded. "Your salon. But also . . . you. I saw the open door and wanted to meet you in person and made up needing a trim." She bit her lip. "Don't run away. I swear my typical moves involve little to no subterfuge."

Tressa Fay smiled and went back to styling Meryl's hair, partly to think, partly to get her hands into the rosy golden mess of it. *I knew about you.* It should have been a red flag, but instead it felt like everything she had been feeling—a gift, a jump through the sky, familiar, sexy, shy, bold. "I have a confession, too."

"Oh, good." Meryl raised a single eyebrow, with a tiny smile.

Tressa Fay handed Meryl her glasses, which she slipped on. Tressa Fay met her eyes in the mirror. "I really liked washing your hair." She raised her eyebrows, too.

"I'm relieved to hear that, because I was for sure not thinking about my split ends when you were washing it." Meryl spun her chair away from the mirror to look right at her.

Tressa Fay reached out and tucked Meryl's hair behind her ear. "So?" she whispered, though she hadn't meant to.

"What do you think about getting a granita and going for a walk?"

"I think *yes*." Tressa Fay thanked her lucky stars for the serendipity of canceled appointments and Mary's tattoo and a pretty day.

Meryl slid out of the chair, forgetting Tressa Fay still had it elevated, right at the moment Tressa Fay remembered it was still elevated and reached out to help. Meryl stumbled forward, her body against Tressa Fay's for a moment as they both laughed.

Perfect timing. All of it.

MAY 6
....

I N TWO MINUTES, SHE HAD THE SHOP LOCKED UP, AND IN AN-
other five, they were through the line for granitas and soft
serve, and then for a timeless interval after that they talked and
walked in the sun along the river, bare arm to bare arm, not yet
holding hands, but with the achy knowledge they could.

The soft inner parts of Meryl's lips were bright pink from
her dragon fruit granita, and the sunlight by the bench they'd
found along the river trail turned her hair the color of a camp-
fire.

"What?" Meryl smiled.

Tressa Fay shook her head. "Nothing. I'm glad you came into
the salon."

Meryl turned her body on the bench to face her. "Me, too." She
looked Tressa Fay over in a way that Tressa Fay could feel behind
her knees. "Are you seeing anyone?"

"Whoa." Smiling, she blew out a breath. Of course she knew
she couldn't flirt with someone like she'd flirted with Meryl this
afternoon without some version of this conversation, but she'd
always loved these very first questions and feelers and awkward *I
like you*s. She shook her head.

"How is that?" Their knees touched. Tressa Fay was smoldering from the inside and might actually catch fire. It had been a while, yes. She had felt, lately, like she might be starting to be . . . ready. Almost ready. She hadn't told anyone except Mary, but telling Mary was a decision in itself, since Mary was legendary for her matchmaking.

Meryl was Tressa Fay's type, sure. But chemistry could make a tall, cool glass of water, or it could make everything explode.

She looked at Meryl, who was studying the river.

Tressa Fay would just ease into this water. That was all. Take it slow.

"Um. No one's asked lately?" Tressa Fay said.

"I'm not, either. Seeing anyone." Meryl gathered her hair in her hand to keep it from blowing in her face. She wrinkled her nose. "I've been doing the app thing."

"Yeah. The app thing." Tressa Fay laughed. "To find someone or to find some*thing*?"

"Mostly the second one. I don't have a lot of faith that I . . . have a lot of faith, I guess. At least, not when it's important to have faith. Important to the other person." She picked an invisible thread off her shorts. "I mean, I'm an engineer, right? The math, the statistics, aren't in favor of the some*one* but are good at finding lots of some*things*."

"That is a very practical perspective."

"To be fair, I have no sense of what my criteria are for swiping right. None. None, none, none. I mean, I *think* I do? But I suspect that there is some kind of dopamine brain squirt that happens when you're on the app, and then you're just, like, backing yourself up to this person as if you came across them in the forest and they smelled fine."

Tressa Fay squealed with laughter.

"I do look over my shoulder once I've backed up. I'm not a complete animal."

"Oh my God," Tressa Fay said. "You are a little scary. I like it. I suspect you're doing better than I am on the apps because you are driving straight at the thing. I've tried them, but even when people are very straightforward in their profiles and when I'm texting them, I get confused when they're right in front of me."

"But this isn't confusing you?" Meryl gestured between the two of them.

Tressa Fay smiled at the sky. It was bluer than blue. "Nope. I've already decided I'm not going to let you kiss me, if we're calling this a first date. Although that's frankly shocking to me, because it's also eighty percent of what I'm thinking about."

Slow*ish*.

Tressa Fay watched Meryl smile and settle back into the bench. Her T-shirt had ridden up and was exposing a soft, freckled strip of belly. Looking at it sluiced lazy desire through Tressa Fay's body.

Slow*er*?

"I should tell you that I very seriously couldn't be in a worse position to start dating right now." Meryl said this to the river.

"You mean dating me, for real, as in you call me or I call you, and we do something else together where I wear as few clothes as possible and rummage around in your nerdy mind for my pleasure? Because you said you were apping about."

"Yes. That's what I mean."

Tressa Fay watched the water move. She liked this conversation, but there *was* something she didn't understand in Meryl's tone, something that flashed a warning in the cautious part of her brain. "Why?"

"There is a lot in my life, coming up in the future, that I

haven't figured out yet, and none of the people I love have been able to help me figure it out."

"At work? With your family?"

"The entire cosmos?" Meryl sighed. "But also, to be honest, I'm only going to try very weakly to scare you off. In fact, this is my whole show. I just wanted to say it in case I fuck up a lot of little things. Or a big thing."

Tressa Fay thought about that. "I haven't seriously dated anyone since my ex, which ended two years ago. I've tried. I really have. And I've wanted to, even if my friends think I don't want to. Except Mary. She knows everything. She runs all the non-hair parts of the salon, but she wasn't there this afternoon, so you snuck through."

"I'm glad." Meryl turned to look at Tressa Fay again. "Mary's a good friend, then?"

"Yes. She's actually the only one of my closest friends who hasn't known me since I was a baby. I think that's why I confide in her the way I do. Linds and Guy are like family, and there's that impulse to protect them. Even from myself."

"I understand that." Meryl took a long pull of her granita. "My best friend in town is James. He was actually my older sister's best friend first. We don't all hang out together the way you'd think. James tried, but he became my friend in the first place because I started dating him."

"Ooh. Like an older sister's best friend kind of trope."

Meryl laughed. "Complete with the annoyance of the older sister. Which we didn't need at the time."

"I see. I mean, I'm an only child, but I'm a hairstylist, so I've heard some things about those dynamics." Tressa Fay looked at Meryl's pretty, freckled ribbon of belly. Her glowing hair. The wrinkle between her eyebrows. She liked this woman. She liked her a little bit too much. It was exciting in the exact way that she remembered her dad never wanting her to get excited—the kind of excitement that could tip over into anxiety or stomachache or tears.

She had never listened to her dad about tamping down that kind of excitement, though.

"My parents split up when my sister, Gayle, and I were really small," Meryl said. "She remembers how it was when they were together, but I don't. I've figured out that whatever that dynamic was, and me missing out on it, drove some kind of wedge between Gayle and me, even though, growing up, I adored her. Our mom was not okay. There was just enough basics, and just enough child support from my dad, to skate us over the surface and keep CPS out of it. I was the one who tried to make Mom happy, and Gayle was the one who fought with her. So of course I fought with Gayle."

"Do you still?"

Meryl gathered her hair again and looked at the water. "I would say we have silent fights. I got hurt, really hurt, by my mom, eventually, once she had gotten tired of using me as a shield and a weapon. Long story short, Mom's in Florida, and Gayle and I are on the same page about her and about how we grew up. But I started dating James when we'd only just started to do better. That didn't help. Then James and I figured out we were better friends, and so I'd say we've all been trying. She loves me. She's proud of me." Meryl shook the icy pink slush in her cup, casting a nervous glance at Tressa Fay. "I am possibly oversharing."

"Nah." Tressa Fay watched two kids, one almost a teenager

and one little, try to get a kite in the air, reminding her of the beautiful, unseasonable day going on around them. "I can return serve with my family history, or we can agree to enjoy the sun and the sugar only. Your call."

Meryl laughed. "Tell me about yourself, Tressa Fay Robeson."

Tressa Fay put her palm against the wood of the sun-warmed bench. "My mom died when I was little, just a baby preschooler. I only remember, really, what she *felt* like. Her neck was always warm and smelled good. I could always get her to pick me up. I have a memory of picnics at Bay Beach and napping on her lap, and I'm not sure it's even real or if it's just what my friend Linds's mom told me. My dad's churchy. We lived in Our Lady parish on the west side, so he got help with the heavy lifting, and he is extremely, extremely, *re-spon-si-ble*"—Tressa Fay drew out the word—"so I lacked nothing, and there were lots of moms around, including Linds's and Guy's. But I wouldn't say Dad and I are going to start a family band anytime soon. We have our routines. Very little changes to make it better, but also, that means nothing gets bad."

"Yeah," Meryl said. "That's how I'd describe where Gayle and I are at right now."

"Tell me, Meryl Whit." Tressa Fay sipped from her granita cup. "About your job. The engineering. The mathing. If you use a protractor, show me a picture."

Meryl tapped the sides of her glasses. "These have that blue light filter in them because, honestly, most of what I do is in front of a computer."

"Don't underplay. This is a date." Tressa Fay waggled her eyebrows.

Meryl laughed. "It's really not that exciting, unless you're me.

I like to take things that don't make sense and find a way to get them to work. I like to make lists, and I like to worry over every possible way that something can fail. When it starts to rain, I'll be awake in bed, listening to the rain hit the roof, thinking about how much water is going to come down and how fast, and how much it will test the city systems. I get to do a lot of this because the stormwater systems in Green Bay are old and failing, and we have two rivers and the entirety of Lake Michigan beating down our gates."

Meryl's voice got more serious and husky when she talked about her work. Tressa Fay couldn't help imagining this might indicate how serious Meryl would be about everything she committed to. That Tressa Fay might someday hear Meryl talk about *them* in that voice.

"Hmm. My dad fishes, and I've been out with him plenty, until I was old enough to have my own thing on the weekends. I liked wandering around finding things in the mud and sand on the bank and looking at weeds and nests and litter, which would frustrate my dad because I scared the fish. That is the beginning and end of *my* knowledge of what you do all day long."

"I love to go creeking," Meryl said.

"Creeking?"

"What it sounds like. Wandering around in creeks, looking, finding things. Spring is such an interesting time for creeks and streams and brooks and rivers. They're taking on more water, breaking up their banks. This time of year is when all the animals come, the frogs spawn, the plants emerge from their beds. It's messy. Creeks are the kind of thing that's more interesting when it's messy."

"What else is more interesting when it's messy?" Tressa Fay

put her hand over her mouth. "I didn't actually mean that as an innuendo."

Meryl laughed. "Problems. More interesting when they're messy. And big."

"Because then you get to stick your hands in up to the elbows and fix it, huh?"

"Yes. Though maybe that's revealing more of my psyche than is strictly a good idea on a first date."

Tressa Fay choked and then laughed so hard, she sounded like a kid. Meryl feigned innocence with her expression, but her eye crinkles gave her away. Whether or not Meryl herself was messy, she was a little *dirty*. "Better to know what I'm dealing with, I think. Didn't you say you're up against a cosmos-level mess in your own life right now?"

Meryl's gaze followed the kite. It had found an updraft and was soaring high over the river. "I did, yes. For sure the biggest mess I've ever had to fix, and it might even be a problem I can't solve. It *should* be taking up all of my mental resources. Every single one."

"Why isn't it?"

When Meryl smiled, it wasn't a smile Tressa Fay had seen yet. It was big and secret and happy. "There's also such good distractions in the middle of this mess."

"Hey-oh." Tressa Fay laughed. "But hear me out. I wonder if the distractions are the answer to your problem. Not to shamelessly bid for a second date or anything, but also, give me your number."

Meryl grabbed Tressa Fay's hand and pulled her up from the bench. "Let's walk a little more, if you have the time."

"I have the time. I have all the time."

Tressa Fay didn't let go of Meryl's hand as they made their way along the river trail, bikes and skateboards and strollers moving past them as they ambled.

"So no end-of-the-trail kiss?" Meryl asked after a while, making Tressa Fay's belly flutter.

"If I kiss you, then I won't be able to feel everything I feel *anticipating* kissing you. I'm inclined to drag out every minute and hour. For example, I haven't had the pleasure of trying to fall asleep while thinking about what it would be like to kiss you, and how could I possibly leave that on the table?"

"You couldn't, obviously."

"Never." Tressa Fay smiled.

"Do you think that what we do now, every little thing, changes the future?"

When Meryl moved her fingers to lace them with Tressa Fay's, she felt it in the pause between heartbeats—a fraction of a second when time stopped. She'd had almost the same thought, earlier, at the salon, thinking about changing Meryl by cutting her hair. "Is this the part where I pull back the curtain on this date to reveal that you're really trying to recruit me into your MLM?"

Meryl laughed. "Didn't you see those life-changing essential oils I left at your station for a tip?"

Tressa Fay slowed her walk and had a moment when the hot sun and the cool river breeze and the remarkable feeling of Meryl's hand in hers felt like something that had always been happening. "Not too long ago," she said, "my dad gave me a box with all of my mom's clothes he never gave away. Those clothes made me . . . not remember, but *know* my mom in a way I never had before. Not even from pictures. This top I'm wearing—she crocheted it. I didn't know she crocheted. She was my size. Her clothes fit me. I didn't know the size and shape of her until I got those clothes, not really. Now I do. I know her favorite colors, and that she shoved change in her pockets, and how she tied and laced her boots because of the wear on the laces of her Doc Martens. I can *see* her. I can smell her Shalimar and Camels, imagine what it would be like to hug her, what bands she listened to."

Tressa Fay glanced at Meryl. She was surprised by how receptive Meryl's expression was. Almost . . . loving. It filled her chest up with a glowing, good feeling that made her shy enough that she had to look away.

"Getting that box of clothes changed so many things about how I felt about my mom, because they made her real, and *I'm* a different person since I've spent ungodly money to have those clothes cleaned and fixed so I can have them hanging up in my closet. I've made different decisions."

Meryl squeezed her hand. "Like what?"

"Like to move on from my last relationship, for real, because my mom didn't get to love my dad for as long as she would've wanted to. Also, to have a better relationship with my dad, because I'm sure that's what she would've wanted, too. I mean, who was she dressing in all these hotness clothes for, right? I haven't really figured out the dad thing yet, but I have hope." Tressa Fay could hear the skepticism in her voice.

"Do you think that getting those clothes and wearing them and wanting to date again is why you're on this walk with me?"

"*You*"—Tressa Fay stopped and pointed at her, laughing—"were the one who confessed to me that you walked in my salon this afternoon because you had a parasocial crush on me. So who's changing the future here, really?"

For a teeny part of a second, a cloud skated across Meryl's expression, and Tressa Fay wondered if she'd offended her or said the wrong thing.

But then Meryl smiled and pulled her down the path again.

"We both are," she said. "We're both changing everything."

GAYLE

SHE WATCHED MERYL LAUGH AT SOMETHING JAMES WHISPERED in her ear. Gayle sighed and pulled another onion ring off the tower in the middle of the table.

"Should we order real food?" Meryl asked, putting her arm around James.

It wasn't that Gayle had a problem if Meryl and James started dating. She knew Meryl had a crush on James. It was probably the first personal thing Gayle had known about Meryl in years. She and Meryl were finally, after all this time, talking. Maybe because their mom had moved to Florida, maybe because Gayle had started dismantling some of her anger with a therapist, maybe because the three of them—Gayle, James, and Meryl—had some surprising friend chemistry, and James had a way of burring off the rough spots in any social situation.

Mainly, Gayle's problem was that she was feeling a way she hadn't felt since she was a kid. Like she was waiting for the other shoe to drop. Their mother was chaotic, and Gayle had spent all of her resources—all of the time she might've done homework or impressed teachers or thought about college or dated—keeping Meryl safe. Making it so that Meryl thought she had a good mother. Making it so Meryl could do homework and impress teachers and go to college. And Gayle had pulled it off, even as she lost Meryl in the process, which hurt so fucking bad there were years it felt like she couldn't breathe. And then their mom had dealt a blow Meryl couldn't forgive, and Gayle hated that even more. Meryl should feel like she had a mom, even if Gayle didn't. As far as that went, even their mother deserved to have at least a little part of what it felt like to be a good mom. Gayle did love her.

She'd been able to find Meryl again in the aftermath. They talked, and sometimes it was even easy. It was so good to think of what it might be like to relax and have the chance to be a *sister*.

Hence the near-constant sensation that it was all on the verge of breaking apart. Their mother's gift to Gayle was to make her forever feel like nothing was going to work out.

She took a deep breath and made herself stay in this moment, the one where she was sharing beer and onion rings with her best friend and her sister. "Is there something you two aren't telling me?"

James looked at Gayle, his eyes sparkling. "Meryl did confess to me about her feelings."

"Hey!" Meryl lightly smacked him on the arm. "Don't embarrass me."

"And?" Gayle couldn't help but join in laughing. James's moods were infectious and almost always good, and Meryl was here. Right here. *Gratitude*, she reminded herself.

"It's not that I'm not flattered." James smiled at Meryl. "And my mother would be thrilled if I brought home an engineer. But I have a bit of news."

"Tell her," Meryl said.

"Tell me what?" Gayle laughed, but her stomach had gone cold and anxious, which was the problem with anxiety. News was always bad news.

"Well. It so happens that I met someone."

Gayle had known James for years. He sounded excited. He was happy, and now that she really looked, he was a bit *different*. "You did?"

Though James was someone Gayle would describe, if she had to choose one word, as *loving*, he was reticent when it came to romance. She had been okay with it, if surprised, to think that he and Meryl might date, but now that he had made this announcement, Gayle realized he likely wouldn't have dated Meryl unless he thought it was serious or he had really almost given up on finding love, because Meryl was Gayle's sister, and James knew how Gayle felt about her.

"I did," James said. "A month ago, actually. Remember when I went to that fancy salon to get these vintage curls done?" He slid his hand over the style he'd been wearing, Jheri curls like his late father's. James had wanted his hair cut to mimic what was usually done with a relaxer, and he'd found a stylist who was game to try it.

"We all do," Gayle said. "You've been very into your hair."

"Mm. The receptionist. Mary. That's who I met. She's fun, she's sharp, she's got common sense, she's gorgeous, and, the most important thing, when I saw her, I knew. I just knew." He gave Gayle and Meryl a little tip of his head.

Gayle put her hand over her mouth. Her eyes stung. This was what James had wanted. Meryl was grinning at Gayle, excited that James had shared his news.

"Mary," Gayle said, trying the name out.

"Mary." James rubbed his hands together. "So I was thinking, what if Mary and I and you and Meryl all went out next weekend? Of course, Gayle, you can bring the husband, if the good doctor can take a night off to party. I want to check out that new place, Speakeasy."

Gayle looked at the two of them, and the knot in her stomach relaxed a little bit. Meryl was here, she reminded herself. James had gotten something he'd always wanted.

"Absolutely," Gayle said, picking up her pint of beer. "To new friends."

OCTOBER 6

. . . .

"TRESSA FAY," LINDS STARTED GENTLY, FOLDING HER HANDS TO-gether. "I know that you must know why Michael got us to-gether here."

They were all at Gayle's house. It was in the fancy Astor Park neighborhood, a big gray Dutch colonial with pumpkins and gourds piled on the front steps. The living room had shiny wood floors and matching leather furniture. There was a lot of art, so it wasn't boring, but Tressa Fay thought Gayle could use some plants.

She'd had long moments to think about things like this while everyone in the room looked at her with various combinations of bemusement, incredulity, and uncomfortable interest.

She *did* know why she'd been told to come here. Ordered, really, in the group chat. It was because of her afternoon with Meryl. "I was supposed to talk to you first." She plucked at the tassels of the pillow on her lap. "I did not do that."

Just yesterday, she had been in her car down the street from her father's house, texting back and forth with Meryl, making their plan, brushing away her fear. Then, this afternoon, exactly five months ago today, Meryl had walked into her salon. Tressa Fay had washed her hair. They'd spent time together. And, of course, Tressa Fay and Meryl's decision to meet had changed reality.

Her life wasn't the only one that had been affected.

She looked up from the pillow to Gayle. "Your house is really nice." Gayle's husband was a doctor. Snort, their labradoodle, had his big, warm head against Tressa Fay's thigh, but he looked at Gayle worriedly when Tressa Fay addressed her.

Gayle nodded. She was sitting with her arms crossed in an envelope of scary silence.

Mary watched Tressa Fay, but she didn't look upset. James didn't, either.

Michael and Guy sat next to each other on a leather sofa. Michael had the deep wrinkle between his eyebrows he got when he was thinking hard. Guy seemed like their usual unbothered self.

"You talked to me about her until two in the morning after your date." Mary said this kindly. "How funny Meryl is, how hot, how smart, how it had been so long since you'd done nothing on a date but walk and sit and talk and get to know each other. It's the strangest feeling, because I sort of *think* it didn't happen, but also I *feel* that it did."

Tressa Fay understood what Mary meant, although the experience she was describing sounded mild in comparison to Tressa Fay's. Today, when her two sets of memories—her two lives—had abruptly crashed into each other at the salon, she remembered everything. Two different sets of everything. Two completely separate versions of her own life.

She'd had to take a five-minute break in the back room, amazed, headachy, and wiping away an immoderate number of tears.

But also, as soon as she'd cried and the shock of the experience had passed—as soon as she'd felt it all—what was left was the story of her life.

Meryl in every part of it.

Linds had been right that first night at Tressa Fay's apartment when she told them that their minds and bodies already knew how to live in this quantum reality. It didn't hurt. It didn't break anything. Even as they were here tonight because she and Meryl had messed up the plan, Tressa Fay wasn't bothered. She didn't feel like she had to keep track or remember the details of every way that her reality had been layered over and rearranged. That wasn't how they were going to save Meryl.

"The only thing that bothers *me* is how lost and moony you've been for the last five months," Guy said, "ever since you had the date of the century none of us here knew you were going to have and then never saw her again."

"Right." Tressa Fay looked up at the ceiling. "I have a sense of that. Somewhat."

It was hard to be bothered with the time paradox when Tressa Fay wanted to kiss Meryl so badly. Her entire imagination was preoccupied with the knowledge of how Meryl's head and neck and hair felt in her hands, with thinking about what her mouth—her soft, smiling mouth—would feel like. What Meryl tasted like. If she made sounds when she started to get turned on from a kiss. These were the two things Tressa Fay wanted to know more than she'd ever wanted to know anything.

They hadn't kissed at the end of their date. Meryl had reached up and hugged her and told her she'd text her that night. Then she hadn't. Because Meryl *couldn't* text the Tressa Fay she'd met in May. When Meryl sent texts to Tressa Fay, her messages went five months into the future. Or they took five months to arrive, crossing over a thousand universes.

But twenty minutes ago, as Tressa Fay was pulling onto Gayle's dark street, thinking about the date that, for a few fleeting moments, felt like it had *just* happened, her phone buzzed, and it was Meryl, with her tongue still pink from her dragon fruit granita, texting Tressa Fay a selfie as soon as she got home from their walk.

Now she knew that Meryl had loved that walk as much as she did. Now she knew Meryl had wanted to kiss her, too. Because Meryl told her so. But reading their texts, back and forth, it felt like she'd always known. Their experiment had made a shifting kaleidoscope of memory and longing and aching and excitement and confusion that made Tressa Fay wish—as she looked at Meryl-in-May's picture and knew she smelled like sunscreen and clean hair—that she could somehow run to her and bang into her house and take her face into her hands and kiss her and kiss her and make *that* be the only thing that mattered.

They'd remade the world. No space fabric had ripped, tumbling Meryl out neatly through a hole in this tidy living room. The experiment's strongest effect was on how Tressa Fay and Meryl felt about each other.

"I'm sorry," she said solemnly.

"Here's something, though." Linds reached over from where she had been sitting on a matching leather ottoman near Tressa Fay's chair. "Remember when we finally talked about Amy?"

She closed her eyes. "I do. God. At the public pool in your neighborhood in June."

"Honey, you *never* talked to me about all that before. You hadn't looked at any of that pain—you were only bearing it, and part of me really thinks that finally opening up about that pain is definitely worth the consequences of your and Meryl's little experiment."

Tressa Fay looked at Linds, surprised to realize it was true.

She left me, Tressa Fay had said, with her head on Linds's thigh, Linds's hand on Tressa Fay's shoulder, the sun hot on their wet swimsuits. *I told everyone we broke up and it was mutual, but that's not what happened. I came home early from the pop-up salon thing in Los Angeles. I was so happy. Linds, I bought a ring, one I'd been designing with a jeweler there, and she had it ready for me to go see it and approve the design while I was on that trip. When I looked at that ring, it made me so fucking happy.* Tressa Fay had put her hands on her heart. *To me, that ring looked like Amy, and all I wanted was to see it on her finger. So I changed my flight and my plans on that last day and came home.*

Linds had run her fingers through Tressa Fay's hair. *What happened when you came home?*

It was very late. I went into the bedroom to get into bed with her. She and her coworker Denay were already there.

Oh, sweetheart.

I knew that Denay was her . . . work wife? You know, someone who understood the grind of the docket and billing hours and dealing with partners. I was so grateful for Denay. I didn't, not once, suspect anything. Ever.

Linds's hand had gone still. Tressa Fay's face had gotten hot.

You knew? she'd asked.

No. Of course not! If I'd known anything, I would have said. It's more . . . when we found out you'd broken up, Guy and I knew something must have happened that you weren't ready to talk about. And later, we heard through Michael and Guy's lawyer grapevine that Amy was with Denay, and we weren't, I guess, surprised. I'm sorry. Linds had smoothed her hand over Tressa Fay's forehead. *It wasn't your fault. You give so much to the people you love. I just don't want you to lose sight of what you need.*

That conversation had unlocked something in Tressa Fay that she could feel now. It had meant she stopped being a hermit and started using the time on her own to think about what it was she needed. What she wanted. What it was about Meryl and their date that had made her yearn and feel so good.

She met Linds's eyes. "So that means the consequences of my connecting with Meryl in person to cut her hair—"

"They're life." Linds was looking around at everyone, her eyes bright with passion.

"You're trying to say that what we're all feeling right now, what we're calling time, is what life is," Michael said. He was still frowning. He didn't like this.

"Yes." Linds nodded.

"That possibly the insights and epiphanies we have along the way, in our lives, are because we're . . ." He shook his head. "Because we're living our lives backwards, forwards, and sideways. At the same time."

Linds took a deep breath. "I really think so. Even right now, this conversation? As soon as I reminded Tiff about our talk at the public pool about Amy, it started to feel like that was simply what happened. The reality where it didn't happen is slipping through my fingers." She made a gesture with her hands, fluid and ephemeral. "But I'm okay with that, because I'm a writer. Every book I publish has been written and rewritten, changed in so many different ways along its road to being finished that ultimately it's almost impossible to remember any version but the one I end up with."

Michael shifted on the sofa. "Fuck."

"You feel it, too," Linds said to Guy.

"Honestly," Guy said, "as soon as we started talking about this, I got lost and thought we were all meeting because Tiff's been so sad the last several months but also doing kind of better, and we were checking in with her."

Linds laughed. "And so what do you think Gayle and James are doing here?"

Guy frowned. "I mean. They're our friends?" He sighed. "Who are also Meryl's friends, which makes zero sense, given that Meryl ghosted after one date with Tressa Fay five months ago."

"Fuck," Michael said. "Again. But also, yeah. I'm not going to give myself a migraine trying to keep an up-to-date reality check-list inside my head of every single change. I couldn't even if I wanted to, and I don't want to."

"We're always doing this—we just don't see it like this. Mostly because we don't want to. Not because it isn't real." Linds looked at Mary. "Your mom remembered. But maybe she remembered because she wanted to remember in order to make things better with you."

"Good *lord*, Linds." Mary fell backward into a cushion on the sofa.

"Confession," James said. "I had no idea why I was called to a meeting on the group chat. That's why I brought chips. I thought this was a hang."

The vintage Bakelite clock on Gayle's mantel ticked out the seconds.

"I really do think," Michael said slowly, "it does depend on how close we are to what changes. Like, Tressa Fay, you must be filled with all of these different memories and feelings because what is happening is about you. But James—"

"I'm mostly preoccupied with figuring out what happened to Meryl."

When Tressa Fay looked up, she was met with Gayle's furrowed brow. "You *saw* her," Gayle said. "You talked to her. I had to meet with the detective today, and honestly I kept thinking how ridiculous he sounded, trying to create a *timeline* for what happened."

Tressa Fay opened her mouth. To say what, she wasn't sure.

"It's okay." Gayle sounded resigned. "It's just hard."

"She talked about you," Tressa Fay said. "She talked about what had come between you and how you were trying to do better. How it felt like it was working, but also, it was still tricky. She talked about how she wanted to be closer to you."

Gayle put her hand over her mouth. "She did?"

"Yeah. She did."

Linds let out a shuddery breath. "And that changes everything. Just you"—Linds patted Gayle's ankle—"knowing that. Right?"

"And we'll probably talk about you more," Tressa Fay said. "Because she loves you. And I'll probably tell her how much you love her. Because you do. And then your relationship gets better way faster than it would've. Or it was always going to get better? I don't know."

"We weren't in a great place when she disappeared," Gayle said.

"Not true anymore," James said. "Yay?"

Gayle sniffed. "Yeah, *yay*." She looked at Tressa Fay. "I mean that. And tell her I love her anytime. All the time, if you want."

"This is giving me a new appreciation for those old-school missed-connections ads that Tiff and I used to obsess over in middle school." Guy smiled at Tressa Fay. "I wonder how many of them were actually burgeoning separated-by-time romances?"

"The last time we met," Linds said, "we were trying so hard to figure out how to keep everything simple. Our hope was to keep a straight line and save Meryl."

"But it turns out that's not how we live," Michael said, leaning forward to reach for the chips James had brought. He opened the bag and held it out to Guy beside him. "We like to think we make plans, but it's impossible to plan. We have feelings, our health changes, other people's schedules and problems intersect with our day, and we ask ourselves, 'What went wrong?' Or, sometimes, everything goes right, and we're so pleased we made such an excellent plan. But that's hubris."

"And Meryl's fearless," Tressa Fay said. "She's not worried about what we're doing here. She feels in control. She has plans of her own. At this point, honestly, I don't think we could stop her if we tried."

"Of course," James said, taking the chips from Guy. "That's Meryl."

Gayle looked at the ceiling. "You know what I'm thinking about right now? About when Meryl got a speedometer on her bike. She'd been begging for one, at eight years old! Oh my God. At that time, we lived in the last house at the end of a dead-end road, and there was a great big dead-end sign, the metal kind, fixed between two wooden poles. Meryl had been racing her bike up and down the street, testing the speedometer. Going fast, slow, looking at what she passed at different speeds. Then she was at the end of our block, and I saw her stand up on her pedals. She started going so fast that her pink bike was rocking back and forth. And I realized she wasn't looking at the road. She was looking at the speedometer, trying to see how fast she could go. Before I could yell at her to stop, she hit the dead-end sign with the top of her head, going eighteen miles an hour."

Tressa Fay gasped.

"Her body flew through the air, and she landed on the street, knocked out cold. I thought she was dead. I started screaming. By the time the ambulance came, she was throwing up everywhere, and her eyes were looking in two different directions. She was okay in the end, after a week in the hospital, but my point is, *that's Meryl.*"

Tressa Fay could see this. She had felt this.

"Meryl is a factor that will intersect with everything. All of us." Gayle sighed. "I think we're just going to have to put our heads down and throw every single power tool at it on the highest speed."

Everyone started talking at once then, throwing out ideas, but Tressa Fay could only think, *Meryl is already doing that.*

Meryl had been over the moon in her texts when she got home from their date.

> There was nothing that could have prepared me for how beautiful you are.

> I want to make you blush over and over.

> I can tell, when you look at me, that you want to kiss me. How long do you think we can hold out?

James had been listening with his elbows on his knees, his head in his hands, his deep brown eyes pinned to the floor. "I think we have to very seriously consider something here."

"What is it?" Michael asked.

"That maybe Meryl wasn't a victim. Maybe no one took her or hurt her. Maybe she's simply not *here* anymore."

"She would never choose to disappear," Gayle said with irritation. "This is something that happened to her."

"But what if it wasn't *something* that happened?" James asked. "What if there was some kind of . . . I don't know, mistake, like a skip in a record that makes it possible for her to be texting Tressa Fay in the future? And she disappears into that . . ."

"Glitch," Tressa Fay supplied.

Then the room fell horribly silent.

"I know." James's voice was patient. "I hate it, too. But I have to mention it."

Gayle stood up. She pointed at Tressa Fay. "You tell her to try whatever she wants to. We'll try everything we can think of. As fast as we can, heads down, no matter what's ahead. We'll break the universe if we have to."

The thought didn't bother Tressa Fay. It just made her wonder, *if* Meryl kissed her, whether she could stand the feeling of not kissing her again for months.

Over and over.

But then she remembered there *was* a Tressa Fay who had kissed Meryl after granitas and a long walk. Or the next day. Soon, for sure.

Tressa Fay realized she was actually willing to break the universe for a lot of reasons.

She probably already had.

I just put so many selfies on IG. My hair is so rarely smooth like this. I had a friend in grad school who called hair like this "princess hair." You know, where it's all shiny and waving in the same direction with curls at the ends. Like cartoon princesses.

shh. I'm looking at these selfies. what is this bare shoulder? are you topless? are you wearing nothing but my haircut and those glasses?

It's a robe.

she says with no regard to my predicament

Are we going to talk about this experiment?

but I have talked about it so much already. angry Gayle is a whole vibe. if I could learn how she does it, I would abuse that power in the worst way. also, she loves you

That tells me enough that I have to ask how YOU'RE doing.

well, you ravishing sweet biscuit, let me just say that I miss you. I miss you, I miss you

OCTOBER 7, 12:55 A.M.

We can absolutely talk about something else.

it's okay. you want to experiment again. I want to see you again. not exactly the same goals, but also the same

Experimenting is about seeing you again. About seeing you again and again and again.

Meryl

Some scientists spend their whole lives finding an explanation for everything that happens. Some scientists find everything that happens IS the explanation. None of this is a reason to doubt that so far, in every lifetime, you're there. Every one of me wants every one of you.

it's math

It's everything.

OCTOBER 8, 3:12 A.M.

epinephrine absolutely understands english. I found him in the alley behind the building where I had my first apartment after I lost everything and he still had his umbilical cord attached so english is the only language he's ever known

Do you think he'll be an only child forever?

are you asking me if I want more children? yes. I have looked at the shelters and the listings. I've talked to epinephrine about it. I would welcome another child. I don't think epinephrine wants a kitten. he would like a sibling who is on equal terms. Meryl, do you like cats?

I had a cat, Justin, from the time I was nine until over five years ago now. He passed away in his little bed at my feet.

oh no. Justin. I am so sorry

I haven't been able to even think about another cat until recently. Now when I walk past the shelter downtown that has the big front window, I look in.

someone's waiting for you. you'll know

I believe that now.

OCTOBER 9, 8:33 P.M.

so I already told you I don't remember not knowing Linds. her mom told me everything my dad never could about my mom, who was her best friend. she made sure my dad knew what kind of jeans to buy and kept tampons under the sink and didn't raise me like a novice nun

And Linds was the one who took all of this in right away.

oh yeah. she was always going to be the one who made us look for the treasure after finding an old map in the attic or walked through the back of the wardrobe into Narnia or discovered she was the lost princess of a far off galaxy

she's seen ghosts and practiced witchcraft and DMs the fourth longest running DnD campaign in the state of Wisconsin. she's polyam, though is single right now

she wrote her first novel when she was ten. it was about teenagers who lived in tunnels after the apocalypse and had never seen the light and so had eyes so pale they were nearly white, and prematurely gray hair

they trained rats and made little leather harnesses for them decorated with the abandoned diamonds of the previous world. then one of them got pregnant and had a baby with bright red hair and green eyes and everything goes tits up

Wow. I really need a mystical queer in my life.

a mystical queer is an important role in every found family. how else are you going to get your tarot read after a breakup? or see someone in a chainmail bikini and fairy wings? who's gonna be your crystal dealer?

I see this now.

get out there and find one. I was born with one, like a familiar, but there are other ways. keep an eye out for moon phase thigh tattoos, hot people in bookstores wearing clothes you don't understand, and anyone who asks you if the design on a tshirt you bought from target is a sigil. then make them tea and love them forever

OCTOBER 10

. . . .

T HE FOUR DAYS SINCE TRESSA FAY AND MERYL'S EXPERIMENT HAD
been a blur of work and long conversations over text, which
Tressa Fay moved into and out of, listening to the soft buzz of her
phone when she was too busy with a client to read what Meryl
had sent, anticipating the moment when she would be finished at
the salon and could curl up at home, post-dinner, and write and
read and flirt late into the night.

Though it wasn't *only* flirting. They talked about Meryl's predicament, too.

I mean, okay, Tressa Fay had written. like, in sci-fi when a character goes to a parallel universe, they find out they have superpow-
ers. or their friends do. or gravity is different. or they are a villain. or
they are incredibly, fabulously rich with a hot wife.

Goals.

Tressa Fay laughed. but in our case, it's lives right next door to
each other. that mostly look the same except they aren't. and I
know, I know, it's way more complicated than that.

Because you have to consider every dimension.

I mean, I don't. I cut hair. I flirt with redheads who consider those things for me and can make a tshirt look like a three-figure-cover floor show, but my point is that all of these different, granular decisions we're all making aren't opening up portals to worlds where we ride bees to work

Never stop talking to me. And yes, I've thought of this, too.

tell me, but go slow

Oh, you can count on me taking my time.

I need to make a chart to see if you ever miss an innuendo

Never. Okay. So I'm thinking about what James said, and my completely disappearing from where you are *does* suggest that time, in more than one universe, is distorted enough to collapse.

wait, Tressa Fay typed. Linds talked about Schrodinger's cat when she talked about collapsing. collapsing means the other possibility is over. so if you're gone here, the possibility you're ever *not* going to be gone is over. I don't like that

> Mm. Okay. Think about it like this, maybe. My sister could give you a rough biography of Meryl, May through September 4.

right, okay

> But I've already done things differently.

because of me

> Because of us. So how many more *us*es can we make? Can we make enough that no us collapses? Forget about whatever happens to me in September. It doesn't matter if we collapse everything but us.

that might be the most romantic thing anyone has ever said to me in my entire life

> Good. I am very competitive. I want to keep collapsing until we're together. And to be clear, I can't NOT do that, because of you, and because I know about September 4. Nothing I do is going to be the same. I'm talking to you over text right now. What would I have been doing if you weren't here with me? Whatever it is, I'm not doing it.

Tressa Fay thought about Gayle's story of Meryl with her new speedometer. Terrible. But also, for anyone who really knew Meryl, comfortingly predictable.

> You know what I was thinking about at work during a very boring meeting?

me

> Absolutely. Always. Especially that picture on your feed I can't believe hasn't been yoinked. I was thinking that maybe James is right and I disappear because of a glitch, but it's also true that, statistically, a bad guy is the most LIKELY explanation. But that doesn't mean I wasn't disappeared by someone not usually in my universe, but who shows up on September 4, making him unfindable and unfightable.

Jesus. you just gave me the worst kind of shivers ever.

Wouldn't that make the cleverest horror movie, though?

if by clever you mean I sleep with the light on for a month, yes

I'll put a pin in that. And hold you if you're scared at night (that's for your chart). But, but, it doesn't scare me because I am confident in my collapsing-everything-but-us plan. The Move Things Over plan. Move ME over. Out of the universe where I disappear.

are you cheerful? you sound cheerful

I really, really like problems. My whole entire job is solving problems about water, and the main rule about water is that it always wins. So.

you're always eighteen miles per hour, heading for a dead end

That is the very worst way to put it, but not wrong, yes.

so what do we do?

Are you ready for a stormwater engineer metaphor?

wait, let me slip into something more comfortable

You are really healing every single one of my nerd wounds. Okay, because our stormwater systems are old, getting older, fragile, and we often don't have good records about what has been done when, we have to start very cautiously. Say we're not getting any movement at the terminal end of a system of stormwater, and a street miles away keeps flooding every time it rains, we might assume there's an occlusion near to that street. Like maybe a big tree root.

in London they have fatbergs, I read about it

We have fatbergs here, too. I love that you read about them. So, we're cautious. We don't want to collapse this system. We don't want to fuck something up farther down the line. We use the smallest tools we can, we go slow, we send in cameras, we stand around and talk about it, someone like me does some back-of-the-envelope math. But nothing happens when we do that. Nothing is fucked up, but also nothing changes. We have exactly our same problem. Great. Then we know we can do more. What happens, then, bit by bit, is that it works or it breaks, but also, we know things.

you are very, very attractively terrifying

I bet you say that to all the girls.

Tressa Fay loved this conversation, because she loved talking to Meryl, and Meryl made it sound easy. Do more. Collapse everything but the moment they were kissing.

But then Tressa Fay was standing behind her last client of the day, styling his hair in the mirror and showing him how he could mess with it to make the most out of the cut, when she felt like she was standing in a new world, her hands full of warm hair.

"You okay?" Her client looked at her in the mirror. He had a kind smile. He'd been thrilled with his cut and very sweet.

"I'm sorry." She tried for a little laugh, but her throat was too tight and dry. "I went away there for a minute."

"No worries. I do that a lot."

Her senses had gone to static. She made herself reconnect with him by turning them back on, noticing his blue eyes, his soft hair, the music, the sticky texture of the hair balm. She managed to stay with him through the rest of his appointment until he left happy.

More, Meryl had said. Try something small, and if nothing changed, try something bigger. Based on the way Tressa Fay felt—like she'd scraped both palms tumbling into another world—Meryl must have tried something pretty big. She wasn't teasing a tree root out of the way anymore.

Tressa Fay walked over to Mary's desk.

"You know what I've been thinking about?" Mary asked.

"That you're ready to try some layers on your crown?" Tressa Fay's voice came out shaky. She leaned over and sifted her fingers through the top of Mary's thick clover-honey hair to try to ground herself.

Mary glanced at her appointment book. "Your four o'clock canceled, so we don't have anybody else coming in. Let's do it. But that's not what I was thinking."

She pulled Mary up by the hand, and while she settled in the chair, Tressa Fay took deep breaths and tried to sort through the soft churn of her feelings. Something inside her was nudging her to think about Linds on the night when Gayle and James had come to Tressa Fay's apartment for the first time.

Mary sprayed her own hair damp with water while Tressa Fay got out her Feather razor. "James and I were talking about you and Meryl," Mary said. "And Gayle. And Linds. And us. Michael and Guy. We actually don't talk about it, not much, except for

Meryl. I've been helping him reach out everywhere we can think of to try to find her. But last night we were trying to talk about *all* of it, and it was almost impossible." Tressa Fay started sliding her razor through the long locks of Mary's crown, and Mary sighed. She studied Tressa Fay in the mirror, her brown eyes huge. "Can't always be about that linear life. James and I think it must be true what Michael said. The closer any of us are to what's happening between you and Meryl, the more it kind of *disrupts*. Sometimes it generates a bigger change in memory, like the conversation you and Linds had in the summer about Amy. But for him and me, it's usually more like a ripple in a pond after someone drops a stone in. Our guess is that the more things change, the less we're going to notice."

"You and James, though." Tressa Fay smiled at her.

Mary smiled back. "It's very easy to talk to him. You know we had the same babysitter?"

"So you guys are way past 'Where did you go to school?' and into your life stories."

"We skipped the favorite-colors questions and got right to the life stuff, actually. That's how it's going, thank you for asking." Mary watched Tressa Fay's hands, then reached up and touched a deep blond wave that had just *shuzzed* off the razor. "It's going to be pretty."

"Your hair is always pretty."

Mary smiled at her lap, a private smile that Tressa Fay could see in the mirror. "I think I've known James in every life I've ever lived. Or every time, maybe. I'm not clear on the physics part. I leave that to Linds."

Tressa Fay's hands stilled. "That's . . ."

"Not something you can deal with." Mary laughed. "I know. But *you* know that what's in my head, like a twenty-four-hour satellite radio station, is the people around me. It's why you pay me so well to work at the front."

"Because you're the best."

"I am. I knew as soon as I sat in your chair the first time that we should be friends, and I should work for you and make this business bigger with you, and then when I met Linds and Guy, it was obvious that I would have to shoehorn myself into your friend circle so we could be together forever." Mary reached up and fluffed a layer Tressa Fay had just made. "But I probably had already done that. Love is probably just like that. Romantic love, family love, friend love—no matter what, we know our people."

"Then I'm glad you've always loved me." Tressa Fay started slicing again, smaller cuts now, looking for how Mary's hair wanted to fall and what she could do to help it find the shape she could see in her mind's eye.

"Me, too. So when I tell you, as someone who has put herself out there and who has met a lot, a *lot* of people, that I feel a connection with James I've never felt before, what I'm telling you is that I trust this, and the only explanation I have is the one I just gave you. I have always known him."

Mary gave her space to work, and Tressa Fay listened to the razor, not really thinking about anything as her feelings drifted and floated and finally settled down. When she glanced at the mirror again, Mary had a determined look that Tressa Fay did not dare ignore, even if this conversation had ventured into territory that gave her a brambly feeling.

"Why do *you* think you left your apartment that night to go to Canyon Tacos?" Mary asked. "For real. Why, after exchanging a handful of texts with a stranger, when you'd already told me and Guy and Linds that you weren't leaving your sanctuary and we couldn't make you?"

"I liked her." Tressa Fay tried to recapture the feeling she'd had when she and Meryl had sent those first messages back and forth. "She was funny. Smart. It had been so long since I liked someone that much right off the bat."

"How long?" Mary raised her eyebrows. "Who was the last person before Meryl you liked so much you'd leave behind soup and Epinephrine and old records on your turntable for them?"

It took Tressa Fay a minute to find the answers to Mary's questions.

Forever.

No one.

Her first date with Meryl in May had been ringed with glitter and anticipation. She'd thought those feelings were created by the energy of what *Meryl* knew—Meryl, who had already talked to the Tressa Fay who occupied a life months ahead—but now Tressa Fay's heart was beating so fast, she had to admit that there was something to Mary's perspective.

When, though? If what Mary was saying was true, *when* had she fallen for Meryl?

The months of longing since May made it seem as though she'd known Meryl a long time. There was nothing here like any of her experiences with anyone before. And wasn't that what people who'd met the loves of their lives said? *It was like I already knew them. I saw her and thought, "There she is." It was like I had been waiting my whole life for him. It didn't matter that it was our first date—I knew she'd be my wife.*

Mary's expression had gentled. "How are we supposed to know how to think about something like this? Especially you. You lost your mom. Your dad is sweet but also the most shut-down specimen of Green Bay Catholic manhood I've ever met, and you've made it clear he took years to get his horses pulling in the same direction after your mom died, so you didn't have permission to talk about your feelings. You had to protect him from your feelings. And then Amy hurt you so much, in a way where your story with her stopped. She cleared her things out of your place when you were at work, blocked your number, and was gone."

Tressa Fay swallowed over the lump in her throat, feeling the nudge again to think of Linds on that day they were all together at Tressa Fay's apartment for the first time. How her sleeves had slid up her arms as she gestured, talking about the multiple realities of time, quantum computers, Schrödinger's cruel treatment of his imaginary cat.

She remembered how Linds had tipped her head and smiled when she said, *But the good news is that I don't have to trust science about this, because I have personal knowledge what we're dealing with here is real and possible. I know Meryl Whit. I've met her.*

The memory was like a dream, hard to catch and pull into focus.

Or maybe it was that she had forgotten the old way that night in her apartment had happened. Because this was a *new* memory.

Meryl must have gone to meet Linds. This day in May. That was what Meryl had changed—while Tressa Fay was at work, Meryl must have walked into Linds's office, introduced herself, and told Linds a story that meant that when Linds came to Tressa Fay's apartment on a dark October night, she'd been able to talk about Meryl as a friend. Someone she'd already met months ago.

"Meryl's making new stories," she said. "Smashing all the old ones."

Mary nodded enthusiastically. "I'm looking forward to remembering when I met her."

Oof. Tressa Fay blew out a breath.

Mary just smiled. "Didn't you feel so much better when you got that first box of clothes that was your mom's, and you took it home in your car and called me to come over, and we spread everything out on your bed and made a plan for getting them restored? Didn't it feel better *because* it changed the past, *your* past with *your* mom?"

Tressa Fay combed her fingers through the short, lifted waves at Mary's crown, watching in the mirror. Her birthmark was bright red, its borders sharp where it met her other skin all along the side of her face, neck, and shoulder, telling her exactly how many feelings must be coursing through her body. "You know what Meryl said?" Tressa Fay laughed, watching her cheeks go as bright as her birthmark. "She told me she'd collapse all the universes except the one where we're kissing."

Mary smacked her hand over her heart and turned around. "What the fuck? Oh my God, Tressa Fay. I can't take it." Mary turned back around, grinning in the mirror. "I get it. I had to take math in summer school two years in a row, but I get it." She pointed at Tressa Fay's reflection in the mirror. "You left your apartment for this woman because the part of you that is in touch with the whole freaking universe had no doubt that this woman was your past and your future."

Tressa Fay reached for the hair balm with shaking hands.

Mary snatched it from her. "I know how to do this part. Go in the back and call Linds. Make her tell you more about what Meryl was like, now that we're all officially gossiping about each other. Also, I look like Brigitte Bardot, right? This is a haircut that is asking me to let my tits breathe under something silky." She turned her head from side to side in the mirror.

Laughing, Tressa Fay went to the back, where they had a tiny table in a room with exposed brick and twelve-foot ceilings. She pulled out her phone from her bag on the table. It was bulky and heavy with its backup power brick on it. She checked her thread with Meryl to confirm there weren't any new messages.

Then she realized she didn't want to call Linds. She wanted to *see* her.

Tressa Fay put her phone back in her bag and grabbed her coat. She went back out front. "I'm going to go over to campus."

Mary was standing in front of the mirror, taking pictures. "Got it. I'll lock up."

It wasn't until Tressa Fay was pulling into a parking spot near Linds's building that she realized she had no reason to believe Linds would even be here. Meryl had talked to Linds in her office in May, and it was fully October. The sky perfectly matched the gray asphalt parking lot.

Except as soon as Tressa Fay fished in her bag for her phone to send Linds a text, she spotted her emerging from the building's door, her long crocheted scarf catching the wind and flying out behind her.

"Linds!" Tressa Fay's voice bounced off the building in an echo.

Linds turned, and then she waved, running the rest of the way down the stairs toward the parking lot, laughing and breathing hard. "Dude," Linds panted. "I was just fucking thinking about you! I was doodling my way through a budget request meeting with the dean, hating life, and then I started thinking that the meeting would probably end about when you and Mary got off work, and we could figure out how to kidnap Michael and Guy from their law firms. There's a new boba tea place where the bead shop used to be on the west side of downtown, and it's amaze." Her smile dimmed. "Hang on, though."

"Yeah?"

"Why are *you* here?"

"I wanted to ask you about when Meryl came to see you in your office last May."

Linds laughed. "So weird! I was thinking about that, too, for whatever reason. Isn't that funny? Meryl is . . . my God. She is something. I was in my office, putting in final grades for graduates. This beautiful woman knocks on my door and asks me if I have some time. I'm thinking, *For you, yes. I have so much time.*"

Linds started to unwind her scarf, then stopped. Tressa Fay watched twenty different thoughts cross over Linds's face, her bright eyeshadow sparkling. She furrowed her brow and closed her eyes. "That was May. It had to be, because I *was* grading the seniors' papers. For sure. And I hadn't met Meryl yet, but you'd had that impromptu date with her, so it must have been then?" Linds looked up at the sky, thinking. "Nope. That's not right."

Tressa Fay didn't rush in to explain.

Instead, she felt her heart go warm, beating hard with a sensation she could identify only as *surrender*. To the universe, maybe. To what Mary had said. To whatever had lit up her phone on a cold night in October and connected her to a person who felt like hers.

"Don't worry about it," she told Linds. "Just tell me about what you and Meryl talked about."

Linds nodded, folding up her scarf. "Hot. She's hot. But you know that. There must be a painting, somewhere, of her naked holding a bunch of grapes. If she were mine, I would be prepping my canvas right now."

"You can't horn in on my time-traveling mega-crush."

"We could share." Linds grinned. Then her face went blank. "Time travel. Gayle. And James. And your phone. Oh, that's why Meryl talked to me." Linds shook her head, then grinned again.

"You're right. I'm not going to worry about the specifics. Linear-schlinear, right?" She leaned on the car next to Tressa Fay. "So I tell her to have a seat, and she tells me she's Meryl Whit, and that she was sorry she had made you angry."

"I wasn't angry. I was hurt." Tressa Fay started buttoning her coat. It was cold standing in the parking lot.

"Don't worry—that's what I said. Then she told me the most incredible story. You know I've been waiting my whole life for someone to show up in my office and tell me a story like that. She showed me her phone, which has pictures of you from what was then the future, when it was cold, wearing a coat I'd never seen before"—she gestured at Tressa Fay—"which is the coat you're wearing now, with your hair grown out from the length it was at the time."

Tressa Fay smoothed her hand down the corduroy collar of her mom's coat. "What did she want?"

"She wanted to talk about you. She wanted to tell me about herself and ask me questions." Linds crossed her arms and slouched her weight into the car. "You know what? She just wanted to meet me and see what happened. That's what I mostly remember."

"She hasn't texted me this afternoon. Probably because, I guess, she was with you in May. Where she lives."

"Whoa!" Linds laughed. "Walk with me? I came outside thinking I'd tromp through this path over by what used to be the golf course. The leaves are so pretty today."

So they walked together. Linds showed Tressa Fay a part of the college campus where a narrow dirt path littered with yellow maple leaves wound through the woods, and she told Tressa Fay about how her life had changed since she met Meryl.

"I had been hurting. For a while," Linds began. "Remember Ren?"

"The guy you were seeing last winter." He was at least six inches over six feet, and he had a beard he styled in long ringlets. Linds had been truly enamored, but she didn't say much about him when people asked questions.

Then Linds didn't talk about Ren at all or bring him around.

"I was so hopeful, Tressa Fay. He got me, you know? My humor, my little routines. He'd bring me huge mugs of spiked tea when I was writing. We'd talk about what love was, what it meant, and I'd connected with him on an app for polyamorous folks, so I felt safe. I felt like we were talking about the same kind of love in every way."

Tressa Fay reached down and took Linds's hand. "What happened?"

"We met someone." She cleared her throat, then swiped at a tear. "Fuck. Fuck all of that. February is the worst month anyway." Linds looked at Tressa Fay. "Don't be so worried. It's okay. I should've talked about this ages ago, but you guys could do better about understanding who I am, sometimes. You could do more to get the incredible depth of polyamory, instead of treating it like it's kind of funny or not quite real."

Tressa Fay felt her heart stutter with the shame that followed a hard truth. "Yeah?" She was embarrassed at how weak her voice sounded.

Linds laughed. "I know. Before I *knew*, I was the same way. I didn't know the difference between nonmonogamy and polyamory or, actually, that there could be a difference that meant something to me. I knew I was queer, like you did."

Tressa Fay nodded, remembering. "You thought you were bi."

"That's as close as I could get at fifteen, even though how I really felt was incredibly turned on with the idea of *kissing* someone who was bi. Who was *more*. Who saw possibility and love everywhere. Look, king-size beds used to make me blush, and not only because of sex. Because of something big I wanted."

"Oh." Tressa Fay tried to think of something to say, but she laughed instead. "*Fifteen*."

"Yeah, and I thought college would make it clear. But I couldn't pull in college. I was a gamer, I hung out with gamers, we were only just learning how to talk to each other. Did I go to grad school hoping for an extension on my sexual awakening? Indeed I did. And it worked. The first relationship I was in that made sense happened by accident. I brought my best friend in the program, April, who I had such a mad crush on—"

"I remember her."

"Yeah, to that open mic where I knew Linh would be reading, because I had the worst crush on her, which I didn't even know, right? I thought I was simply very *fond* of Linh. And the whole way there, I was talking to April about Linh, and April was asking so many questions, looking at pictures on my phone of Linh. One might ask why I had pictures on my phone of a woman who was in my comparative lit seminar, but April didn't ask those questions. She asked me more questions about Linh, which made me so, so happy."

"I have always loved this story," Tressa Fay said. "April and Linh were so good for you."

"Yes." Linds walked for a while, not talking. "April held my hand when Linh started reading. We hadn't held hands. My heart felt *huge*. She leaned over and whispered against my neck, 'Is this okay?' I mean, was I in a novel? Hallelujah! Then April kept whispering to me how beautiful Linh was. What a good writer she was. Did I think she'd sit with us? I died. My corporeal form couldn't handle the heretofore unfelt feelings. Everything finally made sense."

Linds had told Tressa Fay this story, but never in a way that made Tressa Fay imagine herself in the moment, filled with something new that was exactly right.

But also, Tressa Fay hadn't asked for this story.

She hadn't offered the same love to Linds that Linds had offered her. That meant Tressa Fay had left parts of Linds on the table, unacknowledged. Unloved.

She reached out and took Linds's hand to apologize, but Linds shook her head and kept talking.

"It *wasn't* an accident, even though I always tell the story that way, and I wasn't afraid. It's something I thought about after talking to Meryl, how I knew what to do after that night. I had gorgeous, sweet, crunchy apple knowledge, and it led me to a beautiful relationship that taught me about what I was and what I wanted and how much I had to know about myself, how honest I had to be with myself in every part of my life, to have it."

"And Ren?"

"Ren. Beautiful boy, Ren. We had been writing and designing a D&D campaign to open up to new players at Gnome Games. Sometimes these things have a bit of a draggy start, but the group that signed up was amazing. El was . . . well. They were immediately magnetic. And when Ren noticed, too—when Ren couldn't wait to talk to me about them, too—it felt like it was my time to start my epic love story, you know? I was so ready. Tiff, I was thinking about *babies*. My God." Linds's voice was watery even as she laughed over it.

"What happened, honey?" Tressa Fay's chest felt tight.

"Ren had thought he understood about himself. He thought

he'd made that journey, and for a while he tried, but he kept getting hurt, over and over. No one wants to hurt the person they love, and not because of *love*, right? I had all this love for Ren, for El, for me, for us, but it was hurting him. And then it was hurting El. Then it was over before it had even barely begun, before I had talked to any of you, and I just never said anything. Because . . ."

"Because we haven't seen this important part of you."

"Yes." Linds stopped and dropped Tressa Fay's hand, reaching up to hold on to a branch. "'But *how* do you know you're polyam? What if that's not real? What if you're making it up? What if you're fooling yourself?'" She asked these questions in a sarcastic voice that Tressa Fay recognized as the voice of Linds's own self-doubt, turned on her by others. "That relationship shoved me headfirst into the worst second-guessing and gaslighting period I'd ever had, and I was so alone in it, Tiff. It was like I was hurting myself with *staying* alone in it. Until I talked to Meryl."

"Meryl." Tressa Fay's chest lightened.

"Meryl. Time and space and what it meant that she had your picture on her phone. The more I thought about it, the more it felt like I'd been given a glimpse of—of how we know anything, I guess. How we recognize who and what we love."

"Mary just said this to me. Today. Right before I came over."

"I bet. Watching her and James flirt on the group chat like we can't tell what's going on has been something. But in my case, it's knowing *myself*. It's the fearlessness I had, taking April to Linh's open mic, and how I didn't feel that with Ren and El. Can the assurances the multiverse offers that every love is possible explain to a person the shape of their queerness?"

Tressa Fay and Linds had walked so many miles together as teenagers, talking and feeling and complaining and arguing, comparing experiences, trying to figure out how to survive the horrors of growing up, and growing up queer, and growing up queer in Wisconsin. It seemed correct that what was happening with Meryl would be a part of *their* story, too.

Tressa Fay kicked leaves at Linds. "I'm sorry I haven't shown up for you. I'm glad you told me."

Linds looked at the sky, where blue was starting to break through the gray. "Yeah, me, too. And maybe because Meryl led me to thinking about all of that and gave me a chance to heal more, there are some already *possible and new* things happening."

"Reeaally." Tressa Fay bumped her shoulder against Linds's until she let go of the branch and grabbed Tressa Fay's hand again as they started to walk. "You haven't shared."

"You know, actually." Linds took them back toward the parking lot. "Mary was supposed to introduce you to her. At the taproom. But you decided not to go and instead found a time-traveling wormhole, so I feel like this girl is fair game. Probably Mary just misinterpreted the intentions of the cosmic weavers."

"Oh! This is *very* new."

"Brooklynn," Linds said. "Maybe. On the other hand, haven't you been listening? No such thing as old *or* new. But I'll tell you one more thing I just remembered about Meryl's visit back in May."

"What's that?"

"When we were done talking, her plan was to go find you."

MAY 10

"JUST . . . DIDN'T KNOW IT WOULD BE SO SHORT. I THINK."

"On the sides, here?" Tressa Fay feathered the layers that made up her client's new long, wavy shag.

"No, in the back."

"In the back?" Tressa Fay lifted the long waves in the back, fanning them out for the mirror she was holding up so the client could see. "I dusted off about a half inch back here, since you still wanted it mid-back."

"No, not the back. Like, the pieces over the ears, maybe."

"On the sides." Tressa Fay tried not to smile. It didn't disturb her that this young woman was feeling a way about her new cut, fighting unease. Nothing bothered Tressa Fay more than when someone said, *It's just hair. It will grow back.* That might be strictly true, but how a person felt while a haircut they didn't love grew back weighted and darkened that whole era and made it not as good as it could have been.

Hair was important. People had emotional and even sacred connections to their hair. Hair was a part of multiple stories in multiple faiths.

"Yes. On the sides." Tressa Fay's client looked at herself in the mirror, where the new cut had opened up her face. It meant, yes, her eyes looked bigger. Her dark, beautifully shaped brows were highlighted. Her one deep dimple in her cheek and the cleft in her chin were framed lovingly and expensively. But also, she had been using this hair to disguise the texture of the skin on the sides of her face, where it was scarred and pigmented from acne.

Tressa Fay herself found the texture of her client's skin interesting. It had character. She was a very pretty woman. But this wasn't about how Tressa Fay felt.

She heard the door jingle and Mary talking in a low voice to someone up front. She had thought the woman in her chair was her last client, but maybe she'd misremembered. She kept her focus on the mirror, looking into her client's eyes.

"You liked to have your hair along here." Tressa Fay pulled some longer layers forward over the scarring.

Her client nodded. "Yeah. I'm not used to . . ." She put her hands up along her face.

"In high school, I had really long hair," Tressa Fay said, playing with the cut, more to soothe than to style. "And my hair is a lot like yours. I wore it all down, like you did when you came in today."

She met Tressa Fay's eyes in the mirror. "Because of your birthmark."

"Yeah." Tressa Fay touched her temple, where the birthmark started, and smoothed her hand over where it bloomed red along the side of her face, on her neck, a bit over the ends of her collarbones, over her shoulder, down her arm. "Especially here"—Tressa Fay touched her jaw and neck—"where it's darker and a little rough."

"Makeup doesn't cover that kind of thing."

"No."

"When did you cut your hair short?"

"I had been sick in the hospital. I had too many bills and no money. I couldn't make rent. I was sleeping on my dad's sofa because he had already turned my old bedroom into a space where he could tie flies and store his fishing gear. I got really frustrated and sat on the bathroom counter and cut a French bob with my razor, myself, using a picture I found of this old film star, Lillian Gish, who mostly wore her hair long, but it was hair like mine and yours, an unholy mix of curly and thick and wavy, and in the picture I had, she'd cut it like mine."

"You haven't let it grow again?"

"I wanted to for a while. I felt kind of naked. But I had never gotten compliments on my eyes before. Then I did. Then someone complimented my birthmark, and that was something even my closest friends had never talked about, because obviously they could tell I didn't want to. But with it exposed like that, the assumption was that I didn't care, or that I liked it myself."

The client looked at herself. "It's such a banging haircut. It's exactly what I wanted. It's just that I hadn't thought about the other thing."

"It's okay. Do you want to come back in a week and check in? Even if you love it?"

Her client laughed, then sniffed and wiped away a tear. "Yes."

"Okay, let's do it. Hey, Mary? Could we get Katie in here in about a week?"

Mary turned around and gave her big eyes, then motioned over to the bench in the little waiting area.

Tressa Fay looked.

Oh.

It was Meryl, who she hadn't seen or heard from since they parted outside the salon four days ago. Meryl was sitting on the bench, watching Tressa Fay, wearing a black sleeveless knee-length dress and green Mary Jane heels. Work clothes. Her hair was piled up on her head in a big, messy bun, and she had on dark horn-rimmed glasses. If all of this had been calculated as a campaign to destroy Tressa Fay where she stood, Meryl had succeeded. Tressa Fay wanted to put her mouth on Meryl's neck and breathe her in, even while she was hurt that Meryl hadn't contacted her, *at all*, when she'd promised to.

Trouble, trouble, trouble.

Meryl looked at her steadily, leaning forward a little. She raised her eyebrows. Tressa Fay glanced back to Mary, who shrugged.

Tressa Fay finished up with her client, giving her a hug and sending her to Mary to schedule time in a week for any needed adjustments. Once that was done, Mary came up to Tressa Fay, close. "Do you want me to tell her to leave? Do you want me to stay? Take her picture and drag her? Use me." Mary fluttered her new eyelash extensions, which had a lot to serve alongside her pigtails and sequined romper.

"I'm okay, for real. It's possible there's an ordinary explanation. Phones are weird, right? Maybe she put my number in wrong. Didn't pay her phone bill. Maybe she only just recovered her memory after a bout with amnesia." Tressa Fay was not cracking Mary's skepticism.

"You've been out of the game for a while."

"That's true." Tressa Fay felt the strap of her shortalls fall down her arm, exposing the scanty bra she wore with them. She did not adjust, given she could feel Meryl looking at her.

"So, because you've been out of the game"—Mary reached out and pulled up the strap—"I doubt you've recently exercised the self-preservation necessary to survive out there."

Tressa Fay glanced over at Meryl again. She had pulled a *book* out of her bag and was reading. Her knees were as freckled as ever, God help her.

"Look at me," Mary said.

"I can't. She's too hot, and she's right there."

Mary cast her long-lashed eyes to heaven. "You can have any number of hot women, Tressa Fay. You deserve one who calls when she says she will, and, if she can't, does everything in her power to follow up some other way. Especially after hours of conversation and, hello, a fucking free trim. Don't think I didn't notice you comped that."

"I can't charge a client I had active prurient thoughts about while performing a professional service."

"Keep it together." Mary poked her finger into Tressa Fay's chest. "I mean it."

"I will."

Mary narrowed her eyes at her. "You won't. I'll stay up late in case you need help in the aftermath."

"You're a good friend. Go away."

Mary sighed and picked up her bag at reception, shooting a glare at Meryl before walking out the door.

Then it was just the two of them.

Tressa Fay turned to face her, and Meryl put away her book and smiled at her like she was the only reason on Earth *to* smile, which Tressa Fay's heart and clitoris were completely convinced of in the moment, proving that Mary was right and Tressa Fay had no self-preservation whatsoever.

"You can keep reading. I have to clean my station."

"I wouldn't read. I would just watch you. Your outfit looks precarious, and I'm here for it." Meryl crossed her legs and smiled at her again. Tressa Fay was definitely falling for these moves. They were excellent moves. Meryl's moves had lots of corporate domme-y vibes, and so they were easily taking Tressa Fay out.

She decided not to preserve herself. She bent over much more than was necessary and used her strop to polish her razor suggestively. She unbuckled her leather thigh holster like she was getting paid to do it. When her strap fell down again, she did not put it back up, and she told herself that sluttishly gamboling in Meryl's hot, hot gaze was recompense for Meryl's not calling her after their date.

When she'd finished, she walked over to the bench and sat down next to Meryl.

"I'm sorry I hurt you," Meryl said.

Tressa Fay waited for her to offer an explanation, but there was nothing more. She turned sideways on the bench to rest her head against the wall. "It did hurt. I thought we had . . . something."

Meryl smiled. "We did. You're right. I haven't stopped thinking about you."

"What about?"

Meryl closed her eyes. "Everything. I'll think about how your hands felt in my hair, then about one of your funny celebrity stories, then remember when you told me about how you're restoring the clothes you inherited from your mom so that you can wear them. I think about your body and how it moves. Whether I could draw the shape of your birthmark from memory." She opened her eyes. "I think about other stuff, too."

Tressa Fay raised her eyebrows.

Meryl smiled.

She looked a little tired, now that Tressa Fay was close. Her eyelids were puffy. Her freckles seemed to stand out all over her face, and her upper lip—that soft, bitable upper lip—looked like she had been rubbing it.

She'd done that on their walk, rubbing it with her first two fingers when she was thinking hard about something that Tressa Fay had asked her.

"What do you want?" Tressa Fay's body was humming. The music in the salon was still playing, a new Taylor Swift this time, anchoring this moment in the here and now, the light outside pale and bright.

"So many things."

"Pick one."

"Go swimming with me."

"It's May. We'll freeze, even though it's seventy-five degrees out. Unless you mean, like, at one of the indoor places."

Meryl shook her head. "Tell me your address. I'll pick you up in an hour. Wear a swimsuit and shoes that can get wet."

"This doesn't sound like something I'm going to like."

But it did. It sounded like an adventure. The kind with wet hair and slippery limbs and, hopefully, kissing.

The next hour went by in a bright streak, Tressa Fay racing home to feed Epinephrine and mist the plants and try on her swimsuits, one after the next, which was what she was doing when Meryl knocked on her door and the sound zipped through her whole body in the best, best way.

She noticed that she hadn't wondered if Meryl would come. Even though Meryl had said she would get back to her and then had not. Which meant Tressa Fay was as unprotected as Mary feared, but also that she trusted this Meryl Whit.

She answered the door in her red one-piece that was techni-cally one piece, as in one piece of two-inch red spandex flossed through a giant brass ring that circled her belly button. She had managed to dig an old pair of Converse up from the bottom of her closet, which she tied onto her bare feet.

Meryl gasped and shook her head. "No."

She was kitted out in an adorable light blue tankini that was exactly what a marine biology student would wear to a field lab. It covered nearly everything and looked sturdy. The bottoms weren't even swimming briefs, but sensible swimming shorts. Its description in the catalog likely promised long wear. It made Tressa Fay want to lick her.

"This is my swimsuit. Take it or leave it."

Meryl reached out, slid one finger under the strap, and rubbed it over three inches of Tressa Fay's upper chest. It should not have been so completely, utterly killing, but Tressa Fay was in a state. She stepped closer to Meryl. "I like your suit, too."

Meryl looked down and laughed. "Really."

"It is the swimsuit that Lois Lane would wear on a picnic date with Clark Kent when they sat side by side and watched the water and thought very deeply and in extremely dirty detail about what they wanted to do to each other, but only their pinky fingers ever touched, because they are coworkers, and she doesn't know he's Superman yet."

"That is incredibly specific."

"That's really all you need to know to keep me erotically interested. Specificity."

Meryl's laugh was hard and a little shocked, and Tressa Fay savored it like the gift-wrapped present it was.

"Like you said, though, it's not summer yet. You probably want to bring something to wear over it. And a towel. I have a sweatshirt and leggings in my car for after."

Tressa Fay loved how serious and bossy Meryl sounded, like a midwestern mom. She grabbed a hoodie from her sofa and dug in a laundry basket on the floor for a pair of shorts and a towel. She held the shorts up for Meryl's inspection.

Meryl laughed and moved out of the doorway so Tressa Fay could step out and lock up. She noticed Meryl didn't invite herself in or express any curiosity about her apartment. Which was interesting, but also, they'd only had one date.

"Your swimsuit," Meryl said from behind her while Tressa Fay did up the locks.

"Yep."

"There's nothing but *you* back here."

Tressa Fay smiled at the door, then looked over her shoulder. "You're going to see so much more. Are you ready? Because this thing will not stay in place for love or money. It's like trying to bridle a cat."

Meryl was still laughing when they got to the bottom of the stairs and pushed through the door to the street. She showed Tressa Fay to her car, which was the most practical possible Toyota hybrid sedan, navy blue, with gray upholstery. Tressa Fay had to take a moment after she'd buckled herself into the passenger seat. Meryl's car was so clean, it still smelled new. Such a smart-girl car in every way.

"Where are you taking me?" she asked.

"It's a secret." Meryl pulled out of the space. She had a backup camera, but she checked all of her mirrors and did a shoulder check behind her. Tressa Fay could watch her drive forever. "But also, have you ever gone creeking?"

"You're kidding! You're taking me creeking!" Tressa Fay couldn't stop smiling.

"I am. And just so you know the whole plan, because I hurt your feelings and I do feel awful, afterward I am getting you a root beer float."

Tressa Fay wrapped her arms around her middle, looking out the window at the farmland they were passing, feeling as though she had been on a path that led right to this moment, the nice interior upholstery warm against her nearly bare behind, watching Meryl's golden tangerine hair blow around in the breeze.

They passed a farm stand selling eggs and strawberries. It had a big hand-painted sign made by someone who was an artist, and Tressa Fay recognized it. She had been to that farm stand with Amy, in May, though the weather hadn't been this warm and breezy. It was cold and overcast. They'd just had a long argument, tearful on Tressa Fay's part, determined and relentless and full of examples on Amy's. She was a lawyer, after all.

It's an incredible opportunity, Amy had said, looking over the contract Tressa Fay had been asked to consider. *But I'll help you find good representation in LA so this can be reviewed properly. You never want to accept someone's boilerplate contract. It's just an opening.*

Tressa Fay had looked at Amy, her sleek dark hair falling over her shoulder as she flipped through the offer and reviewed a contract from a big studio that wanted Tressa Fay to do a kind of reality show following her days as she cut celebrities' hair. There was talk in the offer about building a lifestyle platform to "celebrate" brands and celebrity wellness experts engaged in "clean, eco-safe, toxin-free" living.

It's not really me, she'd tried to explain. Amy's excitement over something was always so powerful.

But it's exactly you, she'd said. *It's hair. You've worked with celebrities. Several are your regular clients, and you're even friends with them.*

Tressa Fay shrugged that off. She didn't really think anyone could be friends with someone who was around once or twice a year. Texted sometimes. Sent a party invitation. *I've worked hard to build what I have.*

You've built this, too! Amy smiled. *I mean, the way you're doing this, right now, there's a cap, right? Because it's just you and Mary. There are only so many haircuts you can do in a week. You won't even train and hire another stylist.*

I can charge what I charge and pay myself and Mary what we're paid because it's just me. If there were another stylist, we'd be oversaturating the market in this area for what I do. Tressa Fay tried to ignore how thick her throat was. They'd talked about this before.

But another stylist could keep your salon doing what it does while you did this in LA, at least during filming. It would let you diversify your platform, collaborate with brands, which means different income streams. Much, much bigger income streams. Amy sounded like the language in the offer.

It wouldn't actually be me anymore. It would be a lot of other people's idea of me.

You'd still be you. The rest would be business. Smart business.

And there it was, what it always circled back to between her and Amy, which was an unspoken collusion between the two of them to agree that all the different factors and colors and experiences that made Amy who she was were more . . . elite. *More* than what made Tressa Fay.

Amy had never said as much. And Tressa Fay had never explicitly accused Amy of having such an opinion. Sometimes she would *try* to say it, even if it was awkward, but then Amy would simply provide a long list of unimpeachable examples of how her feelings about Tressa Fay were nothing but proud, excited ones, and so then Tressa Fay would end up confused and insecure. The hit to her self-esteem would hang around for days afterward.

That argument had been the first time Tressa Fay directly objected to Amy's personal record of their relationship and persisted in talking about how *she* felt. But somewhere along the way, she'd lost the plot. She'd lost what she was trying to make naked between them so they could fix it, and she'd agreed to Amy's suggestion that they take a drive. *Take a breath.*

They'd ended up at the farm stand, where they bought a half flat of fragrant, early, bright red strawberries.

Every single one had gone soft and moldy, uneaten.

"Tell me about a time when your heart was broken." Tressa Fay looked over at Meryl driving. In the close quarters of the car, she could smell her sunscreen. She could hardly believe she'd asked something so deeply personal on a second date. "But if you don't want to, it's okay."

"I don't mind." Meryl's voice was soft and low. "I'm not going to tell you about the biggest time. I can't yet. But I can tell you about the second worst. I was engaged." Meryl glanced over.

"Oh." Tressa Fay had told Meryl on their walk that she had almost been engaged, that someday she wanted all of that, but she'd only sketched an idea of Amy.

"I told you about my friend James."

"Yes."

"Well." Meryl smiled, taking a turn onto a narrower county road. "After James, there was Kaley. She worked in the mayor's office. She wrote the copy for releases, materials, community education, that kind of thing. Still does, although now she's assistant press secretary."

"Fancy."

"Kaley is fancy. She's charming, ambitious. She's the kind of person that doesn't just *say* it would be a good time to see the Broadway show everyone is talking about, in New York, on Broadway. She books the tickets on her phone the first time she reads about it. On our second date, I mentioned how much I had enjoyed martial arts as a kid, and she signed us up for lessons that we went to for our whole relationship."

"Did she have a lower gear?"

"She definitely did not." Meryl signaled at a four-way stop where the other vehicles were farm vehicles. "If anything at all was scalable, she was ready with an action plan, with money, with ideas. Everything important could always be bigger."

"Oh," Tressa Fay breathed, mostly to herself. *Scalable.* An idea that always seemed to come for her, mostly to make her feel like she was doing something wrong. "Including you?"

"Yes. That's right. And if you were in the middle of the action plan, on your way to more, and you didn't like it, and put it aside or let it go, or changed course, you were a quitter."

A chill had crept into Meryl's voice, a sort of super calm that told Tressa Fay that they had hit a sensitive subject. "Kaley wasn't a quitter," Tressa Fay ventured.

"No. She was a finisher. Always." Meryl's hands gripped the steering wheel, and then she sighed. "But before I sound . . . Here's the thing. She's generous. Being the person who Kaley loved was like breathing pure oxygen, when before you'd just been breathing air."

Meryl turned her car off the road onto a gravel one-lane access path that cut through a field. There was a small metal sign on a pole with a barcode on it, and she stopped her car and stuck her hand out the window to scan the barcode with her phone. "This creek is one we monitor to tell us what the water table is doing. I'll put in a few data points later about anything I notice. My scanning the code just confirms I was here."

"That's incredibly sexy." Tressa Fay laughed, mostly at herself, since she hadn't entirely thought in advance about saying that out loud. "But you didn't get married."

Meryl shook her head. "Here's the part where I won't hold it against you if it changes your opinion about me. We didn't get married, no. Not because she didn't want to. In fact, she planned the most beautiful, amazing, *huge* wedding. Such a huge wedding, completely paid for, that I walked away from two weeks before it was supposed to happen."

The control had crept back into her voice as Meryl said this and parked her car. Tressa Fay could see the creek sparkling through the trees, shafts of light hitting big rocks that the clear water rushed past and around. She could hear the creek. Smell it.

"I think sometimes I would really like to have gone to that wedding," Meryl said. "It would have been something. But I couldn't be a bride in that wedding. I couldn't have told the truth in front of everyone at that wedding. I didn't believe in it. I wanted to. I still often think I *should* have been able to. But I didn't have faith when it counted."

Meryl's tone hadn't let go of any of the tight control. It told Tressa Fay this was something Meryl thought was true about herself—that she wasn't someone who had faith when it counted.

Meryl's hand was resting on the gearshift. Tressa Fay reached over and took it. She had been thinking about doing that for a while.

Meryl turned her palm up and laced their fingers together.

Tressa Fay found it easy to believe Meryl's heartbreak wasn't about faith. She thought instead that this was a woman who'd walked away, two weeks before her wedding, because she couldn't marry Kaley and stay true to herself.

It was the same reason Tressa Fay had torn up the contract for the reality show. The reason behind the worst of her fights with Amy. The truth that Amy wouldn't talk about.

But this felt true. Right here. Holding Meryl's hand.

That was what mattered about living your life, wasn't it?

The story that you, and no one else, could tell.

LINDS

SHE ROLLED HER CHAIR AWAY FROM HER COMPUTER, TURNING on the modem so it could run through all of its startup feelings and she could post the story she had just written online before she had to eat. She could tell by the noises her mom was making in the kitchen that dinner was almost ready.

Her skin felt tight and warm and alive. It had never felt that way before. She knew it was because of the story she'd just finished. Two girls, in love, and *God*, how it had felt to write the scenes where they kissed. She'd been racing home every day after school to write about the girls and about their kissing and about how they were falling in love on this quest. She had known when she started writing that it would be a romance and it would be between two girls, and this had made her feel like she was carrying a ball of pure electricity inside of her rib cage every minute of every day. She wanted to dive her hands into the earth and make the whole world gay. She wanted to see if Tressa Fay would practice the kissing scenes with her, even though they had only just come out to each other and, when they had, they'd mostly cried and talked about if anyone would ever love them.

Linds *wanted*. She just wanted and wanted, and all of that want had gone into this story, so that now, at the end, when her two characters in love came to the part of their quest where they found the lost dragon, prepared to have to capture it in golden chains—in fact, Linds had been ready to write a battle scene where they *did* capture the dragon in golden chains and bridle it to fly back home—but when they entered its lair, the dragon, to both the girls' and Linds's surprise, started talking to them with a low, mellifluous voice. Soon, the three of them were caught up in an amazing conversation about the secrets of the universe and about love, and then the dragon had offered his smooth onyx claw to them, and when the girls touched it, they'd both shivered and been mesmerized by the amber gaze of the dragon, who they knew would be a part of their lives forever.

Linds felt split apart and restless and amazing. It was the best story she'd written, but also, the first story that had taken off on its own, like she hardly had any control over it. It made her think about a girl in her dance class, Emma, who had gotten permission to get a tattoo as a minor from her stepmother and gotten it on her *ass*. The tattoo was of two dolphins in a pink-and-blue yin-yang symbol, and Linds had tried not to stare, but now she thought about tattoos of dragons, with girls in crowns, and rainbows.

Waiting for the computer to finish connecting, she lay down on her floor. She was certain that any minute, a portal would open up beneath her body and she would fall, fall, through a shaft of gay rainbow light into another universe—one where she would meet her characters, including the dragon. Or through a purple, swirling black hole where her body would twist and the entire world would be queer, all through time—everything would have always been queer, always, love in every possible combination and the world filled with thousands of uncolonized villages full of exciting people to meet, and she would do nothing but make out and have sex and write novels.

That was the world she wanted. It was the world she wanted for *everyone*. It was possible. She knew it was. She knew it was *so* possible that, somewhere, it was already happening.

"THE MOST IMPORTANT THING ABOUT WATER IS THAT IT HAS MEM-
ory." Meryl sat on the edge of a large, flat rock that jutted out
into the rushing creek, occasionally bending over to swirl the
sand and mica bottom to investigate a stone. She navigated the
creek as if it were a room in her own home, never slipping, always
oriented, noticing the smallest details.

Meanwhile, Tressa Fay had hardly taken in the layout. She
was covered in chill bumps, her skin reddened and numb with
cold, slipping and splashing in her heavy, wet Converse, laughing
when her swimsuit flashed Meryl and the birds as she tromped
and knelt and fell.

But she didn't feel childish or excessive or in any way *less than*,
and Tressa Fay understood it was because Meryl didn't think of
her that way.

"What does water remember?" Tressa Fay asked.

"Water remembers every place it's ever been, no matter what
people construct to direct it somewhere else, make it something
it's not, or control it." Meryl rubbed silt off a stone with her
thumb. "I will give you an example. In the Pacific Northwest, in
Washington State, people built a dam in order to make a river

into a reservoir and a source of power. The dam was there for a long time."

"How long?"

"A hundred-ish years. It was a big project. And then they decided to take the dam down, and this was going to be one of the biggest dam removals ever. Scientists and engineers and politicians and wildlife managers and rangers and students were talking to each other, trying to figure out what was going to happen."

"When they took down the dam."

"Yep. And at the same time, there were Lower Elwha Klallam people who had not previously been invited to the table—"

"Of course."

Meryl nodded. "And they were reaching out to people like me to say, in a very paraphrased nutshell, 'We know what's going to happen. This river is one of our relatives. We know them well. As soon as they are freed, they have preferences and habits and rituals and journeys that they will take up again.'"

"Because the river has been dammed up, everyone pretending it's, like, some kind of lake, but it was really a restless, caged entity that wanted to go about its usual business." Tressa Fay steadied herself on the creek floor.

Meryl's smile was as wide as a child's. There was a drop of water on her cheekbone. "Exactly. So, of course, the scientists and engineers and managers and rangers and politicians and students made models. And the Elwha people were able to get to a few of them and walk the land with them and show them where the water would go when it went on its journey again, what the land would do. But what the Elwha people said would happen seemed improbable, given what the scientists and engineers had modeled with their equations, physics, and understanding of fluid dynamics. And the

Elwha people—who, by the way, shared a name with the river—were like, 'Cool, cool, but we know our relative.'"

"I'm starting to see the shape of this story."

"Come sit next to me on this rock so I can be more acutely murdered by you in that swimsuit."

Tressa Fay lurched through the creek, laughing, then collapsed on the sun-warmed rock, checking that the scraps of her suit were covering her most important bits. "Then they took the dam down, and . . ."

"The river went on its way. It filled in places that the white people hadn't remembered were riverbanks, that they'd thought were valleys or rock formations. These places made more sense as a riverbank. Several villages were uncovered that had been alongside the river, all of them places the river's relatives said would be there. It overtook places that had been difficult for rangers and managers to keep from having problems with fires or landslides, because they were places that should have always been riverbed. And it didn't go anywhere that its relatives said it *wouldn't* go. The scientific models predicted nothing."

"It's like the whole land was waiting for it to come back." Tressa Fay leaned against Meryl's warm arm, which was a little tacky with sunscreen. The sensation made her breath hitch.

"This is true about all water. It has a memory, even little creeks like this. You know how there's always some parking lot that has a bunch of Canadian geese and sandhill cranes wandering around in it every summer?"

"Yes! There's a parking lot like that at the hardware store my dad likes."

Meryl nodded. "And I would bet my new waders that—"

"You have waders? Like the kind fisherman have with the suspenders?" Tressa Fay traced her finger over Meryl's swimsuit strap, grinning.

"I do. Sure." Meryl narrowed her eyes at Tressa Fay. "That's doing it for you?"

"Absolutely it's doing it for me. Imagine. A short redhead engineer with a fucking fire body in a white tank top and *waders*, barking orders at water guys twice her size while she's standing in the middle of a stream of rushing rainwater. I'm certain there are other details involving what you can see through the tank top, but that's the sketched-in version."

"Hmm." Meryl looked away from Tressa Fay and tried to suppress a smile while she blushed. "Okay."

Tressa Fay laughed.

This was so rare, to like someone this much, to feel so much ease with them. It made her think about how many love stories she'd read where two people met and felt nervous butterflies, which she'd always thought sounded like they were afraid, when obviously *this* was the way she would want to fall in love with someone—to slip into it, warm and happy, excited and joyful.

"You were talking about the hardware store parking lot," she said, giving Meryl a chance to recover the conversation.

"Yes. With the geese and the cranes. I would bet that this parking lot either had a tendency to flood when it rained a lot, or else it had a culvert alongside it."

"It has a culvert."

Meryl nodded. "I think I know the hardware store you're talking about. So that culvert is managing the water. Really, it's draining the water away from the whole property. But what the property actually is, what the geese and cranes know, is wetlands. If we knocked that hardware store down and took up the concrete, dismantled the drains and the culvert, then water would filter into that space. Dormant water plant seeds would sprout, hornwort and duckweed and other oxygenators would proliferate, and it would make a lot more sense why there were geese and cranes everywhere. Someday, if we don't completely fuck it up, your dad's favorite hardware store will be wetlands again."

Tressa Fay liked thinking about that. "So all the water in the world remembers what it is and what it's for and who it belongs with, no matter what. No matter how hard we try to tell it what to do."

"That's right. It remembers everything." Meryl went quiet. "I think that's so important. Because if that's what water does, it means that's what everything elemental does, right? Water, air, fire, earth. They must have a memory of everything, even as other things come and go. We're not good at understanding time. We're not good at understanding how unnatural it is to even try to measure time or observe it."

Tressa Fay looked at Meryl's face. Her glasses were speckled with water, and her eyes were far away. Tressa Fay loved her soft profile. She loved this beautiful date. She hadn't known this woman for very long. She tried to scare up some worry about how big her feelings were on a second date, but she couldn't. There weren't any worries at all. Meryl had just said that people weren't good at understanding time, and right now, that meant that it felt like she'd been sitting on a warm rock in a Wisconsin creek with Meryl for eons.

"I found this for you, speaking of time." Tressa Fay picked up the stone she'd spotted in the creek bed on one of the many occasions Meryl had needed to rescue her from falling. "I think it's a fossil."

She handed it to Meryl, who studied it carefully. "This is such a good find! It's a stromatolite. You can really see the layers on this one. Stromatolites are mats of microbial life, stacked up together."

"Oh! I love that even teeny, tiny things get fossils! You are not forgotten, bitty microbes, even though you were so small." Tressa Fay ran her fingers over the stripy sections of the rough piece of rock.

Meryl handed it back to her. "It should be yours."

"No. I want you to have it. To thank you for this date."

She meant something more than that, although she didn't know how to say it—or, maybe, if it was the right time to say it. She meant that she wanted to thank Meryl for reminding her that they were both part of something bigger than either one of them.

Unexpected for a second date.

"So I was wondering," Meryl said.

"Yes?" Now that Tressa Fay had been sitting a bit and was out of the knee-deep rushing creek water, she was starting to get genuinely cold. She scooted closer to Meryl, whose skin felt furnace hot.

"If you're going to let me kiss you on *this* date?" Meryl tipped her head, and her face caught a shaft of sun coming through the trees, picking up the layers of freckles in her skin. Tiny bits of sun captured forever, like the stromatolite. "Because I'd like to."

The chill Tressa Fay had been feeling washed away in a whoosh of prickling heat, as fast as the creek. "When you imagine kissing me, what do you imagine?"

Meryl reached up and traced Tressa Fay's birthmark where it dipped from her temple to wrap around her jaw and the side of her neck, reminding Tressa Fay of its inkblot shape, new again under Meryl's fingertip. "Is this okay?"

"Hmm." Tressa Fay closed her eyes. "Yes. It doesn't hurt. Nevus flammeus. Port-wine stain. Doesn't bother me. In school it did. Until then, I was around kids in my neighborhood and had Linds and Guy with me, and you know how little kids are—they just kind of accept that what you look like is what you look like. Maybe they ask one question about it. But school is new people. Questions every day. In high school, I tried getting the makeup to cover it up, but I couldn't stand that much makeup over so much of my skin. I did have long hair that kind of covered it up. I actually cut a client's hair today who was dealing with something similar."

"I'm always asked where my red hair comes from," Meryl said. "If I dye it. People would tell my mother it was lucky I was a girl instead of a boy with red hair, I guess because redheaded men are supposed to be less masculine?"

"Sexism is especially revolting when it gets into the gritty details."

"Yes. I also get asked if my carpet matches the drapes. Strangers will stop me on the street or talk to me about it when I'm waiting in line. Red hair is one of those things that people think is permission to talk to someone about things they wouldn't talk to anyone else about."

"People will sometimes ask me what's wrong. If it's a burn. Like I'm supposed to reassure a stranger about my health."

Meryl kept tracing over where the birthmark traveled down Tressa Fay's collarbones. Her shoulder. Part of her upper arm. It felt nice. Studious, as though Meryl were completing an enjoyable assignment.

She stopped tracing and met Tressa Fay's eyes. "Will you?"

"Let you kiss me?"

Meryl raised her eyebrows.

"No." Just saying the word made a deep, terrible throb between her legs. Tressa Fay pulled them up on the rock and wrapped her arms around her shins. "Not this time. Maybe next time."

"Don't you believe in carpe diem? Some people would say we're supposed to live as though this is all the time we have." Meryl didn't sound upset, only amused with Tressa Fay, intrigued by her refusal.

"If it is, then this is how I want to spend it," Tressa Fay said. "On this rock, next to you, anticipating the first time you'll kiss me. You didn't answer my question."

"What do I imagine when I imagine kissing you?"

"Yes, that. Be very, very detailed. I'll close my eyes so I don't inhibit you."

Meryl laughed. "I've imagined it lots of different ways."

"Oh, good. Tell me that you applied true engineer precision to it."

"Shh," Meryl said. "Or I'll get shy, and I won't be able to give you this."

"I will be good." Tressa Fay kept her eyes pressed tightly closed, anticipating, happy that she'd thought to ask this question, because she'd never done this before, never asked a woman she wanted to kiss and hadn't yet what it would be like.

It meant that every possible first kiss was in front of them, hundreds or thousands of possibilities, and the only constraint was what they could think up. They could have all of those kisses. They could decide on which kiss they wanted to have together.

"I've come up with at least half a dozen ways to kiss you this afternoon," Meryl said slowly. "I've thought of how your skin would feel against my body in that swimsuit, and how you'd taste like creek because you've fallen so many times."

"Is it bad to taste like creek?"

"No. It's good, because I brought you here, so it's like I imprinted on you."

Tressa Fay smiled, her eyes still closed. "You're a little possessive."

"More than a little, maybe. I also have a recurring daydream that involves you washing my hair and, not to put too fine a point on it, taking advantage of me."

She laughed. "My imagination *so* did."

"If I want to get off, I start right in the middle of kissing you. Tongues."

Whoa. Her inner thighs got hot as she thought of that, gripping Meryl by her swimsuit straps or rucking up her tankini—whether her skin would be cold from the water, her hair hot from the sun beating down. "I've daydreamed that, too."

"Sometimes we're grabbing each other." Meryl's voice was getting huskier. "And sometimes we're doing a slow manga-comic-like buildup."

"I love a buildup." Tressa Fay opened her eyes. "You might have guessed. This is my best first kiss ever. I'm going to die from the anticipation, and it will be such a happy, horny death."

Meryl snorted, then wiped her hand across her mouth, her eyes on Tressa Fay's. "I probably shouldn't tell you this, but my favorite thing to imagine is kissing you in the snow."

"Yeah? Do you like snow?"

Meryl shook her head, smiling. "I do not. Hate shoveling. Hate winter sports. My skin gets so dry in the winter, and the worst is driving in snow, and the prettiest snow always happens when it's the coldest. But if I'm kissing you in the snow, it means that we made it."

Tressa Fay exhaled in a whoosh. "That's so . . ." She looked at

Meryl, who had gone pink and was watching the creek again. "It's such a not-second-date thing to say, which makes it very sexy and brave. But it also might mean you have to wait longer than you want to kiss me." She grinned.

"Do you even like root beer floats?"

"Yes. Only a monster wouldn't."

"I know where we can get one with Wisconsin-made root beer and soft serve. You'll have to put your clothes on, though."

"Take me there."

Meryl helped her across the creek, holding her hand and laughing when Tressa Fay slipped and tried to keep her swimsuit on, and then they scrambled over the grassy bank on the other side.

She fell asleep on the way to root beer floats, finally warm in her hoodie and shorts in Meryl's car, with Meryl's hand on her thigh.

MAY 11
....

THE TROUBLE WITH BEING WILDLY ATTRACTED TO SERIOUS GIRLS, with the extra convolutions and internal monologues and the labyrinths of their smarty-pants brains, was that they were just a little bit of an enigma.

Tressa Fay considered this while she did her pre-workday chores the morning after spending her whole afternoon in a creek with a hot and serious girl.

Meryl was more than just a little bit of an enigma, and maybe, *maybe*, that made Tressa Fay nervous. But also, Tressa Fay knew, when a woman like Meryl finally kissed you, it really *sent* a person, just because she knew that Meryl was always *thinking*. The idea of how many ways Meryl might be thinking about her had kept Tressa Fay's skin buzzing and her palms aching with tension all through yesterday evening and this morning so far.

And, and! Meryl was a good listener. When Tressa Fay talked to her, she felt so interesting. Meryl asked her questions, and Meryl's questions made her think of questions to ask back. Then Meryl would put her tongue on the back of her teeth and think about the questions while Tressa Fay went breathless waiting for her to answer.

Tressa Fay had tried as she'd fallen asleep last night to be as objective as she could about it. Surely she'd felt this way before. Surely this was the only way a person was even meant to feel when they met someone they wanted to get to know better, to be around, to daydream about. A person they wanted to touch and to be touched by.

But maybe she had never felt this way before. That was what Tressa Fay had been forced to conclude in her bed, thinking about Meryl Whit.

Maybe she had never felt this way *ever*.

Yesterday, the creek was so cold that eventually it numbed their legs to the tops of their thighs, turning their skin bright red, and then the water felt good. It was a wide creek with fast water and tiny falls, one right after another, like steps, and the soft bottom among the smooth rocks was mica and sand, which made their skin glittery and disguised schools of minnows that kept whooshing by their ankles and making them laugh.

Meryl told her about water tables, underground springs, streams, and creeks, and Tressa Fay looked at the trees and grass and plants and the bend in the creek and thought about wild, undone haircuts with not a single piece that matched another, and how a style like that—one made to look like the creek— would blow around in the wind.

She was focused on dreamily reliving the date, sitting on a stool in her kitchen, her knees up under her chin, paging through a trade magazine, petting Epinephrine and drinking coffee, when someone knocked on her door.

"Honey? It's Linds. And Meryl! And—hold on to your butt— Meryl's sister, Gayle."

Tressa Fay put down her magazine, confused.

Meryl had come over? But with her sister. The sister she'd said she struggled to connect with. Had Meryl told Gayle about their date, and then Gayle had insisted on meeting Tressa Fay?

And they'd come at the same time as Linds, who Tressa Fay had kind of expected, since Linds liked to bring fancy coffees and pastries so they could gossip before they both went to work. She was certain what Linds had come to gossip about was her date, but that was okay. Linds would disappear herself once she'd said hello politely and maybe sacrificed the pastries and coffee to a Meryl-and-Gayle-and-Tressa-Fay coffee summit.

Tressa Fay slid back the bolt on her door. There was Meryl, framed by the door, wearing killer high-waisted slacks and a teeny little button-up blouse with miniature sleeves. Work clothes again. Linds was behind her with coffees and a pastry sack, next to a woman who looked a lot like Meryl. Taller, older, but the same hair in a pretty fifties style that matched what had to be genuine vintage pedal pushers. Gayle had tattoos, a tasteful collage of old-fashioned flash over her collarbones and upper arms.

Linds held a coffee carrier with four coffees in it.

Tressa Fay tried to tamp down the unsettled feeling in her stomach. "Hey! Were you guys so surprised when you found yourselves at the same apartment? Obviously, you must have officially introduced yourselves already. Linds, Meryl. Meryl, Linds." She stepped back and opened the door wider to let them by. "And, Meryl? Is this your sister?"

"Gayle," Meryl said. Her eyes were full of apologies. Okay. Tressa Fay was not unfamiliar with family frustration. She would just answer whatever questions Gayle had, make sure Meryl wasn't embarrassed. Hold Linds outside the door with one outstretched palm, then close the door in her face. If that were something she could do kindly.

Meryl walked a few steps inside. "Good morning," she said. Her hair was wavy, curly, and damp underneath, against her nape, where it hadn't dried all the way from her shower. Gripped in Tressa Fay's hands, it would feel like scraps of sweaty silk.

"Good morning." Tressa Fay took her all the way in, her overwhelming realness. "I love your outfit." She reached over and put one finger on Meryl's itty-bitty shirt collar.

Linds stepped forward, breaking the spell. "Good morning, also." Her smile was bemused. Gayle's mouth was firm.

Tressa Fay made more room in her small entryway by closing the door. "Please come in." She gave Linds a warning look.

"I brought coffee!" Linds handed them around, then sat down on Tressa Fay's rocking chair and put the pastry bag on the floor, obviously in no rush to leave. Tressa Fay moved throw pillows off her sofa to make room for Gayle to sit. Epinephrine surprised Gayle by settling in her lap immediately with a big, comfortable purr.

Tressa Fay couldn't stand it anymore. "Why do you have four coffees?" She might have said, *What brings everyone here? How nice to meet you, Gayle! Oh, I'm so glad everyone caught me for breakfast!* But this was a lot after a second date. Even an extremely crackerjack second date.

Meryl touched her arm. "I invited Linds over this morning. And my sister."

That didn't make sense. It made sense that Meryl had talked to her sister, but not Linds. "How do you even know her?"

"I'll tell you the whole story, okay?" Meryl asked this with her big brown eyes on Tressa Fay's.

"Why is there a story?" Tressa Fay sat down on her sofa, glad when Meryl sat next to her, their thighs tight together. "Do you guys know each other from the university or something?" Epinephrine turned on his purr at a high volume as Gayle massaged his ears.

"Meryl came to talk to me in my office yesterday," Linds began. She held up her hand when Tressa Fay leaned forward. "I think it's better if you hold your questions until the end."

"For sure," Gayle said. "You will have at least as many questions as I did."

The coffee was burning Tressa Fay's hands through the paper cup. She kept her attention on Meryl. "I thought everything was really, really good after you dropped me off yesterday?"

"Better than really, really good," Meryl told her. "Because it *was* so good, there are some things I need you to know—"

"Apparently," Linds interrupted, "I have explained everything previously, so I hope I can do a good job this time."

Tressa Fay felt patronized and left out. She didn't want to be left out of something that involved Meryl and Linds. And Meryl's *sister*. "Before you explain anything to me, explain to me why you know Meryl," she said.

"Let *me* explain." Meryl turned her body toward Tressa Fay, her wide-legged slacks draping and slinking against the upholstery. "I tracked down Linds myself to talk to her."

"Why?" The bottom of her stomach dropped out. "Did you have . . . concerns about me?"

"None." Meryl nudged her with her leg. "None at all. I needed to talk to her because of what you told me about *her*."

"What part of what I told you about her?"

"That Linds was receptive and open to even very unlikely ideas and feelings and experiences."

"Did I tell you that?" It didn't sound like something Tressa Fay would say, exactly. She'd be more likely to talk about Linds's delightful witchiness. And she couldn't remember having said it to Meryl. Or anything like it.

"Not in so many words. But you told me about the conversations Linds had with you, and with your friends, and with my sister and James, and what Linds talked to you about helped me understand that she was the person I needed to help me talk to *you*."

Tressa Fay felt a headache starting at her temples. She remembered, suddenly, Meryl telling her in the car that her engagement was her *second*-biggest heartache. She hadn't told Tressa Fay anything about the worst time her heart was broken.

Tressa Fay was afraid.

"I know none of that makes any sense," Meryl said. "I'm wondering, if you knew that I really wanted you to listen to what Linds has to say, if you could?"

It was a question that generated dread. Tressa Fay could feel it—cold, down deep—and she didn't know where it came from or why, because the only other time she had felt it was when she was trying to find a place to sit after her colleague had spilled that texturizing fluid on the floor in the last salon she worked in. She was dizzy, and her vision was gray and spotty, and then, right before there was nothing, there was a feeling that stopped her breath.

But Meryl's knee was pressing against her leg, warm through her slacks, and even though Tressa Fay couldn't get a deep breath into her lungs, she nodded anyway, just to see Meryl's reassuring smile.

"I promise that Linds and I will tell you something for the first time in the history of explanations of ghosting that makes you feel better about the ghosting instead of worse."

Gayle cleared her throat. "To be fair, I didn't sleep a lot last night after Meryl left. But I think there is more good that outweighs the bad. So far."

"Please tell me what's going on." Tressa Fay glanced at Linds, who had on her soft, accepting-of-the-boundless-diversity-of-humanity expression.

Linds started talking, and talking some more, and *explaining*, as the dread spread through Tressa Fay's body in a slow, cold wave.

When Linds had finished, she did not feel better.

Tressa Fay didn't want this choose-your-own-adventure version of a love life. She wanted to kiss Meryl, be with her, cuddle on a sofa with her, go to Canyon Tacos with her. She wanted to have seen her for the first time in her red mathlete T-shirt, sitting at the bar with a pitcher of limeades.

"I get it," Tressa Fay said, having finally managed to understand what they were trying to make her believe. She noticed that her knee was bouncing. "But no. No, thank you."

Now Meryl pulled out her phone. "I have to show you something." She tapped open her Messages app, and then a thread that said *Tressa Fay* at the top of it, with a little picture in the circle that was a picture of her, but not one Tressa Fay had ever seen. Or that Meryl had ever taken. Meryl tapped the picture to open the associated contact info, and Tressa Fay saw her own phone number saved.

So these were messages she'd sent to Meryl and Meryl had sent back to her.

But, of course, she hadn't. She'd talked to Meryl only in person, at the salon, on the trail, driving to the creek, in the water, and now. In her own apartment.

After Meryl finished showing her the messages she'd exchanged with Tressa Fay, the pictures Tressa Fay had sent her *from the future*, Tressa Fay hated two things.

She hated that no version of her was a version with a choice.

And she hated that she was incapable of imagining a solution to this situation that didn't end with her heart getting broken.

"Why did you want me to know about this?" She pointed at

the phone. "That's not me. I'm right here, and I've never seen those messages, which means that's someone else. I don't like the idea that I'm supposed to, what? Take directions from the future? We just met. I *just* met you."

Her cold fingers and forearms were washing over with heat now, and she couldn't make herself believe what she'd just said out loud. Not after yesterday, creeking with Meryl.

Not after lying awake last night, testing her own feelings, thinking so hard about what she felt so she could put her finger right on it, like Meryl's finger on the strap of the red swimsuit.

Tressa Fay had *never before* felt the way she did about Meryl.

"I shouldn't have to know all of this yet." She leaned over Meryl's body to scoop Epinephrine off Gayle's lap, and even though he protested, she needed to bury her face in his fur. "It's too much."

What she meant was that she was in a relationship with Meryl that was much further along, much more serious, than she had understood. The decision had been made for her by Meryl and her unimaginable self, smiling in her mother's coat with a perfectly intact, not damaged and ripped, corduroy collar—a garment that was, right now, at a restorer in Milwaukee, who had made it clear he wouldn't get to it until the end of August.

"Look at this," Meryl said, tipping her phone toward Tressa Fay.

She tapped her finger beside one of the improbable exchanges. This one was from yesterday, late at night, after Meryl had dropped her off at home. And from October. Her stomach wouldn't stop dipping, like the feeling before a roller-coaster drop. Her skin wouldn't warm.

> What was your favorite part of creeking with me?

> when I slipped on the bank in the mud and you came running in my direction and slipped and fell in the creek, and when I looked where I should step to help you, I saw a fossil

> Why?

> because I thought to myself at that moment that we both had to fall on our asses to find something amazing

> I'm going to come and see you in the morning after our creeking excursion. I'll come to your apartment before you go to work. You won't have even a moment to believe I've left you.

Tressa Fay hadn't had this conversation with Meryl. She'd never texted Meryl at all, but she had to remind herself of that, because the exchange felt familiar. That was exactly what she'd thought about the fossil.

Meryl, real and warm and soft, was right against her body, on her left side, even, closest to her heart.

"Meryl said she's already told you how hard it's been between us," Gayle said. "I was shocked when she came over to my place yesterday. I couldn't remember the last time she'd been to my house. Then she told me all this. She showed me what you said about me." Gayle looked at Meryl. "Will you show her what she said?"

Meryl scrolled through her phone, then tipped it at Tressa Fay again, who realized only then that she was fighting tears.

> your sister said the carrier and the tech guys aren't able to get access to your phone account. even though she doesn't have your physical phone, they are supposed to do the spy thing where they look at what you're doing on it. there's a lot of talk about "tower dumps" and "PCMD," the upshot of which is that they can't get a bead on your phone and don't know why

> The universe is at our service. We can sext away.

> I wouldn't care if they were watching

> also Gayle and James have been tromping around in the cold to various lakes and streams you like. Gayle had to buy hiking pants and that is a big deal. she wants to be an expert on your life, because that's the best way to find someone who's missing, she said. to find out everything you can about who they are

> God

but she also said that when you miss someone more than you can possibly imagine when they disappear, you do all the things you never bothered to do and should've done years ago. she said she loves you always but also she *likes* you. she doesn't want to lose you just when she was starting to really get to know you

Tressa Fay looked at Gayle. "That's why I'm here," Gayle said. "Because, like Lindsay told you, the way this ends and the way I get my sister back—not just from disappearing, but really back— is that we join forces with this future and fuck everything up. My whole goal is for September fourth to be a normal day none of us even remember." Gayle's voice had gotten so fierce, the room went quiet. Epinephrine stopped purring. "But I get that you guys just met. And everything."

Tressa Fay coughed out a laugh.

"I didn't have to tell you," Meryl said. "I could've left it the way it was, where you were the only person who got to have time be how it always had been, without thinking about the future or worrying about September. I thought about it a lot, because of something you texted me right before I walked into your salon for the first time. You said you felt sorry for you back in May, having your perfect day, not knowing what was coming for you."

"Which was you."

"Which was us," Meryl said.

"But you have more us than *us*." Tressa Fay gestured between the two of them. "That is what I am struggling with, despite the fact that I just noticed that your belt has little tiny bees on it and is so precious I could die."

Meryl smiled, and her eyes filled. "This doesn't have to change how *we* are. Right now."

"It already has, though," Tressa Fay said. "Even if I didn't know that I had already met you, or I will meet you, whatever you want to call it, I know that you, the right-here you, won't be here after the summer. You'll *disappear*. And that puts a kind of pressure on this, on us, that wasn't there when I was 'accidentally' touching you every chance I got in a creek yesterday, wondering if it would be too soon to ask you to dinner tonight."

"It wouldn't be."

"Well, I know that now, but when I had my coffee this morning, I had only gone out with you twice!"

"So . . . um," Linds butted in, "isn't it kind of good, then? That you can have what you want on an accelerated schedule? Because you know Meryl already really likes you? And you already really like her, if you can accept that the woman wearing your mom's coat in that picture *is* you?"

"But that woman lives in a different universe than me!"

"I mean, she lives in a lot of different universes? But that actually makes my point."

Tressa Fay closed her eyes.

Meryl held her hand.

She'd held Tressa Fay's hand on their first date, walking through downtown, their granita cups sweating in their other hands, and Tressa Fay had loved the way it felt. There wasn't a single awkward knuckle or wrist bone or finger when they held hands. Their hands came together and melted as if their skin were infused with magnets, or like they shared a vessel that had been waiting to connect them together, finally.

It felt like that now, even though she was also angry and her thoughts were blown apart.

She kept her eyes closed and Meryl's hand in hers.

She thought about what it would mean, what it would really *mean*, if she'd met Meryl in October on her phone, and they'd passed those messages back and forth, and she'd told Meryl to come to her salon to meet her in person, and she'd also told Meryl to tell her the truth.

It would mean that in October, she would remember this moment. She would remember holding Meryl's hand. Even though *that* Tressa Fay hadn't held Meryl's hand for a long time.

"More universes," Linds said softly, "is just more."

There was part of Tressa Fay that wanted to push back against Linds for saying that, but she took a deep breath instead and let go of the old reflex. Their whole lives, Tressa Fay had pushed back when Linds said anything that bumped against her self-protection. This time, she just exhaled her held breath, letting herself notice where it hitched and hurt on the way out.

Then she did it again.

And a third time.

"That means there's also more pain," she said. "Because when you texted me the first time"—Tressa Fay was looking at Meryl now—"you were already gone. Your sister and your friend were already frantic, terrified, out of their minds. And I haven't heard anything from the three of you that suggests I won't be out of my mind along with them in just a few months. Why would I get your text just for that? Just to lose you?"

"Because you don't," Meryl said. "Don't you see? I didn't go. I showed up on your phone after no one had heard from me in a month. And now I'm here with you. I've been thinking a lot about this, Tressa Fay, and I think . . ." Meryl looked down at her knees.

Tressa Fay could see the flush race from the collar of her shirt to her hairline. "I think this is some loving world *showing* us, for whatever reason, what it is we actually have. Here. Then. Now. Someday."

Tressa Fay's heart felt wild and feral, hissing like Epinephrine when she'd found him as a wet kitten under the stairs of her building. "You can't say that. You can't. You aren't allowed to say that yet."

Meryl laughed. "I did. I have. Oh my God. Or I've also thought, maybe the energy of us? What we're putting out there? Is pushing back. That's why we can see this and feel it." She cleared her throat. "I don't know. I've been thinking *a lot*. I really, really *like* you."

Tressa Fay's wild and feral heart squeezed, and she thought of something. "My coat."

"Yeah. In retrospect, if retrospect is the right word to use, I'm glad you were wearing it, because it turned out it was a handy bit of proof to—"

"That's not what I mean. I mean, my mom. She died when I was three. I don't remember her, except that I *do.* All the pictures and boxes of clothes my dad kept, and her things, and even sometimes things my dad would let slip, even though he mostly didn't like to talk about her. He'd do something and say, 'Your mother would have said' or 'Your mother would have been proud, or annoyed, or laughed,' and so I got to know her after I lost her. The older I get, the better I know my mom."

"Guy," Linds said. "We've known them our whole lives, never not known them, but they rewrote themself over the Guy we grew up with. Guy coming out made sense of everything that didn't make sense, until it did. And the Guy we have is the Guy we've always had, even when they weren't—"

"Not *weren't*," Tressa Fay interrupted. "Just, they *were*, always. We've always, always had Guy, just as they are."

"Because we act like we're living one day after another," Linds said, "but we're not. Every possible way we could've decided to do anything is happening right now."

Tressa Fay laughed. "You're trying to get me not to worry about it, you weasel."

"I'm right here." Meryl pulled on Tressa Fay's hand. The red spots high on her cheeks made her freckles seem faded. "The only way I'm even getting through this is the idea that if I disappear, it means that I also don't. And maybe there is a reason, a big energy reason, a big universe reason, I'm forewarned." She looked down at their hands. When she spoke again, her voice was rough. "But that's a lie, because there is this other way I'm getting through it, and that's *you*. And Gayle." She looked at her sister, quickly, then looked away. "*All* of us. Those are things I didn't have before. So, for me, I'm just going to keep choosing you." Meryl put a hand over her mouth and looked at the ceiling. "Anyway."

It would be really, really good to kiss Meryl.

That was the thought that stayed still among Tressa Fay's other frantically darting thoughts. If she had a chance to kiss Meryl, she would start with her fuller upper lip and let Meryl's freckles tell her where to go next. She didn't think she could care what universe she was in if her mouth was on Meryl's.

This told her a lot more about what she needed to know than anything Linds and Gayle and even Meryl herself had said.

"So what are we doing?" she asked.

"What do you mean?" Meryl pushed her leg against Tressa Fay's.

"I mean, surely there's a plan?" She looked at Linds. "I get it, I do, that Meryl disappears and also doesn't, but we can't not *do* anything, right? Definitely our October gang must have something cooked up? How do we sign up to be their soldiers?"

Meryl grinned at her. "There is a plan," she said. "*My* plan. It starts with this. Finding Linds. Talking to you. Going to my sister's house. And I have a mission for you, next. I'm going to tell you something you shouldn't know, and then you're going to take that out into your life in whatever way you want and see what happens. I feel like it will only be good."

Tressa Fay tried to let Meryl's smart-girl confidence infuse her with its powers.

Meryl's phone lit up with a text. She smiled at it before she put it away.

That was how Meryl smiled at *her*. Tressa Fay.

It was good to know all the Tressa Fays were on the same page about Meryl. And all the Meryls were on the same page about Tressa Fay.

They chose each other. Every time.

GUY

GUY FELT WHAT MUST HAVE BEEN THEIR ENTIRE SOUL YO-YO through their body, then drop between their legs, where it throbbed so painfully, they never wanted it to stop.

Michael was kissing them.

Michael, in his graduation robe, was kissing them, his hands fisted in their JD hood, like he had to kiss Guy in order to breathe. It wasn't a tender kiss. It wasn't careful. It was hot, like they were in the bathroom of a club instead of a university auditorium. It was the kind of kiss where when Guy licked Michael's bottom lip, Michael bit back and pushed them against the wall, bringing Guy's arms up around their head.

Every muscle in Guy's body was engaged. They could feel sweat on their throat. They could feel where Michael's stubble dragged over theirs, and their breaths were pants and noises so erotic that Guy reached for Michael's ass to bring him closer, to feel him tell them *yes, yes* with the push of his hips.

"Fuck," Guy whispered against Michael's mouth before he came at them again. Guy hadn't known their agnostic, desperate, broken-hearted queer prayers could be answered. They would have to tithe after this. They would have to build an altar. Even if this was the last kiss Michael ever gave them, it was worth an entire temple.

They had *wanted* for so long. Wanted things for themself, so bad, wanted, in their very most protected dreams, this—the feel of muscled chests together, straightforward yearning, the hard thumb against their jaw, the knowledge of a man's smile and his tears even while he fucked them.

They had perseverated for weeks when they first moved into the apartment above Michael's, started taking notes next to him in class, shared pizza with him, felt like they had finally found something forever, even when they didn't know what it was. They would look at Michael, wanting him, wanting him, and beg the universe for Michael to see them, to see *Guy*, to see past everything, even their genuinely epic friendship, and want them in a rush of feelings that he *acted* on, even if he couldn't comprehend those feelings.

Not fair. But the other option was to tell him—to tell someone, finally—and behind that door was the potential for a hundred kinds of notarized disappointment. Guy tells him, and what? Michael says that he knows, he always knew, and touches them tenderly. Or Michael tells them it changes everything. Or Michael tells them that it's no big deal and it changes nothing about their friendship. Or, in the vulnerable, bloody moment when Guy tells him, Michael guesses at something else that Guy feels and gently lets them down.

No.

So it was impossible. They would have to want Michael and be his best friend, his awkward friend from the Midwest, from *Wisconsin*, and, yet again, this would not be the moment for Michael to want Guy. There was never that moment. It was just a constant inflammation of a soul that chafed against their body, but they were used to that, and they couldn't bear any more unknowns or any more awkwardness, not when they were already studying for law school and going to court to change their name, their mislabeled and dusty papers. So they wouldn't, not yet. They would, but not now. By this point, *not now* was as familiar as a sibling. A sibling who wouldn't leave them alone and who rolled their eyes at everything Guy said.

And that was how it would've ended if Guy hadn't come up with the solution. If Guy hadn't thought of something else they might be able to bear, that might be enough, then Guy and Michael would be leaving this ceremony to pack up their apartments, and then Guy would drive away, back to Wisconsin, watching Michael cheerfully wave in their rearview mirror to be a social media thumbs-up dude friend forever.

Instead, Guy had decided Michael would make it possible. Guy would be vulnerable, but by asking for help. *Show me. Show it all to me.*

And it had worked. It had been the most exhilarating three years of Guy's life, with Michael beside them, their friendship better, but in the context of a life that was more than Guy could have imagined. And the more that everything was *more*, and fit, the more Guy felt themself expanding into the world, looking at full lips under beards, feeling a rough hand curl around their biceps at the club, taking their first one-night man to their apartment above Michael's and giving themself over to the miraculous, rough hit of lust consummated.

Even if they would have dreams that were nothing but the way Michael smelled.

Michael pulled back, his lips swollen, his eyes dark. "I should've done that the first fucking day I met you."

Guy smiled and kissed his neck.

They were never not going to do this. They knew that now.

....

WHAT DO YOU NEED?"

This was how her dad always answered the phone when Tressa Fay called him. It no longer hurt her feelings that he assumed that if his child called him, it was to saw off another branch of his giving tree, but it did *annoy* her.

"And how are you, Dad?"

"I just got home from work."

"So did I! I would say this was a coincidence, except that I know better than to call you at work unless I'm dying, and I'm too busy at my work to sit down and take the time to have one of our famous gabfests." As she talked, she fixed Epinephrine's dinner and got a mini pizza from the freezer to microwave.

"Tressa Fay, I'd like to get supper started."

"Do you have a girlfriend?" If he wanted her to cut to the chase, then she absolutely would.

She'd decided on this approach to try to make sense of Meryl, Gayle, and Linds's outrageous conversation with her over coffee yesterday morning. No matter how much she reminded herself of the existence of the texts and photos she'd seen on Meryl's phone, Tressa Fay hadn't really been able to believe in them, not inside her body. But if there was anyone on the planet who she believed was real, solid, and unshakable, it was her dad.

There was a long, long pause, which was an answer in itself, giving Tressa Fay cold goose bumps all over.

They weren't bad goose bumps. Which was interesting. Her dad's failure to confirm or deny the existence of this girlfriend felt more like the answer to a prayer than the outcome of an experiment.

"Where did you hear that?" he asked.

"A friend. You gave me Mom's stuff. Does it matter? I'm your daughter, and unless you're *dating* in a nonexclusive manner, then it would be nice to know about someone new who's important in your life. Of course, she may not be new, but my interest still stands."

"I don't date."

"You've said before."

He huffed out a sigh. "Her name's Jen Sluslarski. Met her at my church group."

Jen Sluslarski was the name Meryl had given her. "How long have the two of you been together?"

"Long enough."

"For what, to trust each other in an apocalypse? To get matching tattoos? Maybe you've started a couples' board game night?"

"We've had a few counseling sessions with Father Cohagan."

He meant premarital counseling, a concept that she was sure was actually anathema to her dad, but it meant he must have either revealed or confessed this relationship to his priest, who would have suggested something like these sessions, and her dad always did what Father told him to do. Doing what your priest told you to do was as foregone a conclusion as aerating the lawn. One did not have to like it for it to be necessary to prevent actual moral entropy, in either the Lord's eyes or those of your Green Bay neighborhood.

"It's serious, then."

"She's a nice woman."

This meant that, first of all, he would never be interested in anyone but a nice woman, and second, a nice woman wouldn't be interested in anything but something serious.

"I see."

"Is that all?"

"No. Let's eat together." Tressa Fay would never know what took over her body and made her say this, but once she had, she realized that she wouldn't back down until her dad said yes.

"You mean tonight?" The incredulity in his voice would be insulting if she hadn't known this man from her literal birth.

"Yeah. We could meet at the diner." She wasn't going to push it by suggesting sushi.

"Why?"

"Neither of us has eaten. It's dinnertime. You're my closest living relative."

"Do you need money?"

Tressa Fay closed her eyes and ran her hand over Epinephrine's soft fur until he purred. She kept her breathing even. "No, Dad. I don't need money. I'd just like to share a meal with you."

"We usually go on the nights they have the meatloaf special. They won't have that."

"Their hamburgers are delicious."

Another long, rough sigh. "I'll see you in ten."

Then he hung up.

Tressa Fay put her mini pizza back in the freezer and sprinted to her car, operating on pure intuition.

She pulled up to the diner at the same time as her dad, and

when he got out of his truck, he was still in his work clothes. He locked the truck up carefully and looked her over in her bright green canvas romper.

"Well, come on, then. Already we're going to have to wait for a table."

Tressa Fay reminded herself that her dad's agreeing to meet her here spontaneously on a non-meatloaf night was the equivalent of another father gripping their daughter in a long bear hug and presenting them with a car wrapped with one of those enormous bows.

Thankfully, there was a booth available in the same row of booths her dad preferred, and the server was an experienced older woman who did not harass him with any small talk or smile at him. He did order a hamburger, but he substituted a house salad for the fries. Her dad did not believe in any food that he considered "empty calories," although he would drink a Coke once a year to break Lent.

Tressa Fay ordered chili cheese fries. "I can't wait to meet Jen."

"She said she'd make dinner at my house tomorrow night, and you should come. Spaghetti."

"You called her before you left?" As far as Tressa Fay knew, her dad called only the numbers written on a yellowed pad, stapled to a wooden board with an apple on it, kept by the phone.

He nodded. "Seeing as you're so *interested*." He cracked a small smile.

Whoa.

Her dad had made a joke. A joke-ish. He seemed pretty relaxed. He hadn't complained about the lack of meatloaf. Also, he'd ordered coffee after four in the afternoon, which was tantamount to skipping mass. Maybe he was glad to spend time with her.

Maybe Tressa Fay should have done something like this before.

Maybe the reason they only saw each other on diner nights and for his trim was because he thought that was the entirety of what *she* wanted.

Maybe. "Tell me about her."

"Jen?"

"Yes, Jen."

"I'll let her tell you herself tomorrow night if you're coming."

"Oh, I'm definitely coming." She watched her dad take a drink of coffee as he looked out the window. He *was* more relaxed than usual. "So, Dad?"

"Yep."

"Why now?"

The advantage to having a father who spoke like he'd been given a quota of words he could say aloud for the year was that he was a man who excelled at both context and subtext, saving his conversation partner from having to come up with words themself. It was helpful at times like this, when her two-word question encompassed the whole of their lives together without Shelly Robeson.

"I noticed her." Her dad put down his coffee and leaned back.

"And you hadn't noticed anyone else? In all these years?"

He shook his head.

Tressa Fay had to look out the window herself in order to focus on fighting back the burn at the inner corners of her eyes that wanted her to let go and cry. "Can I tell you something?" she asked.

"Yep."

That was when Tressa Fay told the single most unlikely person on Earth about what Meryl and Linds and Gayle had explained to her—about *how* she'd found out he was dating someone, and how, when he told her in the future, his first words to her about it would be that he was engaged. She'd taken pictures of the conversations on Meryl's phone, which she pulled up to show him, but he only glanced at them briefly. The rest of the time, he kept his attention on Tressa Fay and didn't interrupt her, not even to say thank you to the server when she brought their dinner. Something he never failed to do.

When she was finished, he picked up the napkin on his lap and wiped his mouth and hands. "I had planned on asking Jen to marry me in the fall sometime, after our counseling sessions were finished. As a matter of fact."

Tressa Fay felt her middle go light. What he meant was *I believe you*.

She did cry then, and even more surprising was that her dad's eyes were shiny, too.

"What is it?" she asked. "What's wrong?"

"Nothing's wrong. I'm thinking about what I'm like in the world where she got to stay with me." His voice was thick. "Somewhere. And what you're like with the mom you got to have. Somewhere."

Tressa Fay gave a watery laugh. "Yeah?"

"Yeah. God is good. You've given me a great comfort that I never thought I would have the chance to feel. Thank you."

"Dad." Tressa Fay blew her nose on her napkin. "You're killing me."

He shrugged. "Did you want to get pie?"

He never ordered pie. "Yes, Dad. I would love to get pie. Let's do that."

Neither one of them said much for the rest of their dinner, and Tressa Fay felt restless, but she couldn't work out why. It wasn't until she was back in the parking lot, waving good night to her dad, the evening cool and breezy and full of the pink light of mid-May, that she realized.

She didn't want to wait anymore. She wanted to be kissed.

Tressa Fay pulled out her phone to text Meryl, and then she stopped. Meryl could receive her texts—at least, as far as she knew—but only October Tressa Fay could get Meryl's.

I don't know where you are, if you're at work or at home, she texted, **but could you meet me at canyon tacos? I've already eaten, but I'll wait at the bar. I'll get limeades like you told me you did.**

She had a hard time finding a place to park, because it was so busy, the front windows open to the nice evening. When she went in, a young woman with long, big, riotous hair styled so she looked like she was mostly eyes walked up to her. "Good evening! I'm Katie. Can I put you in line for a table?"

Tressa Fay stepped more fully into the entry, where it was much lighter from the open windows at the front, and Katie broke out in a grin. "Hey! Tressa Fay!"

"Katie!" Tressa Fay looked a little past Katie's head and saw that there were still spots at the bar. "You look amazing. Like you've made friends with your haircut." *With your whole self*, Tressa Fay thought.

Katie looked down and then back up, and she was fully blushing. "I was more ready than I thought."

Knowing that Katie's hair was helping her cope with her feelings about her skin made Tressa Fay suddenly grateful for literally everything she had ever gone through in her entire life. "Your hair was inspiring," she said. "And don't be afraid to keep your appointment to check in."

"Thank you. I will." Katie smiled. "I don't know what to say."

"Come see me, okay?"

She nodded, looking around the busy restaurant. "I'm going to find you a table."

"Actually, I want to sit at the bar. I told someone to meet me there. Her name's Meryl, and she has long red hair."

"Oh! Hey! She came in like a week ago or so. Maybe longer? And was waiting for you! I remember now. You guys missed each other."

Tressa Fay took a deep breath. "You could say that."

"We'll make sure it happens tonight. Follow me."

She followed Katie, who set her up on a stool and pulled a paper RESERVED tent off her clipboard. Katie set it down on the stool next to Tressa Fay. "There you go. I'll watch for her."

"Thank you! You're amazing."

Katie made her way back through the crowd. The bartender approached, and Tressa Fay asked for a mini pitcher of limeades.

A few minutes after the bartender set the pitcher and two glasses down, Meryl stepped between two tall guys who had been talking near Tressa Fay's barstool. She wore cropped deep red tailored pants and a summery, floaty confection of a top with heels. She had come from work, or she hadn't changed, and as soon as Tressa Fay saw her, she could smell cold creek water and see the river from the bench and feel Meryl's soapy hair through her fingers.

"Hi." Meryl smiled. "The hostess was so glad to see me."

"*I'm* so glad to see you. You got my bat signal."

"I did. I was leaving work, so I came right here."

"I got limeade." Tressa Fay leaned back so Meryl could see the pitcher. "Only, now that I see you, I can't imagine sitting at this bar and drinking limeade. But also, if you just came from work, you're probably hungry."

"I ordered in to my desk over an hour ago." Meryl put her

purse on the stool, knocking over the paperboard tent Katie had put there, and leaned against Tressa Fay's knees. She had on mascara. Her lips were glossy. Her hair was pulled back at her nape with a big, fancy barrette.

Tressa Fay *loved* Work Meryl.

"I'm sorry, but we have to leave," Tressa Fay said. "This isn't where I want you to kiss me for the first time."

Meryl smiled. "No?"

"No."

"Where, then?" She put her hands on Tressa Fay's bare knees.

"I don't care. Where it's just us."

Meryl looked at her for a long moment, her lips pursed as though she might smile, her pretty eyes big behind her glasses, the same softness in her expression that she'd had when she gazed at Tressa Fay at the creek. "You're incredible," she said. "In case no one has told you recently. In case I haven't told you." She smiled. "You're absolutely my favorite person in the world right now, you know that?"

Tressa Fay's smile made her cheeks hurt, it was so big. "Take me somewhere good."

Meryl grabbed Tressa Fay's hand and pulled her down from the barstool. They laced their fingers together and arrowed their way through the crowd. All Tressa Fay could think was *Meryl Whit is going to kiss me.*

When they got outside, Meryl walked them against the headwind from the river, and they made their way to a wide, grassy bank and then a huge granite stone, as big as a garden shed, near the trail along the river. It was a spot far from any business, on a narrow part of the trail, so even on a pretty May evening, there wasn't anyone around except a pelican fishing in the tall grass near the water.

Meryl crowded Tressa Fay until her back was against the warm granite, reaching up to hold her face in her hands. Pieces of Meryl's hair had come loose from her barrette and were blowing sideways. The wind had found the ruffles of her shirt, too, moving them against her skin, brushing them against Tressa Fay's arms when she put her hands at Meryl's waist.

"Are you sure you've waited as long as you want to?" Meryl's body had moved fully against hers, and Tressa Fay had to close her eyes to absorb the pressure, the reality of Meryl right here with her.

Summoned.

Tressa Fay had summoned her, and she'd come. She'd summoned this moment, and now it was here, yet it still had the delicious unreality of the pause before every first kiss Tressa Fay could remember, the moment when neither person knew with absolute certainty that this was going to happen.

And now—now that she'd talked to Meryl and Linds and Gayle about time, now that she knew about one possible future and the infinity of futures, now that she'd had dinner with her dad on a weeknight that wasn't Wednesday without any kind of plan and talked to him about his girlfriend and her mom and he'd acknowledged his loss in a way he never, ever had before—now Tressa Fay thought that maybe this moment felt so big, so impossibly important, because it was one of those moments that split the world in two.

One that changed everything.

The wind made her feel like a creature of reckless excitement, and she squeezed Meryl's waist hard. "Do it!" she shouted, smiling. When Meryl moved closer, her lips a breath away, Tressa Fay said it again. "I want you to do it. I want you to."

And then Meryl was kissing her.

Meryl's glossy, sticky lips dragged over Tressa Fay's. She could feel her smile, and she wanted to taste it, so she put her tongue against Meryl's lush upper lip, her teeth, and Meryl's grip shifted just enough that Tressa Fay could feel the small movement landing in her body as an intensification of desire. She loved this. She loved kissing. She loved the way kissing Meryl started as mouths, hands, bodies, tongues, the shocking experience of closeness, of *contact*, and turned up Tressa Fay's desire until the kissing *became* desire, feeding it and stoking it, taking over so she didn't want Meryl because she was kissing her—she *had* to kiss her because she *wanted* her.

She slid her hands up Meryl's sides, delighted with her warm skin under her Work Meryl blouse, with the way Meryl's fingers had shifted from caressing to gripping her face, guiding the angle at which their mouths met. Meryl's bossy kissing made Tressa Fay go shuddery and urgent at the same time, made her think about Meryl over her, holding her where she wanted her, losing every possible inhibition.

"Hmm," Meryl hummed into Tressa Fay's mouth. "Tell me how it is that this is so good."

"Or you could kiss my neck."

Meryl laughed, and her mouth trailed over Tressa Fay's jaw, licked her earlobe, making Tressa Fay go boneless against the granite while Meryl cupped her head in one hand, rubbed the thumb of the other over the tender side of Tressa Fay's breast, and worked on finding all the places that made her make a noise.

"Come back," she whispered, and Meryl's mouth met hers again. They kissed slow, kissed short kisses, one after the other, until they were just breathing, the wind in their hair, their hearts racing.

"So," Tressa Fay said after a few long moments, "thanks for meeting me."

Meryl laughed. "I'll meet you wherever you want me to, whenever."

"Let's keep doing *this*, though." For the first time, her heart squeezed painfully. "Until we're kissing in the snow."

Meryl put her head on Tressa Fay's shoulder, and they watched the pelican fly away.

WILL YOU HAND ME THAT ONION, SWEETHEART?"

Jen Sluslarski stood at the kitchen counter in Tressa Fay's childhood home, chopping vegetables. She was a small, curvy woman who Tressa Fay guessed was younger than her dad, but by no more than ten years. Probably less, given her references and lifestyle. She had great skin and expensive pale blond highlighting cut into a feathery show of femininity that contrasted interestingly with her Carhartt button-down tucked into jeans.

She was making spaghetti Bolognese, which Tressa Fay knew, for certain, that her father had never eaten before in his life, and certainly not from scratch. Jen's movements in the kitchen were expert and efficient, and balanced on her nose was a wacky set of purple readers with polka dots, which she looked through and over in a way that reminded Tressa Fay of a fast, plump bird on a branch.

Tressa Fay liked her. Even if she couldn't have ever, ever dreamed that anything like Jen or homemade pasta dishes or eating with her dad anywhere but the diner or seeing her dad on a non-haircut or non-diner day would happen.

"So how did you two get to know each other?" she asked. "Tell me everything."

"Aren't you the sweetest?" Jen smiled wryly. "I bet your dad hasn't said a single damn word."

Tressa Fay leaned her hip against her dad's kitchen counter. "Not a breath of a word. Does he talk about me? Regale you with cute stories of when I was a little girl? Go on and on about my successful business?"

They both laughed for a long time, and Jen was wiping her eyes when she said, "We met at church in the Sunday morning adult education class. We've both been going to that class for years, and I got gradually more and more fascinated with the mystery of this man who faithfully attended and never spoke. So I started making him talk to me."

"How does that work? I'm guessing it involves small electric shocks."

Jen hooted. "You're not far off. I made sure that whenever I talked to *him*, I kept my shoulders back." She demonstrated, showing off her impressive rack.

"I like you," Tressa Fay said. "And what he said to you convinced you that you wanted to date him? Because if I got someone to print out on a piece of paper all the words he ever said to me and read it, I don't think I'd be able to tell that whoever said them was my father, versus the cashier at Kwik Trip."

"Oh, God, no. I have friends if I want conversation. My sister. Without sounding sappy, it was what he did, just as consistently as he went to that class. Listened, opened doors for me, showed up to help when I mentioned I had yard work or had to haul something somewhere or a window sash wasn't working, and here's the thing." She pointed the chef's knife at Tressa Fay. "If a man doesn't talk, you know what else he doesn't do?"

Tressa Fay shook her head.

"Complain. Without getting into my entire romantic history, because we've only just met, I will tell you that I'm a woman who can appreciate, more than most, a man who doesn't complain, who lets me live my own life, and who does what he says he's going to."

"I hope you like fishing," Tressa Fay said.

They sat around the dining room table, which hadn't been used in so long that when Jen and Tressa Fay took off its foam protective cover, her dad had to spend some time with a rag and furniture polish to clean off disintegrated foam streaks. Jen lit a candle, of all things, and they ate her delicious pasta. Tressa Fay's dad didn't say a word at any point about anything, but before she left, he gave her a five-dollar bill and told her to have a nice night.

Tressa Fay stood for a long time on the stoop of the house she had grown up in, watching kids ride up and down the street on their bikes, listening to dogs bark. Then she got in her car.

She'd read her conversation over text with Meryl after her dad had told her about Jen. The feelings she'd expressed in the conversation were similar to the ones she'd had tonight. Incredulity. Shock that her dad had permitted a change in his life, let alone had sought one out.

Except that she and Jen had spent some time alone together in the kitchen, and so Tressa Fay had more of a sense of how it had happened. Why it had.

Did it really matter when or in what universe something happened if the feelings were the same?

She started her little Fiat and pointed it in the direction of the address Meryl had given her. It was a small two-story green house in an old neighborhood near the west side of downtown, the kind of house that would have scarred wood floors and creaky four-panel doors that didn't always close completely and a tiny telephone nook carved into the wall.

There was Meryl's sensible car in the driveway. Tressa Fay could see a light on at the back of the house on the first floor, probably the kitchen, and another upstairs. She walked up the drive, knowing that a house like this probably had a side entrance that everyone used instead of the big curved-top front door.

She knocked, her muscles buzzing, her face numb.

Meryl opened the door. She wore a pale pink pajama set, soft T-shirt material, the kind of thing a mom bought a grown-up daughter for Christmas. Her hair was loose, and her glasses were dark, heavy ones, the only saturated color she wore.

"I finished my experiment." Tressa Fay felt the cool air from Meryl's house against her shoulders, swirling with the warm, humid May night. She could feel everything, everywhere.

"What happened?"

Tressa Fay looked up at the light over the door, the moths fluttering around it. "I don't care when or how I met you." She looked right at Meryl.

"No," Meryl said. "I don't, either."

Tressa Fay felt her heart in her ears. "I'm going to lose you no matter what. That's how it works."

"I know. I can't believe we're not completely solitary animals, like the desert tortoise."

Tressa Fay laughed, but she stayed right in this moment she wanted to remember forever, backward and forward. "I was going to wait more. I mean, before I wanted this next part. Not *wanted* it, of course I wanted it. When I washed your hair, well, that was entirely in the neighborhood of . . ." She shook her head. "Wow. Okay."

Meryl moved closer. "What do you want?" She stepped forward, then again, until she had laced one of her legs between Tressa Fay's.

Tressa Fay closed her eyes. She heard a long horn on the river, a mile away. Insects. Meryl's breathing, which was fast. The sound of it flipped a switch inside her that tightened everything between her legs, that made her have to bend her knee and lean in to stay upright, that overrode everything except the idea of skin and pressure and all things wet and fast.

She fisted the fabric of Meryl's pajama top at her waist, her fingertips dragging into soft belly. Meryl made a short noise in her throat.

"Meryl," she whispered. Tressa Fay couldn't figure out how to ask her to make the throbbing connect with something, how to tell her she wanted too much at once and needed something tender and dirty to happen as soon as possible, all over, in a position that allowed leverage.

Meryl laughed and slid her hand up Tressa Fay's body, her fingers catching in the edges of Tressa Fay's clothes, until she put her hand through the back of her hair, over the side of her face, and echoed the grip Tressa Fay had on Meryl's top at the nape of Tressa Fay's neck. When their mouths met, Meryl's was already hot and open, sending such a heavy pulse between Tressa Fay's legs that she pressed herself against Meryl's thigh and moaned, broken.

Meryl's grip in her hair was tight, shooting sharp static down her spine, over her ass, down her legs. As she tipped Tressa Fay's face to better rub their tongues together, she caressed her, slipping her thumb to the corner of her mouth, feeling their kiss.

"God." Tressa Fay moved her hands restlessly over the soft

fabric of Meryl's pajamas. Her body was naked, or nearly, under the thin, soft material, and it was killing, *killing* her how Meryl's hot skin felt through that barrier, how the pajamas slipped and caught over her curves and hips and belly and breasts. She hadn't even touched Meryl's skin yet, and she was aching and wet.

"Come on." Meryl eased her hands away from Tressa Fay's face and hair, sliding her palm down her bare arm, grabbing her wrist. "Come inside."

"Were you getting ready for bed?" Tressa Fay looked around at Meryl's snug kitchen with its original cabinets, everything in different colors of yellow and gold. There was an electric kettle on the counter that was steaming, and one of the cabinet doors was ajar. "I don't want to—"

Meryl laughed. "Nuh-uh. You *do* want to, and when I don't have any plans, I get ready for bed as soon as I come in the door from work." She pulled Tressa Fay through a tiny dining room with a round table covered in binders, papers, and a glowing laptop screen, into the living room, where there was a big sofa in front of a fireplace Meryl had put candles in.

Meryl pulled her down as Tressa Fay collapsed onto the sofa, and then she grabbed Meryl's hand and directed her over her hips to straddle her so that Tressa Fay could take handfuls and handfuls of her if she wanted.

Tressa Fay *wanted*. Meryl's mouth was perfect, sliding, soft, a little bit desperate, and Meryl kissing was a Meryl who was directing her focus and power into taking apart Tressa Fay into her smallest, least inhibited pieces.

"Mm," Meryl hummed into Tressa Fay's mouth, licking into another kiss. "It's you."

"It is." Tressa Fay shivered as Meryl's mouth trailed softly over her jaw, her neck. Meryl kissed her throat and kissed up the other side, lightly dragging her nails over Tressa Fay's sides, which were bare due to the slits on the sides of her tank. "Jesus." Tressa Fay tried to take a deep breath, but she was starting to breathe hard, starting to move her hips against Meryl's, starting to think about naked skin against naked skin and sucking and taking in the slow slide of fingers, grinding against a slippery palm.

Meryl sat back, breathing hard, putting her fingertips on Tressa Fay's mouth. Meryl's bigger upper lip was swollen and pink, yet another layer of freckles Tressa Fay hadn't seen before was glowing against her skin, and her nipples were bunched under her top. "You're here. In my house."

"Under your delicious body." Tressa Fay gripped Meryl's thighs. "I had no idea engineers kissed like you."

"We have to make up for the long dry spells in between." Meryl shifted, forcing Tressa Fay to close her eyes, and Meryl's fingers traced her lips, over her chin, up over her cheeks and eyes. "You're gorgeous."

"What have you been doing?" She didn't want to stop kissing Meryl, touching her, learning the different shapes of her body. She could lose herself there, though—kissing her, fucking her— and not come up for enough air to think about what they needed.

Where they were at right now.

Meryl eased off Tressa Fay's lap, but Tressa Fay didn't let her really get away. She hooked both her legs over Meryl's and leaned her side against the back of the sofa, taking Meryl's hair up in a bunch and smoothing it over her shoulder. Meryl's hands went to Tressa Fay's bare legs, stroking just this side of constant shivers.

"I've been thinking. Science thinking, mostly. And about us."

"What does science say about us?" Tressa Fay wrapped her wrist around Meryl's hair over and over, letting it coil and release, watching how the sensation relaxed Meryl's face. Her caresses over Tressa Fay's legs had moved from her shins and knees to her knees and lower thighs. The sensation made Tressa Fay unwittingly fantasize about Meryl sucking one of her fingers.

Meryl smiled at Tressa Fay's husked-out, sex-drowsed voice. "Can I tell you about it? I promise not to use too many science words."

Tressa Fay touched Meryl's forehead. "I love listening to you talk. I love how when you talk about things, you talk so fast, like you're trying to keep up with your own supercharged brain."

That earned her a small smile. "Can you imagine how many things I must come up with when my supercharged brain thinks about you?"

Tressa Fay's lower belly tightened with a luxurious warning of how little it would take to send her right over with this woman. "Tell me *one* thing."

"I want to watch you use my thigh."

Fuck. Tressa Fay blew out a shaky breath, laughing just a little. "Tell me your thinking thing while I recover from that lethal blow."

Meryl circled one of her fingers around Tressa Fay's knee, smiling. "There's a theory that when two similar universes are made to split, there's a temporary interference between those two universes that eventually goes away."

"Why does it go away?"

"Because the two universes start to become too different from each other."

Tressa Fay thought about that. "What's the interference? Like, what does it look like?"

"Possibly, it looks like the ability to perceive more than one universe at the same time. Like through a connection between two cell phones that shouldn't exist but does." Meryl's eyes were steady on Tressa Fay. One of the lenses of her glasses was smudged from their kissing.

Tressa Fay shook her head. "But you said this interference goes away. When the universes start to be too different."

Meryl nodded, her hands stilling on Tressa Fay's leg. "Right. Then they evolve on their own."

Tressa Fay's hands curled into tense fists. "But aren't they already too different? They're in different places in time. They started with . . . different people in them."

"I don't know," Meryl said. "I'm just trying to understand it."

"No. We're *doing* something, mixing everything up so you don't disappear. So we can kick out the bad guy if there is one, or get everyone knocked into the same universe if there isn't one." Tressa Fay searched Meryl's expression, which was so sweet and soft. This wasn't *interference*! It wasn't fucking interference. Meryl's hands were on her body. Tressa Fay had kissed her. She'd felt her breath fight with hers and her hips push up and heard her noises.

"If it turns out that I go on in some other universe," Meryl said, "I don't think it will hurt. I think it's likely I won't even know." Her hand tightened on Tressa Fay's knee. She was blinking fast. Tressa Fay could see her long auburn eyelashes trying to keep tears from forming. "I think it would just *be*. You'd be where you were, and I'd be where I was, and that would be what it was, only there was no interference anymore, so you wouldn't—we wouldn't—*know*. Right?" Meryl looked at Tressa Fay. "Everything would line up into its own separate universe, and where we ended up would make sense. Even if there was . . . none of me. Where you were."

Tressa Fay had always depended upon understanding time in the sense of "the sun goes up, the sun goes down, all the little mice dance in the town." She hadn't, in all of her life, thought about anything like this. She hadn't looked up in the sky at night and thought about how many galaxies every star represented. She hadn't felt small in a vast outer space.

In school, she'd gravitated toward classes that got her out of her seat, out of her head. Ceramics. Painting. Culinary Arts. She hadn't been coordinated enough for sports, but she'd wandered Green Bay with Guy and Linds, biking, walking, hopping on and off the city bus. She'd discovered sex earlier than what strictly lined up with her Catholic upbringing—as in, when she understood that when she begged the girl in front of her in history class to let Tressa Fay play with her hair during lecture, and she looked at that girl's skin at the nape of her neck and wanted to put her mouth all over it, it meant she wanted this girl. Or another girl.

She wanted. She wanted to see what her body did when it desired someone else, and when she had that for the first time, Tressa Fay had loved it, and she hadn't felt bad about it.

When she found Amy and Denay together in her bed, she'd cried. She'd hurt, right in the middle of her body, right in her chest. Her legs hadn't worked. She'd curled up around the vital middle of herself, on the soft rug in her living room, trying to keep the hurt from tearing her body apart. For days. She was *sore*.

And then she started to move again, and it was okay. She slowly found a way—maybe it was a hurt animal way—of living her life.

That was real. Her life, her heart, her desire, was real. Her body. Meryl's body.

Tressa Fay slid her legs off Meryl's lap and put her hands around Meryl's nape. She thought she would have to ask for the kiss she wanted, but Meryl leaned up and dragged her mouth over Tressa Fay's, her lips already parted.

Meryl's mouth was hot. Her upper lip bumped over Tressa Fay's tongue, and she bit it, just a little. "Tell me what to do."

"Anything. All of it."

Tressa Fay leaned back. "I'll take my top off." She pulled it off, and Meryl laughed, immediately reaching up to brush her hands over Tressa Fay's breasts, making Tressa Fay's nipples go hard so fast, she hissed.

"Too much?"

"No. I like it a little rough there, but it will seem like I don't." Tressa Fay straddled herself back into Meryl's lap, and Meryl steered her into place with her hands at the back of her knees, pulling her tight against her, lifting her hips.

"Do you want me to take my top off?" Meryl sounded *almost* prim and unsure, except that her hands were fully gripping Tressa Fay's high inner thighs, her thumbs sending hot shocks zipping right through her.

Tressa Fay leaned back. "Do I want you to take your top off? That is what you are asking me." She grinned.

"It is." Meryl raised her eyebrows. "Maybe you're not interested in my doing that."

"You, Meryl, are a *hustler*. Here you are, with your librarian glasses and your Lands' End jam-jams, fluttering your eyelashes at me like you don't already know the nuclear power of your tits."

"Take it off me, then." Meryl leaned forward and kissed Tressa Fay's breast to warn her, then sucked her nipple into her mouth, hard, with a little bite on the end. It made Tressa Fay squeal and jump and, in the liquid aftermath, get very, very close to the edge.

"Can't," Tressa Fay breathed. "Dying."

But she scrabbled at Meryl's sides anyway, got two handfuls of jersey, and pulled until there was nothing but Meryl's skin and her hair and her beautiful, glorious body. "Oh no," Tressa Fay said. "I am ruined." Meryl's nipples were tight, a darker shade of the same impossible color of her hair, and Tressa Fay smoothed her hands down the round curve along the sides of Meryl's breasts and closed her eyes for just a second, overwhelmed with her soft skin, the tender shape of her stomach, the freckles everywhere.

"Touch me," Meryl whispered, her hands back to Tressa Fay's thighs. Tressa Fay leaned forward and pressed every part of herself that she could against every part of Meryl, and then she stroked her. Thumbs over her nipples, lifting her breasts and shuddering to feel how they were heavy and soft, and how her touching them made Meryl breathe faster.

Their kissing got rough. It made Tressa Fay feel like she was racing toward the edge of something in the very best way, like her body was made to do this, to touch Meryl, to be touched and stroked and to kiss her with her thumb against her jaw, taking her breath inside her body, her taste, her moans and noises.

"I want to fuck you." Tressa Fay draped her arms around Meryl's head, letting her hair fall over her arms.

Meryl kissed Tressa Fay's throat, licked across her collarbone, making Tressa Fay shiver with the warm, wet glide of tongue against skin and then the hot surprise of Meryl's mouth in her armpit, kissing and sucking. "Yeah."

Tressa Fay had to pull herself away from Meryl's body to shimmy out of her shorts and panties, and she watched Meryl shuck off her pajama bottoms, nothing underneath but more flushed skin and fucking freckles and wet curls. "I want to—" Tressa Fay fit herself over Meryl's body, her thigh. She pressed herself against Meryl's thigh while Meryl stroked her nails up her back, and she was so wet, she slipped against Meryl's skin.

Meryl laughed, her voice hashed up. "Fuck, Tressa Fay." One of Meryl's hands settled at Tressa Fay's low back, pressing, so Tressa Fay experimented to see if it was going to be enough, enough pressure, enough friction.

Oh, it was going to be fucking enough.

They were breathing hard against each other's necks and squirming, kissing sloppy, complaining because they couldn't get enough. Enough skin. Enough touch. Enough kissing between breaths.

"Let me be inside you while I fuck you," Tressa Fay breathed, moving her fingers softly through Meryl's curls.

"Yeah, let's definitely do that." Meryl smiled against Tressa Fay's mouth and then took in a sharp breath when Tressa Fay slid a finger into her, watching Meryl's face.

"Here."

"Yeah. More of that."

Tressa Fay gave her more of that, her other hand around Meryl's nape, looking down at this erotic catastrophe happening in real time. She found a rhythm of short, explicit jerks that was going to get this done, and Meryl put her hand over Tressa Fay's, both of their fingers wet over Meryl's clit, Tressa Fay sliding inside of Meryl in time to her thrusts.

"Meryl." She breathed out, couldn't breathe in, everything winding up tight at that place where she didn't know if she was angry or falling in love or a shameless, wet sex animal, but she didn't care as long as she could come all over this woman until every feeling she'd ever had was wrung out of her and running down her body.

Meryl made a short, low hum that was different, and got tight, and that was it. That was fucking it. Tressa Fay lost it, and Meryl lost it, and maybe they were kissing, or maybe they were biting, or maybe they were fighting for air, but whatever it was, it was good.

"No, don't move." Meryl's arms tightened around Tressa Fay. "Especially your fingers. Don't fucking move them, ever. They live there now."

Tressa Fay laughed, but it was a soft, soggy laugh. "'Kay." She collapsed against Meryl's body.

"But maybe move them now." Tressa Fay could hear the smile in her voice.

She was gentle, but Meryl gasped and shuddered, and then they kissed a little and settled in next to each other with a soft throw around them, the living room getting dark.

After a while, Tressa Fay started hearing a hard, sharp vibrating noise. "What's that?"

Meryl turned her head to look at Tressa Fay. "My phone. It's on the table."

"Oh." Tressa Fay closed her eyes.

"It's probably you."

Her eyes flew open. "Oh."

"Yeah."

Tressa Fay winced. "Should I talk to me?" She did not want to talk to herself. Especially right this moment, which was not a good time.

Meryl laughed. "I have no idea. Do you know how hard it is to cram quantum physics?"

She held her hand out. "Give me the phone."

Meryl got up, and Tressa Fay had the extraordinary pleasure of watching her walk to her dining room table fully nude. She tried to take in as much as possible as a gift to future Tressa Fay.

Meryl put the phone in her hand.

> my dad called me on my cell phone, which
> he has never done unless prearranged

Tressa Fay found she wasn't even curious about what her dad had to say to herself months from now. Months that had Jen in them, months that included dinners with homemade Bolognese. She'd *enjoyed* her dinner at her dad's. She liked Jen. Every muscle in her body was lax. It didn't feel like anything could ever, ever be bad.

> hey girl, hey. Tiff here

Three dots went up, three dots went down. Then again. And again.

Tressa Fay looked at Meryl. She kissed Meryl between the eyebrows, where she had a thinking wrinkle.

"I want you to meet James," Meryl said. "I want him to meet Linds. I want to meet Michael and Guy and talk to Mary when she isn't glaring at me."

A message popped up.

> don't let her out of your sight

I miss you so much. get closer faster

Working on it.

I'm one big ache. like i've been holding onto a mast on a ship with twenty foot waves that have gone on for hours

I'm holding you right now. And I miss you, too.

In the spring, fall feels impossible. Everybody's forgotten that all the leaves fell. We go outside and soak in the tidy greenness, and it feels like it will never happen again.

here, it's getting close to peak leaf color, and I want it to slow down and wait for you

I stare at the sky when it's cloudy and cold and will away the possibility of snow

I don't want to see the leaves fall because then I'll be farther away

OCTOBER 20, 11:13 P.M.

I don't even know how I KNOW to pick up my phone and scroll down my main on IG whenever I've posted a new picture back in May, I even forget what I had posted before, and it's now replaced with a selfie of the two of us, and I can't tell if I remember taking the selfie or if the new post is giving me the memory?

There is a way that all of this throws documentation and observed reality into question, if it hadn't been questioned enough before.

this is why Mary refuses to use a computer booking system and the salon has a landline. fewer variables to run down when there is a problem with time and space

How is your dad doing?

he asks about you now. did I tell you that?
how's Meryl? this question is twofold. it
asks if this relationship is serious, one,
and two, if I have worked out how to keep
you from disappearing, and if not, why
not?

All that?

it is probably also asking me if
I'm going to mass

I'd like to meet him.

you know what's funny? I know for a fact
you will like each other, even as Phil
Robeson has never expressed an opinion
on anyone I have ever dated before

I think that's the most romantic thing
you've ever said to me.

for sure, it is. I was thinking today that
before too long it will be our six-month
anniversary

Here's where this is interesting.

oh, it's HERE that this is interesting?

You have a me that you've been with for six months, and you have a me you've been with for three weeks, and I have a you filled with six months of feelings, and I have a you who has only just started to talk about her feelings.

i know. but is there any one of these ways that doesn't make you want to kiss me?

No. There is no way I wouldn't want to kiss you. Name the hour.

OCTOBER 23, 7:27 P.M.

when do you think you'll meet everyone and I'll meet everyone (before I'll meet everyone in the beginning of October)

We've been talking about this.

yes, but this is the first time I've texted about it

I'm pro for all of it, right now, whenever. Let's rip the fabric of time into ribbons.

242 · ANNIE MARE

you've met Linds. you've been side-eyed
by Mary. I've met Gayle. Am I missing
anyone? I feel like it's all already happened

Linds is still keeping things under her
hat.

it's only my worries for everyone here.
right now, we're just wading into this. as
soon as we're together where you are,
we're in the deep

OCTOBER 27, 3:02 A.M.

You probably won't see this until
morning, but I wanted you to know
that even though you're right here, I
miss you.

OCTOBER 30, 6:22 P.M.

today I went to the spot by the river
where I first kissed you

it was after work, so it was dark, except
for the lights on the trail and from the city.
I needed to feel my feet right on the earth,
like it was as solid as I thought it was, and
watch the water in the river move

none of it was like the movies. nothing glitched or disappeared

My phone did. The headlines changed.

not since

Have you looked?

no, but Gayle does

let's do this

You mean I tell you to get all your people together, and I get my people together, which is something that has never happened before. Not here, not now, which means nothing else after will be the same. For better or for worse.

and we tell them everything, and we make the universe make it all stick together. because you said water knows where it wants to go, and I looked at the river tonight and thought about how many people are making it do what it doesn't want to do with dams and jetties and locks, but it never, ever forgets. it never stops trying to go where it's meant to

what I want is you

NOVEMBER 1, 3:11 A.M.

I keep waking up around three in the morning. James's mother told me that if you keep waking up at three in the morning it means your body is trying to tell you something.

NOVEMBER 3, 11:54 P.M.

I told everyone it's happening when we went to dinner tonight

we all realized we feel exactly the same way we did when we were kids and school got out before christmas and the only thing we could do as kids was wait, literally wait around until THE THING happened

I wanted to tell you tonight that it's been a month and that's enough for me to know.

that even if we weren't burning our way through multiple universes, almost minute by minute, you'd ask me if I wanted to be exclusive?

If I had actually impulsively decided to get a trim that day, I would have asked you to be exclusive before we paid for our granitas. The way you washed my hair was a legitimate ceremony of commitment.

so what do you know?

I'm getting closer to you all the time.

PHIL

HE PULLED HIS TRUCK CAREFULLY INTO THE GARAGE, NOTING that the light over the door that led to the house was out.

When he got out of his truck, he took his step stool down from its hook on the wall, arranged it under the light, and then went to the bin he kept bulbs in, every kind for the house, and found the eighty-watt yellow anti-bug one he liked for this fixture.

He was screwing it in, the old bulb in his jacket pocket, when Shelly opened the door. She wiped her hands on a dish towel, her dark, curly hair the mess it usually was this time of day.

It was as good to see her as it always was.

"Phil." She smiled when she said his name.

"Shelly," he said, stepping off the stool and folding it up. "What do you need?"

She rolled her eyes, but she also stepped down from the kitchen and kissed him, smelling like green dish soap and her perfume. He took a minute to kiss her back like he meant it, and when he pulled away, it was because she had started to smile at him.

"More of that later," she said, "but right now you need to go talk to your daughter."

He picked up the step stool, hung it up, and chucked the dead bulb into the garbage under his shop bench. "What'd she get up to?"

"God, Phil. Nothing. You know she's a good kid, right?"

"I know she's failing algebra" was what he said. But he did know. He'd never say it to Tressa Fay, but he didn't really think there was anything she could do wrong. He didn't want her to get prideful.

"And what did you tell her?" Shelly took his hand and pulled him into the kitchen. "You told her that algebra wasn't the work God had put in front of her to do. And even though the last time Tressa Fay went to mass—or me, for that matter—was long enough ago that I think the priest wouldn't recognize us, it meant something to her. It made her feel better. And she's at the age when her mom isn't always going to make her feel better."

He wasn't sure about that, but he didn't like to think Tressa Fay was hurting. She'd been too quiet lately, all drawn up. Her friends hadn't been around as much. It made him worry, but he didn't see where he could ask her about it outright, either. He didn't like to say what was bothering him until he was ready. Even in confession.

He hung up his jacket and started through the living room to go up the stairs. The house was already dark. He'd been working the seven a.m. to seven p.m. shift, eating the dinner plate Shelly had kept warm for him while he sat next to her on the sofa and listened to her talk about her day. It meant he'd been passing Tressa Fay like a ship in the night recently.

"Hey, Phil?"

He turned around. "Yeah?"

"Don't forget to be grateful she's asking to talk to you at all, no matter what. A lot of parents haven't laid that kind of ground."

This was Shelly telling him that what Tressa Fay wanted to talk to him about was serious. Not good for his heart, but he nodded and winked at Shelly so she knew he wasn't going to lose hold of his composure at this stage in his life, if he hadn't yet.

He found his daughter on her bed, no lights on but Christmas lights she'd hung over her desk. He flipped the overhead switch. He couldn't talk serious in the dark.

"Gah!" Tressa Fay threw her arm over her eyes. "Come on!"

"You'll need glasses if you creep around in the dark like this. Your mom said you wanted to talk to me."

He sat on the end of her bed. She was on top of the covers, not in pajamas yet. Her hair was a bigger mess than Shelly's, probably because it was so long, and she had on a sweater and jeans with more holes in both than he was comfortable thinking about her being seen in public wearing. Like her father couldn't provide nice clothes. He knew it was supposed to be fashion, and he'd gone through his own phase of beat-up Levi's and flannels when he and Shelly went to concerts back in the day, but it was still a bit much.

"I do want to talk to you," Tressa Fay said. "But also I don't."

"All right. Should I go down and get the paper to bring up and read while you think about it?"

His daughter sighed, long and beleaguered. She sounded like his dad, which meant she sounded like him. He'd have to watch that. "I don't want you to be mad."

"Did you talk to your mom about it, or is it only me that has the honor?"

"Yeah. I did."

"Well, was she mad?"

"No." Tressa Fay studied him, and his heart clenched to see how scared she looked around the eyes.

"Come on, now. Go ahead. Get it out all at once, like at confession. If you went."

She closed her eyes, squeezed them shut, really, looking so much like she had when she was little, his heart clenched. "I'm gay. I like girls." She sucked in a breath and held it, not opening her eyes.

Thank you, Lord Jesus.

That was what he thought. That was the first thing in his head, a prayer of gratitude, which meant he could tell Shelly he was a faithful husband for following her advice to be grateful, especially given that he was. Grateful.

Grateful it wasn't anything that would bring Tressa Fay harm, grateful she wasn't hurt, grateful that what she'd told him wouldn't change anything that hadn't already been true, and grateful she *had* told him, though he was a bit worried she'd told him only because she wanted to date a girl in particular, and he'd already made it clear she had to wait until she was sixteen. She was still fifteen. He didn't relish having that conversation again.

"Good to know," Phil said. He hesitated for a minute, a little afraid of rejection, until he remembered he was a grown man and he could take it. "Would you like a hug?"

She finally opened her eyes, and he was glad to see some of the fear gone. She sat up and threw herself in his arms, and he choked out an "oof."

He held her until she let go. Thanked God again.

JUNE 7

. . . .

HERE'S THE SALAD." MERYL PUT OUT A BOWL OF CUBED WATERmelon, diced cucumber, crumbled feta, and a mint dressing that Tressa Fay had watched her make. "I know it seems weird, but it's delicious. Someone at work brought it to a team-builder event, and I got the recipe."

The picnic table in Meryl's backyard was full of food. Gayle had brought chicken burritos. James, who was incredibly beautiful and funny, had made guacamole and brought chips. Guy and Michael carried in a gorgeous cheesecake from Sucre, a bakery near downtown, and Tressa Fay had put together a sangria in Meryl's kitchen with rosé, raspberries, peach schnapps, and her secret ingredient, Sprite.

She had even brought along Epinephrine in his special cat harness, but he'd arrowed toward Gayle immediately and been slow-blinking in her lap, pleased with his friend, who kept feeding him bites from one of the chicken burritos, "to tide him over," she said.

Guy joked it was their first official meeting of the Time Travelers' Club, and Meryl had joked back that it was appropriate it was a potluck, given that they were in the process of bringing completely different things to the same event in the hope that it would turn out well.

"So what's the goal here?" James asked, filling up his plate. "And when is the grown-up coming who will fix this mess?"

"Yes, thank you!" Mary replied, batting her eyelashes at James. "I super-duper hate it when there's a looming deadline over my summer."

"*This* is the goal," Meryl said. "What's happening right now. None of this happened in the original universe."

Michael scratched his fingernails through his dark stubble. "The idea, you're saying, is that in *this* universe, Meryl stays, because we're making her staying more probable than whatever caused her disappearance."

Tressa Fay glanced at Meryl while she filled her plate. She couldn't imagine what it was like for her to hear something like that. Especially today, when it was warm and breezy, the sky perfectly clear, and mostly, they were laughing. James and Mary seemed to be flirting even more than Mary usually flirted with handsome men who were her type. Meryl had just reached over and rubbed a bit of smashed raspberry off Tressa Fay's lip from the icy sangria.

"How's your dad?" Linds asked. "And Jen?" She put her arm around Brooklynn, who she'd brought along to the picnic to meet Michael and Guy.

Mary had met Brooklynn at a plant store, and she'd immediately tagged the tall, criminally luscious, self-declared "plant mom" for Linds—especially after Brooklynn told Mary a story that metaphorized pollination as polyamory. Brooklynn was a sought-after cosplay seamstress for both fantasy/dragon cons and Midwest Renaissance festivals. Tressa Fay and her friends had seen a lot of corsetry lately, on both Brooklynn and Linds, and no one was complaining about the view. They hadn't known Brooklynn was the same Brooklynn a different Mary had met at the taproom and tried to set up with Tressa Fay until Meryl exchanged a funny series of texts with future Tressa Fay that unrolled the entire story.

All of which was to say, Linds and Brooklynn felt extremely *fated*.

Tressa Fay's optimism in the universe was high. "You know, I don't know if it's Jen or talking to him about Meryl, but Dad's good." She met Linds's eyes. "We're good."

"Yeah?"

"Yeah. We're spending more time together. Meryl and I are going fishing with him and Jen."

"What?" Guy laughed. "He's willingly taking you fishing? And not just because he can't leave you unattended at home because you're a child?"

"I know! He's interested in what Meryl knows about water, and probably also in the fishing spots she knows that he hasn't found yet."

"Definitely," Meryl said. "He has his eyes on a trophy at his church's rally in July."

Guy shook their head. "I can't credit it. I've been trying to win that man over for at least twenty-seven years, and he's never said more to me than to tell my mom hello."

Tressa Fay couldn't quite figure it out, either, except that she hadn't known what part of their relationship she had been holding away from her dad. Not that it was her fault. She thought maybe the hurt that had come from not getting the closeness she craved had resulted in her inhibiting more and more of herself around him as time went on. But something had broken between them. It wasn't the same, in such a good way.

"I saw you the other day." Guy was studying Meryl.

"Oh, yeah? Where?"

"Downtown. I was walking a client to the courthouse so they could request a document, and you were crossing the street in front of city hall. I actually was thinking I'd like to talk to you sometime. I have a case I'm dealing with where I'm representing a group of people with properties along the East River that the city condemned. They've been protesting, and the way they went about it got them arrested. I just need to check with my team to make sure if I do ask you some questions, I won't be messing with the city's prosecution unfairly or that you wouldn't need to be deposed."

Meryl pushed her glasses up, which Tressa Fay recognized as a sign of interest. "I know something about what's happening with the East River, and I could likely talk to you, since I don't have anything to do with the city's actions."

Tressa Fay listened to Guy and Meryl casually talk about the case, Michael asking questions, Gayle exclaiming whenever she realized there was something that Meryl did for her job that Gayle didn't know about. James and Mary were in and out, sitting on a metal glider in the yard and definitely invading each other's space. She watched them until Mary noticed and glared at her.

"Hey, James." Tressa Fay leaned forward. "What do you do? Meryl said you work with students at the university."

"I'm the director of student services." His brown eyes were criminally beautiful, sleepy and thick-lashed, and his coral tank against his smooth brown skin made him look like a vacation poster. "A less glamorous job than I make it appear."

Mary sighed, looking at Tressa Fay. "You know, I'm over the moon for you and Meryl, but I'm forever trying to fix you up, and you've never once taken me up on a girl who, for example, isn't trying to avoid a universe where she disappears. No offense, Meryl."

"None taken."

Guy reached over and took Michael's hand. Michael was summer crisp in navy shorts and a grass-green gingham top. He pushed his Ray-Bans into his dark hair. He looked like the secret bad boy on a superyacht. "You know what I've been thinking about, probably because of all these time conversations?" he asked. "After I came home from Michigan's law school prom, second year. I'd gone with this man I picked up at a bar a couple of weeks before."

"In front of me," Guy said.

"Yes. Probably because I'd been so confused, I felt like I had to. But, weirdly, it didn't help to pick this man up and talk to him, take him out just enough in two weeks to get him to come with me to the prom, where I ignored him in favor of dancing most of the night with Guy, who I very seriously contemplated grabbing by their sequined cocktail dress and kissing."

Guy's eyes widened. "You did? I have never heard this. You told me you wanted to kiss me when we ran into each other in Minneapolis and we ended up talking all night at the rooftop thing. I had already transitioned."

"I did want to kiss you then." Michael raised his eyebrows. "And I wanted to kiss you before that."

Everyone in the yard was listening now.

"My point is, I can't really remember a time when I didn't want to kiss you, and I shouldn't have let you go like I did after graduation. I wasn't ready, but I shouldn't have let you go."

Guy smiled. "I wasn't ready, either. Even though you were the very first person I wanted in a way that made sense to me. I shouldn't have let you go like *I* did. Obviously, I never really let you go."

Michael grinned and pulled Guy in for a kiss.

They could do that as much as they wanted now, for as long as they wanted to. It felt to Tressa Fay like an impossible luxury. With the sun slanting away, it was cool, but the prickling sensation over her arms had nothing to do with getting cold.

Tressa Fay pushed the feeling away. She wouldn't think about it, wouldn't let herself become maudlin, because she had no intention of letting Meryl go. She knew that the unimaginable *other* Tressa Fay wanted Meryl with her, too, and the only thing that could possibly mean was that this picnic, this plan, had *worked*.

It had to work.

They talked until it was just starting to get dark, the sky purplish and insects beginning to sing. Tressa Fay's temples ached from her laughing so much and tracking so many different conversations at once.

"Is that what you wanted?" she asked when she and Meryl were back in the kitchen, doing dishes.

Meryl put a bowl away. "I think so. In any event, it's what we can do, right? Look at it, talk about it, research it, science it, hope that time is merciful."

"It would feel so much more real to, like, lock you up in one place where we could watch you and guard the door so we wouldn't have to be afraid that we were missing something easy, like someone we could chase away and tackle to the ground."

Meryl leaned against the counter. Tressa Fay was shocked to see that her eyes were shiny, and she was blinking to keep the tears back. "This feels real. It feels so real to me. But I talk to you *there*, where I'm really, really *not*."

Tressa Fay reached out for Meryl's hand. "But you are, or we wouldn't be here. Which, I know that's a head spinner, but we don't have to let it be. Think about what my dad used to say when I bombed algebra tests." Tressa Fay gently kissed Meryl's forehead. "Whatever you don't understand is for God to know."

Meryl laughed. "You're amazing." She took Tressa Fay's face in her hands. "You are helping me every single day to remember to let the awe happen, you know? Even if there are scary parts and hard parts." Meryl stepped closer. She had put on one of those old-timey sundresses with the stretchy top and tied shoulders and tiers of prairie fabric. It was soft yellow and covered with tiny white flowers, so that the fabric was nearly an inverse of Meryl's skin, with its golden freckles. Her hair was all on top of her head, and she looked sun-kissed and windblown in the best way.

"You're the amazing one. Look at you." Tressa Fay slid her index finger under the first inch of the smocked bodice of Meryl's dress.

Meryl reached up and slid her hand under the skinny tie around Tressa Fay's neck holding up her black bikini top. "Look at *you*."

"Do you have any ideas for what you'd like to do next, and do any of them involve untying things?"

"All of my ideas involve untying things. What *is* this that you decided to wear today? It's so upsetting."

"This is my notion of a Green Bay picnic outfit." Tressa Fay looked down at the black bikini top she'd paired with a sarong skirt, which was really a vintage Hermès scarf of her mother's that she'd tied at her hip.

"I don't know if that says more about you or more about Green

Bay." Meryl kissed her neck. "I want to abandon the rest of these dishes to soak, and I want you to come upstairs so I can show you how easy it would be to tie someone's hands to my headboard, if someone wanted that, and then I'm going to start removing this sartorial sin."

Tressa Fay got fully five degrees hotter than she already was. "We should do that." She slid her hand up Meryl's neck and cupped her jaw, then kissed her softly. "That way, I won't be so jealous that you're sometimes texting her instead of talking to me."

"You are literally the same person. We've talked about this."

"But things have happened to her that haven't happened to me." She kissed Meryl again. "It's confusing. My brain has simplified the problem by deciding to be jealous."

"*That's* why you'd like me to tie you up," Meryl said, smiling. "So you're not jealous. Of yourself."

"Yes. I'm glad you understand."

Meryl laughed. "Go on, then. I want to watch you walk up."

The staircase was adorably old fashioned, with wooden steps and a red runner of carpet, and it ended at a tiny landing with three small bedrooms and a bath opening off it. Meryl's bedroom was the biggest one. It had surprised Tressa Fay with its softness. There was a low, pale wood bed frame with rows of spindles and a fluffy white duvet, a pale pink rug, and filmy curtains. Being in Meryl's bedroom was like being nestled in one of her silky work shirts.

Walking up the stairs, Tressa Fay noticed the fatigue in her legs. The heat and the sun and conversations had made her tired. She wanted to burrow in Meryl's soft bed.

"Are you genuinely in the mood for stern and bossy?" she asked. "Because I could probably dig down and shift my energy, but now that I have climbed one whole entire story, what I'm feeling is much more naked and lazy than what you were talking about downstairs." She flopped backward onto Meryl's bed, letting her arms be loose above her head, her scarf skirt falling open to show her bikini bottom.

Meryl lifted the skirt of her sundress and put her knee on the bed, then crawled over top of Tressa Fay. She kissed her collarbones, her shoulder, the spot where her neck met it. Then she bit the curve of Tressa Fay's neck hard enough that she yelped and clenched against the hard thump between her legs. "I can just spoon you." Meryl reached up and took one of Tressa Fay's wrists, licking into her mouth for a dirty kiss. "That's fine with me."

"Hmm." Tressa Fay closed her eyes. "Possibly I can summon a second wind."

"Yeah?" Meryl focused on the knot at Tressa Fay's hip, breaking it open. "Lift up."

Tressa Fay lifted her hips, watching Meryl, who slid the scarf out from under her and rolled it up carefully, slowly, and then pushed her glasses up her nose, which was what got Tressa Fay wet. After that, Meryl leaned over and very competently tied Tressa Fay's wrists to the spindles of the headboard.

She tested them. They were extremely secure. "Oh no."

"It's a predicament," Meryl agreed, untying the bows at her own shoulders. She looked Tressa Fay over as she shucked off her dress, and then it was Meryl everywhere, all the skin, all her dips and hollows, all of her.

"Gah." Tressa Fay was starting to pant. She brought her knee up to assist her with wiggling and pressing herself against Meryl's body, but Meryl just pushed it back down and slid Tressa Fay's bikini bottom off and began a very slow and torturous process of kissing her way up from Tressa Fay's toes to the arches of her feet, from her ankles, along her shinbones, to her knees, where she licked a circle around her kneecap and blew on it.

"This is very much worse than I thought it would be." Tressa Fay's nipples were so hard. She had her bikini top on and nothing else. Lying on Meryl's pretty duvet cover in her pretty bedroom with a scrap of fabric over her breasts and her hands tied above her head was the most exposed she had ever been.

"Look at you." Meryl repeated the sentiment from downstairs, except this time it was accompanied by a slow rake of her nails from Tressa Fay's belly down to a hip and then over her thigh.

"Please." Tressa Fay decided that begging was the fastest route to getting what she wanted, even if she wasn't sure what she wanted, only that she trusted Meryl would give it to her.

It was *when* Meryl would give it to her that worried her.

"Put your feet flat on the bed," Meryl said softly. "Show me."

"Yes. Okay." Meryl's hands were so gentle over the skin of her legs, her inner thighs, that even though Tressa Fay had wanted to watch, she couldn't keep her eyes from closing. When Meryl's tongue slid into the hollow of her high inner thigh, it was soft and hot, and that was when Tressa Fay knew for sure this was it for her. She wasn't going to survive. Meryl would have to go forward into the uncertain future without her. She hoped November Tressa Fay could take over for her and enjoy more of Meryl's erotic torture.

"Stay with me," Meryl whispered.

It was such a completely ordinary thing to say to the woman you were touching and turning on. A gentle command when everything was getting out of control, good and hot and perfect. *Stay with me.*

Except Tressa Fay felt her throat go tight as Meryl's mouth moved over her, making her throb, making her hips move closer for more. "I want to." Her voice was hoarse. She didn't want to cry, but she hadn't been wrong about her body, and what it wanted was to wind itself around this woman, bind her up in her arms and hold her here.

Instead, she was tied down in one place, with no choice but to trust that Meryl wouldn't leave her. That Tressa Fay could somehow be enough.

Meryl wrapped a hand around her thigh, and then she was at the edge, close and throbbing, every muscle tight, pressing every part of herself she could in Meryl's direction. "Please," she said. She wasn't begging Meryl to let her come.

She was begging Meryl to never go.

She came in a long, slow, endless clench, Meryl right with her, and when she shuddered, Meryl moved over her and slipped the knot on the headboard and gently smoothed Tressa Fay's arms down.

Then she did what she wanted, which was to wrap herself completely around Meryl, holding her. She pressed her cheek against Meryl's temple, and her cheek was wet after all. She kissed her temple, the bridge of her nose, each corner of her mouth.

"Don't cry," Meryl said.

"I have to," Tressa Fay told her. "But it's okay. You don't need to worry about it. I'm very free and easy with my tears."

"I'll just look at you, then."

"Yes. Look at me."

Don't stop, Tressa Fay thought. *Don't ever stop, and let's see if that works.*

THIRD WEEK OF JUNE
....

TRESSA FAY WOKE UP IN THE PITCH DARK TO EPINEPHRINE JUMPing off her bed with a little trill and running out of her bedroom into the living room. She would've fallen back asleep, but then she heard him meow one of his meows with a question mark at the end, and she heard someone softly knocking on her door.

She grabbed her phone. It was after midnight. There were no notifications to tell her who might be at her door—no text from Mary, no voicemail from Linds saying there was something keeping her awake and she needed to talk.

Not one bit did Tressa Fay like this part of living alone, the noises-at-night part and the requirement to either check them out, padding on bare feet over creaking floorboards, or lie awake worried about the murderer who would fling her bedroom door open any moment, and the last thing she'd see would be the glint of moonlight on his butcher knife.

Tressa Fay got up. She pulled on her robe and walked to check the peephole in the door as silently as she could over the pounding of her heart.

It was Meryl.

Meryl had come in the middle of the night, unannounced.

The newness of it made it feel special enough that Tressa Fay opened the door smiling.

"What are you doing here so late?" She reached out to grab Meryl's hand and pull her inside. Meryl's hair was everywhere, and she melted into Tressa Fay's tug willingly. She was so softened, Tressa Fay wasn't sure if Meryl was coming to her tipsy or tired or emotional, but it literally made her knees feel weak that whatever state Meryl was in, she had come to Tressa Fay, seeking her out for comfort or a snuggle or a late-night drowsy talk.

"Gayle and James and I were hanging out, and then I wanted to see you. But I couldn't text. Well, I could, but you wouldn't get it until a long time from now. Also, the you who exists a long time from now maybe wants to break up with me." Meryl made her way to Tressa Fay's sofa and collapsed onto her side. She was obviously tired and punchy.

Tressa Fay slid off Meryl's sensible Birkenstocks, which made her tender every time she spied Meryl's feet in them, and directed her into a comfortable position with a throw, feeling fat with caregiving warmth and indulgence. "There are so many obstacles to separate here." She went into the kitchen and turned on her kettle. "I'm going to make you some herbal tea. Were you guys drinking?"

"No. Well, yes, but that was hours ago at dinner. We kept talking and talking, and I'm just tired now." Meryl put her head on the back of the sofa. The way she smiled at Tressa Fay made her heart lurch, it was so tender.

She didn't want to think about what Meryl had said about future Tressa Fay wanting to break up with her. Meryl had told her that future Tressa Fay was *her* so many times, it felt like an accusation, something that had the potential to start a fight.

She decided to make herself herbal tea, too. It was hard enough on her body to wake up suddenly and be scared without having to figure out what to do about the possible feelings of her future self. "That's a lot of hours of talking." It was hard to keep the questions out of that statement.

Meryl sighed. "So many. But it was good."

"Yeah?" Tressa Fay fussed with tea bags. Meryl didn't seem to have heard her.

Meryl grabbed a pillow to put on the arm of the sofa and leaned back. Epinephrine accepted the tacit invitation to jump onto her belly and make biscuits. "*Oof.* He looks small, but he's so heavy." Meryl ringed Epinephrine's neck with the firm scritches that he loved, and his rough purrs started up. What was it about a woman who knew how to pet your cat?

Tressa Fay came back into the room with the tea and set it on the table near Meryl, sitting down at her feet and pulling them into her lap. "You're friend drunk."

Meryl closed her eyes. "Hmm. It's been a long time."

Tressa Fay pressed her thumb into one of Meryl's arches. Then again. She let Epinephrine's purrs soothe her, too. She almost didn't want to ask the question that was on the tip of her tongue, but she also didn't want to feel this lurch-ache in her heart and stomach anymore. She cleared her throat. "Why do you think I'm breaking up with you?"

Meryl opened her eyes. "You mean future you?"

Tressa Fay ran the heel of her hand down the sole of Meryl's foot, then back up, squeezing her toes. "Yeah. Though you keep reminding me we're the same."

"It's November for her. She's quiet. I don't think she wants to text all the time now that we're together, and you know what it's like here in November. The days are so short and windy and cold and dark."

264 • ANNIE MARE

Meryl traced her fingertips down Epinephrine's spine and didn't look at Tressa Fay when she said this.

Blaming the weather. Tressa Fay couldn't help but think about Amy snapping at her and then apologizing. *It's just that it's hot. Driving in the snow made me cranky.* Maybe she was catastrophizing, but her stomach felt heavy as what Meryl was saying stretched out the distance from now to November. She gently put down Meryl's foot. "Are you sure?"

"Am I sure of what?"

She squeezed Meryl's ankle. "That she's just tired. That the bad weather is getting to her. Are you really thinking she's, I guess, breaking up with you? Maybe you can't reach her the same way anymore, or with as much connection, because . . . because the link that made it possible to talk to her is losing power with the more power we put here, between us? Until what's happening here *is* what's happening."

Please, she thought.

And then she went still, because she hadn't really let herself notice that *please* before. She hadn't let herself admit that even though the link between Meryl's phone and her future self was the reason she'd met Meryl, the reason she *had* Meryl, she'd be relieved if it stopped. If she could just have Meryl and their friends, their people, and none of the rest of this.

In a small, jealous corner of her heart, Tressa Fay wished that the beginning of her first relationship since Amy could be suffused with lust and fun and fascination and limerence—all of the things she had with Meryl, but with no loss. She hated future Tressa Fay because her existence—Tressa Fay's *own existence*, five months in the future—reminded her of loss and tarnish and arguments and the collapse of the world. She couldn't believe she was *meant* for all of that.

But she was meant to feel this way about Meryl.

Wasn't she?

Meryl hadn't answered her, and then Tressa Fay heard a teeny, tiny snore. She gave up and snuggled next to Meryl, which made her stir enough to drape her arm around Tressa Fay.

"Meryl?"

"Hmm?"

"Do you think that if we didn't know you disappeared, if we had met the regular way, we would feel different about each other?"

Meryl opened her eyes. "What do you mean?"

"I mean that every minute I spend with you seems so . . . not regular. It's all bright. It's all good. It makes me feel like I'll re-member forever. Even when we're just hanging out, doing noth-ing special, I *notice* you and me and the weather and how I feel."

"I see." Meryl turned slowly and pushed her feet under one of Tressa Fay's thighs. "No. It wouldn't be the same."

Tressa Fay picked up her mug of tea to steady herself. "No?"

"Mm. Probably not." She ran her palm over the top of Tressa Fay's head and tucked her hair behind her ear. "Not because of you. You're perfect. But my own track record suggests that I hold my feelings closer to the chest than I have with you."

Tressa Fay lifted her tea to her lips, needing to soothe the hurt with warmth, but she hadn't waited long enough for the tea to cool, and it burned her tongue. "People change," she tried.

The statement made her heart feel as tender as her scorched taste buds. Did people change? People *wanted* to change—Tressa Fay's full appointment book was testament to that—but she heard the same kinds of stories, the same fears and complaints, day in and day out.

The skin just beneath Meryl's eyes was dark and bruised

looking. Tressa Fay set her mug down on the table and took Meryl's hands between hers. "You know what? I don't know if it helps to ask these kinds of questions. It's better, I think, to assume we're doing this the way we're supposed to."

Meryl reached up and touched Tressa Fay's cheek. Her eyes were a little bloodshot, those shadows underneath, and her outfit was wrinkled, with what looked like a spot of spilled drink on the bust. "What happens to me, Tressa Fay? What *happens*?" She spoke fast, the way she did when she talked about science, but Tressa Fay had never heard this thread of panic in her voice before. "Will it hurt, or will I even know, or will I wake up and it's a workday and I've never had a sister, or if I do, it's always been someone else? What if there's no you, and I never knew you, and I don't remember you?" She sucked in a breath and continued with barely a pause. "What if in my universe there is no you to even run into," she continued, "to meet you all over again, and meanwhile there's this other place where, at first, a lot of people remember me, and then fewer, and then no one? Or, worse, only one person remembers me after I'm gone and knows what happens to me, and they have to live their lives without me, knowing I'm somewhere, but they can't even talk about me anymore."

"Breathe, okay?" Tressa Fay slowly smoothed her hands over Meryl's shoulder. Her heart was beating so fast. "I didn't know you were feeling all that."

"I can't avoid it. I've been thinking so hard, trying to figure everything out. Doing my 'experiments.'" She made air quotes around the word with her fingers. "But these aren't experiments! You can't experiment with *time*. There's no control. There's no way to observe results."

"We don't have to *observe* them." Tressa Fay couldn't keep the impatience out of her voice. "We're living, right now. We're—"

Meryl shook her head hard, squeezing her eyes shut. Her glasses were smudged. "You're right, we shouldn't talk about this." She tossed her phone on the sofa. "I can tell you right now that *you're* done talking about this."

"Don't do that. Don't say that." Tressa Fay looked at Meryl's phone, almost expecting it to light up with a text, but the screen stayed dark. She hated that phone. "*We've* never really talked about this."

Meryl didn't acknowledge Tressa Fay's distinction between the person she was now and the one Meryl texted. "You know I keep having dreams that I'm driving a school bus? Everybody's in it, you and me and Gayle and James and Linds and Mary and Guy and Michael and even Brooklynn, Epinephrine, and that tuxedo cat at the shelter I liked so much, and Gayle is feeding the cats pieces of her chicken burrito the way she did at the picnic when Epinephrine fell in love with her, and Michael and Guy have a guitar and are writing a song. You're sitting right behind me, looking out the window, commenting on the scenery. Everyone is happy. I'm happy. I have such wonderful friends. I have my sister in a way I never got to. I have you." She crossed her hands over her heart. There were tears in her eyes now. "I have *you*. My Tressa Fay. And then I remember to look at the road, so I turn back to the windshield, and I'm about to drive the bus off a cliff into the ocean."

Tressa Fay laughed, horrified but unable to stop herself. No one was driving a bus off a cliff. They *were* all together. They *were* happy. She looked at the phone and desperately, viciously wished they would go away, the ones who weren't happy. The ones who were messing this up and making it so hard for Meryl.

"It's not funny," Meryl said.

"No, of course it's not. I'm sorry." Now the tears were welling up in Tressa Fay's eyes, too. She'd hurt Meryl. Tressa Fay's *faith* in Meryl, her hope that Meryl could think her way out of disappearing, had put her under the kind of pressure that gave her nightmares.

"I keep thinking, isn't that what we're doing, though?" Meryl asked. "Isn't that what everyone's always doing, being propelled forward until, inevitably, we get to the end? The only thing that's different is that I know when the end is. For me." She sniffed and pressed her fingers against her eyes.

Tressa Fay rolled her body away from Meryl's then and stared at the ceiling with her hand against her throat. She didn't want to panic, and she didn't want to argue, but she understood that Meryl had started saying goodbye.

Her night out with Gayle and James. The way she was throwing herself into projects at work. Her waffling about adopting a cat. How she touched Tressa Fay like no one had ever touched her before.

Meryl had all but said that she wouldn't touch Tressa Fay like she did, or feel like she did, if they'd only met that sunny day in May and there was nothing else. No time-bending. No horrible, cold, dark future.

They hadn't said *I love you*. Meryl had called her *my Tressa Fay* more than once, smiling her good smile, her eyes full of the tenderness that sometimes made Tressa Fay think they were right on the brink of saying words like *mine*, like *love*, like *forever*, and Tressa Fay had looked forward to those words. She'd liked imagining the ways they might say what was in their hearts and how that would feel.

"Everything we've done," she said, "ever since you showed up at my salon, and especially since you and Linds came here and told me what was happening, we've done so that we can be together. You said we have energy, you and me, and it's pushing back on the universe—"

"That was what I *hoped* was true."

"—and you said the phones might be interference, but that doesn't necessarily mean the connection is going to break when you disappear. I get that it wasn't fair to make you be the one who knows everything about everything, I do." Tressa Fay ran her fingers through her hair, searching for what she needed to say. "But, look, Meryl, do *you* understand what you're doing right now? If you start thinking this other way, this fatalist way, you're making that happen. You're making that future. *You* told me that. I saw it happen with the headlines and your phone!"

"But what do I know?" Meryl's voice was loud in the quiet room, as loud as Tressa Fay's had been. Because they were fighting. Crying and fighting about a future neither one of them could control. "I'm not *special*. I don't even know as much as Linds does, and what she knows is mostly from science fiction and fantasy stories. None of that is real."

But what is fucking real? Tressa Fay wanted to shout.

Instead, she made herself breathe.

When she'd been with Amy, they'd argued like this. A lot. So many times, Tressa Fay had wished she could just stay in one place and be quiet and breathe until she could think again, but Amy would accuse her of withholding or of avoiding an important conversation, so Tressa Fay had to cry and stumble through an explanation of what she thought she might feel.

Meryl wasn't doing that. She was sharing her feelings and letting Tressa Fay share hers. There were no accusations. It was only that the feelings they were both sharing were too desperate and hard to be the kind that led to a solution or to new, better feelings. At least not tonight.

So Tressa Fay took one deep breath after another, exhaling through her mouth until she'd slowed her heart down. She picked up her tea and sipped it, careful this time not to burn herself. Meryl picked up her own tea and held it between her palms.

Eventually, Tressa Fay felt calm enough to understand what was happening.

Meryl was afraid. That was all. Meryl was frightened, because she didn't know what would happen to her.

She was allowed to be afraid. It wasn't fair to ask her not to be. It wasn't fair to ask her to drive this bus with all of them on it, to be the ringleader of their hope, and all the while to give her more to miss, more to lose. Tressa Fay had been coasting on infatuation, sex fumes, and faith in Meryl's scientist brain. Faith that someone else, someone who wasn't her, would tell her what to do. But she was afraid, too.

Tressa Fay was afraid she wasn't enough.

She wanted to be the anchor that held Meryl still in the waterways of time. She wanted to be a woman so beguiling that Meryl *couldn't* leave her. She wanted the way she felt about Meryl and the way Meryl felt about her to break time and put it back together again in a different way.

But she was only Tressa Fay Robeson. She didn't know what to do.

Tressa Fay turned back to face Meryl. She touched Meryl in the dark room, hesitant at first, because she couldn't be sure if Meryl was angry with her or sad, if she wanted comfort or to be left alone. But Meryl let her stroke her arm, and she relaxed under Tressa Fay's touch, so Tressa Fay stayed with her. She kept touching her, knowing after a while that she was starting to fall asleep and that Meryl probably was, too.

"You know what I want to do?" Meryl asked, startling Tressa Fay out of a doze.

"Hmm. What?"

"I want us to go to Bay Beach. Today."

Bay Beach was a Green Bay amusement park situated on the shore of Lake Michigan, with twenty-five-cent-ticket rides, concession stands next to a picnic area, and a strip of rocky beach. "Yeah?"

"I want us all to play hooky and go there."

It was the first time Meryl had asked for something that was obviously just for her. Tressa Fay knew it would be another goodbye.

But Meryl was allowed to say goodbye.

"Yes," she said. "Let's do that."

She started planning as soon as she could, beginning with her dad, who got up in the morning at four thirty. He said yes right away. He said he would bring Jen.

It was more than Tressa Fay had asked of her father in years, and he'd said yes.

She caught Mary early, too, so she could reschedule the appointments at the salon, and Gayle was more than willing to meet up anywhere Meryl was. Linds was, of course, over the moon, James had PTO he needed to use, and although Michael and Guy were trickier because of their important lawyer jobs, they told her they would find a way to manage it.

The hours rushed along, so fast, and then they were at the ticket booth at Bay Beach on another warm day, windy enough that clouds raced across the sun over and over, making long minutes of cool weather that brushed the hot sun off their shoulders.

"Meryl," James said, looking over the grassy park starting to fill with kids and families, "we are hitting the Zippin Pippin *now*."

"Yes! Let's try for the front car." She grabbed Tressa Fay's hand and pulled her in to kiss her on the cheek before she ran off laughing with James, who crouched in front of her so Meryl could jump on his back and ride piggyback to the line. Guy, Michael, Mary, Gayle, and Linds set off for the bumper cars, already talking trash about who they were going to corner and surround with the scorching hot smell of sparks. Tressa Fay hated the bumper cars. She didn't like to slam into anyone. She leaned on a tree with her dad and Jen, watching the crowd trickling in.

"When's the last time we came?" he asked, crossing his arms over a short-sleeve plaid button-down. It was new. It was not blue, tan, or gray, but *green*, of all possible miracles, and it made it easy for Tressa Fay to see the young man her dad had been in the photos with her mom—cool, with a sharp jawline and a knowing smile.

Her dad in love.

"I think maybe I was in seventh grade. After that, I went with friends or on those end-of-year school trips."

He nodded and looked at Jen, adorable in a ponytail and a tidy denim skort.

"You know what?" Jen patted her dad on the shoulder. "I raced around so much this morning, I never got my coffee in, and I'm starting to feel the drag. You two don't mind if I head over to concessions and get a cup?" She smiled at Tressa Fay.

"Not at all," her dad said. "I'll catch up to you." He kissed Jen on the temple, and Tressa Fay had to look away. Who knew her dad was such a good boyfriend?

She wondered if he would be as happy if he had waited until October to tell her about Jen.

Jen squeezed Tressa Fay's upper arm and winked at her before meandering toward the concessions booth, her leather slides slapping against her heels.

"So, Tressa Fay." Her dad pushed off from the tree. "Should we do the Ferris wheel?"

Tressa Fay laughed. "Yeah? Because you know we've never done any of these rides together. In fact, I don't think you've ever done any of these rides."

"Sure I have," he said as they took off toward the wheel, making tracks in the dewy grass. "I grew up here, just like you."

Tressa Fay knew that, of course. She remembered her grandparents' small house, filled with cigarette smoke, scrupulously clean, with a crucifix in every room. Her grandfather had died when Tressa Fay was in high school, and her grandma immediately moved to the Mustard Seed Catholic Assisted Living Community near Luxemburg, where Tressa Fay volunteered, cutting and setting hair once a month. Like Tressa Fay, her dad had been an only child at a time when his peers had multiple siblings and families were big. He'd been raised with a lot of structure and rules.

"When's the last time, then?"

"Oh, I must have been about twenty. Took your mom. She wanted to go." Her dad smiled at his shoes, the black Converse high-tops he wore when he wasn't wearing steel-toed work boots or waders. For the first time in their relationship, Tressa Fay felt like she was starting to see *him*. To see where she was like him and where she must be like her mom.

The Ferris wheel was new since Tressa Fay had last been here, much bigger than the old one. After the operator accepted their tickets, they sat on the swinging seat, lowering the bar and then moving up for the car below them to fill. "Did you have fun? When you came here with Mom?" she asked.

"There wasn't ever a time I didn't have fun when I was with Shelly." He smiled. "Everyone had fun when they were with her. So did you. She could make you laugh until you got the hiccups."

Once the Ferris wheel was loaded, it started moving faster, carrying them around and right up to the top, over and over, where the view was across the wide-open bay where the Fox River spilled into Lake Michigan. They talked about what Meryl had told them both about water. He said he'd been lucky fishing at a spot she'd recommended.

He put his arm across the back of the seat. "She's a nice woman."

Tressa Fay was caught off guard. It was the kind of comment from her dad that signaled his certainty. If he'd ever said the same about Amy, she would've been ridiculously happy. She hated that what she felt instead was frustrated.

For all her life, she'd wanted a love as utter and uncomplicated as the love her dad had for her mom. She understood Meryl's preoccupation, her exhaustion, her fear and doubt, but why wasn't having Tressa Fay, *being* with her, enough to give Meryl faith?

Why couldn't it be simple?

"I think she's a nice woman, too," she finally said. Because it was true. Because if all she had left was a handful of months with Meryl, she would take them and not be sorry.

"Good."

Tressa Fay leaned back until she was resting in the crook of her dad's arm, and she didn't fight the swoops the Ferris wheel sent through her stomach. When the wheel came to a stop, they were near the bottom. She could see Jen waiting for them, waving.

"I like Jen."

"Good," her dad said again, but he grinned, an easy grin he gave her rarely, and they stepped out and started toward Jen. "Go on and find your friends," he told her. "Maybe Jen and I will ride the kiddie train."

Jen laughed. "I got a great picture of you and your dad up there," she said. "I sent it to your phone."

"Thanks." Impulsively, Tressa Fay hugged her, and Jen hugged her right back. Tressa Fay had to remind herself that the Ferris wheel ride with her dad and hugging Jen were real things that nothing could take away from her. She would always have them.

She was walking in the direction of the roller coaster when she ran into James and Meryl.

Meryl threw her arms over her head. "We're going to do the Viking swing! We have to hurry so we can sit together on it. The bumper car gang is holding a place in line." Meryl reached her palm out for Tressa Fay's, and they swung their arms as they walked along the gravel path. The concession stand had started making popcorn and cotton candy. The sugar and butter smells wafted over the crowd and through the trees and steel structures of the rides, dissolving in the lake breeze.

It was perfect.

Meryl wore her hair in two braids today. She was sensible as ever in khaki walking shorts, a soft pink polo shirt, and all-terrain sandals. She'd made everyone put on sunscreen at the ticket booth, where she'd paid for enough tickets for the whole group. Her glasses for the day were the kind that transitioned from regular lenses to sunglasses. Tressa Fay could hardly stand it, how much care Meryl gave to others and herself. She guessed that was what was so appealing about smart women. How they so earnestly cared. How they believed there was always a way to make things nicer and safer and more thoughtful, and they went at love and intimacy like it was an important project, worthy of attention and study and experimentation.

"Thank you," Meryl said into Tressa Fay's ear, kissing her

cheek. "I'm so happy we could do this together. This is going to be the best day."

Tressa Fay knew then that she was in love with Meryl Whit.

This nice woman, this smart woman, this woman she should never have met and actually, technically, hadn't even met *yet*, who was sensible but talked about the memory of water, and who was scared but let herself feel and make new friends and be with Tressa Fay. This woman who kissed so hot when they made it to the line for the Viking swing that Tressa Fay couldn't stand it— she gripped the side of her face and kissed her back.

Meryl pulled away, her upper lip a little swollen, and put her finger on the tip of Tressa Fay's nose. "You," she said.

Tressa Fay knew—she really *knew*, because Meryl had told her, and because the version of herself who occupied a different-but-the-same world five months from now had said so—that there was a future where none of this happened.

But it wasn't *her* future.

She'd changed too much. She was someone different than she'd been and someone different from who she was going to be. Her life had its own trajectory, and every step she took in a new direction sent her somewhere farther and farther away from where she'd started.

Tressa Fay didn't have to be resigned to anything. Not one fucking thing.

"We're all riding together," James said to the ride operator, who was lifting the cord for people to get on the swing now that the riders from the previous go-around were off. James had his arm around Mary, and Mary had her finger hooked in one of his belt loops.

"Whatever," the operator said. "Pull down your bar until it clicks."

They raced onto the ride, scoping out the best seats in the stern of the ship so they would be as high as possible on the upswing and fall the farthest.

"I'm starting to worry about how I'll take this at my age," Guy said. "I don't have the stomach I had when I was seventeen." They leaned over and kissed Michael. "Don't laugh at me when I scream."

"Oh, we're all going to scream," Mary said. "Absolutely. We're going to scream it *alllll* out."

They were laughing when the swing lifted up to its very highest point, and then they put their hands in the air and screamed their way down, and the sky was the same color as the water.

MARY

SHE HATED THIS TIME OF YEAR. SHE KNEW SHE WAS SUPPOSED to love fall and cozy sweaters and pumpkin spice lattes and getting lowlights done in her hair, but it was hard to enjoy anything when it was dark before dinner, and there was snow more often than not in Wisconsin, and one didn't have anyone to cozy up *with*.

"Your last appointment canceled." Mary spun around in her chair. Tressa Fay was cleaning her already spotless work station.

"Nice." She did a little dance. It was pretty affecting, given she was wearing only black tights, Doc Martens, and a cropped sweatshirt that peekabooed her black bra every time she raised her arms up, which was all the time, all day long, because Tressa Fay cut hair. "I can go home early and put soup on, turn the music up, and snuggle my cat in a big ol' sweater."

Ugh.

Mary looked out the window in the front of the shop. The bars and restaurants were starting to get busy, their lights spilling out into the street, people meeting each other on the sidewalk and going inside for drinks and dinner.

Light. People. Drinks.

Mary's vision pulled back from the street, and now she saw the reflection of herself in the dark window, sitting at the reception desk, with flat hair and a sad face.

She stood up and walked over to Tressa Fay's station, grabbed her spray bottle, and started wetting down her hair.

"What are you doing?" Tressa Fay narrowed her eyes at Mary. "Because it looks like you're getting ready for a cut, and you already said I was done for the day. I'm going to assume you are merely restyling."

"I said that your last appointment canceled for the day. I didn't say you were done."

Tressa Fay started unbuckling her thigh holster. "Oh, but I am. It's quittin' time. Epinephrine and I have a date with a pot of cheese-tortellini soup. I'm thinking of taking some thirst traps for the 'gram."

Mary winced. "Just some layers on top."

Tressa Fay shook her head. "Nope. Write yourself in tomorrow. I can already smell my new scented candles."

Mary clasped her hands together. "Please? Please, please, please? It's so dark. And I'm so sad. Hair volume would make me feel better, and I'm going out. You should go out with me, but I'm not holding my breath. At least give me big hair to go with the false lashes I'm going to put on with something too low-cut. Pleeeeease." Mary made direct eye contact with Tressa Fay.

"God. Fine. You don't have to Bambi me—it makes my heart hurt. But you're cleaning up after, because as soon as your hair is touching the angels, I'm out of here."

Mary did feel much better on her way home, with fluffy hair and confirmed yeses to go out from Linds, Guy, and Michael. She wanted Tressa Fay out with them, too. The business with Amy had been an absolute grief banquet, and while Mary understood that Tressa Fay shared *some* responsibility for the end of that relationship, Tressa Fay hadn't had a big fat secret affair for Amy to stumble in on after spending thousands on an engagement ring. It had been brutal for Tressa Fay to heal from. Now, though, she *was* healed, only shy about going on the apps or flirting in bars. She wanted, if not romance, a *moment*. A beginning to a relationship that stopped time, at least a little.

Mary had been working on it.

She met her friends at the taproom, which was, first, queer-friendly, and, second, an elusive combination of exciting and inclusive. The music was good but not too loud. There were lots of places to sit and talk and be comfortable, and it wasn't hard to hear a conversation. The bar didn't overserve, and it had delicious drinks *and* snacks. The bathrooms were any-gender and clean.

They had scored a big, long table, which kept them all together but left room for new, fun people to join. Mary was wiggling in her seat, sending her feelers out for time-stopping moments.

It was early when they arrived, so the buzz was very mature, and lots of appetizers were coming out on trays. Guy and Michael played their part by setting bait with their hot mini-makeout sessions, and Linds looked amazing and had flirted with at least three people. Mary was focused on big Your New Best Friend energy in the hopes of snuggling up to a girl who would turn Tressa Fay's head and maybe be open to an introduction.

Then she saw him.

Smooth brown skin, expressive eyes that swept over the room with sexy interest, inky, wavy hair. He wore a soft-looking sweater and *good* jeans and was a man Mary could one hundred percent imagine herself not complaining about staying inside with on a cold night.

But she wasn't here for men. Besides, he had a gorgeous, curvy redhead with him.

She turned to Linds to distract herself from the jolt that was still bonging through her body from looking at that man and caught Linds winking at someone across the room. But it was only a guy Linds had played Dungeons & Dragons with for years who was firmly a friend.

"Invite him to sit with us," Mary said.

"He's with a date. Besides"—Linds looked up—"we're getting some very fire company right now."

Mary turned and accidentally met the eyes of the man she'd spotted when he came in, currently sitting down in two open seats across from her with his date. As he sat, he pushed up the sleeves of his sweater, causing Mary to have some very intense feelings about his forearms.

"Okay if we sit?" He didn't look away from Mary.

"More than," she said. "I'm Mary, this is my friend Linds, and those two huddled together at the end of the table, completely ignoring the world, are Guy and Michael."

He smiled, and Mary's heart sped up. *God.* When was the last time she'd had a reaction like this? She couldn't remember. She was more the type to feel lightning after a warm-up period of getting-to-know-you, and she'd never really believed those stories people told about their partners that started with *I just knew.*

But she had barely touched her hard cider, and she didn't partake of substances, so whatever she was feeling right now was being generated from her unadulterated body or the cosmos or something.

"I'm James."

God.

"And this is my friend Meryl." He put enough emphasis on the word *friend* that Meryl turned to him and raised an eyebrow, but he didn't see, because he was looking at Mary.

He was looking at Mary.

She got stern with herself. Beautiful James was not the person she was here for. She wanted to get Tressa Fay out tonight. It felt a little urgent. It felt a lot like tonight was the night. She smiled at James—her best smile, yes—but then she briskly turned to Meryl to offer her a smile just as good.

And there it was. The potential for a *moment.*

Mary had already noticed this Meryl woman was gorgeous from across the room, but at their table, close-up, she could see Meryl's red hair and freckles and matching red eyebrows and pretty grin and, most of all, her T-shirt, which was a red *Mathlete Champion* T-shirt, and so then Mary spotted Meryl's tidy bag, hooked over the back of her chair, with little square pockets to organize her things, and her perfect, pill-free cardigan, and her glasses, and how her hair, beautiful and curly though it was, hung in one length to her elbows like she was someone who was occupied by other things.

Smart girl things.

Oh, oh, oh. Mary had a feeling. She peeked at her phone on the table. It was still early. If she could get enough intel, maybe she could make it happen. She squared her shoulders and focused.

"Meryl! It's nice to meet you. What do you do?"

"I'm a stormwater engineer for the city."

Engineer.

"Wow. Interesting. You must have to be super smart to do that kind of thing."

"So smart," James cut in. "I have Meryl come to the college all the time to talk to students about career paths with STEM. I work in student services admin at the university."

Oh, James, if I only had time for you, because there you are, piggy-backing so I will pay you some attention. I will get to you, I promise.

"Wow." Mary inched her phone closer to herself. "I guess the math shirt is real, then."

Meryl laughed, such a good laugh. "It's very real. I have three matching ones at home. One for every year of high school."

Ding, ding, ding. "I'm so sorry, could you excuse me for a minute? I forgot I had to make a call." She turned to Linds. "My friend Linds works at the university, too! Linds, let's order these cute people a round." She lasered a telepathic message into Linds's mind with her eyes. *Do not let them leave, even if you have to make it weird.*

"I do work there! Where's your office?" Linds leaned over to talk to James and Meryl, and Mary got up and boxed her way through the crowd to the quiet vestibule by the bathrooms.

"Tressa Fay!" Mary was glad she'd picked up on the first ring.

"I can hear a lot of people in the background, Mary, but I'm already practically naked and have ladled myself a bowl of soup."

"This is an emergency. I've got a hot engineer on the line."

"What?"

"Meryl. She has red hair. She has a messenger bag with organizer pockets. Freckles. Engineer. Tressa Fay, she is wearing a *Mathlete Champion* T-shirt from high school, and let's just say her figure has blossomed since that time."

There was a long enough pause that Mary crossed her fingers and toes.

"Look, I—"

"And a cardigan. Did I mention the cardigan? And that she's gorgeous? Red hair? Has a good laugh?"

"Where are you?"

Thank you, thank you, thank you. "The taproom. It's very low-key. In the key of low. Only dogs can hear, it's so low. Dogs and extremely good-looking people. Come on. I have a feeling about this."

Maybe that was too much. Tressa Fay was not a particularly metaphysical person. Opposite. Mary heard her sigh. "You don't know if she's queer."

Mary didn't, but also, she did. She *did*. "Tressa Fay, the whole world is queer. The whole *universe* is queer. It always has been. It always will be."

There was a long pause. "I'll be there in ten."

"Yay!"

Mary skipped from the vestibule and ran right into a tall woman who smelled like vanilla cookies made in heaven.

"Oops! Sorry," the woman said.

Mary was about to apologize and run, but then her mouth was hanging open. What was it with the super-hot people at the taproom tonight? This woman looked like a silent film star, pale, dark-eyed, bow-lipped, and—yes. *Wearing a pan flag necklace.* All of the matchmaking gifts Mary had inherited from her ancestors were golden tonight.

"No problem!" she said. "Sorry. I'm Mary, and I don't pay attention to where I'm going."

The woman laughed. "I'm Brooklynn, and I can't find a table."

"Brooklynn. Do I have news for you."

The best part of the night wasn't that Brooklynn read Linds's palm all the way up to her mouth, or that James noticed when Mary shivered and then pulled off his soft sweater for her to wear, wrapped up in amber-smelling wool while she looked at him in his tight undershirt and he played with her fingers.

It was when Tressa Fay came in, wearing her lucky jeans, and, when she looked over the crowd, she and Meryl caught each other's eye at the same time.

Mary was there for it. Of all the places in the entire universe she could've been, she was there to see it.

The moment.

JANUARY 13

∙∙∙∙∙∙∙∙∙∙∙∙∙∙∙∙

I'M NOT SURE WHAT TO ASK FOR." THE YOUNG WOMAN IN HER chair was petite, with huge blue eyes and a lot of very coily, bright-red hair that was currently one length, halfway to her shoulders.

"Hmm." Tressa Fay sprayed some water on the woman's hair and squeezed it through, looking at how it wanted to fall and what her curl pattern was. "Has it ever been cut in a style you've loved that you can tell me about?"

She shook her head rapidly, almost violently, and pressed her lips together. "Not ever. No." Tressa Fay noticed the woman shrinking away from herself in her reflection in the mirror, looking at everything *but* her hair.

Tressa Fay avoided her own reflection, too, though she got a glimpse when she tried to catch the client's eyes in the mirror. Hair too long. Dark circles. Too thin.

"Have you taken a look at pictures that you think are inspiring?"

"Sometimes I see something I like, but it's always on hair a lot different from mine."

Tressa Fay smiled at that. "Sure. Not very many people have glorious hair like yours."

Her client sighed. "That's what everyone says, but I kind of hate being a redhead. Everyone always feels like it's license to say something to you. Or even to say something completely gross to you."

Tressa Fay's hands stilled. She could feel a warm rock ledge under her thighs and Meryl's finger tracing over her birthmark. "My girlfriend told me that," she let herself say. To her surprise, it didn't feel wrong. It didn't feel bad or doomed. If anything, that small act of claiming made Meryl feel closer.

My girlfriend. The memories from the creek. The water and the fossil and the cold—it had happened to Tressa Fay.

Her client met her eyes in the mirror. "Your girlfriend is a redhead?"

Tressa Fay smiled, the muscles in her arms and hands aching to think of Meryl, her smile, her body, what it felt like to hold her and to kiss her. "Yeah, she is."

The client watched Tressa Fay's face with shy interest, and then Tressa Fay got it. "Are you looking for a haircut that will speak to feelings around your identity? That can be a really hard thing to explain to a stylist, and also, it's a different haircut for different people, but sometimes there are shared elements."

Her client's expression was big-eyed and soft. "Like, maybe with a part that's . . . shaved?"

"Sometimes. Is it something like that you're thinking about?" Tressa Fay let the client's curls slip over her fingers, looking at her pointed chin and big eyes, the tiny hoop in her russet eyebrow.

"Yeah. I just didn't know what to say, because my hair's so curly, and no cut like that I've seen is. I've looked online, and when I went to Pride, there were so many people who looked so good. Like how I would like to look." She couldn't meet Tressa Fay's eyes in the mirror, but her cheeks had gotten red and her mouth very determined.

Tressa Fay studied the shape of her client's face. "That's true. I feel like a lot of the really cool photo sets you see with an emotionally queer haircut feature very straight, shiny textures, or heavily styled texture that requires a lot of product."

Her client smiled for the first time. "But there can be cool things done with hair like mine?"

"Oh my God, yes. It's my favorite. You have to think about hair like yours as a texture or material that has a lot more body than straight hair. Your hair has more ability to be shaped and sculpted, and you don't have to rely on linear shapes. Can I show you my bestie Guy's hair? They have wavy, thick hair, and I cut it in a masc direction, but still a bit soft."

"Yes."

Tressa Fay showed her the pictures that had been taken back in October at Gayle's house, on a stool in her kitchen, with Guy making their seductive face for Michael, who was behind the camera.

"Oh! That's so . . ." Her client looked at the next photo in the set. "I like that."

"It's very pulled in on the sides. We could even shave or buzz up through here and stack the top all the way back to your nape. A kind of punk mullet? It would grow out cool, too." Tressa Fay showed her by manipulating her hair.

"Yes. I want that. Thank you." Her eyes met Tressa Fay's in the mirror, finally, and they were shiny with tears. "That would be perfect."

"Okay! I'm going to have Mary take you to the shampoo bowl."

Her client slid out of the chair, and Tressa Fay listened to her chatting with Mary while she sat at Mary's desk at reception with her phone cradled in her palm.

In every relationship, there was always an item connected to it that ended up having its own heartbeat. When she was young, it was often a picture or a piece of clothing, and no matter what the outcome of that relationship had been, she'd never wanted to let go of the picture or the T-shirt or the jacket. She'd wanted to have them to revisit, to understand just how far she had come each time she pulled on the shirt or saw the jacket in the closet or showed the picture to a friend. Over time, these kinds of things became more about herself than the other person or even the relationship. They became artifacts of her own life.

Tressa Fay never knew what they would be. She'd thought when her relationship with Amy ended that it would be the engagement ring she'd designed and brought home from Los Angeles, but it wasn't. It was a beautiful bracelet Amy had bought Tressa Fay early in their relationship, too early, really, for a bracelet so expensive—a pure silver cuff set with faceted smoky quartz—but they'd both weathered the blushing self-consciousness of the gesture with a kind of sweetness that Tressa Fay would always associate with what she'd loved best about Amy. What had been lost between them.

She ran her finger down the screen of her phone. She had never let the battery go into the red, not one time since October.

Probably she wasn't the first person managing the bittersweetness of a long-distance relationship who'd started to feel this way about their phone. A bit like it *was* the person they longed for. A lot grateful for it, and a lot resentful of it. Completely sensitive to its noises and alerts, almost like she would be to a child's, and all the while trying to suppress how much she hated it.

She'd hated the phone. Hated the distance. She'd hated the substitution of words for skin. She'd hated how texting distorted meaning and tone and nuance. She'd hated how, no matter how much she talked to Meryl, most of the time the phone was a silent, black, shuttered window that looked in on nothing.

Five months ago, she had woken up next to Meryl in Meryl's room. Epinephrine was asleep at the foot of the bed. She remembered because it was a day she'd had off from the salon for the floors to be polished, and because she'd woken up today in her own bed with Epinephrine, feeling that moment with Meryl all over again. And for the first time.

"Let's go to that new cat café across the street from your salon and eat Korean hot dogs at Pink Guava." Meryl had sat up in bed, pushing her hair from her face.

"Are you sure you actually want to go inside? Because I know few people who can resist a rescue who is determined to be taken home." Tressa Fay stretched, and Epinephrine licked her toe.

"I've decided. I'm going to adopt that little tuxedo cat. I want to name him Spring."

"So you're finally done with flirting with him through the window." Tressa Fay had leaned over and kissed Meryl's neck.

Now she traced her fingertip around the screen of her phone. *I miss you.*

She wished so often that she could be the Tressa Fay in August, even though that Tressa Fay worried, watching the days creep toward September. Even though August Tressa Fay had gotten a little angry with Meryl after she fell in love with that cat, because what if she wasn't there to take care of him? Tressa Fay didn't want a cat who knew her only as the lady who wept into his fur.

The bell over her door rang, and James came in wrapped in a huge silver puffer coat and a dark gray stocking hat that Meryl had knit for him years ago when they dated.

"Hello, you beautiful thing," she said.

"Come here, darling, and give me a hug." He hung his coat up on the hook, and Tressa Fay got up and put her arms around him and breathed in his cold air and spicy smell. "This is a good hug." He squeezed her hard one more time, and, for a heartbeat, everything *James* mixed together. Every meal they'd ever shared, when he had come into her salon for the first time, how he looked at Mary.

She stood back. "Always the best hugs. Your girl is almost done, and you can take her away if you want. I have one more today, and that client doesn't get their hair washed."

"You can take me," Mary called up. "I am almost so takeable." Mary had Tressa Fay's client sitting up, and she was arranging a length of jersey in front of her to wrap around her curly hair.

"I'll get her hair good and hydrated, Mary. You can bring her over after you plop her curls."

Mary walked the client over to the chair. "Let me clean up, Jamesie, and then I belong to you." She kissed him on his jaw. Tressa Fay didn't miss how his eyes closed.

She was fastening on her scissor-and-comb holster and her razor holster, listening to Mary hum while she cleaned up the shampoo station, when James touched her arm. "Catch up with Gayle today, okay?" he asked. "She was thinking about getting everyone together, but I told her to hold up. I really think you should talk to her, though."

Tressa Fay took a deep breath against her instant aversion. "I will, for sure. Are you and Mary still meeting up with Michael and Guy?"

"You bet," Mary said. "We're going to that place that used to be pizza before it was barbecue and is now vegan street food? You know, like way over by Baird Creek?"

Tressa Fay's client turned around to smile at Mary. "That

place is pretty weird," she said. "It was so unexpectedly nice and good, my friend and I wondered if it was secretly fundamentalist."

Mary nodded. "That is always a hard call around here. Will report back." She stood in front of James, who helped her put her coat on, and then she kissed him while he tried to put on his, and they were gone.

James and Mary and Michael and Guy barely seemed to notice anymore the way their mutual past shifted and changed. The changes were no more than ripples, layers sifting in and out of their history together—things they made into jokes or cheerfully bewildered remarks. What Tressa Fay had observed was the same thing she'd noticed after she and Meryl decided to meet each other back in May and Meryl walked into her salon for a trim. The strongest effect of the experiment was on their feelings for each other.

It was how they were able to love each other and hadn't been before.

But for Tressa Fay, it only made her notice more acutely that Meryl wasn't here. She knew Gayle felt the same. The two of them were closest to Meryl, and so they were the most affected by her absence.

She turned up the music and lost herself in the cut. It was easy to do with such beautiful hair and how quietly excited her client was, turning her head to look at the progress whenever she had the chance. By the time Tressa Fay had styled it, letting the coils on top fall forward, running her hands over the buzzed sides and through the trailing curls at the back, her client was ecstatic. Tressa Fay took pictures of her posing in front of the ring light, and she was beautiful and comfortable and had the greatest bouncy, prowling stride of all time. She left walking on air, shoving her hat in the pocket of her coat so it wouldn't smash the height of her curls, and Tressa Fay caught her grinning at her reflection in the salon's front window.

Alone in the salon again, Tressa Fay called Gayle, hoping they could talk while she cleaned her station before her final client of the day came in.

"Hey, Tiff." Gayle had adopted Linds and Guy's old nickname for her. "I'm glad you called. Did James make you?"

"He did. I'm guessing he's looking out for you in some way, so tell me."

"It's . . . I don't know." Gayle laughed the way she did when she couldn't find the right words. "Sometimes I realize I've gone a long time remembering nothing new, and then I remember so much that I have no idea what month it is or where I am or what's happening, you know?"

"I do." Tressa Fay didn't think of time, or of memories, anything like the way she once had.

"Yeah, so, I was steaming some clothes for my shop, and I started thinking about Meryl's case, like, *as* a case, the way I used to before . . . I'm not sure, exactly. *Before.*"

Tressa Fay found herself standing in the open space of the salon, her phone to her ear, staring through the pane of glass in the entry door.

It was getting dark so early now.

"You know how in a dream, your dream gives you some task to do, like a quest, and it feels incredibly important, but when you wake up, it was nothing?" Gayle asked. "Like something silly, like you had to deliver a Christmas ornament to your third-grade teacher to keep your dog from running away?"

"Yes."

"It was a feeling like that, except I'm not asleep. I couldn't stop thinking about how much she loves her job, how many people she works with, and how much impact she has there. She *really* loves her job."

Tressa Fay knew Gayle well enough by now to hear how tough this was for her to talk about. "She does love her job."

"I decided just to close my shop for a bit and walk to where her office is. It's not far. I thought that the cold and the walk would help, and either I would get there and my brain would sort everything out, or at least I would've gotten the exercise in. I think, too, I was hoping that seeing her office would maybe, I don't know, crisscross all the memories and feelings and prove this gap in time is closing up, once and for all. I've been avoiding her office, and even avoiding everyone else who knew she disappeared. Like if I stayed the course that Meryl has put into motion, everything would come together."

Tressa Fay rubbed her arms, nodding like Gayle could see her. She had never been to Meryl's house, a house she knew as well as her own apartment. She avoided looking through the window at the cat café, afraid she would see the tuxedo cat. She knew. She understood.

"When I got to the building, I saw this woman I remembered from some time ago when I went to an office Christmas party with Meryl. I knew she did something at Meryl's work that meant they knew each other, but they didn't work together every day."

"Okay."

"So I told her hi. I said I was Meryl Whit's sister, and she and I had met at the Christmas party a few years ago. She looked at me for the longest time. Then she said, 'Who?' I told her again, 'Meryl Whit. She's a stormwater engineer.' And this lady shook her head. She had no idea who I was talking about. None."

Tressa Fay reached out to brace herself against the wall, dizzy with the implications. "You're positive she was the person you thought?"

"I asked her if she still had the same job she'd always had, and she told me she'd recently gotten her ten-year pin."

"So then . . . what do you think? What is it that we should be doing?" The questions spilled out of Tressa Fay, even as she understood Gayle couldn't have answers. There were no answers.

"Something is broken and messing up, but I don't know if it's what we wanted to break." Gayle sniffed. "And, Tressa Fay, what it *feels* like, in my heart, is that I am letting her go. I don't want to, but I also don't want to let the rest of my life feel like this. Meryl would hate that. But maybe all these feelings are just that it's wintertime and so dark. I don't know."

Tressa Fay closed her eyes.

A few days ago, she and her dad had a rare dinner alone, without Jen. Her dad had come to her apartment, which he had started doing lately, even fixing things that were broken. Tressa Fay had made grilled cheese and soup. She started talking to her dad about Meryl. About how everything, everywhere, reminded her of her and Meryl. Like driving over one of the Fox River bridges and thinking about how high the water looked.

Her dad had listened until she was done talking. Then he'd said, *I understand what you're feeling.*

She didn't think he'd ever said that to her before.

Her dad told her that there were still so many things he never would have known to enjoy without her mom, and that his life was better for that, even though she was gone.

"I understand what you're feeling," Tressa Fay told Gayle.

The line was quiet for a long time before Gayle said, "I think you do. I guess that's some kind of comfort."

Tressa Fay thought of her phone again, so heavy with the

battery attached to it. Meryl's messages. *I miss you.* Something Meryl often texted, even though she had Tressa Fay right there, making plans to adopt a cat. Even though Tressa Fay didn't believe Meryl had ever thought of the woman right next to her in bed and the woman on her phone as different people.

"You know what? You and Meryl are never, ever not going to have each other. You could've gone your separate ways a long time ago, when it was so hard, but you didn't, and that means you're stuck with your little sister forever."

After Tressa Fay and Gayle got off the phone and she'd seen her last client and locked up the salon, she went across the street to the cat rescue and looked in the window. She didn't see the small tuxedo cat that Meryl had been so taken with, so she pushed through the door, the sound of the bell over it making her break out in a cold sweat.

The woman who came to talk to her seemed slightly confused. She couldn't quite understand something about what Tressa Fay was asking her, as though the ripples of everything that kept changing, configuring and reconfiguring around Tressa Fay and the salon across the road, had blurred parts of this woman's life, too.

But there was no way for Tressa Fay to misunderstand what the woman told her.

The tuxedo cat wasn't there.

He never had been.

SEPTEMBER 4, MORNING
....

WHEN TRESSA FAY OPENED HER EYES, SHE TURNED TO HER SIDE to reach for Meryl.

Spring rubbed against her searching hand, and she cracked open her eyes to the cat's sweet black-and-white face looking back at her. Epinephrine was spooning him.

Then she remembered and sat up straight in bed, her heart racing so fast that she started to cough and couldn't get words out. "Meryl." She coughed again, squeezed her hands into fists, and managed this time to shout. "Meryl!"

She heard pounding up the stairs. Meryl appeared in the doorway of her bedroom. "I'm here. I'm right here."

It was the fourth of September. The day Meryl disappeared.

"You scared me." Spring stood up, stretched, and walked into Tressa Fay's lap. "God. You'll have to stay right next to me every second today."

"That's what future you says. 'Tell her I said not to leave your side. Tell her to keep her eyes on you at every moment.'" Meryl smiled, but it was a faraway smile. "Also, my sister. Who is downstairs. I was actually about to make coffee to take with me to work, but Gayle had already let herself into my kitchen and was sitting at the table like a ghoul."

Tressa Fay picked up Spring out of her lap and set him down on the bed so she could swing her legs over the side. "You were going to work? Is there some kind of culvert emergency?"

Meryl shrugged.

That wasn't right. Tressa Fay had known something was off last night when Meryl hadn't wanted to talk about what would happen today and had spent a lot of time on her phone, texting. Last night, Tressa Fay had thought it felt wrong that Meryl, of all people, wouldn't have a plan, but now it struck her as *more* wrong that Meryl had a plan that didn't include her. "Tell me why."

"Why don't you get dressed and come downstairs? Looks like this day has already started." Meryl crossed her arms, drawing Tressa Fay's attention to the fact that she wore one of the no-nonsense button-up shirts and pairs of khakis that she put on when she planned to spend at least part of her workday outdoors, doing things like checking water levels.

She really had been on her way out without waking Tressa Fay up to say goodbye.

"We've done everything different," Tressa Fay said quietly. "Every single world is *different*. What do you know? What were you told that you haven't told me?"

Meryl sighed. "It's not anything like that. I promise I'm just trying to have a day. Just come downstairs, okay?"

When Tressa Fay nodded, she turned and left.

Tressa Fay clenched her fists in the blankets so her heart wouldn't crack in two. She made herself pet Spring between his ears—Spring who, to Tressa Fay, had meant real hope, real progress, because Meryl had adopted him. Epinephrine was purring softly. Tressa Fay tried to keep her heart just as soft. She wanted to be what Meryl needed today.

She got out of bed and put on the clothes she'd been wearing last night, a pair of ripped-up cutoff shorts that were more holes than shorts and a cropped tee. She followed the sound of Meryl's and Gayle's voices downstairs and walked into the middle of an argument.

"I never asked you to be a crystal ball!" Gayle was at the kitchen table, her arms crossed. "I'm simply saying I think we should consider some of the possible outcomes so we can be sure—"

"We *can't* be sure," Meryl interrupted. She was leaning back against the kitchen counter, also with her arms crossed, and her voice was rigidly calm. "We can't be. That's my point. There's nothing we can do today or tonight. You've already tried everything. Tressa Fay told me you said so. You've learned what you could learn about my life, put security cameras on the outside of my house, kept eyes on me this whole day, stayed right next to me, but it didn't work. Not once, ever, has it worked."

"That wasn't *me*, though!" Gayle's frustration was audible. "All I'm suggesting is you let us try to keep you safe. Let us be together. Why wouldn't we do that, no matter what happens?"

Meryl had flushed red from the collar of her shirt to the tips of her ears. She opened her mouth to respond, but Tressa Fay cut in before she could speak. "We are not doing this." She pointed at Meryl. "You. Sit down at the table with your sister."

Tressa Fay waited for Meryl to obey her. Then she crossed to the table and pulled out a third chair for herself. Gayle and Meryl had never resembled each other more than they did in this moment.

In a rush, she realized that all of them—Tressa Fay, Gayle, James, Michael, Guy, Mary, and Linds—had started out where Meryl was ending up right now. The summer had lifted away that fatalism, had given them all hope and a sense of adventure.

But as Meryl engaged with all of them up ahead, in the winter, where she still *wasn't*, she had lost her hope.

"It's the fourth of September," Tressa Fay said. "We're *all* scared. We're going to have to work so hard to take care of ourselves and each other today, but that is what we're doing. We're keeping the faith. We're putting one foot in front of the next. Meryl Whit, you adopted a cat, and you promised that nice lady at the rescue that you'd take care of him for the rest of his life. You *promised*."

Meryl uncrossed her arms. The nod she gave Tressa Fay was tight, but it was something.

"You two are going to have to talk your way through this," Tressa Fay said. "Or else we'll never make it to midnight intact, and it will be because one of you murdered the other. Though, at least then we'll know what happened."

Meryl didn't smile, but her mouth relaxed a fraction.

"I assume you're yelling at each other because you told Gayle you planned to spend the day at work, but Gayle wants everyone to have a stay-up-late slumber party at her house with every door and window locked and the security system turned on."

Gayle rolled her eyes.

"Basically, yes," Meryl said. "But you knew that, because apparently she invited you."

"I've been invited for ages," Tressa Fay said. "I had no idea you didn't know until last night, when you got weird when I tried to talk about today."

"You can't be mad at me for getting everybody together," Gayle said. "It's ridiculous. We don't want to lose you, that's all. *I* don't want to. I just got you back." Her voice broke. "And if I have to lose you, it's not going to be because I took my eyes off you this time."

Meryl's shoulders dropped as curiosity replaced the last of the defensiveness in her expression. "What do you mean, *this time*?"

Tressa Fay also needed this clarified.

"I just mean . . . with Mom." Gayle rubbed her eyes with the heels of her hands. "I didn't even try to understand. I was so hurt by Mom, and you always took her side, so I just let it make me angry. You two had your cute little mother-daughter relationship, I thought, but whatever, *I don't fucking care*. I took my eyes off you. I walked away. And what happened was you got hurt. By Mom. Of course you did, because Mom hurts people. So I told myself, never again."

Meryl shook her head slowly. "If I go, it won't be because you didn't watch me close enough."

"It could be." Gayle recrossed her arms. "We know it could be because you get hurt. We've always known that. We haven't been able to figure it out. If there *is* someone out there who's going to hurt you today, we haven't found even a hint of them, but Linds and I were talking about how so much depends on the life and decisions of this person who could hurt you, just as much as our own."

Tressa Fay expected Meryl to shut down, but she didn't. Her mouth firmed. "I have never, ever been afraid," she told her sister. "I *did* race toward that big sign with my head down. I picked math and engineering even though it was hard and the dudes were the worst, because I wanted that thrill of being good at something hard, and of tromping around in the world where there aren't trails. I've been attacked by so *many* geese, Gayle. You have no idea. Last week, a sandhill crane nearly took me out when I was setting water flow monitors too close to its nest, and I just laughed. Those assholes are four feet tall!"

"You didn't tell me it got that serious," Tressa Fay said. "You told *me* a cute animal story."

Meryl shrugged. "My point is that I feel like I've been jump-scared by the world so many times since May. Not by a crane, but by a shadow in an alley. A weird email. A car that stays parked on my street too long. I'm exhausted with trying to shove off the inevitable future at the same time I'm working with everything I've got to prevent it from happening. But you know what I figured out?"

"No," Tressa Fay whispered. She didn't know what Meryl had figured out. But she *did* know what Meryl was feeling, which was that Meryl wasn't someone who could stick it out. She wasn't a person who showed up when it counted.

She was a runaway bride, a second-guesser, a saboteur.

This was when they most needed to have faith. They needed to believe they had changed the world, that they had changed *many* worlds.

"It's the same as my job," Meryl said. "At work, I'm responsible for taking care of this old, worn-out stormwater system that the city can't afford to properly fix or replace, so really what I do is monitor it and worry about it and try to keep it from falling apart in some catastrophic way that will kill someone, and at the exact same time, I'm looking down at the whole city from, like, the top of the Ferris wheel at Bay Beach, and I can see Lake Michigan, the shoreline, the Fox River and the East River emptying into the bay."

Tressa Fay saw the same view in her head, imprinted in her memory by their summer day at the amusement park.

"I can see the groundwater rising, and the Leo Frigo Bridge pilings sitting on unstable shale that's going to heave up and take the bridge out. I can see those houses along the bay and the East River flooding and displacing the people who live in them. The planet warming. The water going where it inevitably wants to go. Where it *belongs*. And it's *my* job to balance everything. It's *my* job to shove off the persistence of water at the same time that I remember what's going to happen to real people, right now, when the system fails." She turned to look at Tressa Fay. "I'm tired."

"Meryl," Gayle started, reaching for her.

"That's bullshit." Tressa Fay felt her anger as a tingling from her shoulder blades down to her fingertips. "Not the part about your work. You know I love hearing you talk about that stuff. But until now, you've never implied that the entirety of the system is balanced on *your* head. Um." Tressa Fay looked at Meryl, whose brown eyes had gotten big. "Yeah. It's not. You're not any more or less important than that crane. Or me. Or our cats. Okay, how about this?"

"What?" Meryl's voice cracked.

"Those houses on the banks of the East River. The ones that flood every time it rains, because the East River simply can't stay in the banks people gave it anymore? You've had a hell of a time figuring out with a bunch of other smarties how to convince it to stay put so you don't have to displace families from their homes, which, if the city claims eminent domain, means they will have nothing. You talked to *Guy* about it at our picnic, in June? Because they were representing a group of activists? And you know what's happening now."

"There's a new coalition of the homeowners who are working with the city to find a solution."

Tressa Fay pointed at her. "Exactly. And that was *Guy's* work. Not yours. Guy got it off your desk because you met them, became friends with them, talked to them, shared with them, made them a part of your life. Now you *and* Guy are a part of a whole bunch of people's lives and the East River's fate. Everything in that system, just like in a creek, is as important as everything else."

"Are you listening to this?" Gayle put her hand on Meryl's arm. "I like this."

"So what am I supposed to do?" Meryl asked. She wasn't paying any attention to Gayle. All of her nerdy, vulnerable, hot-cheeked, worn-out attention was focused on Tressa Fay. "I love you. I want you to be my Tressa Fay forever."

Tressa Fay started to tremble, and her eyes filled with tears.

Meryl loved her.

She hadn't said it before, even though they'd said so many things that were nearly that, and Tressa Fay had known it in her heart. Meryl Whit loved her. And any minute, Tressa Fay could turn around and discover that she was gone. She'd *said* that on September 4 she always disappeared at night, but there was nothing about the way this worked that made anything truly inalterable, which meant right now, or ten minutes from now, or an hour from now, Meryl could be gone with no warning and no explanation, and Tressa Fay would spend her whole life with her porch light on, hoping she'd come home. Or she could simply move from one breath to the next never aware she had known Meryl.

But she loved Meryl *anyway*.

For as long as Tressa Fay could remember, she'd wanted someone to love her for exactly who she was. Someone who chose to stick by her through good times and bad. Someone she picked for herself, who picked her back, over and over again, forever. But what Meryl was telling her was that having Tressa Fay, loving Tressa Fay, was not enough to give her faith.

"I don't think any of us are supposed to love each other like we'll be here forever," Tressa Fay said quietly. "The point is to love each other like we don't have enough time." She reached over and took Meryl's hand, which was cold. "I love you, too. I love you time after time after time. And not because of . . ."

"The drama," Gayle supplied, sniffing back tears.

"*Not* because of the drama." Tressa Fay laughed. "I met you over text on a night I didn't want to go out, I met you in my salon, I met you after I already knew you, but I always meet you. Right? You always meet me."

The way Meryl looked at her scared her. It made Tressa Fay feel certain she *wasn't* going to be able to stop Meryl from disappearing—not because of the inevitability of the event across time, but because Meryl didn't believe in them. She didn't believe their ongoing love was *more* inevitable.

That day they'd gone creeking, when Meryl had said she wasn't going to tell Tressa Fay about her biggest heartbreak, the heartbreak she'd been talking about was this one.

Tressa Fay couldn't fight that. Only Meryl could.

"You know what I want to do?" Meryl asked. Tressa Fay looked at her beautiful face, her gilded mandarin-orange hair. "I want to go to your salon, and I want you to give me a haircut."

"A haircut."

"I'll pay extra to get my hair washed."

Tressa Fay laughed, refusing to notice how much her heart hurt. "I can cut your hair here."

"I want it to be at the salon."

"What are we . . . What's today?" Gayle asked. "What *is* today? I feel like I've been thinking about this day forever, dreading it, and I will never get to the end of it. I never do. I'm just living in the run-up to this day, never able to make it move and be nothing."

Tressa Fay took a breath, about to try to stumble to an answer, but Meryl reached over and touched Tressa Fay's jaw. "It's okay. I want to talk to Gayle. Go on and get ready for my appointment."

So Tressa Fay had to believe in her own big speeches and leave.

She got into her car. She pointed herself away from Meryl's little house, away from their cats, away from the sheets that smelled like the two of them together, and drove herself over the river. She parked at her apartment, because she wanted to wear something that would make her feel different. She stood in front of her closet, flipping through hangers.

Then she saw a flash of deep, reddish orange like the locks of hair at Meryl's nape. She pulled it out, not having any idea what it was.

Oh.

She hung it from the door and stood back.

It was a dress. A rusty orange baby-doll dress with a black eye-let collar and hem, drapey, with black buttons all the way up the front.

It had been her mother's.

Tressa Fay reached up to the top of her closet to pull down a big photo album. She sat on the floor and opened it to a spread near the front where she had a picture of her mom in this dress, at a party, with her dad. It was one of those overly glossy, slightly out-of-focus photo prints from the nineties. Tressa Fay's mother wore this dress with black lace tights and black boots with thick soles and a fedora. She was grabbing on to Phil's arm and laughing while he looked at her like she was everything, smiling at her in a way Tressa Fay had never seen him smile in real life until recently, when she caught him smiling at Jen.

In this picture, they were both impossibly young. Her dad surely had never, ever been this young or held a beer bottle like that, between two fingers, with a Camel box in the palm of his hand. There were chili pepper lights hung up on the wall behind their heads, and the music had probably been loud.

Tressa Fay peeled up the plastic film in the album and unstuck the photo to turn it over.

Lucy's. October 1990. Me and Shelly.

Her dad's handwriting.

She flipped through the album, pulling out photos and flipping them over until she found the one she wanted. It was a picture of Tressa Fay. A baby, but old enough to be standing up without holding on to anything. She had dark tufts of hair, and her port-wine stain was a deeper red than it was now. She wore a sagging diaper and a T-shirt with Big Bird on it, and she was laughing with her arms in the air.

Her mom's handwriting was neat, with big, girlish loops, and the ink on the back of the photo looked as fresh as if her mom had just written the caption.

My Tressa Fay. 14 mos. Dancing to the Pogues.

My Tressa Fay.

She ran her finger over the letters and looked back up at the dress. She cleared her throat and tried hard not to feel awkward.

"Mom?" Tressa Fay cleared her throat again. "I've never done this before. Not even in my head."

She decided it would be easier if she flipped through the album while she talked to her mom, so she started at the beginning, which was mostly group shots of her parents' friends.

"I want to tell you what I'm worried about." She turned to a page with pictures that looked like they had been taken on the east side of the Fox River. In the background was one of the bridges. Everyone was sitting at public picnic tables, laughing and eating what looked like take-out hamburgers. Her mom was sitting on her dad's lap, feeding him french fries.

"I'm worried I'm not enough." As soon as she said it out loud, her throat filled with tears, and she had to swallow past them. "You know? Did you ever feel that way?" With her finger, Tressa Fay circled her mom's face in another photo, the one where she wore the crocheted halter top that Tressa Fay had been wearing when she met Meryl.

"I wasn't enough to keep Dad from being too sad. Don't worry, I knew he loved me, but I knew he was sad, too. I didn't want to do catechism classes. I knew he wanted me to, but I couldn't, not even to make him happy. And I think I was a lot of trouble for him. He had so many routines and rules, things I knew made everything easier for him, but I was always messing them up. I never got on the honor roll. Or even in the higher reading group. I couldn't sit still."

Tressa Fay wiped one of her tears off the clear plastic covering a new page of photos. "I wasn't enough for school, either. I mean, I graduated, but it just was the alternative graduation for the voc-ed students because I had already started my hair school classes, so I didn't graduate with Guy and Linds. They invited me to a graduation party. It was with all their school friends. Smart kids. Cool kids. So, yeah."

That party was a bit of a core memory for Tressa Fay. It was a bonfire at a kid's house who lived by the bay, and everyone had so many inside jokes and favorite songs to dance to. Linds and Guy were giddy. At the end, everyone had brought their big binders and school papers and spiral-bound notebooks with Sharpiewritten titles like *Honors Bio*, and they threw them into the fire, talking about where they were going away to college.

Tressa Fay had told a lot of girls she could *definitely cut their hair sometime*.

"Then there was the allergy thing." Tressa Fay shook her head. "I don't want to minimize that. It changed everything. It was horrible. It led me to what I really wanted. *That* was horrible. I couldn't even be like everyone else in the career I had picked out, right? I had to do it some other whole way where it always felt like I didn't have anyone to talk to. Years and years, I did it on my own. Linds gone to college and grad school, and Guy gone to college and law school, and me in my crappy apartment making so many mistakes dating. It felt like it was because, yet again, I wasn't enough. I ran into this person I went to hair school with, right before my salon really took off, who told me how much money she was making doing unicorn hair. You know, with all the colors. She asked me what I was doing, and I told her, and it was like, 'You *just* cut hair?'"

Tressa Fay laughed. "And I know. I made it work. I have to explain myself over and over again, but I met so many amazing people, I started traveling, cool and important people wanted me to 'just cut' their hair. I was a bonfire cool kid, right?"

Then Amy, Tressa Fay thought. She tried to tell her mom, say it out loud, but she couldn't. Even though she'd finally talked to Linds about it. Mary. Even Meryl.

Tressa Fay got on her hands and knees and pulled a shoebox from the bottom of her closet and dragged it toward herself. She opened it.

The ring box was small and made of cedar. It still smelled sharply of the woods. When she creaked it open, Tressa Fay was surprised, in a way, the ring was there. It was white- and rose-gold leaves, braided together, a pink diamond like a flower. Amy loved jewelry and scarves and barrettes with flowers on them, and she loved pink. Tressa Fay pulled it out of the box and slipped it on until it hit the knuckle of her ring finger. That was as far as it would go.

"I definitely wasn't enough for her."

Her voice sounded hollow in the empty room.

Tressa Fay put the ring away, the jewelry box in the shoebox, and shoved it back in the closet.

Then she pulled out a small plastic tub and opened it, digging through it until she found the black velvet ring box with a mall jeweler's name on it that held her mom's engagement and wedding rings. There was a thin gold band, along with a simple solitaire diamond in a white-gold setting meant to make the tiny diamond look bigger. She slid them on. They fit perfectly on her finger.

"I think Dad thought he wasn't enough to keep you." Tressa Fay took a deep breath. "And here's the thing that I really want to tell you, because I can't say it to anyone else. Sometimes I don't think I'm enough for Meryl." Her eyes spilled fresh tears. "You're my mom, so you have to tell me that's not true, but I'm so afraid it is. What's how I feel about her in the face of the whole universe? I haven't even loved her long enough to, I don't know, *mature* my love into something bigger and stronger, something that won't get swallowed up by some terrible future. Even though I tell myself there *is* proof we have a future, because Meryl talks to me in the future! But I'm so afraid that the thing that's going to put a literal universe between me and Meryl is me. It's that *I* can't inspire Meryl to have the faith she's looking for."

Tressa Fay twirled her mom's wedding set around her finger. "Tell me how to be enough for this, Mom. It was simple for you and Dad. Maybe you learned something by leaving us when you didn't want to."

She sat on the floor in her bedroom for a few minutes, waiting for an answer that didn't come.

Then Tressa Fay stood up. She pulled the dress off the hanger to put it on. "I wish you were here," she said. "I wish something had held you here."

She was only a few minutes late to the salon, and she burst out of her Fiat and ran down the sidewalk in her Doc Martens, rushing because Meryl was waiting for her outside the salon's door in crisp navy pants and a pale pink crewneck sweater that made her look like the goodest of all the good girls.

"Look at you," Meryl said.

"Look at *you*." Tressa Fay unlocked the salon door and flipped on the lights. "So many indecent thoughts are coming at me right now, one after the next."

"I have this sweater in three colors," Meryl said. "Hot Girl Autumn."

Tressa Fay pulled her to the shampoo bowl and made her sit. "Are they from Lands' End?"

"Talbots." Meryl took her glasses off and handed them to Tressa Fay.

"Marry me."

She'd meant it to be funny, but as she eased Meryl into the shampoo bowl and turned on the water, Meryl opened her eyes, and there was an unguarded moment when Tressa Fay saw more than Meryl usually showed her.

All the love.

All the fear.

Meryl's eyes drifted closed as Tressa Fay massaged her temples. Her cheeks were flushed, her freckles standing out in stark relief to her pale skin. She looked young and scared, like a girl who'd always done everything she could to hold the world together.

Tressa Fay lingered over Meryl's temples, smoothing and smoothing, trying to make the worry disappear. Meryl kept silent as Tressa Fay lost herself in washing her hair, pressing her fingertips over her scalp, scratching with her nails, rubbing circles over her nape, then rinsing the slick mass of it with warm water until the water went from milky to clear. It felt a little bit spiritual, maybe because of the water. It made Tressa Fay conscious of the good she did in the world.

A haircut was never just a haircut. It was transformation. It was self-expression. Bravery. Change. Confrontation. Guy deciding they were ready, and Michael kissing them in front of the salon mirrors. Katie's brave decision to stop hiding her acne scars. Mary's going-out layers that had made her feel ready to start something with James. Tressa Fay gave people something they needed. Something small that changed the world.

That was what Meryl was asking for.

She toweled Meryl's hair dry and led her to the chair and gave her back her glasses. "What do you want?" she asked.

Meryl didn't talk to Tressa Fay's reflection. She turned in the chair and looked at her, just like she had that first day in May. Tressa Fay had the same response she had then. Belly flips, lowdown and delicious thumps, a blushing neck. "You know a lot about this. You're actually an expert. Brilliant, according to a lot of important people on the internet, including that guy who runs that super-fancy hair school in Culver City and tried to recruit you last month. So you tell me, in your experience, do people want to get their hair cut to *mark* something?"

Tressa Fay looked at the mirror, running her hands over Meryl's hair. "Yes. I think it must be a very human thing. A very animal thing, because it doesn't require speech. You can tell people something about yourself with your hair without speaking to them." She lifted the weight of Meryl's hair away from her shoulders and repeated her question. "What do you want? What are you trying to say?"

"I want my hair to take a long time to grow out," Meryl told her. "I want everyone who knows me to do a double take or a triple take. My hair has never been different from this. In every single picture I have of myself, it looks just like this. I want to be able to tell that the part of my life that comes next is *different*." Meryl reached up and put her finger on one of Tressa Fay's black dress buttons. "Kiss me, though. We haven't had one single kiss this morning."

Tressa Fay pushed the lever on the floor, smiling, to raise Meryl up, and then Meryl pulled her into her arms, the short skirt of Tressa Fay's dress rucking up around Meryl's thigh. Meryl's kiss was serious right away, teeth against Tressa Fay's lower lip line, hands at her hips, fisting the dress, and Tressa Fay slid her tongue against Meryl's, and her hips jerked without warning, making Meryl exhale a hot, breathy noise.

Her body needed to lean against something, to lie down, to properly melt into a horizontal surface, but all she could do was push the gusset of her panties against Meryl's slacks and try to find a way to hold Meryl when Meryl was in charge of this, deliciously in charge of it, so Tressa Fay's hands moved over her back, under the little sweater, against Meryl's damp nape, and through the wet weight of her hair.

The moment Tressa Fay started pulling on Meryl, trying to

make her come with her to the back room, to the floor, to a bench, Meryl laughed against Tressa Fay's mouth. "It's a long ways to the ground right this minute."

Tressa Fay pulled Meryl's hair. "I'll catch you. I'll carry you. Do those slacks have one of those fasteners with a button and a little hook? I hope so. It will be like undressing a courtier."

But Tressa Fay laughed, too, and let Meryl kiss her one more time before she bent to the side to turn the chair around.

Tressa Fay squeezed Meryl's shoulders as she looked at Meryl's eyes in the mirror, at her thousands of freckles and her swooping, arching auburn eyebrows, and how both of their faces were flushed and their lips swollen. She thought about how Meryl's throat hollowed out and then sloped downward. Her full breasts. Meryl's shoulders were narrow but rounded with muscles, and her waist pulled in over the softest and prettiest hips, which gave way to legs so strong, Tressa Fay had to ask for breaks when they went on walks, and Tressa Fay was on her feet all day.

She pulled a fresh cape from the shelf at her station and fastened it on, thinking about kissing Meryl, making love to her, hiking along a brook with her, fucking her in the wee hours after teasing each other all day, the clever things she said to Meryl from the future that were on Meryl's phone, things that made Meryl laugh and then lean over and kiss her.

She started cutting.

She cut until Meryl's lashes were the longest she'd ever seen them, and as many freckles were exposed as possible, and her fat upper lip, bigger than her lower, looked like something out of a silent film. She cut Meryl's hair so that her eyes were deeper and darker and another unexpected curve was exposed at her nape. She watched the pieces she left long curl into ringlets, then refined with her razor until Meryl's hair painted itself into its full mosaic of blush and orange and rust and rose gold and sunflower, exposing every color at once, so that it looked like a setting for her beautiful face.

When Tressa Fay was done, she rubbed honey-smelling wax into Meryl's hair and made it messy, messy, and the way it stuck out against Meryl's proper sweater and the dark frames of her glasses made Tressa Fay want to turn her around and kiss her.

She did that.

When their mouths met, Meryl's hands went right to gripping her waist, and Tressa Fay felt everything. The weighty dread of this day, the fourth of September, and the worry on Meryl's face when she squeezed her eyes shut at the shampoo sink, and the way the fabric of this dress that Tressa Fay's mother had once worn felt as it shifted and moved against her skin, and how frightened she was—and, most of all, how much she wanted a future with this woman, not to be her biggest heartbreak.

"It's perfect," Meryl said, pressing her thumb against Tressa Fay's lips. "Exactly what I wanted. You always give me exactly what I want." Meryl looked at her with her brand-new big brown eyes. "You're everything I could ever want, ever, and what I need is exactly you." Meryl's thumb moved to Tressa Fay's chin and held it, making sure Tressa Fay understood.

She did. Meryl was saying that Tressa Fay was enough.

"I love you, Tressa Fay. I love you. I love you. I love you."

Tressa Fay closed her eyes and let herself entertain the possibility—standing in the salon she'd made, with the woman she loved, wearing her mother's dress—that there was more than either having someone or losing them.

That love found a way.

Love found *you*.

MERYL

HER DATE WAS A BUST.

The woman was dragging a churro through a plate of chocolate when she looked up at Meryl after several long minutes of silence that Meryl suspected were awkward only for her. "So you must get busy when the power goes out."

The woman's lashes were long, her buzz cut painfully hot. The creative intensity promised by this mural artist via flirting on the app *should* have been plugging into all of Meryl's sockets—creative intensity was more than a little of what turned Meryl on—but every attempt they made to talk to each other wasn't hitting, as though they were on the same date but in parallel universes.

"Um, no," Meryl said. "It's more city workers and linemen who get busy during power outages."

"I thought you were a city worker?"

"Engineer."

"Huh." The woman nodded. "Is that why you're wearing the math shirt? God, I hated math." Her smartwatch lit up and buzzed, and she looked at it, then started tapping away.

"Yeah," Meryl said, to no one.

The weather was so good, was the thing. Early May in Wisconsin couldn't always be counted on to provide this much sun. The big front windows of Canyon Tacos were open, a cool breeze sifting over the busy dining room. This should have been a perfect night for a first date with a woman who'd made her the right amount of nervous. She'd imagined their date might end with a long walk in the warm twilight.

The woman looked up at Meryl. "Hey, so, this sucks, but I've got to go."

Meryl glanced at the woman's smartwatch, where the logo of a hookup app had just faded from the screen. "I understand."

"Uh, here." Her date dove into the pockets of her tiny denim skirt and pulled out a twenty, waving it over her plate of chocolate.

"Don't worry about it."

The woman grinned, and Meryl felt a deep pang of regret that the first smile of that magnitude she'd been offered on this date had come when she'd said she would pay. "Cool. I'll . . . see you around, maybe?"

"Maybe." Meryl watched her date weave through the crowd, then pulled her wallet out of her purse as the server came over.

"Oh, hey." The server picked up a beanie from the floor near the table. "Is this yours?"

Meryl had watched her date pull off the Carhartt beanie when they sat down. "I'll take it, thanks."

She traded it for her credit card and walked partway through the crowd, looking out the door to see if she could catch her ex-date. Then she got out her phone to send a text.

> I don't see you, and I've done a complete turn of the first floor. You forgot your beanie.

> sorry! I don't think I can help. you've got the wrong number

Meryl closed her eyes in frustration. Online dating was starting to get so tiresome. It would be nice to meet someone literally any other way.

> Look, it's fine to tell me to keep it, or not reply at all, but you don't have to ghost me in disguise. I get that a second date's not happening.

> hey, so ... this is the wrong number, for sure. my name's Tressa Fay, and I'm at home communing with my cat and soup, and I didn't have a date tonight or anytime in the foreseeable future, actually, but good luck out there, it's the level worst

Meryl looked at the number she'd texted at the top. So weird. She'd thought she was replying to her date's last text, but apparently she had somehow started a new thread? !!! I have the wrong number.

> yes

> I just realized. I used the wrong first three digits.

oh, no. numbers are so tricky

I'm an ENGINEER.

remind me not to drive over any of your bridges.

Meryl laughed out loud. At least her wrong number knew what an engineer was.

One collapsed bridge and a girl's got a reputation.

Meryl sat down, waiting to see if she'd get a reply to her joke. She looked out the window at the lavender twilight.

It really was a pretty night.

SLIDING HER HAND INTO HER BAG, TRESSA FAY TOUCHED THE ENvelope again.

It was a plain white business envelope, folded in half, that had gotten soft and wrinkled over five months in her bag from her hand brushing over it again and again. Inside was a long, braided lock of Meryl's hair, fastened at the end with a little elastic band.

"You know what I keep thinking about?" Guy interrupted the silence of Tressa Fay's living room. "A dream I had this week."

"It's rude to tell people your dreams." Mary tucked herself closer to James's chest. "I'll buy you a journal."

Guy stuck their tongue out at Mary. "Tressa Fay was cutting my hair at the salon, and when she finished, she took pictures with her ring light. Then Gayle and James showed up at the salon to tell us that Meryl had gone missing from some bar. But when I woke up, I thought—I *think*—that actually happened."

Gayle sighed, an extensive sigh with a lot of depth to it that was a little funny, because Gayle was their long-suffering friend, too adultish and anxious and stern, but adorable for it, most of the time. "I can remember running into Guy and Tressa Fay in the salon and talking about Meryl, and getting a bunch of food with everyone, but then I can't even remember if that's when we all met?" She directed this question to James.

He dropped a handful of Mary's hair he'd coiled around his fingers. "Don't look at me. I get out of bed every morning, stretch my fingertips to the sky, say my affirmations, and then tell myself to live in the moment. Then I commune with a beautiful woman."

"You know what's happening?" Linds asked. She had come out of Tressa Fay's kitchen with a mug of tea for Brooklynn, who was perched on Tressa Fay's sofa in a red velvet jumpsuit and looked like a painting. "Something is breaking apart like a glacier, right before our eyes." She handed the tea to Brooklynn, who leaned up to kiss her.

"What about this?" James asked. "Today, no matter what we remember, is a day none of us has lived through before. And Meryl *hasn't* disappeared." He gestured at Tressa Fay's phone.

"Wait." Mary suddenly stood up, displacing James so that he had to catch himself. She looked around. "This apartment."

"What is it?" Linds asked.

"*Shhh.*" Mary closed her eyes and held her hand up, bouncing on the balls of her feet. "Meryl doesn't live here. She never lived here. By July, Tressa Fay was already treating this apartment like a closet. She didn't bring . . . Oh, wait. Wait. Wait. Wait! *Epinephrine.*"

Tressa Fay had scooted to the edge of her seat. Everyone was quiet. Mary didn't always make herself the center of attention, but when she did, something always happened.

Mary opened her eyes. She walked to the arm of the sofa where Epinephrine was napping and leaned over, looking incredibly serious. "Eps. Wake up, butternut. Epinephrine!"

Epinephrine's ears swiveled toward Mary. He opened his eyes

a tiny squint. He yawned until he had to arch his back and get a stretch into it.

Mary knelt down in front of him. "Where's *Spring*?" Mary had pitched her voice into cat register, and she was gazing into Epinephrine's eyes.

The air left the room.

Epinephrine, who had always loved an audience, pulled his ears up to full listening mode and released a small, questioning activation trill. *Oooooooh?* He looked around the room. Once. Twice. *Oooooooh?*

Then he stretched his front paws out, clawing the sofa, looked around, and jumped off the sofa arm, making short, sharp, low little meows that Tressa Fay hadn't heard for months and months.

Meows that she'd never *heard*, not out loud. Only in her memories.

It was how he talked to Spring.

She must have made a noise, because Mary looked at her with tears in her eyes. "You talked to the lady at the cat rescue who didn't remember Meryl or Spring. But I remembered being at Meryl's when Epinephrine was there, and Epinephrine and Spring were already buddies. Then I thought, *why* doesn't the cat rescue lady remember? Isn't that from the same universe? She *should* remember." Mary shook her head, smiling, her eyes bright. "What I mean is, this is proof. Look." She pointed at Epinephrine, who was sitting in the kitchen, looking around, getting annoyed in his confusion, still talking to Spring. "It's broken. Really broken. We did something. Linds is right. I mean, as far as Epinephrine is concerned, Spring *is* here, somewhere. He *remembers* Spring, and he could only do that if he knew him. We're losing memories of Meryl disappearing. We're losing memories of exactly how we met each other, which, after all, was because Meryl disappeared, right?"

"Epinephrine's cat. He's here and not here." Linds giggled. "A universe splits from another because of different decisions, yes, but the general trajectory and story of that universe is the same. Or it is the same universe. Schrödinger didn't get that far."

"But where's Meryl?" Gayle asked. Then she shook her head as though to dislodge a confusing thought. "I'm sorry. I know I've asked that a million times before, but this time I mean it, like, both ways, because for a second, I thought, *Why didn't we invite Meryl tonight? Is she coming? Did someone not call her or what?*" Gayle took a breath. "That's how it feels. Like I just need to call her."

Tressa Fay watched Epinephrine walk in a circle around the kitchen, and she couldn't tell if her mouth felt so horribly dry from terror or hope. Every time she tried to work out what Mary's demonstration meant, she felt something like déjà vu—confusion mixed with the certainty that this had happened before.

So she stopped trying to work it out. She started trying to just *feel* it. Feel her heart beating. Feel the truth inside of herself. "It's in our hands," she heard herself saying. "We have to not get afraid. We have to believe they can have what they want. What we want." Her voice was shaking, but she knew she was right. She *knew* it. She put her hand on the phone on her lap. The charger connected to it was warm.

Outside, it had been snowing for days. Tressa Fay had a tough time getting around in her Fiat over the packed snow on the roads. She'd slid around at every intersection.

This morning, she'd found her mom's dress on a hook outside of her closet under three other things that had been put over top of it, and when she buried her face in it, she could smell Meryl. Like burnt sugar. Caramel. Like the honey hair wax. Real.

"This is different." She turned to look at Linds, her fingers tight around the phone in her lap. "Remember? None of this is like how it was. And we wouldn't want it to be."

Tressa Fay's phone lit up.

> I love you. Three people have told me they love my hair.

She took a deep breath, then started typing.

> I wouldn't change anything, Meryl. I wouldn't. no matter what happens, I wouldn't make anything different

> I choose you, and I don't believe I'll ever lose you

Her phone choked out a shuddery buzz, and Meryl's name flashed for hardly a second, indicating she'd tried to call.

It hadn't done that. Not one time since that first night in October.

Even though Tressa Fay's phone had gone quiet, the incoming call no longer visible on the screen, she answered aloud. "Meryl?"

Everyone looked at her, arrested.

Nothing.

"What's going on?" Gayle asked.

Tressa Fay shook her head.

Michael's and Guy's arms were around each other, and Mary

was leaning against James's side. Linds had moved herself close to Brooklynn. Epinephrine was in Gayle's lap now, still alert to the room, as if waiting for Spring to leap out from under a chair, even though Spring had never been in Tressa Fay's apartment.

"Gayle, honey," she said. "Talk to your sister." She handed the phone to Gayle. "Just talk to her, though. Like, regular. Don't get mawkish."

Gayle started typing. She was smiling.

"Hey, nerds," Mary said. "I asked James to marry me, and he said yes. So everyone has to feel happy right now."

"Oh my God!" Tressa Fay jumped to her feet. "For real?!"

James laughed, and then Linds and Brooklynn and Michael and Guy all stood up, and Gayle, too, and they were on James and Mary, congratulating and hugging and cheek kissing and exclaiming. Tressa Fay was part of it all, genuinely excited.

Gayle gave Tressa Fay back her phone, caught up in a laughing conversation with James.

Tressa Fay sat back down on the sofa and folded her legs under her.

> me again. how hard will it be for you to keep this big news to yourself?

> I mean, maybe impossible. How hard is it going to be for you?

> also, possibly, impossible

> But James and Mary would be so so so annoyed if we spoiled their engagement for them.

Tressa Fay looked up from her phone at James running his thumb over Mary's bottom lip and smiling at her before taking a fast, hot kiss.

Meryl believed she and Tressa Fay would have to keep their mouths shut so they didn't spoil the future for James and Mary.

Meryl *believed*, and it made everything snap into place.

> like, extremely very annoyed

> LOL.

And so Tressa Fay had a very, very good moment, in this liminal space she had been dreading—the space between waking up on this day and when it was over—listening to everyone she and Meryl had introduced to each other, texting the woman time had introduced to her, sometimes scrolling back up, up, up to everything they'd said to each other, remembering how their words had disappeared and rewritten themselves depending on their experiences with each other.

And she thought, maybe there *were* worlds where Michael had watched Guy drive away on the last day of law school and never seen them again.

Maybe there were worlds where James and Mary hadn't met.

But maybe, too, her dad was right, and there was a world, somewhere, where Tressa Fay still had her mom.

And definitely, definitely, there was a world where she and Meryl were making out furiously in the snow, everything cold except all the places where they could manage to touch each other. She had never, ever been more certain, now that she knew Meryl was, too.

Epinephrine jumped into her lap with an annoyed grunt-meow and looked at her.

"Don't worry." Tressa Fay scratched his chin. "You'll see him soon."

JEN DEFTLY MANEUVERED THE PAINT ROLLER ON ITS LONG POLE over the ceiling, working away from the corner she'd already covered. Tressa Fay was trimming the baseboards, watching with satisfaction as the shiny paint knit together all the scuffs and chips from years of wear.

"Are you going to tell me how it's going?" Jen asked, moving the pole back down and wiping her arm over her forehead. "Or is your plan to follow Phil Robeson into the storm clouds of silence every time you have a big feeling?"

"Don't tell me you and Dad have fought."

Jen laughed. "Of course we have. We're both grown adults who've been single, doing everything our own way, for decades. We've spent a good part of this month fighting."

"Over what?" Tressa Fay sat on the floor and balanced her brush on top of the paint can.

"This." Jen gestured around the room, which used to be Tressa Fay's but had lately been where her dad tied flies at an old drafting desk and stored things he wasn't sure if he should get rid of. "Making some changes. Moving in."

"Everything you've been doing are things he's thought he should do for ages. I know he's so glad you're here."

"Mm." Jen sat down on the top of a stepladder. She wore a sports bra under a pair of overalls, a bandana protecting her hair, and seemed years younger. "I wouldn't say he's *glad* I'm here. What I would say is that he wants me here but wishes he was a better Catholic and could keep me at courting distance until we got married."

"I'm not sure how he ever could have thought that he could keep *you* at a distance." Tressa Fay looked around at the room. It already seemed so much lighter and brighter than it had been, even when it was hers. "You're a force of nature."

Jen grinned. "I think your dad took in a little more than was necessary of the hair shirt and self-mastery portions of theology and not enough of the parts where love is the point. But at the same time, I wouldn't be here, and I definitely wouldn't have decided to spend the rest of my life with him, if I didn't believe he'd surrendered to love a long time ago."

Tressa Fay thought about that. "I was terrified to come out to him," she said. "But I never thought he'd stop being my dad or yell at me or kick me out. I was scared because I'd fought so hard for every bit of closeness we did have, and I didn't want to lose any of it, but also he'd made me go to so much mass that I couldn't lie to him. I was fifteen."

"That's such a hard age."

"I'm only just beginning to get that. One night I asked him to tuck me in for bed. For some reason, that's how I decided I was going to tell him. From under the covers. I hadn't wanted him to tuck me in and say good night to me for years and years. But he just got up from his recliner and didn't even look at me funny. That's how I knew it would be okay. And it was. I told him, he nodded, and then the next morning he made pancakes, which he hadn't done since I was little."

"He *loves* you."

Tressa Fay looked up at the half-painted ceiling and sniffed, wiping away tears. "Yeah. I think I've only recently figured out that even if he's never been the easiest person to talk to and is so fucking tight and prescriptivist about all kinds of things, he also never tried to make me be anything other than what I was. Which must mean that he actually loves me. For me."

"That's the kind of person he likes, you know. The kind who's exactly who they are. Singular. Not hung up on rules, even the rules he feels like he has to follow."

"Like you." Tressa Fay smiled.

"And your mom."

"So I've heard." Tressa Fay suddenly got goose bumps. "I was this minute years old when I realized that the only stories Dad has ever told me about Mom were the ones where she was particularly outrageous."

Jen laughed. "It makes you think about what he admires most in a person."

"Meryl has rules. I'm not sure that's what she'd call them. She has an old-fashioned code, you know what I mean?"

Jen leaned forward. "I do. She's principled."

"Yes." Tressa Fay picked a thread from the hole in her jeans. "It means she'll never stop talking to me if she can help it. She'll never leave me if she can *help* it."

Tressa Fay thought again of her mom. How her mom hadn't wanted to leave, but she hadn't been able to prevent it. How there were times, especially when Tressa Fay was a teenager and worried about coming out to her dad, feeling like the only lesbian in Wisconsin, certain she would never find love and would definitely die alone, when she'd been so angry with her mom for dying and leaving her with just Phil. She'd wished her mom had fallen in love with someone easier, someone who could have re-covered from losing her with expansive, resilient optimism in-stead of dogged coping and grief.

It had taken loving Meryl and knowing she could lose her for Tressa Fay to understand that her mom had left her with the one person best equipped to love her. The person *she'd* loved the most. Because that meant her mom had never left her and never would.

"Are you mad at Meryl?"

Tressa Fay sighed. "Well, sometimes my feelings and what I can't control have a party, and I get so dug in and stubborn."

"I have no idea where you got that from." Jen put her elbow on her crossed legs and her chin in her hands. "But you didn't stay stuck?"

Tressa Fay cleared her throat. "No. And also, I'm giving her a little time and space this afternoon because I perceived she might have felt the tiniest bit smothered. She has a lot on her mind."

"Oh, Tressa Fay. How is it that you're supposed to navigate this? You're both doing the best you can. But I know that neither your dad or I want you to be left with any regrets."

"You think she's going to be gone," she said softly.

"I don't know." Jen shook her head. "It's out of my depth in every way."

"Meryl said that you weren't even living with Dad when he told me in October that you were getting married."

"Yes. But I was always going to, so it feels like the same thing."

It reminded her of the words her father heard at mass once a week, right before he walked out the door. *As it was in the begin-ning is now, and ever shall be. World without end. Amen.*

Tressa Fay stood up. "I'm going to go find my dad and give him a hug, and then I want to spend as much time as I can with Meryl."

"Come here." Jen opened her arms.

Tressa Fay sank into a long hug with Jen, her first really proper Jen hug. Her arms were strong, and her skin was soft. Her hair smelled good, a gentle scent that didn't close up Tressa Fay's throat.

She stepped back.

"Your dad's in the garage, repairing a bookshelf of mine I was going to toss. I don't think I've ever offended him more than when I told him that I was going to throw away something because it was broken."

"Yeah." Tressa Fay laughed. "You've noticed that this place is a time capsule from the nineties, right? The pristine condition of the creamy-white appliances and hunter-green carpeting?"

"He's shampooing it on a schedule, isn't he?"

"Every August. 'Before the cold weather sets in and it won't dry.'" Tressa Fay imitated Phil's voice.

"Good to know. How receptive do you think he'd be to 'I bet there are perfectly serviceable hardwoods under all this carpet'?"

"Maybe first see if you can get Father to mention they need a bunch of secondhand carpet in good condition to cover part of the floor in the church basement."

Jen laughed. "I'm so glad I have you as a walking Phil Robeson guidebook."

Tressa Fay kissed her cheek and left.

In the garage, her dad knelt down beside the bookshelf, which lay on its side. She smelled sawdust. He had a clamp in one hand and a bottle of glue in the other.

"How's it going?" she asked.

"Almost done. Did you finish up that trim painting?"

"I left Jen to it. She's obviously an expert, and I wanted to hang out with you for a while. Guess what I did today."

"What did you do?"

"I wore Mom's dress to cut Meryl's hair. Look." She fished out her phone and pulled up the photos she wanted him to see. "I found a picture of Mom wearing it to a party. You look about fourteen years old, but the date says you were a legal adult."

Her dad pulled his readers out of the pocket of his shirt and studied the picture on her phone. "I remember that party. It was at Lucy Donmire's. She was getting ready to move to Seattle."

"Lucy Donmire?" Tressa Fay looked at the photo again. "The artist who makes the giant billboard installations? She's famous!"

Her dad pulled a rolling stool over and sat down. "Last I heard."

"You've never told me that you know her. I didn't even know she was from Wisconsin."

"I went to school with her. Kindergarten through graduation. My mom always gave her mom perms."

"You didn't think I would find this information interesting?"

"I never know what you're going to find interesting, Tressa Fay." He laughed. "More than half the time you accuse me of never letting anything change at all, and then you'll make a big fuss because you find a can of Old Bay seasoning in the cupboard and ask me why I have it, because I've never bought it before."

"That was weird," she said. "There has never been anything but salt, pepper, and cinnamon sugar in that cabinet. What was I supposed to think?"

"Sometimes a man wants his Friday fish fry to be jazzed up a little." He raised his eyebrows at her.

Tressa Fay grinned, delighted with him. Lately, she'd been saving screenshots on her phone of haircuts she thought might look good on him, because it had started to feel possible that she might be able to talk him into one.

Although, if he didn't want to change his hair, that was okay. She didn't need him to be anyone but who he was, who he always had been. What felt so good now was knowing that he'd wanted to figure this out, just as much as she had. That was what the monthly haircut appointments and weekly diner meals had been about. They were his way of trying to tell her, *I want to be close to you.*

"I'm glad Jen's moving in. I just wanted to say that, because I happen to know it was a very real possibility that I'd never learn of her existence until you told me you were getting married."

Her dad put down the bottle of glue and settled back on his heels. "Isn't it something?" He looked away, gazing out the open garage door to the street. "I'll be honest, it was hard to hear. But it's been a wake-up call."

"Tonight is the night." She walked over to where her dad had laid a big piece of cardboard out beneath the bookshelf to protect the wood and keep the garage floor clean. She sat down across from him on the cardboard, pulling her knees up to wrap her arms around them.

All at once, feelings rushed over her, and Tressa Fay knew she'd been here before, sitting by her dad on the garage floor.

Sitting by her dad on a boat on a quiet lake.

Standing next to him while he lit a candle in the back of the church for her mom.

Standing behind him, checking that she'd gotten his neckline straight and sharp.

"What is it?" He raised his eyebrows. "What do you need?"

It was the first time he'd asked her that when it didn't feel like an accusation.

"I need to know that how I feel about Meryl is . . . enough." She couldn't say, not to her dad, that she was afraid *she* wasn't enough.

He rubbed his hands together, slow, squeezing his fingers. "It's not," he said, finally. "I had that, plus the candles I lit at the church and all the time I spent on my knees. I can tell you that if the way I felt about your mom wasn't enough to keep her here, nobody's feelings are. I know that's prideful, but I think it's true. Not possible there's ever been a love greater than what I gave to Shelly."

Tressa Fay couldn't speak.

Her dad blew out a breath. "You know, you're a lot like me, Tressa Fay. I don't doubt that you're plenty for Meryl."

She laughed reflexively, almost breathless. "What should I do, Dad?"

He looked out of the open garage door again, then back at her with a smile. "Fishing works for me, but you've never taken to it."

Fishing. She almost made a joke, one of what her dad called her *smart comments*, but the words stopped up in her throat because she'd thought about the water, and being at the top of the Ferris wheel at Bay Beach, and the short walk across the street from Canyon Tacos to the river, and what Meryl had told her about water remembering everything.

Water was something that Meryl was sure of. Like Tressa Fay was sure of what to do with a razor in her hand and a person in her chair who wanted to be made over into the truest version of themself.

Meryl could look at the water moving through a place like Green Bay, where every piece of shoreline along the lake and bounding in the Fox and East Rivers had been engineered— where levees and culverts and drains and underground pipes directed every speck of rainwater—and have complete faith that if all of it was deconstructed, the water would know where to go.

If water was the *only* thing Meryl could be sure of, then Tressa

Fay could damn well get Meryl into the water. Maybe there, she could find the faith she so badly needed.

"It's a nice day," Tressa Fay said. "Probably the last nice day in Wisconsin. I don't fish, but I'm thinking I'll go swimming."

"Wear sunscreen and shower after. Don't want a burn or diarrhea."

"Oh my God," Tressa Fay said. "I'm not ten."

"No, but that night when you were ten after that girl's party at her people's farm pond was a bad one."

Tressa Fay stood up. "You're a good dad. Have I ever told you?"

"I don't need praise for the work God puts in front of me, Tressa Fay." But he smiled. "Come to breakfast in the morning if you want to."

"You bet." Tressa Fay brushed her butt off, even though a person could probably eat ice cream off her dad's garage floor and not have to pick so much as a speck of dust out of their teeth. "You need help getting that back in the house?"

"Nope. Glue has to dry. You can go on. Watch the mailbox on your way out."

She laughed. "Stand up and hug me, though, first." It was only a little bit vulnerable to say such a thing out loud. She wasn't sure when she'd asked her dad for a hug. Probably that was why she'd decided to come out to him from beneath her covers in her bedroom—because part of his routine, when he said good night, had always been to give her a hug.

But he just rose stiffly to his feet as though they'd always done this. He set his clamp on the workbench against the wall and opened his arms.

Tressa Fay hugged her dad, thinking about Meryl and love and what a gift it was to live every day not knowing what would happen tomorrow.

SEPTEMBER 4, 6:47 P.M.

SEPTEMBER 4, 6:47 P.M.

I love you. You're taking me swimming now. I'm saving this to send it in the morning, and when I do, I know you'll get it. Wherever you are.

. . . .

WHO'S GONNA CALL THE COPS?" LINDS ASKED. SHE WAS TOP-less, wearing cutoff jean shorts and a pair of sunglasses, even though it was fully twilight. "The seagulls? That guy we passed drinking beer on the boat launch?"

"Said the privileged white woman." James rubbed his arms and stomped his water-shoe-clad feet in the sand. "You don't even have to have a *who* to call the cops anymore. They have cop-calling robots, and anything can be a robot."

Tressa Fay looked out at the bay, the water meeting the blue-and-pink horizon, stretching way, way out. Lake Michigan touched four whole states.

She hoped it was big enough.

"It's shallow here for a long ways, and even if we go out past the end of that jetty, we'll only be up to our shoulders," Meryl said. She was in a different serviceable suit, this one black, with tiny cap sleeves and a zipper up the front. She also wore new water shoes. Unlike James's, which were lime green and looked like something you'd buy at the pool concession, Meryl's had deep treads and cinched, bulletproof-looking mesh, probably so some kind of Lake Michigan barracuda couldn't eat her toes.

She was so beautiful.

"Explain this to me again." Gayle tugged at the board shorts she'd paired with a red bikini top. "Like I'm five. Without any references to fantasy books or Dungeons & Dragons campaigns."

Linds and Brooklynn laughed. Brooklynn was the only one who could look at Linds full-on. Of course Linds had asked everyone for permission to swim topless, but there was agreeing, and then there was the reality of a topless Linds canoodling with Brooklynn in a swimsuit that had made Tressa Fay's eyes cross but also made her ask where she'd bought it.

"That's *my* line," Guy said. They and Michael had matching Speedos, which had introduced a number of questions on their short hike from the parking lot to the shoreline. The Speedos had something to do with San Diego and a Pride event and their own-ing literally no other swimwear because they were lawyers. "And maybe we could get one more explanation before we all succumb to hypothermia."

"The water has memories," Tressa Fay said. "It knows where it's supposed to go and where it's supposed to be. It's here now, and it was here a long time ago, and it will be here for a long time. It's bigger than us, and it knows about what's been happening to us, because there isn't anything it hasn't seen."

There was part of her that knew this plan was maybe a little bit, or a lot, corny. Or cringe. But Tressa Fay genuinely did not care. She had done a lot, a lot, a *lot* of things in her thirty-one years that other people called corny and cringe and even ridicu-lous, and yet she was still here, living her life the best way she knew how, with her friends. With Meryl.

If that wasn't good enough, Tressa Fay couldn't do anything about it.

"And also I *want* to," Meryl said. "This is where I want to be more than I want to be anywhere else, and you guys are who I want to be with."

When Tressa Fay had told Meryl her idea, she'd worried Meryl wouldn't get it, or that it was too mystical a take on what Meryl had taught her about water, or that she'd have a lot of practical objections related to breaking into Bay Beach Amusement Park after the season was over to gain access to the swimming beach near dark.

But instead, Meryl had listened. She'd told her it was a good idea. She'd made Tressa Fay feel right. More confident than she should on this night.

Meryl always made her feel right.

Before they left, Meryl had typed a text, then set her phone down on the kitchen table. Before Tressa Fay could ask, Meryl had kissed her and told her that she had everything she needed. Everything she'd always wanted.

"I've walked the whole swimming beach area," Michael said. "I checked the changing hut and used my flashlight in the trees. I don't think anyone's here." He leaned down and picked up a shopping bag. Michael had put himself in charge of monitoring the area for bad guys and had in fact walked up to talk to the man who was drinking on the boat launch, obtaining his name and contact information. The man ended up asking Michael for his card in order to help him with a legal issue related to late property taxes. "And I have these."

Michael passed around what looked like a car's electronic key fob attached to a lanyard to each person. "It's a personal alarm. Push the button, it makes an unholy noise, and we know one of us needs help. It's waterproof. I had to go to that weird trail cam and gun shop by the chicken wing place that gave Mary food poisoning last year to get these, so you have to wear them."

"Strong swimmers should fill in around the weaker ones," Meryl said. "It's going to get darker fast, but the security lights in the park are on all the time. They'll seem brighter when we're out in the water."

Mary adjusted her lanyard. Tressa Fay knew she was nervous. Mary hated swimming. Her retro swimsuit hadn't even seen the water. It was for sunning only.

"You okay?" Tressa Fay asked her.

"Yeah," Mary said. "I am. I'm okay. I can do this." She looked out over the water. "I don't want a fish to touch me, but Meryl said it wasn't deep, and it's easy to walk, and probably there's not a lot of fish in the sandy swimming part. But this feels too much like we're Navy SEALs getting ready for some kind of drill. Or Meryl's water-testing interns. I feel like there should be a metaphysical vibe? Or some words."

"Like at a funeral?" James asked.

"*James*," Mary chided. "But yes, something real like that."

Something real, Tressa Fay thought. What was more real than nine people who loved each other who had come to the edge of the water to keep everyone together?

"We should just be us," Tressa Fay said.

She reached over and took Mary's hand, and that got everyone moving toward where the lake water sloshed against the wet, dark sand, frothing as it receded. The lake smelled cold and stony and a little fishy, and their group started laughing and whooping as the near-icy water slapped against their shins, then their knees. It was hard to walk in the soft mixture of fine sand and lake mud in her old Converse, the ones she had worn in the creek, but they were moving slowly, getting loud, then shushing each other, pushing forward, the lake bed giving way to a firm matrix of coarse sand and pebbles.

Then they were up to their waists, and the light from Bay Beach broke over them where it had been touching the water farther out.

"Oh," Mary said. "You can see better." Her hand slipped from Tressa Fay's, and she moved toward James in the outer circle. Meryl was laughing and splashing Gayle. Michael looked like he was counting all of them, over and over, while Guy slipped along, trudging awkwardly toward where Linds and Brooklynn were experimenting with floating on their backs.

Tressa Fay turned to see behind them where the park sat on the shore, the wooden roller coaster huge and dark, the paths lit by the security lights. She skimmed her hand over the surface of the water, white blue with reflected light. Her legs had moved from numb to almost warm feeling, but everywhere else she was cold in the wind over the lake, so she bent her knees and knelt down into the water until it hit her chin.

Then she held her nose with two fingers and took a sharp breath and dunked all the way under.

The sounds of her friends immediately dropped away, replaced with watery silence and her heart racing from the cold.

When her lungs started to burn, she stood up, water sheeting off her hair. She looked down to check her suit, surprised by how dark the navy fabric had gotten in the water. When she'd taken it out of a little tote bag she'd found in the bottom of a box of her mother's things, the spandex suit was starting to gray, and the green stripes over the straps and sides had sun-bleached to mint from what must have once been a bright kelly green. But she'd wanted to wear it because it was the only item of clothing she could remember her mom wearing. She had a memory of being at the pool, her arms wrapped around her mom's leg, her hand stretching up to touch her belly, feeling this smooth navy spandex.

Then she looked up, waving at Phil on the shore with Tressa Fay, who was so cute in her tiny red suit and sun hat, smacking her dad's thigh. From here, she couldn't hear if Tressa Fay was squealing, but she bet she was. Phil noticed her waving and waved back, grinning. She should've worn her sunglasses. The sunlight was glaring on the water and giving her a bit of a headache, but it was so good to get out of the house like this. Tressa Fay was a handful. Even the teachers at the church's nursery school thought so.

She lifted up her feet and kicked out, floating on her back, listening to the families on the shore and the noise from Bay Beach, hit with a sudden rush of love for her husband and daughter.

She stood up again, squeezing out the water from her hair, feeling clumps of it turn to ice in the cold as snowflakes melted on her sun-hot skin and then stayed as she chilled. The water was thick with icy slush. She waved at her dad on the beach, wrapped up in a coat, but he didn't see her. He was flinging snow into the water. When it sailed over the wind and clung to Tressa Fay's skin, though, it wasn't snow, but ashes.

She turned to show Linds, who held on to a pool noodle, her lashes dripping with water, a stripe of the white sunscreen her mother made her wear on her nose.

"Look," Tressa Fay said. "It's my mom."

Linds kicked over, splashing water everywhere. "Yeah," she agreed. "She's waving at you with my mom."

Tressa Fay turned her attention back to the shore, where her mom and Linds's mom were sitting on the blanket together. Guy's mom was putting sunscreen on them while nursing Guy's little sister with her swimsuit pulled down, which was so embarrassing.

"Wanna race?" Linds asked.

"Yeah. Where's Mary?"

"On the Viking swing with James and everybody else." When Linds pointed, Tressa Fay saw the ride, lit up bright against the darkness, already tipped high into the sky. Mary, James, Gayle, Linds, Guy, and Michael had their hands in the air, and they were screaming, shouting, falling.

"I wish I could've been there," Meryl said, nudging Tressa Fay with her shoulder, wet and warm from the water and sun. "It looks like fun."

Meryl's hair was in two long braids, dark with lake water, dripping onto her light blue suit. "You were there," Tressa Fay said. "Remember? You were the one who made us go."

But Meryl shook her head. "That couldn't have been me. I always disappear."

"Not this time."

"It's the one thing that never changes. I'm talking and talking to the future, but no matter what I do different, I never make it to where you are."

"You can't keep telling yourself that story, honey." Tressa Fay's chest was hot, her lungs overfull, her whole self brimming over with how much she loved this woman. "It's breaking your heart."

Meryl shook her head. When Tressa Fay tried to touch her, she retreated beyond her reach. "You know, I really hurt Kaley when I walked away from the wedding. I don't want to hurt you like that. I love you so much."

"Then stay with me. Choose me."

Meryl looked devastated. "I'm sorry I won't be there to meet you at Canyon Tacos," she said. "I love how they do the limeade in mini pitchers."

Tressa Fay could barely hear Meryl now, she was so far out in the water, and it was hard to tell, but it looked like there might be a dark shadow around her, moving with her, out past where it was safe to be. Tressa Fay tried to get closer, but the water was hard to walk in, dragging against her legs. She wasn't strong enough. When she lifted her head again, there was nothing but black water.

"Meryl!" she shouted.

No one answered.

"Meryl, don't you dare! Don't you dare!" She planted her feet and turned in a circle, looking everywhere. There was nothing to see. No lights on the shore, no people. Just Tressa Fay, alone in the water.

The shore had gone. The waves lapped gently against the tops of her thighs.

She'd lost her. She'd lost them all.

"Meryl!" she yelled again. "Gayle! Mary!" She drew out Mary's name, heard her hoarse voice crack, heard the grief in it. "Linds! Guy! Michael! James! Where did you go?"

Tressa Fay spun around, and every time she turned, the light and the water changed. There were people on the shore, families crowding the beach. The Ferris wheel was huge and bright, a thousand colors, then smaller like it had been when she was a kid, then gone. The beach disappeared. The trees crowded in.

"Mom!" she shouted. "Dad?"

She tipped her head back, her tears hot against the side of her face, on the cool skin of her birthmark, and she watched the stars blink on and off, the clouds skate over the moon.

There was no such thing as time.

The world filled up with her beating pulse and her body spinning and her restless, insistent self. Her heart. Her.

Her.

She knew who she was. In every universe, she was Tressa Fay Catherine Louise Robeson. She was a beloved child for no other reason than she existed. She had so much love to give, it ached in her chest.

She'd spent so much of herself thinking all she wanted to do was eat soup and take lingerie selfies and hang out with her cat, listening to old records, soaking in nostalgia, pushing off her friends' attempts to drag her out into the world, then musing about the kind of love she wanted but had never been able to find.

She should have remembered she had *already* found love. She'd figured out how to love herself. She'd learned to give herself everything she needed.

That was when she found Meryl, and Meryl found her.

It didn't matter how or why it happened. In every time, every different way, the number Meryl misdialed was Tressa Fay's.

So she was taking Meryl Whit with her, no matter what.

She stopped spinning. "Meryl," she said. Conjuring her up. Summoning her from the water.

There she was. Not with dripping braids, but with shorter hair, *different* hair, because Tressa Fay had made her different.

Loving Tressa Fay had changed her.

"It's you," Meryl said. "My Tressa Fay."

She took hold of Tressa Fay's elbow as their feet left the lake bed, and they heaved up in water that was freezing, marine, rushing. Tressa Fay couldn't find the beach. There were only wide, shining fields of land crisscrossed with running water and huge pools. There were birds everywhere, all kinds, all sizes, and they were incredibly loud, diving in and out of the water and resting on the patches of land and rock. The water she floated in carried stones and dirt that abraded her skin.

"Oh, wow." Meryl wrapped her arms around Tressa Fay, holding her up in the strong current. "That's the Laurentide ice sheet." She turned them away from the land to look at the horizon, which was drawn with a thick blue-white line that Tressa Fay couldn't make sense of. "A glacier. We're swimming in a lobe of what will be the bay of Green Bay! When there is a Wisconsin." Meryl had to shout over the sounds of the birds, grinning. Tressa Fay felt something brush against her Converse and looked down to watch a dark, smooth shape, bigger than a car, glide under the water flashing with rocks and mica.

"A sturgeon!" Meryl laughed. "And see here?" She lifted her hand up from just underneath the surface. A heavy and dripping membrane of slick greenish-brown slime slid over her wrist, then back into the water. "A healthy microbial mat. Maybe it will be a stromatolite someday."

Tressa Fay reached out, trying to touch the mat before it could float down into the depths. She caught the corner of it and lifted it out of the water, pink with the coming sunset. The fossil had smooth edges where the water had worn it away, and the rows and rows of tiny circles stacked up on each other were easy to see in the wet stone. She lifted it up to show her friends on the beach, but no one was there. The Ferris wheel was turning, though. It looked orange in the light of the late-fall sunset. Her dad waved and nudged Tressa Fay, who sat next to him and waved back at Tressa Fay. They wore coats in their swinging seat, and autumn leaves swirled around the paths.

She could still hear the birds screaming. Couldn't she? Or the sound of the ice breaking away from the glacier.

The security lights scattered white streaks on the surface of the dark water around Meryl's black swimsuit. She was still smiling, her new haircut messier than even Tressa Fay had made it, her glasses spotted with water. Tressa Fay let go of the fossil, and as it sank in the water, she cradled Meryl's face with her hands. "Meryl Whit. I thought you'd left me."

"Tressa Fay Robeson," Meryl answered. Their friends were nearby, making ripples everywhere. Their splashing seemed loud in what was now full dark. "Never. Never, never." Meryl reached up and put her hands around Tressa Fay's wrists. "You were right. I was doubting myself into a bad ending, driving my own bus right off the cliff. I'm so sorry I ever made *you* doubt, because here's the thing—I was so certain I didn't have faith that I totally missed all the faith. Maybe I was too distracted by your hotness."

"*You* were right," Tressa Fay corrected. "I shouldn't have ever believed you didn't think I was up to it. That I wasn't enough. Of course I am."

"Of course you are. You're everything." Meryl pulled Tressa Fay in and kissed her, their lips cold and their mouths warm, the air sweet and mossy and too cold to be swimming in September.

There was a loud, piercing noise, the same noise Tressa Fay had been hearing, the calls of the birds, the screams of her friends on the Viking swing, the crack of the ice, but now it was Michael and Guy. The personal alarms.

They were right there in their matching Speedos, shoving their bodies through water up to their chests, calling out her name.

"September fifth!" Gayle screamed out. She had her arm up in the air, pointing at her black watch. "It's September fifth!"

And just then, Tressa Fay felt the shift. A little hitch, like a tug on a tablecloth, it smoothed out the fabric of everything.

SEPTEMBER 5

. . . .

EVERYONE WAS SHOUTING, FALLING OVER EACH OTHER, THE waves picking up a little, the moon high overhead, and as Tressa Fay buried her face in Meryl's neck, she was surprised to feel her chest catch with grief.

She'd seen her mom. Her dad. Her friends, so many ways and times, and she missed them already. There hadn't been enough time with any of them. Her whole life was moving so fast, she almost wished she could live it like she had been, in more than one direction at once. That way, she wouldn't miss *anything*. She wrapped her arms around Meryl tighter. "I love you."

"I love you." Meryl pulled away, and Tressa Fay took her in, her spikes of wet hair and glasses and perfect Merylness. "We should get out of the water. Go home."

She felt like she'd only just walked into the water. She wasn't even cold, certainly not cold enough for the hours from twilight to midnight to have passed. Time had collapsed, just as they'd hoped it would.

Gayle ran up to the both of them and pulled Meryl away from Tressa Fay, wrapping her arms around her. "I've missed you so much. That's how I feel, like I missed you, and now I'm seeing you again. Where have you been? Don't ever do that again."

Meryl buried her face in Gayle's neck. "Thank you for waiting for me. You've waited for me so many times, and for so long."

"We waited for each other." Gayle pulled herself away but kept her hands on Meryl's shoulders. "And now we're here. Let's keep it that way."

"Meryl!" James ran up, wrapping Meryl in a huge hug that Mary piled into, and Guy's arm caught Tressa Fay's waist, until they were all there, hugging, laughing and ecstatic to have made it to the other side of this scary thing that had brought them together.

By some mutual agreement, they started trudging toward the shore, and Tressa Fay's limbs felt heavy and useless on solid ground as she toweled off and shivered and laughed. Everyone had a story to tell about what they'd seen in the water. None of the stories made sense, exactly, but it didn't matter. That was life. Things happened every day that didn't make sense or didn't fit together. Time rippled and warped, crossed over itself in the course of its cosmic dance, and showed you new possibilities.

Or that was the story Tressa Fay had decided to tell herself. The love story she'd conjured up.

With one last hug and a promise of brunch after they'd all had a chance to sleep, finally, finally, she was in the passenger seat of Meryl's snug Toyota, the dark roads by the bay rising up in front of the headlights until they were pulling into Meryl's driveway.

Once they were inside, witnessing the miracle of a lamp on in the living room, of Epinephrine and Spring snoring together on the sofa, Tressa Fay felt shy. She wasn't sure what to do with her whole, wild self.

Meryl laughed. "Um. How about I shower down here, and you use my bathroom, and we meet somewhere in the middle after we've unweirdened ourselves?"

"Mm-hmm, mm-hmm." Tressa Fay nodded. "I hear that, agree, and admit to having enweirdened." She waved awkwardly at Meryl and raced up the stairs, her bare feet still wrinkled from the water. She relished the rough texture of the staircase carpet under her feet, how ordinary it was, and when the warm water poured from the showerhead and melted into her bar of soap, she started at her toes and lathered everything deliberately, all the way up.

She wanted to be the *next* Tressa Fay when she stepped out from behind the shower curtain, blotchy and pink, her surfaces buffed, the last layer of skin she'd worn swirling down the drain.

When she walked into the bedroom wrapped in a towel, her phone on the bedside table buzzed.

> I love you. You're taking me swimming now. I'm saving this to send it in the morning, and when I do, I know you'll get it. Wherever you are.

She looked at the text for a long moment, and she remembered that part of the exuberant joy she'd felt exiting the lake had arisen from the moment she looked at Meryl and discovered she knew everything about their falling in love—and not just from the moment Meryl had walked into Tressa Fay's salon on that pretty day in May until she was in her arms in the water on September 5. *Everything.* She knew the Meryl who'd sent her the misdirected text in October. She remembered all their late-night sessions texting and sexting and falling in love, every single one of them. Tressa Fay under the covers in the dark. Cold nights of autumn and winter, missing Meryl's touch. Meryl in sunny May, and Meryl in the summer with all of their friends.

It seemed absurd that she had ever been jealous of future Tressa Fay. Maybe she hadn't *felt*—not yet—that she was falling in love with Meryl from every timeline at once, but she had been.

She came down the stairs in a T-shirt and underwear to find Meryl in the kitchen in her robe. "What are you wearing underneath that?" She was delighted with the cold tiles of Meryl's kitchen under her bare feet and the half-damp fuzzy mess of Meryl's new hair.

"The point of a robe like this is I don't have to be wearing anything underneath it, and no one will ever know. So that I can pick up a package off the porch or answer the door for the Avon lady."

"No one would know? Really?" Tressa Fay asked with false incredulity. "That sounds like a challenge." She stepped closer and put her hand on Meryl's robe tie. "If you're naked under here, it means you have ideas, because I *know* you have spare loungewear in the downstairs bathroom closet. You are a painfully organized person."

Meryl took a step back and picked up a glass of water from the counter. She sipped it, very cool, looking Tressa Fay over. "It could be that I have ideas. You would have to investigate."

Tressa Fay reached out, quick as lightning, and deftly untied Meryl's robe, pulling the fronts apart. "Oh my God! You *are* naked under there!" She dropped to her knees and pressed her mouth against Meryl's freckled stomach, kissing her, then blowing a raspberry while Meryl laughed and pushed at the top of her head and tried to put her water glass safely on the counter.

"How did you do that so fast?!"

"I have so many talents." She dipped her tongue into Meryl's navel and trailed kisses down her stomach to the tops of her thighs.

"Tressa Fay." Meryl was clearly trying to make her voice intimidating, but it was not a successful effort. "Get up off the floor."

Tressa Fay slid her body up Meryl's as slowly as she could, making sure as much of herself touched as much of Meryl's self as possible.

"I'm standing up. Now what?" Tressa Fay kissed Meryl's neck, slow, with lots of tongue and soft bites.

"Upstairs?" Meryl sounded a little far away.

Tressa Fay raked her fingers up through Meryl's soft, much shorter hair, gratified to feel Meryl shiver against her. "Now we're on the same page. But first." Tressa Fay reached into Meryl's robe pocket and extracted her phone. She'd felt its weight when she'd pulled open the robe. Now she yanked off the charger and smacked it on the counter. "Why don't you send a brunch time to the new group chat? The one I just put myself into?"

Tressa Fay watched, fascinated, as Meryl opened her mouth to say that Tressa Fay couldn't get a text from her. But then a spot under each eye went pink, and she swiped open her phone, pushing a tear away. She poked her phone. Tressa Fay watched her look at the text she'd sent her that Tressa Fay had just received while upstairs, the one that Meryl had meant to go to a worried Tressa Fay in the future.

Meryl looked up at Tressa Fay. "You're you." Meryl held up her phone. "I don't know how to explain it, but *you* are *you*." Her eyes were dark and wide as she waved the phone back and forth, starting to grin.

Tressa Fay's body recalled the moment in the water when everything smoothed out, tugged into place. "I remember. You couldn't help doing one last experiment, huh? Writing a text to send in the morning. Clever, you goose."

"You *remember*," Meryl whispered. "How?"

"You were right. I was always me. I don't know what to tell you, honey. Time doesn't play by the rules. When I walked out of the water, I could remember *alllll* the texts, even if *technically*, officially, none of them has happened yet." Tressa Fay felt warm and alive and afraid of nothing. "But you know how I told you that when the memories double, they start to fade and blur into a single story?"

Meryl nodded, her eyes big.

"We're just us. You didn't lose her. I'm here. Turns out we always have been."

Meryl shook her head and looked back at her phone. Her thumbs flew over her screen.

The phone that Tressa Fay had set down at the end of the counter when she came into the room buzzed. The group chat.

She took a deep breath and let it out, one second at a time.

"I don't know what happened for you in the lake, but you were there with me," Meryl said. "In the water, the whole time, you were there, and it was the first time I truly believed it was *all* you. I was so afraid of losing all the different times of you. The you that I pulled over text, somehow, like a miracle, and the you who seduced me at your salon." Her laugh was shaky. "But you were there, all of you, and I got it. *We* got it. We saw what we needed to see and felt what we . . ." Meryl swallowed and opened her eyes. "Anyway. You were always there, and it was easy to trust that I wasn't running away. I wasn't taking myself out. I had faith. It was easy."

"I think it's supposed to be easy," Tressa Fay said. "I've had so many clients in my chair tell me 'the timing was wrong' for some epic romance, and I'm thinking, I don't know, it sounds like maybe you guys just didn't get your shit figured out, and that's what blew everything up."

"Is that stylist wisdom?"

"It's vintage Tressa Fay wisdom, in fact. Choose love over fear. Figure your shit out. Give yourself what you need so you can have what you want. Watch the mailbox on your way out."

Meryl snorted. "You're feeling big with yourself now."

"I bent time to get to this moment. The least you can do is meet me upstairs. You won't need a robe." She skimmed off her underwear and shirt and, grinning, ran away to the bedroom.

Meryl came into the room and knee-walked onto the bed and put her hand on Tressa Fay's hip. Tressa Fay pulled her down and over until she was in contact with Meryl's skin. So much skin. Not a stitch of clothes on either of them, and her body so warm, Tressa Fay's eyes drifted closed.

Meryl pushed on Tressa Fay's shoulder and rolled her onto her back, and then she was above her, her hard thigh coming between Tressa Fay's, her mouth finding Tressa Fay's, kissing one corner, her chin, her jawline. "I like my hair." Meryl's hand slid up Tressa Fay's side, following the dip of her waist, the curve of her breast.

Tressa Fay laughed. "Yeah?"

"Yeah. It will be so much easier to deal with when I'm out on jobs and in the field." She kissed behind Tressa Fay's ear, her hand wandering up over her nipple, making her gasp and arch up, but Tressa Fay ruined it a little by laughing again.

"I don't think anyone has ever liked a haircut I've given them because it was practical. I'd say my dad did, but I can't, because I have no idea if he likes the haircut I've been giving him for fifteen years. He's never said."

"Shh." Meryl hushed her, laughing too, then slid her fingers down Tressa Fay's belly, urging her thighs apart. "Let me touch you." Meryl moved her hand without hesitation, sliding through where Tressa Fay was warm and wet, making her mouth fall open and her hips lift. "Turn on your side."

Tressa Fay was very lucky that outsmarting the multiverse made Meryl feel bossy.

She turned, and so did Meryl, facing her, so she raised her leg to hook over Meryl's hip and dropped her shoulder to reach down and find the damp juncture of Meryl's thighs, the slide of her fingers so fast and easy that she felt her eyelids get heavy at Meryl's sharp inhale. Their mouths met, a little uncoordinated, more than a little urgent, and Tressa Fay forgot about how she'd teased Meryl in the kitchen, in the bed, and got lost in Meryl's body, the way she gasped and moaned, the way she felt against the pressure of Tressa Fay's fingers, the way her own body wound tight and tighter as Meryl touched her and she forgot to pay attention, absorbed in Meryl's skin, licking over Meryl's mouth, until all of a sudden she felt every sensation she'd failed to notice at the same time—Meryl's breasts, her hard thigh, her clever fingers pressing right where Tressa Fay needed them.

"God. God. Meryl." Tressa Fay shifted to take Meryl's fingers deeper, hitching up her hips, then biting down on Meryl's shoulder when everything got tighter and tighter and closer until she was coming, or she was coming *and* coming, she couldn't exactly tell. It was good, though, it was so good, and as she was floating down, she realized both of her hands had moved up to Meryl's breasts and Meryl was shifting restlessly, her thighs moving, kissing Tressa Fay's shoulder and neck a little frantically.

"I forgot about you," Tressa Fay breathed. "Oh no."

Meryl laughed into her neck. "No worries. I'll just suffer."

Tressa Fay moved over Meryl's body, and Meryl looked up at her, her skin doing that thing where it revealed layers and layers of freckles under her flush, as if Tressa Fay could see every sunny day that Meryl had ever had, all the way back to when she was little.

Maybe she could.

"I don't want you to suffer, though. At least, not like that." She gave Meryl a very soft kiss that made her frustrated, if she was going by how tightly Meryl gripped her hair when Tressa Fay pulled away.

"Tressa Fay." Meryl reached up and took her face in her hands. "Please fuck me. It's an emergency."

"Should I fuck you with my fingers some more, or should I fuck you with that very terrible vibrator you've got in your second drawer that I saw when I was looking for the lip balm you said was in there?"

"You found Pinky?"

"That is a surprising name for something so awesomely intimidating." Tressa Fay leaned over and opened the drawer, and her fingers knocked into a bottle of lube she had also noticed. She put both of them on the bed, and Meryl pulled her knees up by Tressa Fay's hips, so Tressa Fay kissed her.

Meryl's mouth was clever and desperate, and every time their tongues met, Tressa Fay felt every muscle in her body go loose and then start to tighten up again in a delicious unending sensation that was going to lead to something.

But first, Meryl.

She took a long time, stroking and kissing her way down, before she pulled one of Meryl's nipples into her mouth and they both made a noise.

"Tressa Fay," Meryl breathed. "It's so good."

She smiled against Meryl's belly, running her hands over every inch of skin she could reach, scratching her nails down Meryl's sides and over the fronts of her thighs, watching the muscles clench. "I want to taste you," she said. "Just a little."

Meryl laughed. "Just a little."

But then Meryl slid her hands into Tressa Fay's hair and bossed her around more than a little, and Tressa Fay was humming against Meryl, tasting her, feeling how hot and wet she got against her mouth, getting close again, leaning into the sting of Meryl using her hair as a handle.

Tressa Fay reached over and grabbed the bottle of lube, and Meryl eased up. Tressa Fay met her eyes and licked up her center as she clicked open the lid and then made Meryl wetter, so wet Tressa Fay couldn't resist sliding her fingers through Meryl's rosy curls just to feel everything like this.

"I love you," Meryl panted.

Tressa Fay kissed Meryl's thigh and turned on the vibrator. "I love you, too."

It was so hot—how her hips moved, how the bright pink vibrator looked against her clit and then sliding inside Meryl, then back up again, every time harder and deeper until Meryl was fisting the blanket and Tressa Fay kept everything exactly the same, over and over, praising her, kissing every part she could reach, and when Meryl came, she laughed at the peak of it, her head thrown back, one of those *oh my God* laughs that comes from amazement at one's own body and what it's capable of.

Tressa Fay moved to her side, next to Meryl again, glad when Meryl started kissing her as she shuddered, glad when Meryl took Tressa Fay's hand that was still holding the vibrator and eased it between her legs, kissing her softly until she fell over the edge in a lush second orgasm.

"Whoa," Tressa Fay whispered against Meryl's mouth. "Mercy."

Meryl rolled onto her back. "Never. But maybe a merciful break. I can grab up a snack. Then maybe a nap."

She smiled and reached out to hold Meryl's hand. "We've got time."

They dozed. Tressa Fay felt Meryl shift to pull the covers up over them. "There's a pond my coworker told me about that I've never been to. It fills from the water table below and has the clearest water he's ever seen. Up in the woods near Minocqua." Meryl's voice was sleepy, and she moved Tressa Fay into her nook.

"We'll go."

"It's a couple of hours away."

"I love road trips." Tressa Fay could feel sleep coming over her again. She squeezed Meryl's hand. "I love you."

"You do. You will, too, I think," Meryl whispered back.

"I have. Lots and lots of times I've loved you."

They fell asleep and slept until they woke up suddenly, together, realizing how late it had gotten, and then Tressa Fay was rolling out of bed and laughing, tossing clothes at Meryl and pacing the floor to find her own, and they had barely gotten dressed when Gayle knocked twice and walked in with a bag clinking with champagne bottles.

It wasn't long before the rest of their people had arrived, and Tressa Fay couldn't imagine wanting to be anywhere else except right inside this moment.

This very, very one.

TRESSA FAY LAUGHED. I will be there so fast, Meryl.

> You better! Everyone is here. Everyone is coupled. Well, Linds is throupled, because Harper showed up! I finally met zir! When Brooklynn and Linds introduced zir, it was adorable. Also, also, I changed after work, and I'm wearing my brand-new math T-shirt just for you. It's pink with a calculator and says SHOW YOUR WORK.

Tressa Fay jumped up from the sofa with so much urgent intention, Epinephrine and Spring complained at her.

"I know, babies, but this is an emergency. I have a funny engineer on the line, and you know how I feel about redheads, also. You, Eps, for example." She scritched his head and then dashed up the stairs and into the bedroom she shared with Meryl, digging through their closet until she found her lucky jeans and a clean button-down.

She had been taking pictures for Insta in an extremely horny black mesh and brown velvet bodysuit, very strappy, and she decided to put both the jeans and the button-down over the bodysuit in the hope this decision would have favorable results when she and Meryl got home. She pulled on her boots and was on her way to Canyon in less than ten minutes.

Tressa Fay cursed downtown parking but eventually found a spot for her tiny green Fiat. Even with the cold, damp weather, people were spilling out of the restaurant. She jogged to the narrow two-story building, which sat in the same row as the old theater. On warm days, Canyon would open its entire front wall of windows to let people sit at an open-air bar looking out at the street, but right now it was closed and fogged from the people and food inside, the light casting a square on the dark sidewalk and the smokers huddled there.

It was packed. She looked over the bar and didn't see Meryl at first glance.

"Can I help you?" The hostess widened her eyes. "Oh! Hi. Um, Tressa Fay? Is it you, the woman who cut my hair and changed my entire life?" She grinned.

"Katie!" Tressa Fay had to shove her hands in her own pockets to keep from fixing one of Katie's curls near her face. "You're here! Yay!"

"Yes! You remember. I love this haircut so much. I have never loved my . . ." She gestured around her face. "Not ever. But I've felt completely different since I left your chair."

"Can I?" Tressa Fay reached out.

"Yes!" Katie leaned forward, and Tressa Fay played with the hair near Katie's face, changing her part, then stepping back. "You're amazing. What can I help you with? Oh! You must be meeting the big party that I just—"

"Tressa Fay!" James shouted over the crowd, waving from a huge table in the corner.

Katie laughed. "Let me bulldoze the way there for you."

Tressa Fay put her hands on Katie's shoulders from behind, and they crashed through the crowd to the table, where Mary was on James's lap, Gayle pored over the menu, Tressa Fay's dad was laughing at something Jen had said in his ear—which gave her a good view of his new look, the hair getting longer and curling on top, shaving years off his appearance—and Michael was playing with Guy's hair. She'd just given them a haircut yesterday, one they realized they were ready for after starting testosterone. They looked like a snow fairy in a fantasy novel, and it was obvious Michael liked it.

When Tressa Fay had shown a picture to Meryl at work, Meryl had written back, **Oh! I've always loved that cut.**

As she sat down, Meryl, Linds, and Linds's two baefriends, Brooklynn and Harper, broke through the crowd from the direction of the restroom, and Meryl skipped to Tressa Fay and wrapped her arms around her. Her new T-shirt was just as tight and sexy as Tressa Fay could have wanted.

"It's you," Tressa Fay said, dropping a kiss on Meryl's lips.

"I just looked at your Insta when I was waiting for the other folks in the bathroom. Um. Those are going to get so taken down."

"I used Post-its!" Tressa Fay protested. "But even if they do get taken down, it doesn't matter, because I'm wearing that bodysuit right now." She pulled her collar aside to reveal the black strap.

"Let's go," Meryl said, grabbing her hand as if to pull her into the crowd.

Tressa Fay laughed. "No. You promised me churros and limeade in your text, and churros and limeade I shall have."

Tressa Fay and Meryl squeezed in around the table just as the appetizers started coming. None of them could really hear each other, but it didn't matter. They did this once a week when they could, trying out new restaurants and revisiting old favorites. Not everyone could always come, but tonight Mary had group-chatted everyone and insisted so that they could all meet Harper, who was so charming and made Brooklynn and Linds so *right*.

Tressa Fay had wondered if Mary and James were going to make an announcement, but then Meryl told her no, because she'd already talked to James about it a couple of weeks ago, breaking the promise they'd made to each other not to tell James and Mary they were going to be engaged in February. Meryl said that James and Mary had been delighted but had decided to hold off and give their future selves something good for their moment.

Tonight, it was just that Mary wanted to make sure no one acted too hermity now that the weather had gotten cold.

"Isn't Harper so fine?" Mary yelled at Tressa Fay from across the table. "Did I tell you it was me who made this match? I met zir at the taproom, and I was like, if you're, you know, poly, I have two I'd like to introduce you to. I'm a genius!"

"You are!" Tressa Fay laughed, watching James kiss Mary's temple in a very delicious manner, the vintage Jheri curls she'd given him glossy in the low light.

Tressa Fay ate her weight in churros and chocolate ganache. She didn't realize she'd been staring into the middle distance, letting the noise crash around her, until she felt Meryl's mouth against her ear. "Let's get out of here."

She turned and smiled at her beautiful, darling, hot, smart girl Meryl, who took such good care of all of her people. Including herself. "Yes."

Of course, it took more than a moment to extricate themselves from the table and say goodbye, and by the time they walked past the big red coat rack by the entrance and pushed through the door into weather that had turned decidedly cold, it was dark and very late.

There was only the sound of the wind from the river and Meryl's hand warm in hers. Tressa Fay took a deep breath of the cold air.

"It smells like snow already," Meryl said as they walked to Tressa Fay's car.

It did. There was that indescribable ozone bite to every gust that whistled down the street, and the black clouds in the deep violet sky looked heavy. Tressa Fay had just decided to outrun the bitter cold to her car when she saw it.

A snowflake.

Then another.

Just a few, spinning in the wind, not even anything you could call a flurry. But she stopped anyway.

"You wanted to kiss in the snow. We wanted to. We wanted to get to there." Tressa Fay tugged Meryl's hand.

Meryl smiled at Tressa Fay, then stepped close. "We did get there. We're right here. The night we met."

Tressa Fay put her arms around her, suddenly overwhelmed, but Meryl grabbed the placket of her shirt and pulled her down until their lips were almost touching.

"You're going to kiss me." Tressa Fay smiled against Meryl's mouth.

"So much, I'm going to kiss you." Meryl rubbed her bottom lip against Tressa Fay's.

"When?" But Tressa Fay couldn't help but pull Meryl's irresistible upper lip into her mouth, and then they were kissing slow, so hot compared to the snowy wind whipping around them and their chilled hands reaching for each other, touching every soft place they could find around their coats and hats.

Such a good kiss.

Best one so far.

THE END

(except there is no such thing)

ACKNOWLEDGMENTS

I started this book without knowing what would happen to it, if it was part of a journey to someplace else or a book that was asking me to have faith. It wasn't long before this story and its characters became very alive and embodied, and I knew I had to have faith, and then I read a paper that suggested a multiverse could unfold from an author's imagination—a scientist absolutely suggesting that our characters are real, inhabiting a universe that we have called into being.

A lot of the research for this book gave me chills, but most of all I wanted to speak to the experiences we have of when the universe feels much bigger and the only thing we can explain is love. So I want to thank the physicists, astrophysicists, thinkers, mathematicians, and poets (including Cyndi Lauper) whom I consulted and then ghosted to invent the science of this book. Science has made my world both bigger and smaller my whole life, and always more beautiful.

I owe the existence of this book to my gorgeous and brilliant wife, Ruth, who had no patience for doubt or cruel self-talk, and who, every single time the writing of this book made me cry, loved me until I went in again. She is, as Tressa Fay would say, "one of those smart girls" with the folders and pens and shiny,

368 • ACKNOWLEDGMENTS

unbound hair, and Tressa Fay and I share similar feelings about these girls. Thank you, Ruth, you criminally hot woman who lives in my house and loves me.

Thank you to my kids, August and James, whose nerdery is inspiring, whose jokes about the multiverse kept my thoughts to scale, and who face a different universe than I ever did, but with the kind of compassion that changes the world. Thank you for being cool with the loss of our dining room table to writing. I will always watch you do a video game run.

Susan is my family, my biggest fan, and has offered me support for everything I've gotten myself into since we met as work-study students in college. There is nothing like having a history with someone you love.

My agent, Tara Gelsomino, read this book in its first, tender draft and called it a "brilliant, beautiful mess," giving me real hope. She showed me where the heart of the book was and stuck with it even though she isn't ordinarily a fan of "time-y shenanigans." She made it ready for the world, championed it, expected it to triumph, and strategized on its behalf. It's not easy to find someone in this business who listens to you when you bring your most extra ideas to their door, but I did. And it's so much fun.

Esi Sogah at Ace is, I have *no* doubt, the editor of this book in every possible possibility of this universe. Listen, she sent me back to revise and resubmit with the edict to show her its romance, and then she found a way to get an entire publishing team to rally behind it, and every edit we wrote and talked through uncovered something brave and romantic and real. Esi is very sharp, very smart, celebrates this genre with every book she brings to its readers, and maintains an easy sense of humor and calm all the while. Romance readers are so lucky they have her.

Genni Eccles, first, you have made this process so easy. You are juggling fireballs and kittens at the same time and making it look fun. Second, your editorial note to give the book even more worlds made me fall in love with it again after a long year of work. You're an editor who sees the magical forest for the trees, and I'm so happy to get to work with you!

I'd like to thank Juniper, my stylist. She was one of the first people I told about this book and this idea, because Juniper is your stylist who, like Tressa Fay, finds a safe place for the queer community to land and shows them how beautiful they are. Her compassion and significant talent has healed so many gay little hearts all over the Midwest by celebrating the gorgeousness they've missed, lost, or had taken away from them. Your salon *is* the multiverse hair salon.

And to the vascular birthmark community! I love you, I love you, I cosmic love you.

ANNIE MARE (she/they) writes in the queer contemporary young adult and romance genres. With Ruthie Knox, she also cowrites mystery (as Annie Mare) and romance (under the Mae Marvel pen name). Their romances have been critically recognized and bestselling. Annie Mare lives with her wife, two teenagers, two dogs, multiple fish, one cat, four hermit crabs, and a bazillion plants in a very old house with a garden.

VISIT ANNIE MARE ONLINE

AnnieMare.com

Ready to find
your next great read?

Let us help.

Visit prh.com/nextread

Penguin
Random
House